Born in the Lo... ...tor
Pemberton is a su... ...er,
as well as being the author of six highly popular London
sagas, all of which are published by Headline. His first
novel, OUR FAMILY, was based on his highly
successful trilogy of radio plays of the same name.
Victor has worked with some of the great names of
entertainment, including Benny Hill and Dodie Smith,
had a longstanding correspondence with Stan Laurel,
and scripted and produced many of the BBC's 'Dr
Who' series. In recent years he has worked as a producer
for Jim Henson and set up his own production company,
Saffron, whose first TV documentary won an Emmy
Award. He lives in Essex.

Goodnight Amy

Victor Pemberton

HEADLINE

First published in 2000
by HEADLINE BOOK PUBLISHING

First published in paperback in 2000
by HEADLINE BOOK PUBLISHING

10 9 8 7 6 5 4 3 2

ISBN 0 7472 6125 3

Printed and bound in Great Britain by
Clays Ltd, St Ives plc

Typeset by CBS, Martlesham Heath, Ipswich, Suffolk

HEADLINE BOOK PUBLISHING
A division of Hodder Headline
338 Euston Road
London NW1 3BH

www.headline.co.uk
www.hodderheadline.com

For John Tydeman
whose friendship and encouragement
has meant so much to me
and to so many others.

PROLOGUE

Hyde Park was at peace with itself. It was in one of those rare moods that didn't last very long, for there was a war on, and it wasn't easy to remain tranquil when the sky was raining death and destruction all the time. But tonight was different. Tonight, the giant leafless oak, elm, and chestnut trees were covered in a thin layer of frost, and the air was crisp and free. No wailing air-raid siren to crack the peace, no rumble of anti-aircraft guns to wake the cockney sparrows and their big pigeon cousins, no glare from searchlights crisscrossing the sky like some vast illuminant kaleidoscope. This was a park that radiated peace and calm. It rejoiced in it.

Down by the Serpentine lake, the usual cluster of down-and-outs had retired for the night to their own individual territory, which usually meant a park bench, or a clearing in a sheltered clump of evergreen bushes. They were a motley bunch, mostly middle-aged-to-elderly men who, for one reason or other, had turned their backs on a world that they were unable to come to terms with. By day they shuffled around the park, from Piccadilly to Knightsbridge, from Marble Arch to Bayswater, protected from the biting cold by two or three layers of flea-infested woollens and jackets, which had long since been donated by the Good Samaritans of the Salvation Army.

Sometimes, in the vain hope that some well-to-do person would take pity on them and give them a few coins or even some leftover wartime rations, they would cross Park Lane and venture out into the surrounding streets of classy Mayfair, or if their feet would carry them as far, they would drag themselves off to trail along the entire stretch of nearby Oxford Street, hoping that they could make enough before the special constabulary made an appearance. Their main problem was that in the event of a daytime air raid, there was no way that they could take shelter down in the tube stations with everyone else. With the thunderous sound of ack-ack fire and bombs exploding above ground, the stench of brown ale or methylated spirits was just too much for the well-washed to take.

But tonight, the park was safe. Not even the distant rumble of traffic along the blacked-out Park Lane could disturb the pitch-dark of London's acknowledged premier back garden. Even the surface of the Serpentine's ice-cold water was still. Now, the spidery shadows of the brigade of lost souls had disappeared into the luxury of their own nests, leaving only one figure to settle down for the night behind the old boathouse at the water's edge. But this was no ordinary figure, not one of the flock. This was Aggie, 'Ma' or 'Aggs', as they called her, wrapped up in woollens, raincoat, headscarf, and a mangy old eiderdown. She was barely visible in the dark, but her small, beady eyes could see more than most. They could see the stars bright and clear, sparkling high in the sky above, and the sinister shapes of the tall trees casting their eerie shadows across the water beneath the glare of a crescent-shaped moon. They also saw the past, and a life before. It was a time for recalling nights just like this. It was inevitable. It was past midnight. It was Christmas morning.

CHAPTER 1

The Christmas truce didn't last long. The year of 1941 had hardly breathed its last breath when the skies above London were once again reverberating to the roar of enemy aircraft dodging in and out of the protective shield of barrage balloons. Like so many parts of the capital, Islington had had its share of bombs during the height of the Blitz just a year or so before, but even though the air raids had become less regular, they were always taken seriously. Once 'Moaning Minnie' had wailed out her warning from the roof of Hornsey Road police station, people went straight down into their shelters, whether it was the poor old smelly Anderson in their back yard, the crowded tube platform, or one of the many public brick shelters scattered all around the borough.

Like all the small communities around the main Holloway Road, Enkel Street had somehow survived the worst of the Blitz – apart, of course, from the regular inconvenience of having all the windows blown in, tiles catapulted off roofs, and plaster ceilings collapse under the blast of nearby high-explosive bombs. One such occasion had been during the night when a row of shops in Seven Sisters Road had been wiped out by an aerial torpedo. It was a lucky escape for all the

3

surrounding streets. Especially for the inhabitants of number 16 Enkel Street.

The Dodds family had lived at number 16 for nearly ten years. At the time they moved there, Amy, the eldest of the four kids, was barely eleven years old, and her sister, Thelma, was four. Arnold, who turned up a couple of years after they'd moved in, was no more than a twinkle in his dad's eye, and as for little Elsie – well, when she arrived three years later, she was really a bit of a mistake. When Amy and Thelma were born, their mum and dad, Ernie and Agnes, were living in digs at the top of a four-storey terraced house in Axminster Road, no more than a stone's throw away from Enkel Street. Times had been hard in those days, for, as Ernie had no real skills to fall back on, he'd spent the best part of two years on the dole. If anything, life was even harder now. Apart from having to survive bringing up a family during a war, the only real breadwinner in the house was Amy, who worked as a waitress in Lyons Tea Shop just round the corner in Holloway Road – for the paltry sum that her dad earned each week as an attendant at Hornsey Road Baths was hardly enough to pay the rent. Each morning, as she rushed around getting breakfast ready for the family, and struggled to get her brother and sisters off to school, Amy constantly prayed that her mum would one day come back home and look after them all.

''Onestly, Else,' Amy grumbled, as she wiped her small sister's running nose with a piece of paper torn out of the *Evening News*, 'if yer keep losin' yer 'ankies like this, we'll 'ave none left.'

The greasy bit of newspaper was all that was left from what had been used to wrap up the family's usual Friday night fish and chips. 'Why don't yer just tuck it up yer knickers or somefin', then yer'd know where ter find it.'

Elsie, the five-year-old, didn't take too kindly to that suggestion, especially as the newspaper not only ponged of cod and stale lard, but it was also very rough on her nose. 'I don't want no bleedin' 'ankie,' she raged, stamping her foot. 'I can use me 'and!'

Amy gave the child a gentle whack on her bottom. 'Don't you let me 'ear you say words like that again!' she growled. 'Yer know wot you'd get if Mum was 'ere!'

Humiliated, Elsie pulled away. 'Well, she *ain't* 'ere!' she snapped back, on the verge of yet another of her tantrums. 'So why should I care?'

Amy had no answer to that. Her young sister was right. Why should she care what her mum thought, when they hadn't even seen the woman for over a year? What with their dad stuck in the boozer most of the time, and their mum God knows where, Christmas had been a pretty bleak time for the Dodds family; even as she spoke, the remains of the badly home-made paper chains were coming unstuck across the back room ceiling. There were times when Amy felt absolute despair as she wrestled with the uphill task of standing in for her mum. Try as she may, she couldn't help but resent the fact that if she didn't do it, no one else would. After all, her dad was weak and useless; he didn't have a clue how to bring up a family on his own. Time and time again, Amy tried to work out in her mind what the quarrel between her mum and dad had been all about on the night Mum had walked out on them all.

'Go and get yer coat on, Else,' she said now, busily clearing away the breakfast dishes from the kitchen table. 'I don't want you being late for school again.'

Elsie didn't have to be told twice. Grabbing a piece of left-over bread and jam from her plate, she rushed out of the room, her feet thundering on the stairs in the passage outside, as she made her way up to the room she shared with her two sisters.

Amy took the breakfast things out to the scullery, and quickly washed up. As usual, her brother, Arnold, and her second sister, Thelma, had gone off to school without washing up their own dishes. But over the past year, Amy had got used to running the house single-handed, which she deeply resented. After all, in a few weeks' time she would be twenty-one, *only* twenty-one, and here she was shouldering all the responsibilities of a ready-made family. As she glanced from the old stone sink, and saw the reflection of herself in the window overlooking the small back yard, all she could see was a face racked with anxiety. To her, there was no sign of those large dark blue eyes, round dimpled chin, and clear honey-milk skin. All she could see was someone who looked tired and drained, with not a chance in hell of one day meeting a boy who would sweep her off her feet and get her away from her daily life of drudgery. She hadn't even found time to trim the fringe of her dark brown hair, which settled precariously across her forehead, and which always needed at least ten minutes' attention each morning.

'Don't fink I'll go in terday.'

Amy suddenly noticed the reflection of her dad standing behind her. She turned with a start.

Ernie Dodds looked terrible. Wearing only an old pair of black serge trousers held up by an army belt and thick, frayed braces, a long-sleeved woollen vest, and black socks with holes in both big toes, he ran his hands through his uncombed brown hair.

'Don't feel up to it,' he yawned. 'Reckon I'm comin' down wiv the flu or somefin'. You'll 'ave ter go in an' let Farrar know for me.'

Amy sighed. She was sick to death of having to tell lies for him to his supervisor, especially when she knew only too well the state her father had come home in from the boozer the night before.

'Why don't yer 'ave a wash and brush-up first, Dad?' she said, looking at the thick stubble on his face, and his shabby appearance. 'Yer might feel better.'

Ernie ignored what she said, turned away, and went into the kitchen. 'Wot 'appened ter my fag?' he called, looking around for one of his dog-ends.

Amy found it for him. It was in its usual place, perched on the edge of the mantelpiece above the black metal oven grate. She was much smaller than her dad, with a round face as opposed to his, which was long and narrow. Amy had always been secretly pleased that, with her slightly dumpy figure, she was more like her mum than her dad. 'I was wonderin', Dad,' she asked, rather impetuously. 'Is there any chance yer could let me 'ave a bob or two? Else needs a new pair of socks, and Arne says his teacher's told 'im ter get anuvver exercise book for 'is 'omework.'

Ernie lit his dog-end without looking at her. 'Not this week, Ame,' he replied, going to the table. 'I'm a bit short.'

'I've got ter get it from somewhere, Dad,' Amy persisted. 'I only got paid me wages last night, an' most of it's got ter go on stockin' up the rations.'

Ernie took the cosy off the teapot, and poured some lukewarm tea into one of the cups that still had dregs left over from breakfast. 'I told yer, Ame,' he said, adding some of the made-up dried milk into the tea, 'I ain't got nuffin' left over this week.'

'But it's only Friday,' replied Amy, quietly insistent. 'Don't yer get paid ternight?'

Ernie gulped down his tea. He was always a mild-spoken man, and was forever determined not to get riled. 'Yer mustn't ask me questions like that, Ame,' he said, almost apologetically. 'My wages is me own business.'

As he sat down at the table, Amy went to stand over him. Although she knew better than to challenge him, she just had to say, 'Dad, I don't make enough ter keep the family goin' on me own, I just can't.'

Ernie flicked a quick glance up at her, and without a shred of guilt, replied, 'Yer mum did.'

It was this kind of remark from her dad that had always angered Amy. Just who the hell did he think she was, she asked herself. She wasn't her mum. She was no skivvy. Why should she be expected to shoulder all the responsibilities of a woman twice her age?

'Mum ain't 'ere, Dad,' she replied as calmly as she could. 'An' even when she was, she didn't 'ave ter go out ter work ter look after the kids.'

Ernie looked up at her, and gave her a reassuring smile. 'I know, Ame,' he said, covering her hand with his own and gently squeezing it. 'I'm very grateful to yer.'

Amy could have hit him. It wasn't his gratitude she wanted. She wanted his help, *any* help. Things couldn't go on much longer the way they were now. If the family was going to survive, her dad was just going to have to pull himself together, and give them the support they so desperately needed. 'When, Dad?' she asked for the umpteenth time. 'When can yer let me 'ave somefin'?'

Ernie stalled for a moment, and took a puff of his dog-end before replying. 'Soon, Ame,' he said, with yet another infuriating smile. 'Soon.'

Once she had walked with her little sister to the gates of Pakeman Street School, Amy headed off briskly towards Hornsey Road Baths. On the way, she stopped briefly to chat with old Gert Tibbett, who lived on the ground floor of one of the terraced houses in Roden Street, and who had always been a great pal of Amy's mum. Every time they met, Gert invariably had plenty of advice for Amy, especially where Amy's brother and sisters were concerned. But Gert's advice today was a bit worrying.

'Keep an eye on your Thelma,' said the old girl, touching the side of her nose with one finger as a sign that she knew something. 'She's a one fer the boys, ain't she?'

Amy did a double take. 'Wot d'yer mean, Mrs Tibbett?' she asked anxiously.

The old widow's eyes gleamed. Ever since she lost her husband ten years before, from heart disease, her only escape was gossip. 'Always got a bunch of 'em round 'er, little devil,' she said, pulling her hairnet tight over her curlers and moving close to Amy. 'One or two's all right, I suppose, but when there's that many . . .'

''Ow many?' Amy asked tentatively.

'A bunch or so,' replied Gert. 'They're always waitin' for 'er outside the school gates durin' the dinner break. Gord knows where they all go to.'

Amy bit her lip, and sighed.

'I only tell yer 'cos I know wot yer dear mum would've

said. I mean, when yer live this close to the school, yer can't 'elp but notice these fings, can yer?'

Amy tried to smile appreciatively, but it wasn't easy. 'Fanks fer tellin' me, Mrs Tibbett,' she said. 'I'll 'ave a word wiv Thelm when she comes 'ome.'

The widow smiled, and went back into her house. She was well satisfied with her morning's work.

Amy hurried off down Roden Street, turning over and over in her mind what the old busybody had told her. In one way, hearing about Thelma's behaviour was not exactly a surprise, especially when it came from someone like Gert Tibbett. But there was no doubt that her sister was, and always had been, a problem child. God knows, their mum had ranted at Thelma enough times in the past. But Amy knew that something had to be done before things got out of hand. Although Thelma was only fourteen years old, she looked older, and with her sensual good looks, she could easily become prey to any Tom, Dick, or Harry.

A few minutes later, Amy was striding off past the school gates into Pakeman Street. It was only when she turned into Mayton Street that she realised how many front rooms still had Christmas trees in their windows, and how sad it was that, because of the blackout restrictions, it wasn't possible to see the coloured lights on them after dark.

By the time she reached Hornsey Road, a long queue had formed outside Dorners. The reason for this was most probably because the popular butcher shop had managed to get in some beef, which, like lamb and pork, had during the past year become almost unavailable. Despite their German origins, Dorners had managed to keep faith with their Holloway customers, mainly because their service was friendly and helpful, and their hot saveloys and pease pudding were great bolsters to wartime rations.

Every time Amy crossed the main Seven Sisters Road, her mind raced back to the time during the height of the Blitz when she'd got caught in an air raid, and had seen an enemy fighter shooting down a barrage balloon. It had been a terrible but exciting experience, for the great 'silver cigar', as it was known, had suddenly burst into flames, sending large fragments of burning material fluttering wildly into the midday sky.

On the other side of Seven Sisters Road, Amy quickly made her way past the bombed-out shell of the police station, which had been destroyed during a fierce air raid the previous year, and finally reached the adjacent Hornsey Road Baths. It was an imposing red-brick Victorian building, which, although badly damaged during the bomb explosion on the police station next door, nestled proudly beneath an impressive clock tower. The public baths themselves were separated from the indoor swimming pool, and, because so many buildings had been destroyed during the air raids, the local Borough Council had no money to maintain the services properly, and relied totally on the staff. That was one reason Amy hated the number of times she had had to make feeble excuses for her father.

'I'm sorry Dad can't come in, Mr Farrar.' The words stuck in Amy's throat. 'I fink it must've been somefin' 'e ate. 'E's been up all night on the lav.'

''As 'e now?' replied Ernie's superintendent, Bert Farrar, who as usual, didn't believe a word of it. Despite the fact that he looked quite tough, Farrar was a kind-natured man. A victim of a gas bomb attack in the trenches during the previous war with Germany, he had been left with breathing difficulties.

'Suffers quite a lot wiv 'is bowels, do 'e?'

Amy didn't know where to look.

'Well, don't ferget, Amy,' he said, 'if 'e's off fer longer than three days, 'e'll 'ave ter let me 'ave a doctor's certificate.'

'Oh, I don't fink that'll be necessary, Mr Farrar,' Amy replied quickly. 'I'm sure 'e'll be back termorrow.'

'I 'ope so, Amy,' said Farrar, who was not much taller than she. 'I do 'ope so. It's difficult enough keepin' the shifts goin' 'ere wiv the air raids an' everyfin'. When yer dad's not 'ere, I 'ave ter cover fer 'im.' Then he added pointedly, 'I'd 'ate ter lose 'im. 'E needs the wages ter keep the family goin'.'

Amy smiled anxiously, then turned to go.

As she did so, Farrar called to her, 'Any word from yer mum yet?'

Amy turned back to face him. 'Not yet,' she said bravely. 'I'm sure it won't be long now though.'

Farrar shook his head sympathetically. 'Poor woman,' he said, speaking in short breaths. 'Somefin' must've turned 'er 'ead, all right. It's you an' yer bruvver and sisters I feel sorry for.'

Amy smiled gratefully. 'Oh, we're managin', Mr Farrar,' she said unconvincingly. 'At least I've got my job at the tea shop.'

Farrar gave her a supportive smile, and went back inside through the men's entrance.

Amy watched him go. As he opened the door, the smell of cheap soap and steam came gushing out. But as Amy turned to leave, she caught a glimpse of a middle-aged woman at the cashier's desk at the female entrance. Amy gave her a stern look. She knew only too well who the woman was, and quickly moved off.

As Amy returned to the road outside, Bert Farrar's words were ringing in her ears: *'Poor woman. Somefin' must've turned 'er 'ead, all right.'* He knew. Of course he knew. So did everyone else.

A few yards along the road, Amy came out of her trance. She was just passing the section house, the temporary home for the new police station, and as she came to, the first thing she saw was a police car turning into the front yard. She stopped a moment, to let it pass, then carried on. But Bert Farrar's words suddenly returned to her, and quite impetuously, she turned back and strode briskly into the yard. It wasn't the first time Amy had been there; during the past year she had entered the bleak building more than a dozen times. She hated everything about the place: the smell of police uniforms and floor polish, the white distempered walls, and the sound of a typewriter in constant use in a back room.

''Allo there, young lady,' said the duty sergeant, as he looked up from his work at the reception desk. 'Long time no see?'

Amy ignored his jibe. She knew only too well that they were all sick to death of seeing her, but she was a determined girl, and she was not going to let anyone rest whilst her mum was still missing. 'Any news?' she asked, imperiously.

The sergeant suddenly felt a bit guilty. He knew the distress Amy had been going through for the past year, and he was sorry he'd teased her. 'Nothin', I'm afraid,' he replied, with a sorrowful shaking of the head. 'But we're on to it, don't you worry.'

'Yer've been on to it for a whole year,' quipped Amy, getting her own back.

The sergeant smiled. He knew he deserved that.

'I want ter speak ter Inspector 'Anley,' she demanded. 'I've got something I want ter ask 'im.'

''E's up to 'is eyes in it, I'm afraid,' replied the sergeant. 'We've got a lot goin' on at the moment.'

Amy looked at her watch. She still had half an hour before she was due at work. 'I'll wait,' she said haughtily.

The sergeant sighed. 'Wot's the point, Miss Amy?' he said. ''E won't be able to tell you anythin' more than me.'

Amy stood her ground. 'Would you at least tell him I'm here, please?' she demanded. Without waiting for his response, she turned, and sat down on a bench next to a woman and a teenage boy.

The sergeant, realising there was never any point in trying to argue with Amy, put down his pen, left the counter, and went into the back room.

At this time in the morning, the station was buzzing with activity. Special constables were hurrying in and out of the place, and there were the sounds of telephones and walkie-talkies coming from the back office. Amy, sitting erect on the bare wooden bench, kept her eyes lowered all the time, determined not to make any kind of contact with the couple sitting next to her. In any case, the woman and the teenage boy, who was most probably her son, never opened their mouths to each other; they sat in stony silence, eyes turned in different directions.

'You can come in, young lady.'

Amy looked up to see the sergeant opening a door at the side of the counter for her. She stood quickly and entered.

'Must be your lucky day,' he said, as he closed the door behind her. Then he led her to another door and knocked on it.

A moment later, Amy was sitting at a desk facing Chief Inspector Rob Hanley, a handsome, middle-aged man, whose greased-back blond hair was already merging with streaks of grey. 'Sergeant Rugby says you've got something to tell me,' he said, in a slightly middle-class accent. 'Something new, I hope?'

'I told him I had something to *ask* you,' Amy replied.

The inspector eased back into his chair. He made a mental note that he would give his overkind sergeant hell. 'Go ahead,' he said, collecting his half-finished cigarette from the ashtray in front of him on the desk.

Amy looked him straight in the eyes. 'I want ter know if yer've found out anyfin' about my mum yet?'

The inspector took a deep puff of his cigarette, exhaled, and returned it to the ashtray. 'Now, Amy,' he replied, leaning on the desk towards her, 'if we did have any more news, you know very well you and your father would be the first to be told.'

Amy was not impressed. 'It's been a whole year,' she chided. 'She must be somewhere.'

'Perhaps.'

Amy felt a momentary cold streak shoot down her spine. Not for the first time was she aware of how bleak and airless the tiny room was, and of the bare white walls with very little furniture.

'Wot's that s'pposed ter mean?' she asked.

'A lot of things.' The inspector got up from his desk, picked up his cigarette, and went to stare out of the window. After a brief moment's silence, he turned back to her. 'Amy,' he said, cautiously, 'have you ever considered the possibility that your mum might not still be alive?'

Amy was outraged. 'Never!' she growled, springing up from her chair. 'Wot're you tryin' ter tell me?'

The inspector came across to her. 'Now just be calm, Amy,' he said, trying to pacify her. He gently eased her back into her chair. 'Believe me, I'm not trying to tell you anything specific. But after such a long time, it would be foolish to rule out anything from our investigations. Let's face it, there is a war on.'

'Wot's that got ter do wiv it?'

The inspector perched on the edge of his desk. 'People die, Amy,' he said wearily. 'They get killed. In this borough alone, an awful lot of innocent people have lost their lives. Your mum left at the height of the Blitz. Anything could have happened to her.'

Amy was prevented from getting up again by the inspector's hand resting on her shoulder. 'She ain't dead, if that's wot you're sayin'. My mum knows how to take care of 'erself.'

'I'm sure she does, Amy,' said Inspector Hanley. 'But these are things that we have to take into account. We can't dismiss the possibility that she was caught up in an air raid. Since the air raids over London began, hundreds of people have quite literally disappeared without trace. It's a gruesome thought, I know, but we can't ignore it.'

'But in one year,' persisted Amy, 'yer 'aven't even 'ad one single clue as to where she might be.'

'Not entirely true,' replied the inspector, returning to his seat. 'As you know, we did have a few sightings soon after your mother disappeared. But there was nothing positive about them. Mind you –' he stubbed his cigarette out in the ashtray, and looked up at her – 'it might have been more helpful if you and your father had been more – shall we say – forthcoming.'

Amy looked blank. 'Wot d'yer mean?'

Hanley leaned across the desk to look closely at her. 'There must have been a reason for her walking out that night, Amy. What really happened? Did she have a row with your father?'

Amy looked away. She had had quite enough of this line of questioning, and she was fed up to the teeth with it. And yet she knew that this man had every right to ask the question, because it was true. Yes, of course her mum and dad had quarrelled on that ill-fated Christmas Eve just over a year before. Although she and her brother and sisters had been out in the Anderson shelter in the back yard at the time, she could hear her parents' voices raised in bitter conflict. At one moment, her mum's voice was so shrill, Amy was convinced that the woman was going to have some kind of a fit. But although she couldn't hear precisely what the row was about, she had a good idea. And that was something she had decided never to reveal.

With her face turned away from him, all she could say was, 'I'm sorry, Mr 'Anley. I'm afraid I don't know wot you're talkin' about. I don't know nuffin' about no row.'

Hanley had been all through this before, so now he quickly brought his meeting with Amy to a halt. 'Well then,' he said briskly, 'if you should remember anything, you know where I am. As I've told you before, the moment we have any clues, we'll let you know. Good morning, Amy.'

Amy got up from her seat, and made for the door. As she opened it, she turned. 'If anyfin *'as* happened to 'er – you know – like the way you said, 'ow would yer know?'

Hanley looked up from his desk. 'By checking the

descriptions of victims killed in air raids all around London – people lying in hospital mortuaries, still waiting for someone to identify them.'

Amy shivered. The thought unnerved her. ''Ow long will somefing like that take?' she asked, painfully.

Hanley paused before answering. 'There are a lot of them, Amy,' he said. 'We're doing our best.'

She nodded, and left the room.

In the reception area outside, the teenage boy was in tears, and being comforted by his mother. Amy was glad she didn't know what it was all about, and quickly made for the outside door. On the way, she took a glance at one of the many posters pinned on the police notice board. She had seen it plenty of times before, of course. In fact, she had seen it every time she had called at the station over the past year. Even so, it still sent a chill down her spine, for below the large print legend 'MISSING' was an old snapshot of her mum.

CHAPTER 2

Considering there was a war on, Lyons Tea Shop in Holloway Road did pretty good business. There weren't many luxuries, of course; gone were the days of hot bacon rolls, delicate full-cream pastries, and buttered scones. But with a clever juggling of the rations, rock buns were a constant favourite, and chocolate cake was sometimes available, despite the fact that it had to be made with cocoa rather than real chocolate. None the less, the good old cuppa remained the number one attraction, and the girls who served it made quite sure that it reached the customers' tables piping hot.

It wasn't only her job as a waitress that Amy loved, but the fact that, for a few hours a day, it gave her the chance to get away from the burdens of looking after her family. She was very popular with the customers, for she had a cheerful way of dealing with them, besides looking very pert in her black dress, white apron and cap. She was also greatly liked by Mrs Bramley, the larger-than-life cook, and Marge Jackson, her supervisor. But her great mate was Hilda Feathers, who was the only other girl waiting on tables with her. Hilda, who had a mop of bright ginger hair packed with tight curls, came originally from the posh part of London – Knightsbridge – but because of her parents' financial difficulties, had had to move with them into more modest accommodation in Islington just before the start of the war. Much to Amy's amusement, Hilda had retained her cut-glass accent, and practically anything she said sent Amy into fits of laughter. The two girls got on like a house on fire, and during the past year, Hilda had been the one person Amy could rely on for support.

'Well, you can't really blame the police too much,' said Hilda, as she and Amy waited at the counter for Mrs Bramley to prepare customers' orders. 'I mean, he's right, isn't he? There must be millions of missing people from the air raids. Trying to find your mum must be like trying to find a needle in a haystack.'

'I know,' said Amy, laying a tray with two cups and saucers, a knife, and a milk jug. 'It's just that lookin' after the family on me own all this time is beginnin' ter get on top of me.'

'As I've told you before, and I'll tell you again,' replied Hilda, in her best plum-in-the-mouth accent, 'you should get that father of yours off his back side. Just tell him one night you're going out, and he'll have to take over.'

Amy laughed. 'That'll be the day!' she said. But when she realised that some of the customers were looking at her, she quickly lowered her voice. ''E wouldn't know where ter start.'

They were interrupted by Marge Jackson, a handsome woman in her late forties, who was never seen wearing anything but her rather severe, long-sleeved black supervisor's dress. 'Come on, you two,' she called quietly, as she approached from the till at the far end of the counter. 'They're getting impatient!'

The two girls quickly collected their trays, and took them

to their respective customers. As it was mid-morning, the place was only half full, mainly with local shopkeepers taking a quick break. The long, narrow shape of the tea shop meant that most of the tables had to be set against one wall, competing with the counter on the opposite side. The tables down the centre of this area were the least popular, mainly because most people thought there was very little privacy. Apart from at the front, there was also very little natural light in the place, especially at the rear, where there were no windows, which meant that, despite the shortage of power, the electric light was on practically the whole day.

The big advantage for Amy was that the rear shop entrance led out on to Enkel Street itself which meant that it was no more than a couple of minutes' walk to work each morning.

Amy and Hilda didn't have a chance to talk much until just before closing time that afternoon. By then, they'd carried more trays of tea and chicory coffee than they cared to count. They had also repeated their endless, pat answers a dozen times: 'Sorry, sir. No cakes today, only rock buns,' and 'Sorry, madam. We've run out of sugar, there's only saccharins.' Hilda, who had written out her last bill for the day and handed it over to the customer, finally flopped down into a chair at one of the tables to the rear of the shop. 'My poor feet!' she sighed, slipping off her shoes, and wiggling her toes to freedom. 'I'm bursting for a fag!'

Amy poured them both a cup of tea at the counter, and brought them across to the table. 'It's a bit stewed,' she said, with an exhausted groan, as she sat down with Hilda.

'Who cares?' said Hilda. 'At least it's wet and warm.'

As they sat there, Marge Jackson was just seeing the last customer out before locking the front shop door.

'Did I tell yer I saw 'er again this mornin'?' Amy asked.

Hilda was lighting her Craven 'A'. 'Who?' she asked, taking a deep puff of smoke, and then blowing out the match.

Amy stirred the saccharin tablet in her tea. 'That woman,' she said caustically. 'The one at the baths.'

Hilda turned to look at her. 'Oh, *that one*,' she replied, equally caustically.

'If looks could kill,' Amy said, sipping her tea, 'I'd be dead as a duck.'

'I hope you did likewise?' asked Hilda.

Amy exchanged a wry smile with her mate. 'Wot der *you* fink!'

They chuckled.

Hilda kept quiet for a moment. As she watched Amy sipping the now lukewarm tea from her cup that she clasped in the palms of both hands, she knew only too well what was racing through her pal's mind. 'D'you really think there is something going on between them?' she asked tentatively. 'Your dad and her?'

Amy shrugged, and continued to stare at the floor.

'Have you asked him about it?'

Amy thought for a moment before answering. 'I wouldn't know 'ow,' she replied. 'It isn't easy fer a daughter ter ask those kind of questions.'

It was at times like this that Hilda wanted to go round and tell Amy's dad what she thought of him. During the time they had known each other, Hilda had embraced the true cockney spirit of loyalty to one's friends. As far as she was concerned, nobody was going to upset *her* best mate. To Hilda, it made no difference that she was tall and skinny, and wore enough make-up to hook a good-looking bloke at twenty paces, or that Amy only came up to her shoulders, was on the podgy side, and couldn't afford to buy make-up. No. There was a bond of true friendship, and Hilda would be prepared to take on anyone who ever tried to come between them. 'Well, what are you going to do, Amy?' she asked tenderly. 'If this woman was the cause of your mum walking out on you all—'

'I don't know that, 'Ild,' Amy quickly replied. 'Well – not fer sure, anyway.'

'But you suspect?'

'I suspect all sorts of fings,' said Amy, peering aimlessly down into her teacup. 'Trouble is, I'm all mixed up. I don't know wot ter fink any more.' Then she suddenly looked up. 'But I intend to find out – one way or anuvver. I've decided.'

So far, it had been quite a good day for old Aggs. When she finally emerged from her hiding place behind the boathouse that morning, the first thing she noticed was that someone had dumped a half-eaten slice of bread in one of the litter bins along the lakeside path. She couldn't believe her luck, and the bonus was that the slice was still smeared with a scrape of jam, probably home-made, Aggs reckoned. Even more surprising was that she was the first to find it; most days the 'parkies', as the Hyde Park tramps were known, were first to clear out the bins, and by the time the morning commuters had crossed the park to their various offices, everything left behind had been snapped up.

There had been a light sprinkling of snow overnight, but there were pinpoints of grass everywhere, desperately trying to reach up for what there was of the early morning sun. Aggs had her usual cat's lick of a face wash, dipping her hands into the ice-cold waters of the lake, then drying herself on an old tea cloth she had found behind a WVS van parked in the street during an air raid. For Aggs, more detailed ablutions came once a week at the Seymour Road Baths, a ritual she always made quite sure she never missed.

Today, she had an important mission ahead of her. Today, she was going to follow up the chance of getting a job, only as a part-time cleaner in a pub, but a position that would at least give her a few bob a week, enough to buy her something warm to eat at night.

'Need yer furs on terday, Aggs.'

The parkie who joined Aggs on the bench, where she was trying to rub some life into her frozen feet, was wearing two threadbare overcoats, and a knitted hat, which was pulled down tight over his ears. Aggs ignored him. 'Scrounger', as he was called, was a bit too forward for her.

'Your big day, Aggs?' he asked, through the last few of his own natural teeth, which were stained brown with fag smoke. 'Don't ferget ole Scrounger when yer get yer first pay packet, will yer?'

Aggs didn't even bother to look at him. 'You'll be lucky,' she replied, struggling to put her plimsoll back on. In some ways, she had quite a soft spot for the poor old codger. Scrounger had been a soldier in the First World War, and, despite his scruffy appearance, he always wore a row of campaign medals across the lapel of his overcoat to prove it. 'If I pick up 'alf a crown fer a day's work,' Aggs said, in her low-pitched, husky voice, 'I won't be doin' bad.'

'A good ol' piss-up, eh, Aggs?' chuckled Scrounger, with a gleam in his eyes.

Aggs ignored his remark, which she resented because it was too close to the truth. She got up from the bench, and tried to make herself look a bit more presentable. It wasn't easy, for her clothes looked as though they'd come from a rag bag, and her long, mousy-coloured hair, which was streaked with grey, was draped over her shoulders, and completely lifeless. So she tucked it under the collar of her coat, took out a scarf from her pocket, covered her head with it, then tied it under her chin.

As soon as Aggs started to move off, Scrounger got up quickly from the bench and followed her. 'The Kid was askin' after you last night,' he called. 'Nearly got 'imself nicked yesterday mornin'.'

'Nicked?' called Aggs over her shoulder as she shuffled on ahead of him. 'Wot for?'

'Same as before,' answered Scrounger, hurrying along to catch up with her. 'Selfridges.'

'Bloody little fool,' snapped Aggs. 'Ain't 'e ever goin' ter learn? If 'e gets caught, the boys in khaki'll be down on 'im like a ton of 'ot bricks.'

'The Kid' in question was one of the new parkie recruits, a young deserter who couldn't take another minute of army life after surviving the bloody evacuation of British troops from the beaches of Dunkirk during the summer of 1940.

'That's wot I told 'im, Aggs,' said Scrounger, who had stopped briefly to pick up a dog-end he'd found on the cement path. 'I told 'im you'd 'ave a go at 'im when yer saw 'im.'

Aggie suddenly stopped dead, and turned on him. 'Wot d'yer mean, *I'd* 'ave a go at 'im? Wot's The Kid ter me?'

Scrounger looked up at her. 'Come off it, Aggs,' he said. 'You're the nearest fing to a mum 'e's ever 'ad.'

This infuriated Aggs. Her eyes suddenly glared from her round pallid face, and looked as though they were about to pop right out of their sockets at the old codger. 'I'm *not* 'is bleedin' muvver!' she growled. 'I'm nobody's bleedin' muvver! Once an' fer all, Scrounger – d'yer understand that?'

The old codger shied back from her. Despite all the bloody military battles he'd been involved in, he knew better than to cross Aggs. There wasn't much of her, but she had a will of iron. 'Sorry, Aggs,' was all he dared to say. 'It was just that, well – The Kid sorta – looks up ter you.'

'That's 'is bad luck!' snapped Aggs, turning and shuffling off angrily.

The moment she'd left Scrounger, Aggs felt guilty. The poor bugger was harmless enough. He was just a bit of a pest at times, that's all. As she went, she resisted the urge to glance back over her shoulder at him. She knew what he'd be doing. She knew that he'd be off on his relentless prowl, searching for discarded dog-ends, scraps of food, and anything else that might help him to survive the winter.

It took her almost ten minutes to cover the distance from the Serpentine to Marble Arch. As she went, she was unaware of how beautiful the park was looking, a vision of white tinged with blue reflected from the sky above, and snow from the branches of trees fluttering down in a gentle breeze. In her mind's eye, she could see not only Scrounger, but all the other parkies who roamed that bleak urban landscape. Even though they often squabbled with each other over such things as territorial rights and humble personal possessions, they were all basically one large family, who, in the face of an outside threat, would fiercely defend each other. In fact, they were the only family Aggs had now, even though she was the odd one out – a female, and not really one of them. But in their own way, they respected her, and she respected them. She didn't mind a bit that they called her Aggs the hag. In fact, she liked it.

Walking today wasn't easy. She had to take it slowly, carefully. It had been a heavy drinking night the night before. Too much brown ale. Just like always. Her brain was fuzzed. She couldn't think straight. She hadn't thought straight for a long time. She couldn't really think too much about what her life had been before she came to the park. It was all a cloud, a fog. But then, she didn't want to know. By the time she had reached Speakers' Corner, she was out of breath. Ahead of her lay Marble Arch and Edgware Road. She liked this part of London. Oh yes. West London. More money, more freedom to breathe. Not a bit like – whatever part of London she had come from . . .

As usual, Thelma was late home from school, so it was left to Arnold to bring his small sister, Elsie, back to Enkel Street. Luckily for Thelma, Amy didn't get home herself from work until at least an hour and a half later, so 'what the eye didn't see, the heart didn't grieve'. However, Uncle Jim, the lodger upstairs, knew. In fact he knew a great deal that went on when Amy wasn't there. There were a lot of things he could tell Amy about Thelma's goings-on, but, close as he had always been to the family since he and his late elderly sister had moved in before the war, he felt it was not his place to interfere.

By the time Amy did finally get home, Thelma was already doing geography homework in their room on the first floor. Well, that's the impression she tried to give, but in reality, she was looking at make-up advertisements in a women's magazine which she'd nicked from the staff room at school.

Once Amy had checked that Arnold had drawn the blackout curtains properly, she went straight upstairs to her room. 'Right!' she growled, the moment she saw Thelma. 'So wot d'yer fink you're up to then?'

Thelma, crouched cross-legged on her bed, looked up with a start. 'Wot d'yer mean?' she shot back, all wide-eyed innocence.

'Yer know bleedin' well wot I mean!' Amy barked, going straight across to her, her jaw fixed firm. 'Yer've bin 'angin' round them boys again.'

Thelma had quickly concealed the magazine she had been poring over. She snapped back, 'I don't know wot you're talkin' about!'

'Don't yer?' asked Amy. 'So yer don't know anyfin' about this bunch of louts yer've bin 'angin' round wiv, when yer should be bringin' yer sister 'ome from school?'

Thelma was furious. 'It's not my fault if yer listen ter that old cow in Roden Street!'

'Don't you talk about people like that!' snapped Amy, pointing her finger angrily at her sister. 'I don't know wot's the matter wiv you lot since Mum left!'

'*I* ain't done nuffin'!' complained Elsie, who had come into the room behind Amy.

'Look, Thelm,' said Amy, doing her best to calm down, 'I don't want ter keep goin' on at yer. But since we ain't got Mum around, I've got ter try an' keep us all goin'. But if you keep makin' life difficult for us . . .'

'Yer mean, I'm making life difficult just because I chat wiv some of the boys from school on the way 'ome?'

'That's *not* wot I mean, Thelm, an' you know it. Just

remember, you're still only fourteen. You'll 'ave plenty of time fer boys when you're older. But till then, keep yer distance.'

Amy turned and made her way to the door.

'An' if I don't?' came Thelma's question.

Amy stopped and looked back at her. 'If yer don't, Thelma,' she said, quietly but firmly, 'then you'll not only be lettin' all of us down, but Mum too.' With that, she left the room.

On the landing outside, she paused a moment, deciding what to do next. Then a thought occurred to her and she began to go upstairs. Before she reached the top-floor landing, she called out, 'Uncle Jim! Are yer up there?'

Almost immediately, one of the two landing doors opened, and Jim Gibbons appeared. 'Yes, Amy,' he said. 'Come in.'

Amy followed him into his kitchen parlour. It was a meticulously neat little room, with a table in the middle, which was covered by a floral-patterned tablecloth laid over the top of another, woollen and fringed. In a corner by the window was a small oven cooker, and there was the last glow of a fire in the narrow fireplace. The magnolia-patterned wallpaper seemed to be as fresh and new as the day he and his late sister, Lil, had last decorated the room, before the war, and, because Uncle Jim was an avid reader, in another corner of the room was a home-made wooden bookcase containing dozens of old books, most of which were about Uncle Jim's passion for railways.

'Just getting myself ready for me night shift,' he said brightly, in a much better-spoken voice than his appearance might have suggested. 'Anything wrong?'

'No, no,' said Amy. 'Just wanted a bit of advice, that's all.'

Uncle Jim breathed a mock sigh of relief. 'Ah – thank goodness,' he replied. 'I thought you'd come to put up the rent!'

Amy smiled. 'Oh no, nuffin' like that,' she said. 'If you're just goin' out, I can come back later.'

'Sit yerself down, love,' he said. 'I'm not due on for half an hour yet.'

They both sat in easy chairs by the fire, Amy taking the one that had been used by Uncle Jim's sister when she was alive.

'Uncle Jim,' said Amy, tentatively, 'I've made up my mind to go and look for Mum.'

Uncle Jim sat back in his chair. He was an ample man in his late fifties, with a perfect head of almost completely white hair, and kindly grey-green eyes that shone out of a puffy face which was edged with a double chin. Now those eyes looked wary. 'How are you going to do that, Amy?' he asked.

'I don't know,' replied Amy. 'But I've got to do something. I'll go mad if I don't. If she's dead—'

Uncle Jim did a double take. 'Dead? What makes you think that?'

Amy sighed. 'I saw Mr 'Anley at the cop shop terday. He says we shouldn't 'ope fer too much. He says, it's just possible that Mum might've bin killed in an air raid.' She sat on the edge of the chair and looked hard at him. 'Wot do *you* fink, Uncle Jim?' she asked anxiously.

He thought hard for a moment. 'I would've thought it's most unlikely.'

'That's wot I say,' said Amy, trying to convince herself. 'But we have to admit, it is possible.'

'Possible,' said Uncle Jim, 'but unlikely. Your mum is far

too practical to let anything happen to her.'

Amy flopped back in her chair. 'Not practical enough ter stop 'er runnin' off the way she did.'

Now it was Uncle Jim's turn to lean forward. It wasn't easy for him to try to allay Amy's fears. He'd known her for quite a few years now, and felt very protective towards both her and her brother and sisters. But he had also known Amy's mum, knew how ill she had become during that final year before she disappeared.

'You know, Amy,' he said, 'some people do things that others can't quite understand. If they feel that they're in – well, some kind of a rut, then they look for a way out. It's much easier to face up to things if you have someone you can talk to.'

Amy sat up in her chair again. 'She could've talked to me,' she said forcefully. 'I'm her eldest daughter. I could've helped her.'

'Helped her to do what, Amy?' he asked gently.

Amy shrugged her shoulders. 'If she'd told me wot was wrong, I'd've kept my eyes on 'er.'

'You knew she was drinking?'

'Yes, course I did,' replied Amy. 'We all did. But a lot of people drink, an' they cope wiv it. I mean, just look at Dad. 'E spends most of 'is time round the boozer, but at least 'e 'asn't walked out on us.' Even as she said it, Amy felt that perhaps it might have been a good idea in some ways if her old man had been the one to walk out on them.

Uncle Jim lowered his eyes awkwardly. When he looked up again, he could see Amy watching him intently. She wanted some answers – some good, logical answers. But he had none to give her, and it pained him. It pained him a great deal.

'Amy,' he said, 'when someone is ill – I mean ill like your mum is – they don't really know how to think straight. They just shrivel up and withdraw into their shell. Like an ostrich really, burying its head in the sand.'

Amy didn't really know what he was talking about. But she trusted him. Uncle Jim was one of the very few people that she *could* trust. 'I won't know 'ow ter 'elp 'er, unless I know where she is, unless I know whevver she's alive or dead.' She leaned across and placed her hand on his. 'Uncle Jim,' she said, with a look of desperation, 'will you 'elp me find Mum?'

In the back garden of number 16 Enkel Street, the Anderson shelter was full of water. This was what happened every time there was either persistent rain or a thaw after a period of heavy snowfalls. There had been quite a lot of rain towards the end of the previous year, which meant that the ground was saturated, and the water levels high. Therefore, until someone – and it was usually young Arnold – got the stirrup pump working to drain the shelter, and then dry it out with a paraffin heater, the place was virtually uninhabitable. Luckily, the air raids on London were no longer as long nor as frequent as they had been at the height of the Blitz in 1940, so the Dodds family were able to spend more time in their beds. But since the Christmas 'truce', there had been one or two haphazard raids which had been more of an irritant than a threat. None the less, nobody could take any chances, and when, during one of those night raids, the going got a little too rough, Amy roused her sisters and brother out of their beds and made them head round the corner to the public brick shelter alongside the Savoy cinema in Loraine Road. Despite his so-called severe attack of flu, their dad was round the boozer at the time, and so, as usual, Amy had to cope on her own.

The Loraine Road public shelter was, true to form, packed to suffocation. Amy hated the place, mainly because it was practically airless, and smelled of people with wind problems. Like many others, she had misgivings about the wisdom of taking shelter in such a place. Since their introduction just before the Blitz, there had been a lot of criticism in the newspapers about brick shelters being 'death traps' if there were to be a direct hit, and this had been proved right on several occasions during some of the fiercest air raids. But at least they were a protection from one of the greatest hazards: shrapnel from exploding ack-ack shells, which frequently rained down from the sky during a heavy raid. And because they were reinforced with concrete, the public shelters did, to some extent, protect them from distant bomb blast.

'Over 'ere, Ame!'

'Plenty of room, Ame!'

Amy's heart sank, when the first people she laid eyes on, the moment she entered the shelter with her brother and sisters, were 'the Dolly Sisters', Mabel and Doris Hardy, who were given their nickname after a Hungarian singing act who had been internationally famous during the First World War. The formidable twins lived next door to the Dodds family, and had the distinction of not only looking alike, but thinking alike, and acting in perfect unison.

''Ere you are, Ame!' said Mabel, who was older than Doris by two and a half minutes. 'You can all share our blanket.'

'You can all share our blanket,' repeated Doris.

Thelma and Arnold groaned, and reluctantly squatted down

33

on the carpet that the twins had spread out on the cold cement floor. Elsie, who was huddled up to Amy, was half-asleep, and didn't really know what was going on.

'It's very good of you, Miss Mabel, Miss Doris,' said Amy, trying hard to sound grateful, but not succeeding very well.

The twins moved over, practically pushing a large fat man out of the way, and made room for Amy and Elsie.

'Nice 'n comfy cosy,' said Mabel.

'Comfy cosy,' repeated Doris.

The two sisters, who, like everyone else, were wrapped up against the cold like Eskimos, never stopped smiling. Both they and the Dodds family were now propped up against the wall.

'We got in early,' said Mabel, tilting her head towards Amy.

'Soon after tea-time,' said Doris.

'We'd never've found a place if we hadn't,' said Mabel.

Both sisters nodded in mutual agreement.

After a moment or so, the sound of anti-aircraft fire heralded the approach of the first wave of enemy bombers. Everyone automatically turned their eyes towards the shelter roof, watching, waiting apprehensively. In the background, a man started to sing 'Run, Rabbit, Run'. Within seconds, several people had joined in. It was a desperate attempt not only to keep up their spirits and drown out the deadly sounds above them, but also to keep warm. On the other side of the shelter, Amy could smell cocoa spiced with rum, which a young mum was pouring from a vacuum flask, and who, to Amy's astonishment, was giving sips to her son, who looked even younger than Arnold. But then she thought, what does it matter? After all, when she looked around the cold, bleak surroundings, who could blame anyone for the way they attempted to cope? None the less, this was Amy's idea of hell. In her mind, she damned everyone, from Herbert Morrison – the so-called Minister of Security, who was responsible for subjecting them to such hellholes – and Adolf Hitler, for starting the war, to, in one rash act of judgement, her own mum, for leaving her to cope with a family that she clearly didn't want.

'Cat's pee!' said Arnold, immediately slapping one hand over his nose and mouth.

'Arnold!' Amy gave her young brother a hard nudge.

'I tell yer, I can smell cat's pee!' insisted Arnold, speaking through his fingers. 'It's terrible!'

He was of course right, for during the day most of the shelters were left open, and they were a haven for stray cats. But what they did not expect was to hear the sound of a moggy mewing, coming from somewhere between the twin sisters.

Mabel and Doris exchanged quick, guilty looks, then turned to Arnold and motioned to him not to draw attention. The reason soon became apparent. They had brought their pet cat, William, with them, tucked in a large woollen bag between them. And William was clearly not happy.

Mabel said quietly, 'We couldn't leave 'im at 'ome in the middle of a raid. Could we, Ame?'

'Could we?' repeated Doris.

'After all, 'e is one of the family,' said Mabel.

'One of the family,' repeated Doris.

Amy smiled back at them, indicating that she agreed. But by now she felt as though she was going out of her mind stuck in such a place, and decided that next time she would sooner take her luck at home in an air raid than subject herself and her family to such torture in public.

But her attitude soon changed when Mabel suddenly said, 'Your dear mum did so love our William. Just before she went last year, she told Doris and me that if she'd 'ad the chance, she'd've taken our William wiv 'er. Isn't that right, Doris?'

Doris nodded. 'That's right, Mabel.'

Amy sat up with a start and turned to face both of them. 'Yer mean – yer knew Mum was goin' ter leave 'ome?' she asked, in disbelief. 'She – told yer?'

Mabel turned to Doris, and Doris turned to Mabel. 'Well, of course she did, Ame,' they replied in unison. 'Didn't yer know?' the Dolly Sisters' smiles had disappeared. It was most unlike them.

CHAPTER 3

Aggs didn't care much for her new job. But then she didn't care for any jobs, and only thought of them as a means to an end. However, a quid a week wasn't to be sneezed at, especially the way she was living it out rough on the streets, so she decided to grin and bear it – at least until something easier came along. The job in question was at a pub called The Turk's Head, which was tucked away in one of the seedier streets behind Paddington Station, and involved scrubbing out the three main bars and washing over the tables and well-worn leather bench seats. It also meant mopping out the two lavatories, which was Aggs's least favourite task, especially as they always smelled of stale urine after the previous night's booze-up. The best part of the job was that it was only part-time, from eight in the morning, until the pub opened at midday. The worst part was the landlord, Charlie Ratner.

Ratner was a weedy little man in his fifties, a good head of well-preserved black hair, and dark glasses to match. When Aggs first met him, she was convinced that if she breathed on him too hard he would fall over backwards. However, even on her first day there, she was already beginning to see quite a different person, for Charlie Ratner was clearly as hard as nails. Her assessment wasn't only based on the cardboard notices pinned up behind the counters in all three bars, which read in very large menacing letters, 'NO CREDIT – FOR ANYONE', but also in the domineering way in which he talked to both his wife, Josie, and to his young daughter, Maureen. But Aggs didn't expect what the pub landlord said to her that first morning there, whilst she was scrubbing the floor in the Private Bar.

'Oh, by the way,' said Ratner, who was never without a fag end protruding from the side of his lips. 'In case I didn't mention it, all the booze in this pub is closely monitored.'

Aggs looked up briefly to see him behind the counter, wiping the upturned bottles of measured gin and whisky. She sniffed. 'I never touch spirits meself,' she said, very pointedly.

'I said, *all* the booze,' replied Ratner, without even turning to look at her.

Aggs sniffed again disdainfully, wiped her running nose with the back of her hand, and carried on with her scrubbing. She resented his remark. If he didn't trust her, she said to herself, then why had he taken her on? But she had already sussed that one out the moment he'd given her the job. Running a pub wasn't this ratbag's main line of business, she reckoned. Oh no. There was a war on, and whatever his sideline, it would suit his purpose to have a down-and-out on his payroll rather than someone with more prying eyes. Even when she'd come for the interview, she'd been surprised, and relieved, that he hadn't given her appearance more than a casual glance, and hadn't bothered to ask her one single question about where she'd worked before.

'You're the one they call Aggs, ain't yer?'

Aggs stopped scrubbing. She hadn't expected this. 'Where

d'yer 'ear that then?' she asked, trying to sound as though she didn't care.

'Oh, I don't go round wiv me ears closed,' he said, stubbing out the remains of his fag end, and immediately lighting up another. Then, with his elbows on the counter, he smiled, and asked, ''Ow do they take to the idea of one of their lot gettin' a job then?'

'Don't follow yer.' replied Aggs, carrying on with the scrubbing.

Ratner grinned, pulled on his fag, and, despite the fact that it was only eleven o'clock in the morning, poured himself a measure of rum from a bottle he kept beneath the counter. 'From what I've 'eard, most of the scruffs in that park prefer to cadge.'

'Oh really?' replied Aggs, without turning. 'You know more than I do.'

Ratner grinned. 'I wouldn't be at all surprised,' he said. It sounded more like a warning than a comment. 'Anyway, Aggs, you look after me, and I'll look after you. Savvy?'

Aggs looked up to find him standing over her. He had a broad, false smile on his thin, chiselled face.

Amy was determined to have it out with her dad. If it was true, if the Dolly Sisters – and God knows who else – knew that her mum had been on the verge of leaving home, then why didn't *she* know? Had something happened between her mum and dad that she hadn't been told about?

The first opportunity Amy had to tackle her dad was on Friday bath night. During the time when her mum was at home, the family had had to use the old tin bath, which was kept hanging on a hook outside in the back yard, and which was brought into the scullery on Friday nights. But it was such a chore, heating up the water in a bucket on the stove, and by the time the bath was anywhere near full, the water was usually lukewarm. So after her mum disappeared, Amy decided that her brother and sisters would have to do like most other people, and go round to Hornsey Road Baths. After all, their dad worked there, for goodness' sake, so why shouldn't he at least do something for the family and get them in free?

After Thelma, Elsie and herself had finished taking their baths in the officially regulated few inches of water, and Arnold had caused his usual mayhem by singing at the top of his voice in his bath in the male baths area, Amy sent them all home, and waited for her dad. He wasn't due to finish work until ten o'clock, and by then the air-raid siren on top of the police station next door had wailed out, practically deafening everyone close by. But the moment he'd locked up, and turned off all the lights in the male bath area, Amy started to question him.

'I've told yer before, Ame,' replied Ernie, when Amy asked him for the umpteenth time why her mum had left home. 'Yer mum was ill. You know only too well wot she was like wiv the booze.'

Amy was not accepting this as an answer. 'Even if she *was* ill,' she persisted, 'there must've been a reason why she started drinkin' like that. There must've been a reason why she was prepared to give up 'er family an' walk out on them.'

Once they'd left the baths, they headed slowly along Hornsey Road. With the distant rumble of ack-ack fire heralding the approach of enemy aircraft, the streets had emptied, and as the sky was covered by a thick mass of wintry night clouds, the only way to move along was by torchlight.

'Yer've got ter realise, Ame,' said Ernie, who was no more

than a dim figure beside her in the dark, 'yer mum was like that. She was always a one for suddenly doin' fings, wivout no rhyme nor reason.'

Amy didn't go along with that at all. In her eyes, her mum was a kind, considerate person, who would never have done anything to hurt her family – unless there was a reason why she couldn't help herself. 'Dad,' she said, bringing him to a halt on the corner of Seven Sisters Road, 'did you know that Mum was goin' ter run off like that?'

Ernie took a deep sigh. 'Don't be so daft, Ame,' he replied. 'Course I didn't.'

Amy came back at him immediately. 'Everyone else did.'

'Who's *everyone*?'

'Miss Mabel. Miss Doris.'

'Come off it, Ame . . .'

Amy grabbed his arm to prevent him from moving on. 'They're not the only ones, Dad,' she said, refusing to allow him to dismiss what she was saying. 'It sounds as though everyone in the neighbour'ood knew wot she was goin' ter do, except us. Did *you* know, Dad?'

Ernie was relieved that Amy couldn't see his expression in the dark. She knew he felt cornered, for he suddenly lit a dog-end, which briefly illuminated his face. 'Yer mum wanted time ter sort fings out for 'erself, Ame,' he said. 'I fink we should give it to 'er, an' get on wiv our own lives.'

'Give 'er time!' Amy couldn't believe what he was saying. 'She's been gone for a whole year! Are we just goin' ter let 'er go, an' do nuffin' about it?'

Ernie was getting irritated with her. 'Listen ter me, Ame!' he said, trying hard not to snap. 'Yer mum'll come back – when she's good an' ready!'

'When will that be, Dad? When?'

It was so pitch-dark, that the only thing Amy could really see of her dad was the glow from his fag end. 'I'll see yer later,' he said.

Amy knew he had gone, for the sky was suddenly illuminated by a vast crisscross of searchlights, and she could just see the outline of his figure hurrying off along Seven Sisters Road, heading for his usual rendezvous at The Eaglet pub.

The air raid was now becoming a bit dodgy, and with a barrage of ack-ack fire now directly overhead, Amy's main task was to get back home to her brother and sisters as fast as she could. As she quickly made her way past The Eaglet, she resisted the urge to peer round the door into the Saloon Bar, for she knew that without any doubt at all that her dad would be there with his mates, propping up the bar, offering drinks all round. After all, it was Friday – pay night.

Once she had turned off Hornsey Road into the deserted, pitch-dark confines of Mayton Street, her pace quickened, and the dim light from her torch flickered precariously. Suddenly, all hell broke loose directly above her, as ack-ack fire managed to pinpoint an enemy aircraft caught in the crossbeams of a vast pattern of searchlights like a fly in a spider's web. She started to panic, and her trot quickly turned into a run. The relentless, blinding glare from the ack-ack barrage lit up the entire street. Amy tried to shield her eyes, but as she did so, she lost her footing, and tumbled off the kerb into the road, where, she let out a loud yell as something hit her on one side, sending her reeling to the ground. Dazed, but not seriously hurt, she quickly struggled to get up, but as she did so, she felt someone's arm around her shoulder, trying to help her to her feet.

'Are y-you all r-right?' called what sounded like the voice of a young bloke with a stutter.

'Bloody fool!' Amy groaned as it quickly dawned on her that, luckily, she had only been hit by a bicycle. 'Why don't yer look where you're goin'?'

'C-can't see you in the b-blackout,' called the voice. 'I'm s-sorry. I'm r-really s-sorry.'

'So yer should be!' snapped Amy ungraciously. 'Yer could've killed me!'

'Are you h-hurt badly?' asked the anxious voice. 'Can I do anything?'

'I'm all right!' Amy shouted above the deafening sound of ack-ack gunfire. 'Which is more than I can say for me torch.' She tried to turn it on, but the bulb was completely dead. 'It's 'ad it!'

The young bloke quickly took the torch off the front of his bike. 'Here!' he said, without a second's thought. 'Take mine.'

Amy practically snatched the torch from his hand and immediately turned the beam on to the boy's face. He was about the same age as herself, but as he had a woollen scarf tightly wrapped around his neck, apart from a bright red slightly pointed nose and thin metal-rimmed spectacles, it was quite difficult to make out his features. Even so, for one passing moment, she felt she had seen him somewhere before.

'I'm s-sorry,' the boy repeated. 'I'm really s-sorry. Can I t-take you home?'

'Over my dead body!' growled Amy. As she spoke, there was an almighty explosion in the near distance, and the whole street shuddered.

Without another word, Amy turned and ran off as fast as she could.

'I'm s-sorry!' called the boy yet again. 'S-sorry . . . !'

By the time Amy got home, the air raid was in full swing. Her brother and sisters were already in the air-raid shelter, and doing their best to get some sleep amidst the constant barrage of ack-ack gunfire overhead, bombs screeching down in the distance, and the sound of fire engines and other emergency vehicles, with sirens and horns blaring, rushing back and forth along the main Hornsey and Seven Sisters Roads.

It wasn't until she had settled down on the bunk alongside little Elsie that Amy began to feel a bruise beginning to form on her left hip, on the spot where she had been struck by the bicycle. As she lay there, she cursed the young fool who had collided with her, despite all his repeated apologies. After a while, the raid gradually abated, and it wasn't very long before she could actually hear the sound of Arnold snoring. When she eventually felt safe enough to turn off the paraffin lamp, she lay there in the dark pondering how much longer she would have to endure the hardships of bringing up her family. Oh, how she hated the dark. Even though her eyes were wide open, she could see nothing. The dark made her feel so vulnerable, so lost, so utterly alone. She felt much safer in the light. The sun gave her confidence.

'I'm firsty.'

For one brief moment, Amy was startled by the sound of little Elsie's weary voice cutting through the eerie silence. 'Go ter sleep, Else,' she whispered, trying hard not to wake the others.

'I *can't* sleep!' persisted Elsie, tetchily. 'I wanna drink. I'm firsty!'

Amy suddenly remembered that not only had she forgotten to bring a jug of water down into the shelter, but she had also not made their usual flask of hot cocoa. 'All right, all right,' she whispered directly into her small sister's ear. 'I'll go an' get yer one. But don't wake up the uvvers!'

After nearly tripping over the extinguished paraffin lamp, Amy finally managed to extricate herself from the dark, and find her way out of the shelter. Although it was dark outside too, there was a restless half-moon rushing in and out of the sombre night clouds, and the sky over the rooftops at the end of the back yard was a shimmering red glow, which indicated that some poor soul over Muswell Hill or Highgate had probably copped it during the air raid. She was just about to enter the house by the back yard door, when she suddenly noticed that a chink of light was filtering through a small gap in the blackout curtain at the window of Uncle Jim's back room on the top floor.

Rushing into the house, she made straight for the stairs, where she stopped, and called out, 'Uncle Jim! Yer've got a light showin'!'

She waited briefly for a reply from the top floor. But there was no response.

'Uncle Jim!' she called again. 'Can yer 'ear me?'

Receiving no reply, she rushed up the stairs as fast as she could. When she reached the first-floor landing, she called out again as loud as she could, 'Uncle Jim! Are yer up there?'

Still no reply, so she quickly climbed the last stairs. It was so unlike their lodger to be negligent, she thought, so unlike him.

Once she had reached the top-floor landing, she could see the chink of light under the kitchen door. Once again she called out, knocking on the door at the same time. 'Uncle Jim! Are yer in there?' There was still no response, so her only course was to go in. She gently opened the door, and peered in. 'Uncle Jim?' Although the electric light was on, the room was deserted. So she went straight to the window, and corrected the offending chink in the blackout curtain. Then she turned round to take in the room.

It was the first time she had ever entered the lodger's room without him actually being there, and she suddenly felt guilty. But where was Uncle Jim? She knew that he had been on night shift all the week in his job as a post sorter at the nearby Bovay Place GPO sorting office, but it really was careless of him to leave the light on during an air raid. It was only pure luck that they hadn't been caught out by an ARP warden, for as sure as God made little apples, it would have meant a heavy fine. She quickly turned off the light, left the room, and closed the door behind her. But just as she was about to make her way down the stairs in the dark again, she noticed another light under the door leading up to the attic. 'Uncle Jim!' she called out, simultaneously banging hard on the door. 'Are yer up there?' But once again, there was no reply. Taking a deep breath, she slowly opened the door, and peered up the stairs which led to the small attic room above. 'Uncle Jim?' she called, even though she knew by now that he was not at home.

As she slowly climbed the steep and narrow wooden stairs, the first thing she noticed were the hoards of second-hand books piled up all over the place. Although the electric light was on, the blackout curtain had been drawn across the window set high up in the sloping ceiling. The last time she had been up there in the attic was long before the war, when she was no more than a bright-eyed kid. In those days, nobody had yet occupied the place, and it was something of an adventure to spy out such a deserted, mysterious room, which in Amy's childlike mind was probably full of ghosts. It was also to this same airless room, in those happy days, that her mum and dad would come whenever they wanted a few moments alone together, away from the prying eyes of their inquisitive young daughters. It all seemed to be such a long time ago, when the Dodds family really knew how to get on with each other. But now?

She sighed deeply, and turned to leave. But just as she was about to go down and switch off the light at the bottom of the stairs, she stopped abruptly. She could smell something burning. She turned back, and looked around the cluttered room. A thin funnel of smoke was twisting up from an ashtray on the small table Uncle Jim used as a makeshift desk. Going straight to the ashtray, she found a half-smoked fag smouldering. It puzzled her, for when Uncle Jim was on night shift at the sorting office, it usually meant that he had to leave home soon after five in the evening. But it was now well past ten, so how come his fag was still burning in the ashtray? Without a second's thought, she picked up the remains of the fag, and stubbed it out.

For a moment or so, Amy just stood there, looking around her, thinking about Uncle Jim, and what a strange and lonely man he must be. She thought about his relationship with his elderly sister, Lil, which some of the more prudish neighbours had often considered 'unhealthy', an opinion formed only on the basis that they lived together. But even Amy did ask herself why someone like Uncle Jim had never got married, nor seemed to have any female acquaintances. Then she suddenly felt guilty. People shouldn't have to answer questions as to how they wanted to live. '*Everyone to their own*,' as Amy's mum always used to say. Nevertheless, there was no denying that Uncle Jim *was* a very self-contained man.

After a moment, she came to, and suddenly felt quite awful for trespassing on the lodger's part of the house. An Englishman's home is his castle, she thought to herself. She had no right to come charging up to his private room while he was away. But her split second of guilt was unexpectedly put to the challenge when something caught her notice on the makeshift desk in front of her, something which was concealed behind a shadow cast by a tall pile of books. For some inexplicable reason, it sent a cold chill down her spine. It was a small framed snapshot of a man and a woman standing arm in arm, laughing at the camera.

The snapshot was of Uncle Jim, and Amy's mum, Agnes Dodds.

Aggs hadn't felt so flush for ages. At the end of her first day scrubbing floors and cleaning out the lavatories at The Turk's Head, she had picked up a cool three shillings and fourpence, which to her, in her present circumstances, was nothing less than a fortune. On her way back home to her patch in Hyde Park, her first inclination was to blow the whole three bob on a few good bottles of booze, nothing fancy – she had never been much keen on spirits – but a couple of bottles of stout, which to her was like living in the lap of luxury. However, her first priority was to get some grub inside her, so the place she made for was a fairly seedy street just behind Paddington

Station, where she managed to buy herself a loaf of bread, some apples, and a small pork pie. But her big treat came when she got a whiff of fish and chips coming from a small corner shop, which had had its windows boarded up after a bomb blast, and now carried a huge chalked scrawl, 'BISINESS AS USHAL'. When she reached the place, there was, inevitably, a long queue so she decided to go into Woolworths first to buy herself a penny bar of soap.

For a threepenny and sixpenny store, this particular Woolworths had currently very little to offer within that price range. On a good day there was always a queue of women of all ages waiting in hope to buy a pair of quite ordinary woollen stockings, and even though they had the money, they had to make sure that they hadn't left their ration books at home. Today, there was no queue, but Aggs sniffed contemptuously as she passed a group of women shoppers searching in vain for a lipstick or some face powder amongst the pile of junk on what was laughingly called the 'Make-Up' counter. Some of them scattered when a rather pungent-smelling Aggs pushed her way to the counter and called mockingly to the young, heavily made-up assistant, ''Ow many coupons fer some beauty cream, mate?'

Turning only briefly to look at Aggs's yellow-stained teeth, the girl replied, 'It's not beauty cream you need, missus – it's a good bath!'

Aggs waited for the women's laughter to subside before answering, quick as a flash, 'Wiv your brain an' my looks, who needs a barf?'

Amidst gales of laughter, the humiliated shopgirl turned her back and went to serve customers on the opposite side of the counter.

Once she had purchased her soap, and fish and chips, Aggs made her way back to the park. There was still a couple of hours or so until it got dark, so before collecting her bundle for the night, she made her way to one of her favourite daylight benches, which was situated just across the road from the Royal Albert Hall, close to the massive Albert Memorial. Here she could rest without interruption, her only companion being a selection of grey squirrels who relied on her to provide any tasty titbits she might have retrieved from any of the litter bins. The bench itself was surrounded by what had once been some beautiful ornamental floral gardens, but in keeping with the war effort, they had been replaced with allotments containing all the essential vegetables such as carrots, cabbages, turnips, green beans, and just about anything else that was edible. As it was now mid-winter, however, the ground, although turned over by the park gardeners, was practically bare – cold and hardened by endless ice and frosts.

Despite the fact that it had been almost an hour since she had bought her fish and chips, Aggs settled down to eat them. In fact she preferred them cold. She always had, she said to herself, even on Friday nights back home, when Amy used to go round to Andersons in Hornsey Road to collect the usual six pieces of cod and chips for the family. She suddenly stopped chewing on the cold chip with her loose front teeth. She was thinking about the past again, and that was something she had vowed not to do. But it wasn't easy, not at times like this, not with a mouthful of fish and chips. No matter how hard she tried, she could see them all – Amy, Thelma, Arnold, little Elsie, and yes, Ernie too. They were there as clear as daylight itself, as though they were standing right in front of her. If she had ever thought that she wanted to get away from them, away from every part of her life during those hell-on-earth years, then it wasn't going to work. It couldn't.

'Give us a chip, Ma.'

Aggs looked up with a start to find The Kid standing over her. 'Bugger off!' she growled, quickly shoving another chip into her mouth. 'An' don't call me Ma. I ain't nuffin' ter you!'

The Kid grinned. 'That's where you're wrong,' he said cheekily, as he sat down beside her. 'Yer mean a lot ter me.'

Aggs turned away from him, tore off a bit of cold cod, and shoved that into her mouth with the chip she was still chewing.

Mischievously, The Kid sat as close to her as he possibly could. 'You're about as near ter 'ome as I'll ever get – or want ter get.' For someone who had survived one of the great horrors of the war at Dunkirk, he managed to look amazingly well and alive. 'If my mum was like you,' he said, peering over her shoulder at the newspaper containing the fish and chips, 'I'd still be there now.'

Aggs turned only briefly to look at him, and the moment she saw what should have been the exuberant blue-grey eyes of a nineteen-year-old, but which were now grey and looking at least ten years older, she couldn't really be angry. 'You bin nickin' again,' she said, picking up a chip and reluctantly giving it to him.

'Don't believe everyfin' people tell yer,' replied the boy, whose pallid face was only just visible beneath a black woollen scarf which covered his head and was tied beneath his chin. 'Especially old codgers like Scrounger.' He popped the cold chip into his mouth and chewed it like he hadn't eaten for a long time, which he probably hadn't.

'Wot 'appened?' asked Aggs.

'Nuffink.'

'Wot 'appened?' growled Aggs.

The Kid swallowed the remains of his chip, then leaned back against the bench. 'It was this stupid sod – in Selfridges, in the Men's Department. 'E caught me puttin' this tiepin in me pocket.'

'Tiepin!' said Aggs incredulously. 'Wot d'yer want wiv a bleedin' tiepin?'

'Nuffink,' replied The Kid. 'I just liked the look of it. I wanted somefink I didn't need, that's all. I wanted to feel it inside me pocket, so's I could roll it round in me fingers every so often, and imagine wot it might be like ter be well off.'

''Ow much was it?'

The Kid adjusted his mittens, then thrust his hand into his duffel coat pockets. 'Oh, I dunno. One an' six – somefin' like that.'

Aggs swung round to look at him. 'One an' six? You took all that risk, fer one an' six?'

The Kid had a gleam in his eyes as he leaned his head back on the park bench and stared up into the darkening sky. 'It wasn't 'ow much it was, Ma,' he said, 'it was just the feelin' that I had as much right to it as anyone else.'

Although Aggs found it difficult to take in what he was trying to say, she had a great deal of sympathy for him. To her, The Kid wasn't like the other parkies. His reasons for being there were different; he wasn't only running away from his family, he was running away from life.

''Ow d'yer get away?' she asked.

'Wiv difficulty!' he grinned. 'As soon as I saw this ponce lookin' at me, I just belted off down the stairs, and got me arse down Oxford Street as fast as I could.'

'You're a stupid bugger!' said Aggs, turning away from

him and stuffing herself with another piece of cod.

'Aw, come off it, Ma,' said The Kid. 'Ain't you ever done a dare in yer life?'

'Never!'

'Pull the uvver one!'

Aggs's face stiffened. 'No matter 'ow much I want, I don't take stuff that don't belong ter me.'

The Kid broke into a wide grin. When he did so, Ma was always infuriated, for she knew that he was taking the piss out of her. None the less, the boy's grin was infectious, and it made her feel protective towards him. 'Sounds ter me like yer've never left 'ome, Ma,' the boy said provocatively.

'Wos that s'pposed ter mean?' snapped Aggs.

'Yer've still got principles,' replied the boy. 'Means, you'll go back 'ome – one day.'

'Stupid sod!' said Aggs, haughtily.

The Kid knew he was riling her, so he leaned in towards her. 'Why d'yer do it, Ma?' he asked riskily. 'Why *did* yer leave 'ome?'

Aggs refused to look at him. She wanted to remind him that the unspoken rule of the parkies was that no one ever asked questions about someone's past. To them, it was only the present that mattered – not yesterday, nor tomorrow, only today. 'Mind yer own business!' she said, getting up from the bench.

As she moved, a flurry of grey squirrels came rushing towards them, each of them sitting up expectantly. Fish and chips may not have been their favourite titbits, but there was a war on, and even they had to make do.

''Ome is only a place,' said Aggs, as she wrapped up the fish and chips into a bundle. 'If I ever lived in such a place,

I'd remember. The fing is – I don't.' Without another word, she shoved the parcel of fish and chips into The Kid's lap, and made off.

The Kid watched her go. He couldn't make up his mind if she was really as old as she looked, if she was married, if she had any kids, or why she had shunned the past to live the way she was living now. In fact, there were a lot of things that puzzled him about Aggs. But he respected her too much to push her too far.

One of the many squirrels who had gathered round him suddenly leaped up on to the bench alongside him, and bobbed up and down anxiously, waiting for an evening treat.

The Kid opened the newspaper, and tucked in. Yes, he had a lot to be grateful for to Aggs. He still wished he'd been given her as a mum rather than the one he'd got.

CHAPTER 4

Amy had never seen Uncle Jim embarrassed before. It had not occurred to her that he was anything but a pillar of cool respectability, someone who wouldn't have anything to be embarrassed about. None the less, there was no doubt how ill at ease he was when she tackled him about the lights he'd left on the night before.

'I'm a stupid nit, Ame,' he said falteringly. It had clearly unnerved him to find Amy waiting for him in the passage as soon as he walked through the front door on his return from night shift. 'I usually go round last thing, always do a final check. It's so unlike me. Must be old age creepin' on.'

Amy was not convinced. 'But you left boaf lights on,' she persisted. 'An' when I went upstairs ter check, there was a fag burnin' in the ashtray.'

Uncle Jim felt his inside tense. He dreaded the implication in Amy's remark. 'Oh – did I do that?' he asked, in as matter-of-fact a way as he could. 'I tell you – I'll forget me own head one of these days.' He took off his flat cap, and ran his hand nervously through his flock of white hair. 'Thing is, I came back for a bit – in me supper break. Just twenty minutes. I like to get away once in a while – stretch me legs a bit.'

Amy shrugged. 'There was an air raid on.'

'Not when I came back,' replied Uncle Jim, immediately replacing his cap on his head. 'You know it's only five minutes' walk back home. It was dead quiet when I came. You was all in the shelter.'

Amy wasn't too sure how he knew that she and the family were in the shelter, but she let it pass. She also let pass the one question she really wanted answering. But that would have to wait for a more suitable moment.

'Well, I'm sorry I went upstairs, Uncle Jim,' she said. 'I didn't mean to intrude. It was just that—'

'I know,' he interrupted. 'The blackout. I'm sorry, Ame, I'm really sorry to have put you to so much trouble.'

Amy smiled. 'See you later,' she said, returning to her back parlour.

'You can come up to my place any time you wish, Ame, you know that,' he said, before Amy had disappeared. 'There's nothin' private up there.'

Amy smiled sweetly. 'Fanks,' she said, closing the door.

For a moment, she stood with her back against the door, listening to Uncle Jim as he made his way upstairs. She waited until she heard his kitchen door close on the top floor. Something was wrong, or at least there was certainly something odd going on. She tried to work out why Uncle Jim had come home during the night. It was so unlike him, she said to herself, for in many ways he was quite a lazy man, who rarely seemed to use his feet to go anywhere, except to work at the sorting office, just a few minutes' walk. No, he must have had a reason for coming home. As she stood there turning things over in her mind, all sorts of questions started to concern her. She didn't know why. For all she knew, there was a perfectly good, simple answer to the mystery she was beginning to build up in her mind. After all, apart from leaving a chink in his blackout curtain, Uncle Jim hadn't actually done anything wrong. But then she remembered that snapshot photo of him, arm in arm with her mum . . .

On the top floor, Uncle Jim switched on the light and went straight upstairs to the attic. The first thing he did was to pull back the blackout curtain, which was fixed on a piece of wire above and below the sloped window. For one brief moment, he looked out, and took in the skyline view of North London on a surprisingly bright and sunny morning. In the distance he could just see the glass dome of Alexandra Palace glistening in the watery sunlight, and beyond that a hint of the suburbs of Palmers Green and Enfield. But this was only a minor distraction; his thoughts were now concentrated on far more important matters, which took him straight to his makeshift desk. He immediately grabbed hold of the snapshot of himself with Amy's mum. He stared at it anxiously for only a brief moment, then quickly opened a drawer at the bottom of the desk, and popped it in. Then he took a key from one of several on a keyring in his coat pocket, and locked the drawer.

For a moment he stood there, staring at the locked drawer as though it might suddenly open again of its own free will. Then he turned round, and looked towards the stairs.

He only wished that he could have prevented his stupidity of the night before.

That same morning, Hilda Feathers was waiting for Amy when she arrived for work. 'We've got two free tickets for the hospital dance at the Town Hall,' she said excitedly. 'That gorgeous young doctor gave them to me. You know, the one who comes in regular as clockwork on Tuesday mornings. Ooh, he can look me over with his stethoscope any time he likes!'

Amy was baffled. 'Don't be daft, 'Ilde,' she said. 'We can't go to an 'ospital dance. We're not nurses.'

'You don't have to be a nurse to go to a hospital dance, you fool!' her friend sighed. 'It's in aid of the Red Cross.' She looked carefully round the tea shop to make sure no one could hear her, then added, 'It'll be full of servicemen. I might meet my destiny, a general or something.'

Amy laughed.

'You can laugh,' said Hilda. 'These things can happen, you know.'

'Not to me, they don't,' replied Amy.

'How d'you know if you don't go hunting?'

Amy was puzzled. ''Untin'?'

Hilda growled like a dog, and with a nudge and a wink replied, 'Come off it, Amy. *You* know . . . !'

The next opportunity they had to talk was after they'd taken the first orders of the day, and passed them on to Mrs Bramley, the cook. It happened when Amy only just managed to prevent Hilda, who was carrying a full tray of tea for four, from bumping into Marge Jackson, their supervisor. It was a frequent hazard for Hilda, who usually sacrificed safety for vanity by quickly removing her spectacles every time a presentable male customer came into the shop.

'It's on Saturday night,' whispered Hilda, as she met up with Amy again after delivering her tray of tea.

'What is?' asked Amy.

'The dance!' snapped Hilda. 'We'll have a wonderful night out. It'll do you the world of good!'

Amy shook her head. 'Can't manage it, 'Ild,' she said, with a sigh.

'Why not?'

'I can't leave the family that long,' she explained, loading up her tray at the counter for the next customer. 'There might be an air raid or somefin'.'

'So what?' growled Hilda, who suddenly realised that taking off her spectacles hadn't made her invisible. 'So what?' she repeated, lowering her voice. 'They can go down the air-raid shelter, can't they? Your Thelma's old enough to keep an eye on them.'

'Oh yes!' laughed Amy. 'An' who's goin' ter keep an eye on 'er?'

Hilda sighed irritably. 'What about your father?'

Amy lowered her eyes and shrugged guiltily. Then, after collecting her tray containing a stainless-steel pot of coffee and chicory, well-worn cups and saucers, and two plates of bread and marge, she hurried off to some customers at the front end of the shop. On her way back to the counter, however, she was somewhat unnerved to be waylaid by Marge Jackson, who beckoned that she wanted a word with her.

'If you want ter go ter that dance, Amy,' she said, voice low, 'I'll come an' keep an eye on your lot at 'ome.'

Amy was dumbfounded. 'Marge!' she said, quite taken aback. 'I couldn't ask yer to do a fing like that.'

'Yer didn't ask,' replied her supervisor. 'I offered. I'm not doin' anyfin' on Sat'day night. I can easily baby-sit for yer.'

Amy was overwhelmed. Even though she had always been on the best of terms with Marge, their relationship had really only ever been a professional one. But she had clearly underestimated this quiet, unassuming woman, who, despite only being in her mid-thirties, was already widowed, her young husband killed fighting in the Spanish Civil War.

'It's really kind of you, Marge,' Amy said, 'but even if I wanted ter go, I couldn't. I 'aven't been on a night out since me mum left over a year ago.'

'Even more reason why you should go now,' replied Marge. 'It'll take your mind off fings, 'elp yer ter ferget about tryin' ter find yer mum.'

Amy stiffened. 'But I don't want ter ferget about tryin' ter find 'er. She's my mum. I love 'er.'

'Of course yer do, Amy,' replied Marge, comfortingly. 'An' I know wiv your persistence, yer *will* find 'er sooner or later. But you're not an ol' woman, Amy. Yer can't afford to lose these kind of chances when they come along. Yer deserve more.'

Amy didn't know what to say. She wasn't used to someone taking an interest in her, someone showing her even a modicum of kindness. 'I must say,' she said, weakening, 'I do love dancing. Bit out of practice, mind. But I ain't got nuffin' I could wear. Not even a good pair of stockins'.'

'Well, if that's all you're worrying about,' said Hilda, who had suddenly joined them, 'then your problem's solved. My sister's got a dress that would just fit you. And as for stockings, well – all we need is a good packet of Bisto!'

Amy didn't like Dr Ferguson. In her opinion, there was something smarmy about him, a sense of his own importance, a bit of a show-off. Ever since she was a kid, she remembered being dragged round to his surgery in Arthur Road by her mum, and sitting in that dreary little waiting room full of out-dated magazines and people sniffing with colds, and groaning about aches and pains of every description. Even though Dr Ferguson had been the family's GP for years, the only thing Amy could ever remember about him was the way he treated her and her mum as though they were nothing more than a hindrance to his daily routine. A Scot from Glasgow, Dr Ferguson had an air of superiority that owed more to his feeling of guilt at having been brought up in the rough Gorbals area, and his attempts to conceal that he was, in reality, from no better background than most of his own patients. However, Amy had no choice but to go and see him, for he knew practically everything about the health of the Dodds family, and that included the mental state of her mum.

'You're only asking me what I have told the police a dozen times, young lady,' said the doctor, officious and businesslike. 'A practitioner is under no legal obligation to reveal the personal medical details of his patient.'

Amy was having none of it. 'Well, she ain't just your patient,' she replied firmly. 'She's my mum.'

The doctor sat back in his leather-covered swing chair. His smile contained a faint touch of condescension. 'Quite so, my dear,' he said, adjusting the small red carnation on the lapel of his black three-piece pin-striped suit. 'But life is never simple. Your mother had many problems. It can't have been easy for her bringing up a family single-handed.'

'She wasn't single-handed,' Amy reminded him. 'She 'ad me *an'* my dad.'

The doctor ran his hands through his greying hair, then smoothed back his grey, pencil-thin moustache with the thumb and first finger of his right hand. If he knew anything about Amy's mum that she didn't know, then he was clearly not going to reveal it. 'A difficult situation,' he said. 'How long has she been missing now?'

Amy sighed. 'Just over a year.'

'And she still hasn't made contact?'

Amy shook her head, and lowered her eyes.

The doctor thought for a moment then asked, 'Have you checked with any of your relations? She may be hiding out.'

Amy looked up sharply. 'I've checked wiv every one of our relations that I know about,' she said. 'I'm pretty sure that if she *was* wiv 'em, they'd tell me.' Getting impatient, she sat forward in her chair, and stared the doctor out across his desk. 'Dr Ferguson,' she said intensely, 'before she left 'ome, Mum came an' saw you quite a few times.'

The doctor raised his grey, bushy eyebrows. 'Oh really?' he asked in apparent surprise. 'And how would you know that?'

''Cos I saw 'er,' she replied without a moment's thought. 'Lots er times.'

The doctor sat up in his chair, clenched his fingers together, and rested his hands on the desk. 'There was nothing physically wrong with your mother, Amy,' he said. 'In fact, in many ways she was quite a strong woman. What she was suffering from was a state of mind. Putting it simply, I suppose you could call it an inability to cope. In some ways, it *is* a kind of disease, especially in wartime.'

Amy was hanging on his every word. 'So you fink she ran away, because of the war?'

'No, Amy,' said Dr Ferguson. 'That's not what I'm saying.' He got up from his desk, and stood at the window, which was covered with fine white net curtains. 'Every time your mother came to see me, she was – how can I put it? – disturbed.'

'Disturbed?'

'Disturbed, restless – call it what you will.' He turned and looked at her. He was a far more compassionate man than his appearance and manner suggested to Amy. He was desperate to tell her the truth, the real reasons why the mind of this perfectly ordinary woman had suddenly snapped, leaving her with the only solution – to get away. 'Whatever it was that happened to your mother, Amy,' he said, unconsciously abandoning his unconvincing London brogue, 'whatever it was that pushed her to that final point of desperation, was nothing less than a cry for help.'

'But *I* could've 'elped 'er,' Amy said firmly. 'If only she'd confided in me . . .'

'You're the last person she could have confided in, Amy,' said the doctor, coming back to stand at his desk. 'The very last person.'

Amy was hurt. 'But I'm her daughter, her eldest daughter. She *knows* she could've trusted me.'

'There is only one person she should have been able to trust, Amy,' said Dr Ferguson, quietly intense. 'And that was your father.'

Amy's entire body seemed to go quite numb. So she was right. Something *had* happened between her mum and her dad, something so awful that Mum had had to get far away from him, without any regard as to what might happen to the rest of her family.

As he watched Amy staring despondently into her lap, the doctor's professional superciliousness was gradually beginning to melt. 'But, you know,' he continued, coming round to perch on his desk in front of her, 'there is one redeeming feature about all this. One ray of hope, if you like to see it that way.'

Amy looked up at him.

'The fact that she came to me for help.'

Amy was puzzled.

'You know, I've had to attend patients who've tried to kill themselves. But in many cases – not all – they've given some kind of indication what they'd planned to do. It was the same with your mother. Coming to me all those times was her way of saying: unless you can help me, I'm going to break. If I blame anyone for what has happened to your mother, Amy, I blame myself.'

Amy found it difficult to take in what Dr Ferguson was trying to tell her, and it took her a moment or so to respond. Finally, she asked, 'So what do I do?'

'Find her,' said the doctor. 'Believe me, she's out there somewhere, waiting for you. She may not know it, but she needs you. Oh yes, she needs you all right. She needs you so desperately.'

Thelma Dodds slipped away from school shortly after roll call. It wasn't the first time she'd done it, for once she realised that she could get away with playing truant without anyone taking too much notice, she was well away. She was taking a risk, of course, for on two or three previous occasions she had been hauled before the strict headmistress, Miss Neville, who had received disturbing reports from Thelma's form mistress, Miss Hatton, that the girl was simply not concentrating on any subject she was supposed to be studying. Consequently, Thelma's time at Pakeman Street School had been extended by a year to give her a chance to catch up on the scholarship exams. However, with her continuing disregard for anything or anybody who wanted to improve her educational qualifications, the girl's chances of moving on to Highbury Hill Girls' School were practically nil.

The trouble with Thelma was that she was growing up too fast, for at fourteen, she could easily pass as someone three or four years older. Having already reached puberty, she was looking for something more than English grammar, maths, geography and ballet classes, and it didn't matter to her one bit that both her mum and her sister Amy had been called in to see Miss Neville on at least two occasions. In fact, as far as Thelma was concerned, her mum's disappearance had been a godsend, for not only was her dad totally disinterested in his kids, but, in her mind, because Amy had to go out to work, do the shopping, the housework, and all the other chores, she didn't really have enough time to keep an eye on her wayward young sister. No, for Thelma, things were going just right, and she hoped that the longer her mum was missing, the better it would be all round. At least, that was the impression she tried to give, even if it wasn't entirely true.

Kenny Silver and Rich Buckley were waiting for Thelma at the number 14 bus stop outside Woolworths in Holloway Road. She arrived just in time, for the moment she got there, a bus appeared from around the corner of Seven Sisters Road, and all three jumped on.

Luckily, the two front seats on the top deck were free, so Thelma and Kenny took one of them, and Rich sat across the aisle. The two boys were in buoyant mood, and immediately brought out the fags.

'Fawt yer weren't goin' ter make it,' said Kenny, who, at sixteen, was the older of the two boys, a half-caste, whose mum was married to a merchant seaman from Trinidad. 'We was just goin' wivout yer.'

'Don't believe 'im, Thelm,' said Rich, who had only just turned sixteen, and who had a baby face, and unkempt blond hair that needed cutting. ''E's bin waitin' ter get 'is 'ands on yer.'

'Ha!' sniffed Thelma, throwing her head back haughtily. ''E'll be lucky.'

''Ope so,' retorted the half-caste boy, with a gleam in his eye. He offered his mate a fag first, which the boy took. Then he put the packet to his mouth, and pulled out a fag with his teeth.

'Wot about me?' asked Thelma, irritably.

'Gels shouldn't smoke,' said Kenny provocatively. 'Specially *young* gels!'

Irate, Thelma snatched the packet from him, took out a fag, and shoved it between her lips. Then she flicked the packet back into his lap. This only made the boy laugh as he brought out a box of matches from his pocket, struck one, and held it out for Thelma. She almost choked as she tried to inhale. Both boys laughed, then lit up.

'So, wot d'yer do wiv yer satchel?' asked Kenny, as he leaned back in the seat, and perched his feet on the ledge in front of him.

'I 'id it in the gels' lavs in the playground,' replied Thelma, recovering from her coughing fit.

'Cor!' said Rich, who had joined the others by perching his feet on the window ledge in front of him. 'I bet it'll pong when yer get it back!'

All three roared with wild laughter.

Kenny took a deep puff of his fag, turned towards Thelma and blew smoke into her ear. She didn't object. Then he slid his arm over her shoulders. Again, she didn't object. 'So wot's yer big sister goin' ter say about all this?' he asked, quietly.

'Who cares?' replied Thelma, talking with the fag in her lips, as though she was some seductive film actress. 'She ain't my keeper.'

'Free as air, are yer?' mocked Kenny.

Thelma puffed a small amount of smoke, turned, and blew it straight into the boy's face.

'Don't fink your mum would approve, would she?' asked Kenny, intimately.

'My mum's dead,' Thelma replied. But then she qualified what she had said. 'Well, ter me she is. She never cared fer me, so why should I care about 'er?' She turned to him. 'So wot's all the big interest about me mum?'

'Nuffin' really,' replied Kenny, fag in mouth, as he ran his hand through his head of tiny, cropped, black curls. 'I don't like my mum eivver,' he said. 'She bosses me around too much. Finks she knows everyfin'. But I like my dad. 'E says boys should be left ter get on wiv fings their own way.'

'Wot about gels?' asked Thelma.

'We're all boys in my family,' replied Kenny.

'Right!' called the conductress, who was standing over them. 'Where yer goin' then?'

Kenny looked up casually, put his hand into his pocket, and took out some coins. 'Two ter the Circus,' he said, handing them over. 'One fer me, one fer me luvely lady friend 'ere.'

'Same again,' called Rich from the next seat.

'I presume yer mean Piccadilly Circus,' said the conductress, who was clearly not amused. 'Unless you're joinin' yer mates down Bertram Mills?'

'Ha! Ha!' sneered the half-caste boy. 'Very funny!'

The conductress put their coins in her leather satchel, took out three tickets, and punched them in the ticket machine strapped to her shoulder. Then, as she gave all three tickets to Kenny, she barked, 'An' while you're at it, take yer feet down from the window. Wot d'yer fink this is – a bleedin' doss 'ouse?'

The bus moved on along Caledonian Road, past King's Cross Station, and gradually headed towards the West End of London. On the way, the signs of a city at war were everywhere – gaps in the terraces of houses and shops which had been struck down during the great aerial onslaught of the winter of 1940 and 1941, windows either boarded up or covered with protective cross strips of sticky paper, and signs on many street corners pointing the way to the nearest air-raid shelter. On the approach to Piccadilly itself, Shaftesbury Avenue still played host, despite the war, to morale-boosting plays and musical shows. A line of glistening red double-decker buses waited their turn to drop passengers off in the Circus, which, by the very fact that it was thronged with army, navy, and air force uniforms from so many Commonwealth countries, was bristling with life. Although it was still only mid-morning, there were long queues of people waiting to get into the London Pavilion and Paramount cinemas, and at the New Gallery cinema in nearby Regent Street, the current wartime pin-up, Rita Hayworth, was proving to be a magnet to soldiers home on leave.

Once they had got off the bus, Thelma and her two companions made their way to the milk bar alongside the Pavilion cinema, but as milk was now in short supply, they all three had to settle for a very watered-down orange squash. Despite the fact that it was freezing cold outside, none of them seemed to feel it; the sheer thrill of being in such an adventurous and pulsating place kept them warm. There was so much to see, so much going on around them. It was all so different to the dull routine of living in Holloway.

Thelma's great kick came after they had made their way along Leicester Square, and crossed over Shaftesbury Avenue into the red light district of Soho. It was Kenny's idea that they went there, and as they gazed in awe at the street girls, hovering round the doors of the faceless, carefully disguised strip-clubs, they gradually ambled back towards Piccadilly. Rich felt a bit out of it with Kenny and Thelma flirting like mad, so he kept his eyes open, just in case he saw someone for himself. After a quarter of an hour or so, they found themselves at the Piccadilly entrance to Hyde Park.

Down by the Serpentine, all kinds of people had stopped to watch the home colony of wild ducks, geese and swans. It was a tranquil scene, far removed from the tensions of the day, with servicemen and their girlfriends linked arm in arm, oblivious to anyone around them.

After a while, Rich decided to go off on his own, fed up with being the odd one out. Once he had gone, Kenny led Thelma to a bench overlooking the lake, but the moment she sat down, she realised that the seat was not only ice cold, but wet. Not to be put off, Kenny wasted no time. Wrapping his arms around Thelma, he kissed her hard and full on the lips.

''Ere!' said Thelma, pushing him away. 'Who d'yer fink you are?'

'Wos up wiv yer?' Kenny said, put out. 'Wot d'yer fink we come 'ere for – ter feed the birds?'

Thelma suddenly felt guilty. Yes, of course she knew why he had brought her here, and it was what she wanted. It was just that she didn't want to be a pushover. And so, as he lit up a fag, she slipped her arm through his, and kissed him gently on his cheek.

'Watch it,' he said sarcastically. 'Wot d'yer fink yer mum would say if she was 'ere now?'

'Why do we 'ave ter keep talkin' about my mum?' she said, suddenly pulling him towards her and kissing him hard and full on the lips. 'She dumped us,' she continued sourly, 'so she'll 'ave ter put up wiv it.'

Kenny was smiling at her. 'I wanna see yer again, Thelm,' he said.

'Why?' she asked teasingly.

'Yer know *why*,' he replied, staring straight into her eyes. 'Wot about Saturday?'

Thelma shrugged noncommittally. 'Dunno.'

'Afraid?'

She swung him a glance. 'Wot of?'

'Yer big sister – or yer mum?'

Furious, Thelma threw her arms round him, and kissed him hard again.

As they sat there, locked in each other's arms, someone passed them by with hardly a second look. Someone who had far more important things on her mind than a couple of sex-crazed kids who wanted to do everything they wanted to do in public.

Aggs didn't approve. No. She didn't approve at all. They were sitting on her favourite park bench.

CHAPTER 5

Amy didn't know what she had let herself in for. Lipstick for the first time in her life, eye shadow, a small mole on the right side of her chin highlighted with something that looked like black paint, drop pearl earrings, and a neat hairdo with a silk bow stuck on the back of her head. When she looked at herself in a hand-mirror in the bedroom she shared with Thelma and little Elsie, she squirmed in horror. The cause of all this transformation was, of course, Hilda Feathers.

''Onest, 'Ild,' Amy said, peering up at her best mate's reflection in the mirror behind her, 'I can't go ter the dance like this. I look like a West End tart.'

'Wot's a tart?' asked little Elsie, in what seemed far from innocence.

'Never you mind,' said Amy, glaring at her youngest sister, who was sitting on the edge of her bed, swinging her feet back and forth in unison.

'Don't listen to your sister, Elsie, dear,' said Hilda, in her cut-glass accent, admiring her own handiwork in the mirror. 'Amy looks absolutely gorgeous!'

'Wot's gorgeous?' asked Elsie, her feet swinging faster and faster.

Hilda decided not to encourage this dialogue any further.

'Go downstairs and finish yer tea,' Amy called, over her shoulder. ''An tell Arn not ter finish off all them buns I brought 'ome from work.'

Elsie didn't wait to be told twice. Jumping down from the bed, she rushed to the door, yelling, 'Yer do look like a tart!' as she went. The slamming of the door behind her shook the entire house.

'Quite a character, that one!' said Hilda.

Amy swung round on her chair and, with a look of desperation on her painted face, said, 'I can't go like this 'Ild. I wouldn't feel comfortable.'

'When you're looking for a man,' Hilda said firmly, 'you're not expected to feel comfortable. Just take the best on offer, and enjoy yourself!'

Amy wasn't convinced. 'I 'ope you're right,' she said, with a deep sigh. 'Let's face it, I'm not exactly Hedy Lamarr.'

Hilda put her arms round Amy, and gave her an affectionate hug. 'Now you listen to me, Amy Dodds,' she said, as they looked at their joint reflection in the mirror, 'you're worth a hundred Hedy Lamarrs.'

Amy shook her head. 'Look at me, 'Ild,' she said. 'D'yer really fink some bloke's goin' ter go for a podge like me?'

Leaning over Amy's shoulder, Hilda pressed her cheek against Amy's. 'There's someone for everyone in this world, Amy,' she said reassuringly. 'It has nothing to do with how podgy or thin you are. People see what they want to see. Believe me, there's a bloke out there for you somewhere. He just needs a bit of encouragement, that's all!'

They both laughed.

'But first,' said Hilda, pulling her mate round to face her, 'we've got to add the final touch.'

'Wot d'yer mean?' asked Amy, puzzled.

'Where's that Bisto?' asked Hilda, taking off her signet ring, and putting it down on the tiny dressing table.

'I can't!' objected Amy, trying to stand up. 'Please, 'Ild. I'd look a real charlie!'

'Absolute rubbish!' said Hilda, gently easing Amy down on to her seat again. 'You've got a smashing pair of legs, and you're going to show them off to the hilt.' She suddenly found a small basin on the window ledge behind the dressing table. 'Ah!' she cried. 'Is this it?' She picked it up quickly, and found the Bisto powder that Amy had already mixed to a thin paste before she'd lost her nerve. Removing the spoon, she used both hands to refresh the mixture. 'Right!' she commanded. 'Pull up your dress.'

'Please, 'Ild . . .' begged Amy.

'Amy!' Hilda was determined to get her own way. 'Since there's not a chance in hell of getting you a decent pair of nylons, this will do just fine.'

'Owch!' protested Amy, as Hilda slapped a handful of Bisto paste on to one of her legs.

'By the time I've got this stuff on,' said Hilda, as she rubbed it all over Amy's leg, 'you'll look good enough to turn the head of every red-blooded male on the dance floor. Whatever you may think the rest of you looks like, I'd die for a pair of legs like yours!'

Amy blushed. Regardless of how mucky her leg was feeling, her mate's enthusiasm was raising her morale no end.

For the next few minutes, Hilda slapped the Bisto paste on to both Amy's legs, smoothing it out as delicately as she could, using her fingers and palms to produce a fine finish. There was only enough in the basin to cover an area from the feet to

73

just above the hemline of Amy's dress, and because the mixture was quite thin, it was drying almost as she applied it.

Once she had finished, Hilda stood back to take a distant look at her handiwork. 'Yes,' she announced, with satisfaction. 'Not bad. Not bad at all. I'll just go and wash my hands. Stay right where you are,' she called, as she wiped her hands on a piece of newspaper, and made for the door. 'I'll be right back.'

Amy had no intention of moving an inch. Utterly bewildered, she stared down at her legs, hardly able to believe what she had allowed Hilda to do to her. The only time she had ever used gravy powder was when she was lucky enough to get a piece of meat for a Sunday roast, and yet here she was, feeling like the roast herself. But she did what Hilda had told her to do, and kept her dress held up over her thighs, waiting for the awful mess to be absolutely dry.

Suddenly, Elsie was peering round the door. 'I 'ope yer don't give us any more gravy on Sundays,' she called.

'Out!' yelled Amy.

The door slammed immediately. Then it opened again, as Hilda returned. 'Right!' she said. 'Now for the finishing touch.'

'Wot now?' asked Amy nervously.

Hilda went straight to her handbag, which she'd left on Amy's bed. After a quick search through the contents, she produced something which she held up for Amy to see. '*Voilà!*' she announced, triumphantly. 'One eye pencil.'

'Wot's that for?' asked Amy.

'Don't be silly, Amy,' replied Hilda, as though what she was about to do was something she had been doing every day of her life. 'Whoever heard of stockings without seams?'

Acutely aware how short-sighted Hilda was, Amy was beginning to dread how straight the seams were going to be on the back of her gravy-covered legs.

Aggs gulped down a mouthful of stout from the bottle. It was still her favourite booze, for it was heavy and nourishing, and as far as she was concerned, it was the one thing that really kept her warm during the interminable winter months. It also helped her to get through Saturday nights, which, despite her endless efforts to forget her former life, brought back too many memories. In her younger days, in those early years of her marriage to Ernie Dodds, there was nothing the two of them liked better than to go dancing at the Majestic Dance Hall in Upper Holloway Road. Oh, it was an expensive night out all right – sixpence each, not including the shandies for her and the brown ale for him. But to Aggs, it was worth every penny; for one night a week she felt like someone important, as she and Ernie turned heads gliding round the floor in a waltz or a quickstep, and kicked and twisted their legs, and flapped their hands frenziedly in the charleston, just like all those 'bright young things' of the upper classes. Aggs and Ernie may not have been able to afford the beads and tasselled dress and stylish tuxedo, but what they lacked in money, they made up for in the sheer joy and exuberance of their dancing. These days, Aggs couldn't care a fig for Saturday nights. As far as she was concerned, Saturday was now no different to any other night of the week. She didn't want to have memories, she didn't want to recall anything, not even the names of her kids, or of her so-called husband.

Aggs couldn't define her bitterness; all she knew was that for the past couple of years, she had been consumed by it.

Even now, as she settled back in her own bit of 'territory' down by the boathouse, urging her mind to slip away in a haze of stale stout, her bitterness with life itself just refused to let her go. With her head leaning back on a pile of old newspapers, which she used as a pillow, she turned her gaze across the Serpentine where she could just see the distant, dark silhouette of the smart buildings of Knightsbridge on the other side of Rotten Row, where, even during wartime, the rich were able to exercise their horses in grand style. For one brief moment, it inspired her to imagine what it would be like to be rich, to be driven around in a big car, covered from head to foot in furs and jewels. But the thought of it only made her chuckle to herself; it wasn't the high life she had ever wanted, just love.

''Evenin' Ma.'

Aggs immediately snapped out of her haze. A torch beam was suddenly blinding her, and two people were standing over her in the dark. 'Who is it?' she growled. 'Wot d'yer want?'

'You're all right, Ma,' called a quiet, gentle, male voice.

'We're not going to hurt you, mate,' added a second.

Only then did she recognise the voices of the two regular special constables, Sid and Roy, who patrolled the park for what seemed to Aggs like twenty-four hours a day.

'Wot yer want?' she growled again. 'I'm trying ter get some kip!'

'Plenty of time for that,' came Constable Roy's voice. Both he and his companion were now crouching beside her.

'It's only half-past seven, mate,' said Constable Sid, trying to direct the torchlight without blinding her. 'I bet you haven't had your four-course dinner yet, have you?'

'Cut the double act!' snapped Aggs, shielding her eyes from the light. 'Wot d'yer want?'

'We've been asked to have a few words with you,' said Sid, the older of the two men, whose tin helmet was halfway down his forehead. 'Can you spare a minute?'

Aggs felt her insides fall apart. This was the moment she had been dreading. It had been her recurring nightmare ever since she had left home – the thought that, sooner or later, the law would catch up with her. But despite the haze she had boozed herself into, she was determined not to panic. 'Wot 'ave I done this time?'

'Just a little co-operation, Ma,' said the younger constable. 'We'd like to know about one of your park mates. A young bloke they call The Kid.'

At the Town Hall, the dance in aid of the Red Cross wasn't at all what Amy had been expecting. For a start, the average age of each member of the four-piece band seemed to be about ninety, and Amy thought they looked as though they should be playing at a tea dance rather than for a whole bunch of young people. But that was the other surprise. As there was a war on, there was clearly a shortage of men, for most of the girls and older women were dancing with each other. Amy thought it all looked most peculiar, especially as the small sprinkling of men that were there looked either not much older than her brother, Arnold, or were much the same age as her grandfather. As far as she was concerned, any hopes of a passionate romance were practically nonexistent.

'Don't look so glum,' said Hilda, as she partnered Amy in a quickstep. 'It's not as bad as it looks.'

'Oh yes it is!' grumbled Amy, who was crushed up against

her mate, and practically swamped by the surging mass of dancers. 'An' my bleedin' legs are itchin' like mad!'

'For God's sake don't scratch them!' begged Hilda, raising her voice above the pensioners' version of Glenn Miller's 'In the Mood'. 'You'll give the whole game away.'

'Wot diff'rence does it make?' yelled Amy. 'Nobody can see them!'

'Don't you be so sure!' Hilda assured her.

When the music stopped, they fought their way off the floor, and made for the makeshift bar at the back of the hall. Sweat was seeping through the shoulder blades of the pale blue dress that Hilda had borrowed for Amy from her own younger sister, and Amy's fringe, which had been so carefully cut and shaped by Hilda before they came, was stuck fast with perspiration to Amy's head. Incredibly, however, Hilda looked as cool as a cucumber, and not one of her crop of tight ginger curls was out of place. Amy bought them both a shandy, and Hilda took out of her bag a packet of Craven 'A'.

'Cheer up, Amy,' Hilda said, placing a cigarette between her lips. 'Just enjoy yourself for one night. My motto is "Forget about everything, and have a good time."'

'I *am* 'avin' a good time, 'Ild,' said Amy, suddenly concerned that she was being ungrateful. 'Mind you, I 'ope Marge knows wot she's let 'erself in for. She's got 'er 'ands full lookin' after my lot.'

'Stop worrying,' said Hilda, who was searching around in her handbag for a box of matches. 'Marge's got her head screwed on the right way. She wouldn't offer if she wasn't certain she could cope.'

Amy took a sip of her shandy. She was still not convinced. 'It's Thelma I'm worried about,' she said. 'I never know what she gets up to. Since Mum went, she's gone her own way. I just know she's going to get herself into trouble one of these days.'

'You're not her mum, Amy,' said Hilda, still rummaging for the matches. 'She'll have to be like the rest of us – learn by our mistakes . . . oh!' To her surprise, someone had provided her with a light for her cigarette. 'Thanks very . . .' Her face suddenly beamed when she saw that the lighted match was being held out for her by a middle-aged army officer. She quickly lit her cigarette and blew smoke past him. 'Very kind of you.'

Within minutes, Hilda was being accompanied on to the dance floor with her new beau, leaving Amy to prop up the bar on her own. Amy wasn't entirely despondent; it was no more than she had expected. It wasn't long before she began to feel the effects of the stifling atmosphere of the place, for the hall itself was now jammed from end to end with people, so taking her glass of shandy with her, she started to ease her way back towards the main exit. It was, however, quite a task, for people were shoving and pushing all the way, totally oblivious to the poor creature trying to get past them. Never had she felt so aware of her height; it was as though everyone in the entire hall was towering over her.

By the time she had reached the exit, there was very little shandy left in her glass, so she left it on the nearest table she could find. As it was pitch-dark and freezing cold outside, she decided to put up with the hot, steaming atmosphere of sweating bodies and fag smoke, and make herself as inconspicuous as she possibly could. Nearby, she spied a long bench against the wall on which were seated a line of young girls, all waiting to be asked for a dance. Luckily there was one space available right in the middle of the bench, so she pushed her way through the crowds of dancers who were just standing around in small groups, chatting and boozing. When she got there, she tried smiling at some of the girls sitting there, only to be greeted frostily. As she sat down, the girls on either side moved away from her, and turned the other way, showing that they had no intention of opening a conversation with her. Despite all Hilda's efforts, Amy had never felt so much of a frump in her entire life. In the distance, she could just see Hilda and her army captain doing their best to smooch around the crowded dance floor to the strains of the pensioners' interpretation of 'I'll See You in My Dreams'.

Feeling thoroughly out of place, Amy leaned her head against the wall behind her, and stared up aimlessly at the mass of different coloured balloons that were waiting to be released at an appropriate moment. But her thoughts were miles away, wondering where and what her mum was doing at that precise moment, and how much the poor woman used to love going to dances just like this. She remembered how, when she was young, her mum and dad used to dance around the front parlour together, to the music of Victor Sylvester and his orchestra, on the wireless. It was always so lovely to watch them, for they seemed to be so much in love. She sighed deeply. Oh, what went wrong? she asked herself. Why do married people always have to start looking for things wrong in each other?

She was suddenly jolted out of her reflections by someone tripping over her feet, and landing with a thump on the floor. She immediately sat up, to find a tall thin bloke sprawled out across the floor in front of her.

'Blimey, mate!' she gasped, getting up from the bench to

help him. 'I'm sorry! I'm really sorry!' The rumpus she caused amongst the crowd immediately cleared the other girls from the bench. 'Are yer all right, mate?' she cried anxiously, as she and some of the crowd helped the young bloke to his feet. ''Ave yer 'urt yerself?'

'N-no thanks to you and your big f-feet!' replied the bloke, as he turned round, still clutching his empty beer glass. However, the moment he caught sight of Amy, he did a double take. 'B-blimey!' he said shamefully.

The boy's stammer and his metal-rimmed spectacles gave Amy a bit of a shock too, for there was no doubt in her mind that he was the person who had knocked her down on his bicycle during the air raid in Mayton Street a few nights before. 'You!' she gasped. 'Wot're *you* doin' 'ere?'

'S-same as you,' replied the boy. 'L-looks like you've got your own back.'

Amy suddenly saw the funny side of what had happened, and she found herself laughing. To her relief, the boy did likewise. 'Well, it's my turn ter say sorry now,' she said. 'You're not 'urt, are yer?'

'No,' replied the boy. 'What about you?'

Amy shook her head.

'Can I buy you a d-drink, Amy?' he asked, shouting above the pensioners' rendition of 'Yes sir, That's my Baby!'

Amy looked at his empty glass. 'Looks like I owe *you* one,' she bellowed, trying to compete with the amplified dance music. But her expression suddenly changed. ''Ere, 'ang on a minute,' she said suspiciously. ''Ow'd yer know my name?'

'I used to go to Pakeman Street School,' he shouted. 'You were in Miss Hatton's class, and I was in Mr Piper's. My name's Tim. Tim Gudgeon. Don't you r-remember me?'

Amy slapped her hand against her forehead. 'I knew it!' she said. 'I knew I'd seen yer somewhere before.'

The rather sulky girls who had moved away from the bench where they had been sitting with Amy, glared at her. They were also puzzled to know what that brown, soggy mess was on her forehead.

Fortunately, the distant wail of the air-raid siren saved the day.

Amy's sister Thelma hadn't reckoned on the air-raid siren. When it came, her back was pressed up against a hard brick wall in the school playground, her arms coiled round Kenny Silvers' neck, her lips resisting too much pressure from his. Getting out of the house whilst her sister's mate Marge Jackson was supposed to be 'baby-sitting' had been a piece of cake for someone with Thelma's cunning. All she had to do was to say that she was going to bed to read her *Filmgoers* magazine, and then to wait for the innocent 'baby-sitter' to settle down in the back parlour, listening to *In Town Tonight* and *Music Hall* on the wireless. The lavatory window on the first-floor landing was her usual method of escape; although it was small, she was lithe enough to climb up and squeeze through, and once she was out on the scullery roof, it was easy for a girl like her to flit off along the back yard walls to the relative safety of nearby Hertslet Road. The only thing she was not too happy about was scaling the playground wall with Kenny for the caretaker, Mr Mitchinson, had eyes like an owl, and if he caught them, then there'd really be trouble. The other problem was the air-raid post on the other side of the play-ground, which was used as a meeting place by the wardens, especially during air raids. Tonight there was plenty of activity over in that direction, for, from where Thelma and Kenny were hiding near the outside lavatories, they could see the constant flashing of torch beams as the wardens gathered to assess the latest approach of enemy aircraft.

'I'd better get back,' said Thelma softly into Kenny's ear. 'If this old cow goes inter my room and finds me gone, there'll be all hell wiv Ame.'

'I fawt you said your youngest sister was goin' ter cover for yer?' whispered Kenny, whose body was pressed hard up against Thelma's.

'Elsie'd give me away at the drop of an 'at,' she replied. 'As it is I 'ad ter bribe 'er wiv my sweet ration.'

'Why don't yer tell the troof?' said the half-caste boy, deliberately riling her. 'You're piss scared of yer big sister.'

'Get off!' she snapped angrily, trying to push him away. 'I ain't scared of no one, and that includes you, Kenny Silver!'

Kenny chuckled, and resisted her attempts to push him off.

'I've got ter get 'ome!' insisted Thelma.

'Why?' Kenny complained. 'Don't yer like bein' wiv me?' He kissed her ear, and gently bit the lobe. 'Not scared, are yer?'

'Scared?' she asked. 'Wot of?'

'You know.'

Thelma felt his hands trying to pull her dress up beneath her coat. 'Pack it up, Kenny!' she growled as loud as she dared, at the same time pushing his hands away. 'I've told yer I don't want none of that.'

'Why not?' he replied irritably. 'Wot's the matter wiv yer?'

Thelma adjusted her dress. 'I just don't wanna do it, that's all.'

Kenny pulled back from her. 'Then why d'yer come out?' he sniffed, indignantly. 'Why din't yer stay at 'ome wiv yer baby-sitter?'

To his surprise, Thelma stretched out her hands and pulled him back to her again. ''Cos I was 'opin' you'd 'elp me,' she said.

Kenny hesitated before answering. 'Wot're yer talkin' about?' he asked suspiciously.

Before Thelma could answer, there was a crack of anti-aircraft gunfire in the distance. On the other side of the playground, voices were heard, as some of the ARP wardens came out of their hut to look up at the sky, which was now patterned in a web of searchlights.

Despite Kenny's nervousness, Thelma pulled him close and whispered into his ear, 'I was 'opin' you an' me could talk about gettin' away from this place.'

Kenny felt her arms wrapping themselves round his neck, her hands reaching up to feel his head full of hard, tight curls. Then, to his surprise, she kissed him full on the lips. But this time, it was he who prised her away. 'Wot d'yer mean – get away?' he asked cagily.

'I'm fed up wiv 'Olloway,' she replied, trying to pull him back to her again. 'I'm fed up wiv livin' at 'ome, wiv two sisters an' a bruvver. You an' me could go anywhere we like, Ken.' She tried to pull him closer again. 'We could go up West, 'ave a really good time.'

Kenny suddenly saw red, and pushed her away. 'Always somefin', ain't there, Thelm?' he replied, not really concerned if he could be heard or not. 'Wanna get away, do yer – just like yer mum? Well, let me tell yer somefin', Thelma. I ain't doin' yer dirty work for yer. There's a war on. Sleeping out rough on the streets is a mug's game – no rations, shrapnel fallin' down on yer in the middle of the night.' He now moved right away from her. 'If you wanna make a dope of yerself, go right ahead,' he called, 'go right ahead. But don't fink *I'm* goin' ter 'elp yer!'

Then he was gone, and within moments she could see his shadowy outline climbing up the playground wall, then disappearing into adjoining Roden Street outside.

The first burst of gunfire nearby came as quite a shock. But Thelma refused to panic. She never had, and she never would. That's the way she was. That's the way she'd always be. Sooner or later she'd get away from number 16 bloody Enkel Street. And if the little worm with the tight black curls wouldn't help her, she'd find someone who would.

The Town Hall air-raid shelter was jammed to suffocation. It was not surprising, for there had been nearly three hundred people at the Red Cross dance earlier in the evening, and when most of them made a dash for the official shelter beneath the building, a crush was inevitable. However, most made the best of it, and after the first few minutes, one of the pensioners from the four-piece band started a singsong, which continued the happy-go-lucky atmosphere that had prevailed during the dance. Amy wasn't really surprised that Hilda had used the stampede as a good excuse to go off and be alone with her army captain, for she imagined that by now the two of them were probably enjoying themselves taking shelter in the air-raid shelter of some pub. To her surprise, Amy was enjoying herself too. She had taken quite a shine to Tim Gudgeon, the boy with whom she had already had two near-calamitous encounters. She loved his sensitivity, and found his stammer positively endearing.

'You must come round the tea shop some time,' she said, as they sat crouched on the cold stone shelter floor. 'If yer play yer cards right, I might even get yer a free cuppa.'

'It's f-funny,' said Tim, 'I've p-passed that p-place dozens of times, and never once g-given it a thought that you worked there.'

'Why should you?' asked Amy. 'Yer din't even know me.'

'Oh, I've always kn-known you,' replied Tim. 'Ever since w-we were at school together, you've always b-been on my m-mind.'

Amy blushed. She didn't think she was capable of doing such a thing, but she did. She flicked her eyes up to find him waiting to stare into them. 'Wot about you?' she asked, a little tongue-tied. 'Wot sort of work d'you do?'

Tim sighed, and released his eye contact. 'By r-rights,' he said, despondently, 'I should've been c-called up. But I get these b-bouts of diabetes – nothing serious – but it's enough to p-put them off. So I w-work as a clerk upstairs in the T-Town Hall. I'm a k-kind of local c-civil servant.'

'I'm glad,' said Amy, warming to him with every word he said.

'That I'm a civil servant.'

'That yer don't 'ave ter go in the army.'

He smiled back, shyly.

Both of them now leaned their heads back against the stone wall. The whole place smelled of face powder and cheap cologne. Some of the younger couples, taking advantage of the low-voltage electric lighting, and in defiance of the stern looks they were getting from some of the older generation, snogged in whatever confined space was available. Most people tried to ignore the rumble of ack-ack gunfire thundering above their heads outside, even though they knew what was going on. It was also an odd feeling to know that there were no children taking cover, for the dance in the hall upstairs had been strictly for adults. For some inexplicable reason, that only made matters worse; the lack of kids meant that this was not the family sheltering together. And without the family, there was a sense of being disconnected from the real world.

When she emerged from her reverie, Amy realised that Tim had his head turned towards her. 'You m-must think a lot about your m-mum on nights like this.'

Amy was startled. 'Wot d'yer mean?' she asked, puzzled.

'I knew your mum,' he replied. 'Shc was always very n-nice to me.'

Amy couldn't believe what she was hearing. 'You *knew* my mum?'

'Well, I d-didn't exactly know her,' replied Tim, guardedly. 'But I knew that she was your m-mum, so whenever I saw her in the street, I used to – to ask her about you.'

Amy turned right round to face him. 'You asked my mum – about me?'

Tim, embarrassed, lowered his eyes. 'Yes.'

'Why?'

'I l-liked you.' He raised his eyes again. 'I've always l-liked you. I used to watch you in the school playground. I w-wanted to get t-to know you. I just didn't have the nerve.' Once again he lowered his eyes, but in a sudden brave moment, flicked them up again. 'I always thought you were the best-looking girl in the school. I still think you are.'

Amy didn't know what to say. She couldn't believe that someone was saying such things to her. She couldn't believe that someone actually admired her. It was such an odd feeling, something she had never experienced before. She was suddenly conscious of every part of her face, every blemish, every mole, her lips, her ears – a face that she had always considered to be podgy, and totally unattractive to every male in the world. Her cheeks flushed, and her dark blue eyes flicked awkwardly over everyone else except the boy she was talking with.

'W-wot did my mum used to tell you about me?' she asked, for want of anything better to say.

Tim thought hard before replying. When he did, it was with some difficulty. 'She often s-said what a good d-daughter you were. She s-said you were one in a m-million, that you d-didn't deserve a m-mum like her.'

Amy clasped a hand to her mouth. She was shocked.

Tim now felt confident enough to turn to face her. 'The l-last time I s-saw her,' he said, 'was the day before she d-disappeared. When I heard, I wasn't surprised. She w-was so upset. S-something had happened. I d-don't know what. But I knew she was d-desperate to g-get away.'

In the background, the All Clear sounded. Almost at once, everyone moved to make their way to the exit stairs. Amy, however, was too stunned. She just remained where she was, her head leaning back against the wall again.

Tim, worried that he had upset her, came closer. 'The thing is, Amy,' he said, trying to be heard over the excited chatter and shuffling of people's feet, 'I think I may know where your m-mum went to.'

Amy sat bolt upright, and turned to look at him.

Tim stood up, then helped Amy to do the same. Staring into her eyes through his metal-rimmed spectacles, he said,

'Of course, I'm n-not absolutely sure, but I've got a p-pretty good idea. I'd like to help you, Amy,' he continued falteringly. 'If you'd l-let me, I think I know where we can f-find her.'

During the brief moment that Amy was considering this, Tim took a handkerchief from his trousers pocket, and gently rubbed the gravy smudge from her forehead.

CHAPTER 6

Speakers' Corner was just as lively as ever. Despite the war, the place was rarely deserted on a Sunday morning, and this was no exception. The usual crowd were there, including the 'Bible punchers' who endlessly predicted that Jesus was about to return to Earth to punish the human race for their inability to get along with one another, the Bolsheviks, who did their best to rouse their working-class listeners into the belief that a red-coloured revolution would be their only salvation, and the pacifists, many of whose members had refused to fight in the war, and had registered as conscientious objectors. Missing, of course, were the British Fascists whose dangerous but charismatic leader, Sir Oswald Mosley, had been sent to prison in 1940. Speakers' Corner had always been a great tradition for anyone who had something to get off their chest, be it a political plant or an ordinary down-to-earth female parkie.

'Down wiv ration coupons!' yelled a very shrill voice, from the middle of the crowd, as one of the impassioned orators, perched on a soap box, tried to rally support for the return of the three miles of iron railings which had been removed from around the perimeter of the park soon after the start of the war. What ration coupons had to do with the subject under discussion, nobody knew, but Aggs's intervention, as always, prompted a wave of robust laughter. 'Bring back steak an' kidney pud!' she yelled again, provoking more laughter.

'This Government,' countered the poor trilby-hatted orator, who was battling to retain his dignity, 'has ruined every park in the land! Look around you. Just look at what was once London's own beautiful back garden – ruined by allotments, unused trenches, pigsties and demolition dumps.'

'Give us back our liquorice allsorts!' yelled Aggs, to gales of laughter.

Undaunted, the orator pointed his finger menacingly towards Aggs, and yelled above the din, 'Yes, my friend – and the likes of you too! Look at you – you and your scruffy mates – do anything you like – wandering around at ease, fouling the footpaths like mangy dogs!'

'Wot about the workers?' yelled someone else in the crowd, for no apparent reason, and to thunderous applause and laughter. As usual, Aggs had managed to reduce the proceedings to sheer farce.

Aggs was about to respond, when a voice in her ear said, 'Got ter talk to yer, mate. Urgent!' It was Scrounger.

Reluctantly, Aggs pushed her way out through the crowd, closely followed by her fellow parkie.

'The Kid's bin up to 'is tricks again,' said Scrounger, as he and Aggs slowly strolled off across the open park. 'Nicked a pig from the sty over at the cop shop.'

''Ow'd yer know it was 'im?' asked Aggs, without turning to look at him.

Scrounger smiled to himself. ''E's the only one who could get away wiv it. Anyway, Laurel an' 'Ardy are out gunnin' for 'im.'

'I know,' replied Aggs, quickening her pace. 'They came ter see me last night.'

Scrounger was shocked. 'Sid an' Roy? The bluebottles?' he asked, now finding it difficult to keep up with her. 'Wot d'yer tell 'em?'

Aggs was now striding out at her own shuffling speed. 'I told 'em nuffin'. 'Cos I don't know nuffin',' she sniffed airily.

'They come ter me too.' This time the voice came from behind them. It was Tiny Tim, another parkie, a great big lanky man whose hair was so long it had to be tied with a bit of string behind his head. 'I told 'em ter sod off!'

''Ow subtle,' replied Aggs scornfully, still on the move.

'Wot I can't understand,' said Tiny, his thin, gaunt face numb with the cold, 'is 'ow The Kid managed ter nick a pig an' get away wiv it. An' where'd 'e take it to?'

'Must've sold it,' said Scrounger, scratching the lice on his head. 'Everyone knows about those pigs they keep over at the cop shop. I've often thought about 'avin' a go at nickin' one meself.'

'They make a pretty profit when they sell that lot, I'm tellin' yer,' said Tiny.

Aggs suddenly stopped and turned to face both of them. 'It's got nuffin' ter do wiv the bleedin' pig!' she growled. 'The reason the nobs come ter see me last night was 'cos The Kid's a deserter. There's a feeler out for 'im from the army.'

Scrounger and Tiny Tim exchanged puzzled looks. 'Yer mean, they're gunnin' for 'im?'

'D'yer know wot they do to deserters?' Aggs reminded them. 'They put them up against a wall, an' shoot 'em.'

Tiny Tim shuddered. 'That's terrible,' he said, pinching a

dewdrop from the end of his nose.

'It's bloody murder!' added Scrounger. 'We've gotta do somefin' ter 'elp 'im.'

'Too right,' said Tiny. 'But wot?'

'Keep yer bleedin' mouvs shut,' snapped Aggs. 'That's wot yer can do.' She turned to go, then turned back to them. 'An' if yer see 'im, tell 'im ter keep 'is 'ead down. Unless 'e wants ter get it shot off!'

She strode away, leaving Scrounger and Tiny to watch her go in puzzlement. So Aggs had a heart after all. The only problem was that she had no intention of admitting it.

Ernie Dodds was having his usual Sunday morning lie-in. Ever since his wife had left home, he had made it a rule never to get up early on the one day of the week that he didn't have to go to work. But that didn't mean it was a sacred day to him. It merely meant that he'd been boozing until chuck-out time at The Eaglet, and his eyes couldn't bear the sight of daylight streaming through the curtains until he'd got over his customary hangover. But today was different. Today, the row his two elder daughters were making downstairs in the back parlour was shaking the very foundations of the house.

'Bloody 'ell!' he roared, bursting into the parlour, wearing only his trousers and vest. 'Wot's all the bleedin' row?'

'Talk to 'er, Dad!' shouted Amy, pointing at Thelma. 'Tell 'er wot a stupid little cow she is!'

'You're the cow – not me!' bawled Thelma.

Amy, face blood red with anger, raised her hand to slap the girl across the face. But Thelma ducked out of the way.

'Stop it, Ame!' countered their father. 'Stop – boaf of yer!

Just calm down, and tell me wot this is all about.'

'It's *'er* fault!' yelled Thelma hysterically, close to tears. 'She won't leave me alone! She keeps on at me all the time! I'm fed up wiv 'er! I'm fed up the way she keeps pushin' me around!'

'Fer Christ's sake calm down, gel!' demanded her dad and, turning to Amy, asked, 'Wot's goin' on 'ere? Wot's it all about?'

'Well you may ask!' snapped Amy. 'I go out fer one night – just one night off – and wot 'appens? She sneaks out on 'er own!'

Ernie, bewildered, shrugged. 'So wot's wrong wiv that?' he asked.

'Wot's wrong wiv it? Wot's *wrong*?' Amy looked as though she was about to burst a blood vessel. 'She's fourteen years old, Dad!' she bellowed. 'She's only a kid. If she starts gettin' mixed up wiv the wrong people at 'er age, it could ruin 'er fer life!'

'I'm not a kid!' shrieked Thelma, her face all screwed up with anger and frustration. 'I'm almost fifteen!'

Amy yelled back at her, 'As far as I'm concerned you *are* a kid! An' you're heading straight into the dustbin!'

'That's enough now, Ame!' said her dad, clutching his head in a desperate attempt to calm his daughters and his hangover. 'That's enough from boaf of yer! Now just tell me exactly wot 'appened.'

Amy took a deep breath, and tried to contain herself. 'I got Marge Jackson from the tea shop ter come round and keep an eye on 'em – just fer a few hours while I went to a dance up the Town 'All wiv 'Ilda. When I came back, Marge said this stupid little cow 'ad slipped out durin' the air raid. The poor woman was out of 'er mind wiv worry. She searched all the streets fer this – this stupid little cow!'

Thelma was about to protest, but her dad spoke first. 'Is this true, Thelm?'

Thelma was quick to reply. 'Yes, but—'

'Where did yer go?'

This time, Thelma hesitated before answering. 'I went round ter see my mate, Rita.'

'Where?'

'In Isledon Road. I was only gone an hour or so.'

'Little liar!' snapped Amy.

'I'm not!' Thelma yelled back at her.

Amy was practically eyeball to eyeball with her. 'You were out wiv some of those bleedin' louts you've bin knockin' around wiv.'

'I wasn't! I wasn't!' sobbed Thelma, hysterically.

Ernie put his hands up to silence them, then gently sat down in a chair at the parlour table. 'Yer should've told yer sister or someone where yer'd gone, Thelm,' he said.

'I did,' insisted Thelma. 'I told Elsie.'

'No you didn't!' called her younger sister, from the scullery door. 'Yer din't tell me nuffin'!'

Thelma swung an angry look to the door. 'Lyin' sod!' she screamed.

Elsie made a quick getaway by slamming the scullery door.

'All right, Thelm,' said her dad. 'I don't want ter 'ear any more about this. Get yerself upstairs an 'ave yer wash.'

By this time, Thelma was sobbing her heart out. With one last hateful look at Amy she rushed out of the room and stomped up the stairs.

'Yer've got ter do somefin' about 'er, Dad,' insisted Amy.

'If she isn't taken in an' soon, I don't know wot's goin' ter become of 'er.'

'I fink you're tryin' ter take on too much fer yerself, Ame,' said Ernie, putting a dog-end from behind his ear between his lips. 'She's goin' frough wot every gel of 'er age goes frough. She'll be all right.'

'No, Dad!' said Amy, thumping her fist on the table in front of him. 'Don't you understand? She's out of control. This 'ole family's out of control. If we don't do somefin' ter stop it, we're in trouble, real trouble!'

'Becos Thelm goes out for an hour wiv one of 'er mates?' replied Ernie, lighting his dog-end.

'It's not like that, Dad!' insisted Amy, leaning towards him, both hands on the table. 'Thelma looks older than her age. One of these days, someone's goin' ter take advantage of 'er. An' yer know wot that means, don't yer?'

Ernie rubbed his eyes, and looked up wearily at her. 'Amy,' he said, with a deep sigh as he exhaled smoke, 'you can't get blood out of a stone. Yer can't keep an eye on them every minute of the day. You're not their muvver.'

For a brief moment, Amy stared at him. Then she backed away from the table, and made for the door, where she stopped and turned. 'If anyone else says that to me,' she said, opening the door, 'I'll walk right out of this 'ouse, an' never come back.'

On Monday morning, Hilda couldn't wait for Amy to get into work. There was news, important news, for both her and Amy, and she was bursting to tell her. 'We've got the interviews!' she spluttered excitedly, the moment Amy came in through the Enkel Street back door. 'They want to see us next week.'

'Wot interviews?' she asked, not knowing what the hell her mate was on about.

'The Corner House!' squealed Hilda, shaking with excitement, and hardly able to contain herself. 'They've accepted our application forms and they want to see us.'

Amy was beginning to think her mate was going bonkers. '*Wot* application forms? Wot're yer talkin' about, 'Ild?'

They were interrupted by Marge Jackson, who stopped briefly on her way to open up the tea shop for the day. 'The job you applied for, Amy,' she said. 'To be a waitress at our Corner House branch in Coventry Street.

Amy gasped. 'Wot!' Her face was a picture of shock and disbelief. 'I din't apply fer no job up West.'

'Oh yes you did!' insisted Hilda. 'I filled it in for you – over a month ago. Same time as my own.'

Amy was now convinced that Hilda was bonkers. 'You filled in an application form fer me?' she asked, incredulously.

'Of course, darling,' replied Hilda, quite shamelessly. 'I don't want to take on the job without you.'

'It's a wonderful opportunity, Amy,' added Marge. 'It's not all that much more money, but you'll meet all kinds of people, important people. Our Coventry Street branch is one of the biggest in London.'

'Just think who we might wait on at table,' chirped Hilda, gleefully. 'Actors and actresses, MPs, film stars . . .' She gasped. 'We might meet Clark Gable! He's in the army. He might pop in for a grilled Dover sole.'

'If Clark Gable pops in fer anyfin',' bellowed Mrs Bramley, the cook, from behind the counter, 'it won't be fer Dover sole!'

Amy, stunned, slowly lowered herself into a chair at one of the tables. She couldn't believe what her so-called best mate had done to her. 'I don't want to wait on film stars up West,' she said, poignantly. 'I like it 'ere in 'Olloway.'

Hilda sighed. 'Don't be so unadventurous, Amy,' she said. 'This is the chance of a lifetime.'

'Hilda's right,' added Marge. 'In a way, it's a kind of promotion, a step up.' She lowered her eyes, and tried to put on a brave face. 'But I can't deny, I'll miss yer both.'

'Yer won't 'ave ter miss me, Marge,' replied Amy, ''cos I'm not goin' anywhere.'

'Oh, Amy!' growled Hilda, exasperated.

'No, 'Ild,' Amy said. ''Olloway's my place. I've got commitments 'ere, a family ter look after. I can't just walk off an' leave 'em.'

'That's just wot yer should do!' barked Mrs Bramley, from where she was cooking some black-market bacon, the appetising aroma of which was filling the shop. 'It'll teach 'em ter stand on their own two feet, ter do fings fer themselves. An' that includes yer ol' man!'

'That's not fair, Mrs B,' chided Amy. 'Dad's a complicated man, but since Mum left, 'e's suffered just as much as the rest of us.'

Mrs B grunted, and returned to her bacon.

'Mrs B's right, Amy,' said Hilda. 'You're always doing something for someone else. This is your time now – our time! Everyone should be given the chance to grow.'

Amy laughed that one off. 'At my age,' she chuckled, 'I reckon I've grown about all I'm goin' to!'

'Oh, come on, Amy!' complained Hilda. 'You know what I mean. You know that as long as you stay chained to that family of yours you're never going to be able to live a life of your own.'

'Hilda's right,' added Marge. 'Chances like this only ever come once in a lifetime. If yer miss 'em, yer'll always look back wiv regret.'

They were interrupted by the first customer, who was tapping on the front door, peering in between the protective strips of glued paper tape, frantically miming in an effort to find out if the shop was about to open. Marge waved back, and hurried to let the customer in.

Amy immediately got up from the chair and moved off to the counter with Hilda. She felt utterly bewildered and confused.

'Don't look so downhearted, Amy,' said Hilda, putting an affectionate arm round Amy's shoulders. 'You deserve a break. There's a lot more to you than slaving away to bring up your own brothers and sisters.'

'They're my family too, 'Ilda,' replied Amy, mournfully. 'I don't want ter be like my mum. I don't want ter leave 'em in the lurch. Whatever hassle they give me, they're still me own flesh an' blood.'

Hilda gave her mate's shoulder a tight squeeze. 'You know,' she said, 'sometimes I think blood can be just a little too thick. Once in a while, it needs to be thinned out a bit.'

The Kid was already at 'The Dump'. Aggs knew she would find him there because just before sunset was always his time for sorting through the vast mountains of old iron, wood and all kinds of paraphernalia that had been taken from bombed buildings around central London, and just dumped there. Placed alongside fashionable Rotten Row, these great piles of demolition were a monument to the insanity of the human race, and an eyesore to the beauty and grandeur of what was once a beautiful London park.

'Found anyfin' fer me then?' called Aggs, as she approached the youngest of the parkies, who was trying to chip off some cement from a length of lead pipe.

The Kid didn't even bother to turn round. He could tell Aggs's voice a mile off. 'Not unless yer want a bit of broken lavatory pan,' he replied. As Aggs climbed up to join him, he picked up a chunk of piano keyboard, and held it out in front of him. 'Or maybe yer've got an ear fer music?'

'Nah,' replied Aggs. 'I ain't musical. But if yer find a good pork chop, I won't say no ter that.'

As the boy turned round to her, he had a grin on his face. 'Am I in fer a lecture?' he asked.

'Not at all,' replied Aggs. 'But you're takin' a chance out 'ere in broad daylight, ain't yer?'

The boy did his best to look as though he didn't know what she was talking about. 'No more than usual.'

''Ow much did yer get fer that pig?' she asked, ignoring his feigned innocence.

The Kid dropped the chunk of piano keyboard back on to the rubble, and rubbed the dirt off his mittens. 'Why is it people always jump ter conclusions?' he asked.

'Dunno,' replied Aggs, who kept her distance just below where he was perched. 'No smoke wivout fire, though.'

The Kid looked away from her and surveyed the surrounding area. There were very few people left in the park, and the wintry sun had already sunk low behind the tall Knightsbridge buildings in the distance. His eyes finally came to rest on the darkening sky. For one fleeting moment, it reminded him of the sky above Dunkirk, the night before that fateful evacuation from the white, sandy beaches that were left covered with the blood and remains of so many of his army mates. 'I s'ppose it's no use tellin' yer that I din't nick that pig?' He turned to look at her. 'Is it?'

'Yer can tell me,' replied Aggs, who had a huge dewdrop hanging from the end of her nose. 'But I don't 'ave ter believe yer.'

'Just like the rest of my life,' said the boy. 'People never believe anyfin' or anyone they don't want ter believe.' He came down from the rubble to join her. 'As a matter of fact, Ma, I 'ad nuffin' ter do wiv it. But, if it's any interest, I know who did.'

Aggs shrugged noncommittally. 'It don't make no difference ter me,' she said, wiping the dewdrop from her nose with the back of her hand. 'But like I said, yer're takin' a chance 'angin' round 'ere.'

The boy grinned again. 'The rozzers won't miss one ol' pig down on 'is luck,' he said, flippantly. 'They got plenty more over in that cop shop.'

'It wasn't the pig I was talkin' about. They're out lookin' fer you, fer quite diff'rent reasons.'

The Kid gave her a knowing look. Then he turned to survey all around him. He was relieved that there seemed to be no one in sight, unaware that someone was in fact watching them from behind a huge oak tree alongside the old lido café nearby.

'It seems the army don't take well ter deserters,' said Aggs. 'Or so they tell me . . . Oh, don't worry, I don't blame yer,' she continued, bending down to pick up something protruding from the rubble. 'After wot you lot went frough, I'd've done the same.'

Despite her reputation amongst the parkies for not caring a damn for anyone other than herself, The Kid's predicament was, in some strange way, restoring the spark of maternal instinct in her.

The boy recognised this and he was grateful. 'Fanks, Ma,' he said.

Aggs held up the twisted brass object she had uncovered. It was the remains of a long toasting fork. 'Come in useful fer me breakfast,' she said, with a grin.

The Kid laughed. 'Bacon, eggs, bangers, and plenty of ketchup, eh?'

Aggs smiled, threw the toasting fork back on to the rubble, and turned to leave. As she went, she called back over her shoulder, 'Keep yer 'ead down,' and nodded towards Sid and Roy, the two special constables, who had just come into sight in the far distance, out on evening patrol.

The Kid took note and made a quick retreat.

Aggs strolled off at her own pace along the north side of the Serpentine. The wild bird population was already kipping down for the night on the island in the middle of the lake, but as darkness started to squeeze out the day's final light, the Muscovy ducks were determined to have one last grumble with each other before turning in.

Aggs made her way slowly over to the northside bridge, unaware that she was being followed by the same person who had been discreetly watching her and The Kid a few moments before. He was a well-built man, who, for the time being at least, was keeping his distance.

By the time Aggs reached the opposite side of the Serpentine, the twilight was thin and obscure, leaving her no more than a dark, moving shadow, weaving in and out of the hundreds of other shadows that were cast by the tall trees and thick foliage. She stopped briefly to look at the surface of the gently rippling water. By this time, she was perfectly aware that she was being followed, and merely waited for his reflection to join her own.

'You're late,' she said, sharply.

CHAPTER 7

Arnold Dodds didn't get on well with his sisters. In fact, if he'd had his way, his parents would have produced three brothers rather than what he had been lumbered with. He didn't mind Amy so much, because she didn't hassle him when he was doing something, like dissecting a moth, or reading a book from the library about how to climb Mount Everest. She was also the only one who listened to what he had to say, and knew how to make his favourite bread and marge pudding. But his other two sisters, Thelma and Elsie, were nothing more than a pain in the neck, nosy, and always going on about something or other. Boys were much more fun, Arn reckoned; they knew how to keep themselves to themselves and have a good time by just getting on with their lives without worrying about stupid things such as dolls and dressing up in their mum's clothes. Although Arn thought a lot of his mum, he had learned to do without her, and the fact that she had walked out on them without notice had never really surprised him, for during that last year or so that she'd been there, he had often heard her screaming and shouting at his dad.

His real hero, however, had always been his dad, not just because he was a bloke like him, but because he had once

105

helped Arn to build a pyramid out of a pile of used matches, which to Arn was the pinnacle of creativity. Unfortunately, since that one solitary occasion, the only time that the boy had any real contact with his hero was when they met over bread and jam at breakfast time. Now Uncle Jim upstairs was the only person who took any real interest in him, and that was only because, for the past few months, they had been working on a huge jigsaw together, which Uncle Jim had bought at the Emmanuel Church annual bazaar the previous summer. The jigsaw, a sprawling picture of the great ocean liner the *Queen Mary*, had over three thousand pieces, and had remained, growing exceedingly slowly, on the polished table in Uncle Jim's front parlour since the day it was bought.

'The only thing about jigsaws,' remarked Arnold, as he searched for an elusive piece that would fit into the flagpole on the aft section of the liner, 'is they take so long ter finish.'

'Ah!' replied Uncle Jim, who had his spectacles perched on the end of his nose, searching in vain for a piece of the ship's funnel. 'That's the beauty of it. It gives you time to think, to work things out.'

'Pity my mum didn't do jigsaws,' replied Arnie, quite unselfconsciously.

The boy's casual but shrewd remark took the lodger by surprise. With a careful sideways glance he said, 'How d'yer mean, Arn?'

The boy shrugged. 'She always did things wivout finkin',' he said. 'That's why she ran away.'

Uncle Jim was intrigued. 'So what didn't she think about?' he asked, cautiously.

'Us,' was the boy's blunt reply. 'Me an' my sisters. An'

me dad,' he added, with just a quick flick of a look. 'She didn't care about any of us.'

Uncle Jim thought about this for a moment, and continued to search for the missing pieces of ship's funnel. Eventually, and just as casually, he said, 'Maybe she couldn't help it.'

'Who?' asked the boy, who had almost forgotten what he had said.

'Your mum. Maybe she was ill or something.'

'If she was ill, she should've told us,' said Arn, trying a handful of jigsaw pieces to the missing flagpole. 'When I 'ad the measles, I told *everyone*.'

Uncle Jim smiled to himself. 'It's not quite the same, Arn,' he said tactfully. He had always had a great admiration for the boy, not just because he was practical-minded like himself, but because, unlike Thelma and Elsie, he had a way of seeing things intuitively. For a boy of eight, Arn had remarkable perception; he often worked out things like someone many years older than himself. He also had an inquisitive mind, which was good. In Uncle Jim's eyes, wanting to know was a great asset, especially for kids.

'Do you miss your mum, Arn?' he asked, again casually.

'Sometimes,' replied the boy, who was not concentrating as hard on the jigsaw puzzle as he appeared. 'My mate Mickey Dunstan asked me that at school the other day. I told him if she don't come back one day, I'll forget what she looks like.' Flicking another quick look at Uncle Jim, he added, 'But she'll come back, sooner or later.'

'How do you know?' Uncle Jim asked.

'She must want ter know 'ow we're gettin' on,' he replied. 'It's obvious in't it?' Then he turned back to the jigsaw puzzle. 'But I still love 'er,' he said, without any emotion.

To his great jubilation, the last piece of jigsaw in his hand fitted perfectly, successfully completing the *Queen Mary*'s flagpole.

Amy was beginning to take quite a shine to Tim Gudgeon. Since she'd met him properly at the Red Cross dance, she was gradually coming to realise that he was not only a thoroughly nice bloke, but also genuinely interested in helping her to find her mum. Tim had taken to turning up at the tea shop just before closing time in the evenings, much to the delight of Hilda, whose own brief encounter with the army officer had turned out to be something of a nonevent. Marge Jackson also approved of Amy's boyfriend, and did her best to encourage him by giving him a free cup of tea and a rock cake every time he turned up. About a week after they had first met, Tim told Amy that he had talked to someone in Annette Road whose husband had been sure that he'd recognised Agnes Dodds coming out of a pub in Paddington. Although the man, who worked as a ticket collector for Great Western Railways at nearby Paddington Station, didn't know Agnes personally, he had seen her out shopping with Amy many a time in Seven Sisters Road, and felt certain it was her.

The blackout curtains were already drawn by the time Amy and Tim had wandered into The Turk's Head up near Paddington Station. It was early evening, and Charlie Ratner the guv'nor, had left his wife Josie to serve at the Saloon Bar, whilst he looked after what he considered to be the more superior type of customer in the Private Bar.

'What'll it be, darlin's?' asked Josie, wiping spilled beer from the counter as Tim and Amy approached warily.

'Half of c-cider and a g-ginger beer sh-shandy, please,' replied Tim.

'Blimey!' chuckled Josie, exchanging a grin with two of her regulars who were propping up the bar. 'You're livin' dangerous, darlin's!' She was used to playing to the gallery.

Tim smiled back, attempting to share the joke with the two regulars, but he decided to let the missus go and get the drinks and not join in her repartee. For a moment or two, he and Amy stood where they were, looking around the bar, which was filling up fast. It was one of those pubs which seemed to be a meeting place for some of the nefarious types who lived in the dingier streets behind the Great Western railway station. At least, that's what Amy thought, and by the look on Tim's face, he felt the same way. To them, the customers were like a brotherhood of thieves, although they had no real grounds for knowing exactly why they should think such a thing.

'Are yer sure this is the right place?' Amy asked Tim, nervously.

'It must be,' replied Tim, voice low. 'The T-Turk's Head. This is where he saw her coming out.'

Both of them felt decidedly uncomfortable, as though dozens of pairs of eyes were looking at them. In point of fact, most of the customers were more interested in the frenzied game of darts being played by a couple of thick-stubbled men on the other side of the bar.

Amy kept as close to Tim as she possibly could, trying to ignore the thick palls of fag smoke that someone was blowing her way from nearby. 'I can't believe Mum would ever come to a place like this,' she said. 'She didn't like pubs. She preferred to drink at home.'

'One cider, one ginger beer shandy.' The missus plonked

the two glasses down on the counter, and wiped her hands on a tea cloth. 'One an' tuppence, please.'

Tim dug into his trouser pocket, produced a half-crown, and handed it over. The missus took the coin, rang up the correct amount on the cash till, and gave him his change. She was about to go off to serve another customer, when Tim stopped her. 'S-sorry to b-bother you,' he said, as fast as his stammer would allow, 'but we're looking for s-someone – a l-lady.'

The missus did a double take. 'A lady!' she blurted. 'The only one of them you'll find around here is me!' She roared with laughter at her own joke, which encouraged some of her regulars to join in.

'This one's a real lady,' said Amy, suddenly tired of the pathetic jokes. 'She's been missin' for nearly a year, an' someone we know thought they might 'ave seen 'er comin' out of this pub.'

'Did they now?' replied the missus, who hadn't taken too kindly to being answered back by a fat girl. 'An' what does she look like – this *lady*?'

Amy was ready with her mum's description. 'She's just a bit taller than me. Same colour eyes – dark blue; brown, short-cut hair, round face, and a mole on the right side of her chin. She disappeared from 'ome just over a year ago. We ain't seen 'er since.'

The missus looked suspiciously at Amy for a moment. Then she took a swig from her half-finished glass of gin on the ledge beneath the counter. 'An' why are you so keen on findin' this – *lady*?' she asked tartly.

'She's me muvver,' replied Amy.

The missus suddenly swung her a look. An answer was on

her lips, but before she had time to give it, a voice boomed out from the Private Bar curtain further along the counter: 'We don't know anyone wiv that description.'

Amy and Tim turned with a start to find Charlie Ratner, the pub's landlord, moving slowly towards them. 'Like the wife says, we don't encourage single ladies in The Turk's Head. It might give the wrong impression.' His wife looked at him as though he was up to something. But when, once again, she tried to speak, he shut her up. 'Why don't you take a turn in the Private, dear,' he said, fixing her with a look of steel. She clearly knew better than to protest. 'I'll take care of fings 'ere,' he added.

A short time later, Amy and Tim left the pub. They were only too glad to get out of the place, with its stifling atmosphere of cheap fags and draught bitter. As they walked up towards Edgware Road, for a few minutes neither said anything to the other. They both sensed something about The Turk's Head that was just not right, but whether it had to do with Amy's mum or not was quite a different matter.

'I don't believe for one minute it was Mum that was seen coming out of that pub,' Amy said, as they strolled towards Marble Arch. 'That landlord alone would be enough ter put 'er off.'

'He p-put me off!' agreed Tim.

'An' yet . . .' said Amy. Quite unconsciously, she slipped her arm through his.

'And yet?' asked Tim.

'Oh – I don't know. In a funny way, I *felt* 'er presence there.' She sighed. 'Wishful finkin', I s'ppose.'

Tim stretched his arm round her shoulders, and they slowly strolled on.

A few minutes on, they reached the junction of Edgware Road and Oxford Street. Although by day Marble Arch was a familiar landmark for Londoners, after dark the blacked-out streets had reduced it to no more than a silhouette, framed against an evening sky dotted with silver barrage balloons. The outer fringe of Hyde Park was a sombre sight, and the few cars whose fuel tanks were lucky enough to have whatever petrol was available on ration coupons or the black market, made slow progress in the dark, their dipped headlights only just visible through the regulation wartime slats. But there were still delights remaining to warm the heart and stomach on a cold January night, for despite the constant threat of air raids, the hot chestnut sellers were immovable, their indomitable spirits raised high with every customer.

At the open entrance to the park itself, Tim stopped to buy a bag of those chestnuts for Amy, and, most of the park benches removed for the war effort, they managed to perch on the remains of a brick wall which had once supported a section of the park's iron railings.

'The more I fink about it,' said Amy, taking a chestnut that Tim had peeled for her, 'the more I know that Mum would never've gone in a pub like that. She 'ad too much pride.'

Tim was in the middle of peeling another chestnut. 'P-people do funny things when they don't f-feel well.'

'It's not just that,' continued Amy. 'It's this place. It's just not our part of London, that's all. Islin'ton's diff'rent. The people are diff'rent. Even the smells in the streets are diff'rent. I remember, just before the war, Dad brought us up 'ere one Sunday mornin'. We went to some place round 'ere called Speakers' Corner. There were all sorts of people hollerin' at one anuvver. They was all gettin' so worked up about the most stupid fings. I 'ate the place. The streets are too clean, an' the people walk round wiv their nose up in the air.'

As if to illustrate her point, a well-groomed woman walked briskly past, with two equally well-groomed white poodles.

'B-bit unfair, don't you th-think, Amy?' suggested Tim, chewing the hot chestnut. 'Different doesn't necessarily mean worse, does it?'

'Maybe not,' replied Amy, glaring at the woman and her dogs as they disappeared along Park Lane. 'But you don't know my mum. She was set in 'er ways, an' nuffin' an' no one could change 'er. If they tried, Gord 'elp 'em!'

'Is that what happened b-between her and your d-dad, Amy?' asked Tim. 'Did she run off – b-because he tried to change her?'

For a moment, Amy was a little taken aback by Tim's suggestion. 'No,' she answered finally. 'She ran off becos – becos 'e was knockin' around wiv some uvver woman.'

Tim swung her a shocked look. 'Oh no,' he said with concern.

'It's this cow 'e works wiv down the baths,' said Amy. 'I've known fer ages that somefin's bein' goin' on between 'em, 'cos every time I go there, she glares at me.'

Tim put his arm round her shoulders. 'There are s-some things we can't d-do anything about, Amy,' he said. 'My d-dad left my mum years ago, s-soon after I w-was born. I d-don't even know what he l-looks like.'

Amy turned to him. She suddenly felt a deep warmth for him, so much so that she felt confident enough to slip her arm round his waist. 'Sounds as though *your* mum's 'ad a bad time too,' she said, guiltily. 'Left all on 'er own ter bring you up.'

'Oh, she m-managed all right,' said Tim, with just a touch of irony. 'She d-didn't lose everything. She still had m-me.'

Amy took in what he'd said. This was the first time he'd really mentioned his mother to her, and she was curious.

'I th-think the best day of my m-mum's life,' continued Tim, 'was when I got turned down for conscription. You d-did know I have diabetes?'

Amy looked up at him in the dark. 'Wot does that mean?' she asked, anxiously.

Tim smiled and hugged her close. 'N-nothing to worry about,' he said, reassuringly. 'T-too much sugar in my b-blood, that's all. But at least it gave M-mum a good excuse.'

'Excuse?'

He hesitated before answering. 'To k-keep me to herself.'

Amy's mind was racing. Tim's mum sounded quite a handful. She certainly wasn't looking forward to meeting *her*. 'I'm sorry, Tim,' she said. 'I'm so wound up wiv *my* problems, I ferget uvver people 'ave 'em too.'

Tim leaned his head on top of hers.

'Trouble is,' said Amy, staring out into the dark, 'I took my mum too much fer granted. I could see the state she was in long before she left 'ome. I could've stopped 'er. I *should've* stopped 'er, but I let 'er go.' She looked up at him again. 'If only I'd known, Tim. If only I'd known what she'd bin goin' through. That night, just as I was goin' up ter bed, she asked me ter give 'er a kiss. It's a fing she 'adn't done since I was a kid. I should've known then. All she said was, "G'night Amy, g'night." An' that was the last time I saw 'er.' She snuggled her head up tight against his chest. 'All I can say is, wherever she is now, I only 'ope she finks of me 'alf as much as I fink of 'er.'

114

Behind them, silent figures were wandering in and out of the long, dark shadows – birds to their nests, and humans to whatever patch of dry territory they could find.

The inhabitants of London's favourite back garden were already settling down for the night.

Sylvie Temple locked up the female side of the baths for the night. She'd been on duty for nearly ten hours, and not only was she dead on her feet, but she was desperate for a drink. Not that she was a heavy drinker, but after a long day, a glass of 'mother's ruin' gin and tonic always proved a far better pick-me-up than a cup of tea. For someone in her middle forties, she was pretty good. She wasn't a bad-looking woman, with violet eyes, and jet-black hair that had always convinced old Gert Tibbett from Roden Street that she was a dago. Sylvie's worst characteristic was that she had a hard and determined little face, with lips that pressed up tight against her teeth whenever she couldn't get her own way. But there was no doubt that she had striking looks, which is clearly what attracted Ernie Dodds to her.

'Do I get a drink ternight then?' Sylvie asked Ernie, as she watched him lock up the men's entrance. 'I'm parched.'

'Mind if we give it a miss ternight, Sylv?' replied Ernie, pulling up the collar of his raincoat. 'I'm not too flush this week. Got a lot of expenses.'

In the dark, Sylvie's face tensed. 'You're not the only one,' she replied acidly.

'Gospel,' said Ernie. Although he couldn't actually see the expression on her face, he had a good idea what it was. 'Maybe we could go round The Eaglet Friday night?'

'Can't wait that long, Ern,' replied Sylvie. 'I could do wiv a quid or two meself. Fings've come up.' Her request was more anxious than threatening. 'It's not easy on the pittance yer get at this place.'

'I know, I know,' said Ernie sympathetically. ''Ow much d'yer need?'

Sylvie hesitated a moment before she replied. 'Actually – three quid.'

Ernie nearly had a fit. 'Three quid!'

Both of them withdrew back into the darkness of the baths entrance, as the beam from a torch flicked across the pavement.

''Night, Ernie!' called a man's voice. ''Night, Sylvie!' It was Bert Farrar, the baths superintendent.

Ernie replied sheepishly. ''Night, Bert!'

Sylvie waited for Bert to go before speaking again. 'Fings're gettin' tight fer me, Ern,' she said, voice low. 'I've got bills that've got ter be paid. I can't hold out much longer. Yer promised ter pay me gas and 'lectric. Yer 'aven't given me a penny towards anyfing for ages.'

Ernie could feel the chill in the air more than ever before. It was causing his stomach to ache, and he, like Sylvie, was now longing for a drink. He knew he had a duty not to ignore this woman, knew that he had a responsibility to help her out. But how? He had a family at home who also needed looking after, needed clothes on their backs and food in their stomachs. Lousy father that he was to all of them, he just couldn't desert them at a time when they needed him most.

'If yer could just find a quid now,' continued Sylvie, moving up as close as she could to him, 'just ter tide me over till pay day . . . ?'

Ernie's mind was in torment; he had no idea how to deal

with this situation. Where did his loyalties lie, he asked himself – to his own children, or to the demands of this forceful woman whom he had once loved? For the moment then, there was only one thing he could do. Taking hold of her cold hand, he pushed a crunched-up pound note into it. 'I'll get yer some more next pay day,' he said, voice low. 'I don't know 'ow, but I'll try.'

Sylvie sighed with relief. In the dark, she sought out his lips, and kissed him. 'I love you, Ernie Dodds,' she said softly into his ear. 'I've always loved you.'

Ernie hesitated before answering. 'I love you too, Sylv,' he replied, but with very little conviction. 'Yer know I do.'

CHAPTER 8

In December 1941, soon after the Japanese made their surprise attack on the United States naval base at Pearl Harbor, the Germans felt confident enough to declare war on America. It was a bold move, for, throwing down the gauntlet to one of the world's greatest powers immediately brought the English-speaking peoples together as never before. But there were grim times ahead, for during the following few months, both the British and the Americans suffered catastrophic losses on land, sea, and in the air. Two of Britain's mightiest warships, the *Prince of Wales* and the *Repulse*, were sunk by Japanese bombers off the coast of Malaya, Allied merchant shipping was being destroyed in the English Channel, and in the Far East, the Japanese war machine was threatening to engulf American dependencies throughout the Pacific. Prime Minister Winston Churchill warned of the dangers now facing the British Empire, and appealed to the British people to welcome the armed forces of our 'American cousins' with open arms.

It was therefore no surprise to Amy and Hilda that as they were making their way along Coventry Street from Piccadilly tube station, the streets were already bristling with the khaki uniforms of the new-found allies from the other side of the

Atlantic. In fact, Hilda's eyes were quite literally bulging with lust, and by the time they reached the white and gold façade of Lyons Corner House, Hilda had almost forgotten the reason why she and Amy had made the journey 'up West' from the tea shop in Holloway Road.

'If we get this job,' she said, 'I only hope we get to wait tables on some of this lot!'

Amy was too nervous to be amused by her best mate's remark, for the very sight of the prestigious restaurant was churning her stomach over. She still had misgivings about applying for this job as a West End waitress, and secretly hoped that her very appearance would exclude her from the ordeal of going through the interview. The moment Amy saw the grandeur of the ornate entrance hall, with its wide staircase leading down to the Salad Bar, and up to the main restaurant, her instinct told her that this was not for her.

It was almost lunchtime when they arrived, and the place was already a hive of activity. Despite this, however, there was no sense of panic, and although the place was brimming with what Amy assumed were the rich and famous, none of the staff moved at anything more than a natural pace. At the entrance door, a man in a grey Lyons uniform and cap directed them to the administrative office downstairs, and as they made their way there, Amy was certain that her legs were about to give way beneath her.

It was nearly forty minutes later when Hilda came out of the office where she was being interviewed by the Personnel Manager. During that time Amy toyed with the idea of just getting up from the seat where she was waiting, and going straight back home. After all, she kept telling herself, this wasn't her idea; she never asked to be a 'nippy' or whatever they called the waitresses in this place. She was perfectly happy with being just plain Amy Dodds, who served tea and rock buns at Lyons Tea Shop in the Holloway Road. She didn't want, didn't need this kind of so-called 'lift up' in the world.

'In you go, Amy,' said Hilda, as she came out of the office where she'd just been interviewed. Then she lowered her voice. 'There's two of them, quite nice – on the whole. Nothing to worry about. Just be yourself. They wouldn't dare turn you down!'

Amy got up from the chair. She wanted to run out screaming, but decided not to, took a deep breath, and after a supportive kiss on the cheek from Hilda, she went to the office door and gently knocked.

'Come in!' boomed a man's voice.

Amy opened the door and went in.

Just prior to her appearance, the two people sitting there had clearly been in deep discussion about the next applicant, for the man behind the desk was poring over one of the two applications forms. He was in his fifties, a smoothie if ever there was, with dark greasy hair combed back with a razor-thin parting down the centre of his head, a scrubbed clean, hairless, glowing red face, and wearing a plain black suit and gleaming white shirt, complete with a striped old school tie.

'Good morning, Miss Dodds,' he said, his lips hardly moving. 'Sit yourself down, please.' He indicated a chair on the other side of the desk, directly facing him. 'My name is Pearson. I'm in charge of personnel at this branch.' And with an aimless flourish of his hand he added, 'And this is Miss Fullerton, who is the principal superintendent of our catering staff.'

The woman seated on one side of the desk gave a slight nod towards Amy, which only remotely acknowledged the girl's presence. She was in her mid-to-late forties, with an elongated face, tortoiseshell-rimmed spectacles, and hair secured severely with a comb behind her head. As she was wearing a plain black dress with a row of simulated pearls, Amy rather thought that she and the man looked like a couple of undertakers.

'We've had a very good report about you from your supervisor at Holloway, Miss Dodds,' said Pearson. 'It appears you are a very conscientious worker.'

Amy tried a weak, grateful smile. It wasn't very convincing.

'Are you happy in your work at Holloway, Miss Dodds?' asked Mr Pearson, fixing her with a puzzled look.

Amy gulped before answering. 'Yes, sir. Very much, sir.' She was only just audible.

'Then what attracts you to service in the West End of London?'

'Sir?'

Pearson tried to exchange a look with his colleague, but Miss Fullerton resisted the temptation and kept her eyes focused on Amy.

'I take it that Holloway is your home?' Pearson continued.

'Oh – yes,' replied Amy. 'Yes, sir. Born an' bred.' She was suddenly intrigued by a framed photograph on the windowsill behind him. It was a posed studio portrait of what must have been his family – a woman and three young children. The extraordinary thing was, they all seemed to look like carbon copies of Pearson himself, even his wife.

'What are Holloway people like, Miss Dodds?'

Amy looked at him as though he was stark raving mad.

'They're just – people, sir,' she replied, unsurely. 'Like anyone else.'

'Ah, but not *all* people are the same, Miss Dodds,' said Pearson. 'Take the people who come to eat in our restaurant here. They come from all walks of life – professional people, politicians, the theatre, the cinema, the armed services. But they all share one thing in common. They are well-bred customers. They can afford to eat in a place of high quality.'

Amy was mesmerised by his every movement. She watched in awed fascination at the way he picked up his pipe from an ashtray on his desk, pressed the tobacco down with his finger, then lit it.

'What about *your* customers, Miss Dodds?' continued Pearson, in between puffing smoke through his pipe. 'Would you say there is a difference between them, and the type of person we serve here?'

For a brief moment, Amy mulled this over. What was he getting at? Was he trying to tell her that West End people were better 'class' than her own back in Holloway? She had to fight hard to keep her temper. 'I s'ppose it depends on the person, sir,' she replied, 'not on 'ow much 'e can afford.'

Pearson smiled graciously. 'Quite so,' he conceded. 'Quite so.' At this point, he referred to Amy's application form on the desk in front of him. Then, glancing at his own notes, he asked, 'How much do you know about food, Miss Dodds?'

Again, Amy thought for a brief moment before answering. With a shrug, she replied, 'We serve all kinds of food down our tea shop, sir.'

'Such as?'

Aware that this was at last her chance to shine, Amy rattled off, 'Sausage rolls, rock cakes, fish-paste sandwiches. Mrs

Bramley – that's our cook – her real speciality is Welsh rabbit. Only when we can get the cheese, of course.'

Mr Pearson looked despondent.

'Our chefs also make a very good Welsh rabbit, Miss Dodds.' This time, the woman in the smart black dress was speaking. 'But we have a variety of other dishes for our customers to choose from. Roasts are always very popular.'

'Oh – with me too!' spluttered Amy with great enthusiasm. 'I sometimes do a bit of roast mutton for the family on Sundays. My bruvver, Arnold, goes mad, 'specially if there's roast spuds as well.'

Pearson nearly choked on an overdose of pipe smoke.

'Desserts?' asked Miss Fullerton.

'Pardon?' asked Amy. 'Oh no, don't tell me. We call it "afters" down our way.'

Miss Fullerton took a deep, exasperated breath. 'If I was to ask you to describe a baked Alaska,' she said, 'would you know what I was talking about?'

Amy thought for a moment. 'Somefin' ter do wiv meringue, ain't it?' she replied.

Miss Fullerton sneaked a glance at Mr Pearson, who was busily scribbling notes.

'I know 'ow ter make a good bread an' marge puddin', though,' said Amy. 'Before the war, my mum used ter make it wiv real butter, but since the ration—'

'We're not asking you how to cook things, Miss Dodds,' said an increasingly impatient Pearson. 'We have our own team of experts to do that. What we want to know is if you are capable of identifying items on a menu. A Lyons Corner House nippy is a household institution. She is expected to know what food she is offering our customers.'

Amy looked down at her lap for a moment, then quickly looked up again. 'I'd soon know, once I'd learned about them. The one fing I do 'ave is a good memory. I take after my mum like that.'

For a moment there was complete silence from the black-attired interviewers. Pearson rubbed his chin, chewed the end of his pipe, and scratched his nose, whilst Miss Fullerton sat straight-backed in her chair, hands folded, eyes staring down noncommittally into her lap.

Pearson spoke quite suddenly. 'Let me tell you what we expect of a nippy, Miss Dodds,' he said, replacing his pipe in the ashtray. 'A nippy is a Lyons Corner House waitress who is not only a renowned figure in our own country, but internationally. Before the war, tourists from around the world who ate in our restaurants returned home full of admiration for the professionalism and dignity of the young ladies who served at their tables. Nippies not only look superb, but they also know how to give good service to their customers.'

Sitting as upright on her chair as she could manage, Amy suddenly became very conscious of her appearance. How, she asked herself, could she possibly pretend that she looked 'superb', or that she really knew anything about food – food that they ate 'up West', and not what she served in her beloved tea shop in the Holloway Road. As she looked at the two impassive faces in front of her, she knew that she was fooling no one. She was no slender young beauty. She was an overweight, ordinary-looking girl from the wilds of Islington, and no matter how she tried to pretend, there was no getting away from it. However, she had nothing to be ashamed of, and in any case, she had never wanted to be a so called 'nippy' in the first place. As far as she was concerned now, she was going to take Hilda's advice and 'be herself'.

Pulling herself up to her full height, which wasn't very much, she looked straight across at Pearson and said, 'Well, sir. I do realise that I'm not really suited for a job like this. After all, I'm no oil paintin', an' I wouldn't want ter go round scarin' all yer very important customers.' At this point, she got up from the chair.

'How old are you, Amy?' Miss Fullerton's question was the first attempt by either her or Pearson to show any sign of warmth.

Amy, a bit taken aback by hearing herself referred to by her Christian name, replied, 'Twenty, miss.'

'Plenty of time to learn then?' contributed Pearson.

Amy looked puzzled. 'About what, sir?'

'About life,' said Miss Fullerton.

Amy smiled wryly. 'Oh, I know all about that, miss,' she replied. More than *you'll* ever know, she thought to herself.

As Amy left the office, Hilda was waiting eagerly to hear her news. 'What happened, Amy?' she asked excitedly.

Amy adjusted the neat little hat on her head, the one she had just borrowed from Hilda's sister. 'Oh – nuffin' ter worry about, 'Ild,' she replied. 'It was a cinch really. They obviously don't want me, any more than I want them. At least I know me place – right back there in 'Olloway Road.'

A few days later, Amy heard from Marge Jackson that she had received a telephone call from Personnel at Lyons Corner House in Coventry Street. It appeared that both Amy and Hilda had received favourable reactions from their interviews, and they were being transferred to their new jobs as nippies on the first Monday in February.

* * *

Aggs arrived for work at The Turk's Head at her usual time. It was fortunate that there was no one around then, for she had something important to do. It wasn't going to be easy, for the door she was looking for was somewhere behind the counter itself, and that was the part of the Saloon Bar that Ratner had made out of bounds for her, and, presumably anyone else.

The first thing Aggs had to do was to make sure that neither Ratner, his wife, Josie, nor daughter, Maureen were around. This she did by checking the Saloon and Private Bars, both male and female lavatories, and the small yard running alongside the pub, which was reserved for anyone who might still be lucky enough to run a car. The hardest part, however, was to come, for on her way to the pub that morning she had already taken the decision to go behind that bar and find the door she was interested in.

First, she had to go to the cupboard under the stairs near the side door, and bring out her bucket, soap, scrubbing brush, and cloths. Then she filled the bucket with cold water from a tap situated just outside the yard door. Once that had been achieved, she double checked the two bars again, then quietly raised the counter flap, and went behind. When she heard voices, she stopped dead. For a moment, she couldn't quite make out where they were coming from, but eventually her eyes looked up towards the ceiling, as she realised she could hear Ratner talking to his wife on the floor above. She slowly moved on, until she found the door she was looking for. It was situated behind a curtain between the two bars, and after one final look over her shoulder, she opened it and went out.

She found herself in a large yard, flanked on all sides by high stone and brick walls. It had clearly been designed with privacy in mind, for it would have been quite impossible for anyone in the car park to see into the yard. The most immediate impression Aggs got was the surprise of finding such a large area attached to the pub, especially in a built-up area so close to a mainline railway station. Her curiosity now fully aroused, she carefully made her way across the yard towards the place she was really looking for. This was a fairly large shed with a corrugated iron roof and no windows. The door was made out of planks of wood, and although it had a padlock fastened to the latch, it was not locked. After one more quick look over her shoulder, she pulled back the latch, opened the door and went in.

Despite the rough type of life she was living, she was repulsed by what she saw inside. The place was little more than a junk shop, for there were tools of every description scattered around the hard concrete floor. Tools for what? she asked herself, although it wasn't too hard to work out, for there were sealed tea chests, wooden crates, and cardboard boxes piled up everywhere, clearly brimming with every type of black-market goods imaginable. Several of the boxes were clearly marked in bold black letters: 'PBX STORES. FOR SALE TO USAF MILITARY PERSONNEL ONLY.' This didn't shock Aggs, for it was no more than she had expected, but what did horrify her was the stench, the sour and revolting smell of blood, seeping through a thick layer of sawdust which covered the floor. The source of that blood was coming from the poor, huge, dead creature who was trussed up, and hanging by the feet from a large hook in the ceiling. It was a pig. Despite her revulsion, covering her nose with her hand, Aggs drew closer. It reminded her of the two cockerels Ernie had once kept in their back yard at Enkel Street, and how distressed she and the kids had been when he eventually had to slit their throats to provide two Sunday meals for the family. As she stood there, all she could think of was the injustice levelled against her young fellow parkie The Kid, for there was no doubt now about who had been stealing the pigs from the Hyde Park police sty. Even though it was no more than she had suspected, questions remained. Was Ratner part of a black-market gang? If so, who were these people and how many of them were involved? Despite her chosen life style, Aggs still had a sense of fair play; she had no intention of letting The Kid take the blame for something he hadn't done. The boy had gone through quite enough already.

'Yer shouldn't be here, Ma.'

Aggs swung round with a start. Standing in the open doorway behind her was Ratner's daughter, Maureen.

'If Dad catches yer in here, he'll flay yer alive!' The girl checked the yard outside, and made sure that her father wasn't at the upstairs window of the pub, then quickly, quietly closed the door. 'Yer've got ter get out of here,' she said, voice low, coming across to Aggs. 'This is nuffin' ter do wiv you.'

Aggs glared at her. 'You're wrong,' she said icily. 'It's got a lot ter do wiv me. Your ol' man's a crook. The law's tryin' ter collar one of my mates fer this. I won't let 'em.'

Maureen drew closer. She was a pretty girl in her twenties, with blonde hair that just touched the top of her shoulders, and blue eyes that matched the colour of her cardigan. 'I beg yer, Ma,' she said, 'don't get involved. *I* don't. It's not worf it.' Unlike her father, the girl had a kindly face, and Aggs was in no doubt that what she was saying was for Aggs's own good. 'A lot of fings go on here, a lot of fings that could get Dad into a lot of trouble. He does dang'rous fings, Ma. You don't want to get involved.'

For a moment, Aggs didn't reply. Then she looked up at the slaughtered pig, the blood still dripping from the large slit in its throat. ''E's nicked this pig.'

'No, Ma,' insisted the girl. 'Somebody else did that. Dad's just a kind of – agent.'

'Where I come from,' replied Aggs, 'someone who nicks gets put inside.'

'Where *do* yer come from, Ma?' asked the girl doggedly.

Aggs was put off by that question. It was unexpected from a girl like this. She refused to answer.

Maureen came closer. 'Someone come into the pub the uvver day,' she said pointedly. 'She was lookin' fer someone like you. She said she was – this person's daughter.'

Aggs's face tensed. She looked shocked. 'I ain't got no daughter,' she snapped.

The girl nodded. 'When Mum told me, I felt sorry for the poor woman – whoever she is. She sounds as though she's been goin' through a rough time. I felt sorry for the girl too. She says her mum ran away from 'ome, from all 'er family.'

Aggs glared at her. 'Leave me alone, will yer!' She tried to push past, but Maureen blocked her way.

'Dad ain't all bad, yer know,' she said. 'When the bobbies come in ter ask fer everyone's identity card, 'e covered for yer, told 'em you was very absent-minded, always leavin' yer card back 'ome. 'E may 'ave his bad sides,' she added, 'but sometimes 'e does 'elp people.'

''E's still a crook,' replied Aggs.

'An' 'e's still my dad,' replied the girl.

Aggs picked up her bucket, and left as she had come.

On Friday evening, Ernie Dodds kept his promise and took Sylvie Temple for a drink in The Eaglet. Just lately, he had been thinking quite a lot about their relationship, and, in particular, about how his feelings had changed towards her. There was no doubt in his mind that he still fancied her, for she was a very attractive woman. But fancying wasn't love. Despite the fact that she had deserted him, Aggs remained the only woman in the world he would ever really love. After all, they had spent most of their adult life together, and Aggs had given him four kids. However, his dilemma was heightened not only by the fact that his job at the public baths earned him such a pittance, but also that, to his way of thinking, the work itself was so demeaning. Even so, his relationship with Sylvie had lasted a long time, and for that reason, if no other, he owed her at least some degree of support.

For her part, Sylvie was definitely still in love with Ernie; at no time in their sixteen-year relationship had she ever given up hope that one day he would belong to her, and her alone. But things hadn't turned out like that, and there were now increasing signs that her frustrations were beginning to test both her patience, and her endurance. All she knew was that she wanted him, and whatever happened, she would never let go.

'Stay wiv me ternight, Ern,' she said, as she sipped a glass of 'mother's ruin' at the same table in the Public Bar of The Eaglet that they had retreated to so many times over the years. 'I get so lonely at nights. Yer don't know wot it's like ter lie there in the middle of a double bed, no one ter talk to before I go ter sleep, no one ter share my troubles wiv, no one ter make love wiv.'

Ernie shook his head slowly. 'I can't do it, Sylv,' he replied. 'I can't leave the kids on their own at night.'

'Yer've got Amy, 'aven't yer?' said Sylvie. 'She's grown up now. Surely she can look after 'em?'

'Amy's not their mum, Sylv,' Ernie reminded her. 'She does more than her bit, but it's not fair ter load all the responsibility on to a young gel.'

Sylvie sighed, sat back into her chair, and pulled on a fag. 'My, my,' she said sourly. 'Suddenly we've become a caring dad!'

Ernie took a puff of his fag and stretched out for his half-full pint glass of bitter. 'That's not fair,' he said.

Sylvie suddenly felt guilty. 'I know,' she replied with a sigh. She leaned forward and squeezed his arm. 'I'm sorry, Ern.'

Ernie shrugged.

'But it's not easy,' continued Sylvie. 'Fings can't go on like this. Yer know they can't. Sooner or later, you're goin' ter 'ave ter make up yer mind one way or anuvver.'

Ernie suddenly felt self-conscious, and took a quick glance round to see if anyone was watching them. Then, keeping his voice as low as he could beneath the raucous pub banter in the background, he said, 'I'll see yer all right, Sylv. Yer know I will. I'll give yer anuvver pound next week.'

This irritated Sylvie. 'It's not just money, Ern,' she said. 'It's us. It's – wot're we goin' ter do wiv our lives. Do we go on pretendin' it's not 'appenin', or do we come out in the open an' face up to everyfin'?'

Again Ernie shook his head. 'I 'ave more ter lose than you, Sylv, yer know I do. I can't just walk out on my family. Not now, not just yet.'

Whilst they were sitting there, an elderly woman with hair in curlers hobbled in through the front door. It was Gert Tibbett from Roden Street, in to collect her nightly jug of stout. As she made her way to the counter, most of the regulars made room for her to pass, one or two of them giving her a pat on the shoulder, and a wry greeting of ''Ere she comes! 'Olloway's answer ter Betty Grable!' As usual, the old girl ignored them, and thumped her empty china jug on the counter. Whilst she waited for Jenny, the barmaid, to fill it up for her, her beady little eyes scanned the bar to see who was in for the evening. She scowled at anyone who dared to catch her eye, and cursed when one of her new Woolworths curlers fell out, leaving a strand of white hair dangling like a piece of string over her nose. Quickly hooking back the offending hair, the first thing she saw was Ernie and Sylvie sharing a table in a recess on the other side of the bar. By the time she had managed to focus, however, the couple had already got up from the table and were making for the door. Slamming her eightpence down for her refill, Gert picked up her jug of stout, and quickly pushed her way towards the pub door.

Ernie and Sylvie emerged from behind the blackout curtains in the pub entrance, and for a moment stood together in the velvet-dark street outside, their voices low and intimate.

'Come 'ome with me, Ern,' whispered Sylvie. 'Just this once. I won't make it difficult for yer, I promise.'

Ernie sought her lips in the dark and kissed them hard. 'Just give me a little time, Sylv,' he said, as he pulled his lips away from hers. 'Give me time ter sort fings out.'

The pub door suddenly opened, and for a brief moment, a shaft of light fell directly on them. They quickly stepped back into the doorway of the dairy shop next door, and disappeared into the dark. Gert Tibbett came out of the pub, firmly clutching her jug of stout. She paused a moment, to readjust her eyes to the dark. But, disappointed that she couldn't see who she was looking for, turned on her torch and tottered back home to Roden Street.

A few minutes later, Ernie and Sylvie kissed one last time, then went their separate ways, Sylvie to her flat in Axminster Road. Ernie, however, was far too unsettled to go back home to Enkel Street. He had so much on his mind, and he needed time to breathe. So he turned round, and made off slowly in the opposite direction, crossing Seven Sisters Road, and up past the public baths which had become such a dismal part of his life.

As Ernie ambled along, the glow from his fag end was like a minute beacon in a vast wilderness. But the dark winter clouds were moving fast, like giant creatures rushing home to bed, and as the ice-cold moon did its best to avoid colliding with those creatures, from time to time it bathed Hornsey Road in a dazzling fluorescent glow. If anything, the few quiet moments alone gave Ernie the chance to mull things over in his mind. It was something he rarely did, for putting things off was part of his nature; he didn't want to know when the going got difficult.

For a moment, he stopped outside the Star cinema, one of the best-loved bug hutches in Islington. After the tragic bombing of nearby Mitford Road just a few months before, the poor old picture house had been closed, but he couldn't resist standing there for a moment or so, peering inside the iron trellis gates which now flanked the entrance. Good old days, he thought to himself, recalling the times when, as a kid, he and his older brother Alf came to every Saturday morning picture show, watching Western serials with great stars like Tom Mix and Gene Autry. Yes, good old days! Not any more, though. The Star was closed, and the entrance full of rubbish and smelling of cat's pee. So he moved on.

He crossed to the other side of Hornsey Road, and made his way along the busy Tollington Road, which eventually led to the posh suburbs of Stroud Green and Crouch Hill. After strolling on for a few moments, he realised that he had reached St Mary's church, where he and Agnes had been married over twenty-two years before. At first, he had no intention of hanging around, for the memories were now so complicated, so painful. But the more he walked, the more he painted pictures of Agnes in his mind.

He could see her in those early days, fresh-faced and half-pint size, eyes gleaming in her cheap, home-made wedding dress. And he thought about their honeymoon, a long weekend at a boarding house in Southend, and the hours and hours of love-making in the double bed with the brass head and knobs. She loved him so much, he knew that – he'd always known that – so why had he done what he'd done? Why had he betrayed her, why had he betrayed his family just for the sake of an infatuation with another woman? And then, as he stood there, with the moon flicking back and forth across his rough, stubbled face, another picture entered his troubled mind. It wasn't Agnes this time, and yet, in a way it was. Amy. Dear, loving, sturdy-as-a-rock Amy. Just like her mum – warm, good-natured, and always to the point. Oh God, he thought, his mind in turmoil, how *could* I have done this to her, to all my kids – to *myself*? The moon appeared briefly again, reflecting in the tears that were welling in his eyes.

At that moment, Ernie was distracted by a worrying sound,

something that he could not at first identify. But as it grew closer and closer, the air along Tollington Road was suddenly pierced by the shrill sound of police and ARP whistles. This was immediately followed by a deafening explosion, coming from somewhere around the Nag's Head, in the distance behind him. Following that, but already too late, a chorus of voices echoed around the streets, yelling out frantically, 'Take cover!'

Ernie, with no time to bring his mind back into focus, was totally bewildered. There had been no air-raid warning, so what was going on? Where was this bloody Jerry coming from? He had only just started to move, when the sound he had heard just a few moments before, droned into reality. Just appearing at the end of the road, skimming the rooftops, was an enemy plane, machine gunning randomly down at the streets as it came.

The roar of its engines were deafening, terrifying, and at the precise moment that the raider had reached the spot where Ernie was running for his life, there was an enormous blue flash, an almighty bang, and a woman's voice screaming out hysterically from the distance: 'Ernie! Ernie . . . !'

CHAPTER 9

It was almost three o'clock in the morning when Amy left her brothers and sisters in the Anderson shelter, to answer a constant loud banging on her front street door. When she got there, she found a special constable waiting on the doorstep to tell her that her father had been badly injured in a bomb blast in Tollington Road during the night, and that he was unconscious. Leaving Thelma to look after Arnold and Elsie, Amy was driven by the constable in a police car straight to the Royal Free Hospital in Gray's Inn Road. The first person she met as she entered the casualty ward was Sylvie Temple, who was in floods of tears.

'It all 'appened so quick!' sobbed Sylvie, who was still in a state of shock herself. 'There was no warnin'. This plane just come down from nowhere an' dropped a bomb in a front garden right near where yer dad was runnin'. I fawt 'e'd 'ad it, I swear ter God I fawt 'e'd 'ad it.'

Amy clenched her teeth, glared at Sylvie with a look of absolute hate, and tried to push past.

'It's not like you think,' pleaded Sylvie, her eyes red and sore. 'We 'ad a drink tergevver. I wanted 'im ter come 'ome wiv me, but 'e wouldn't. I knew 'e was in a state, so I followed 'im.' She was close to tears. 'An' then . . . it 'appened . . .'

Amy ignored her, pushed past, and turned straight through the ward doors.

Ernie had been placed in a bed behind screens at the far end of the ward, but despite the fact that it was the middle of the night, there were doctors and nursing staff everywhere, applying emergency treatment to the most badly injured air-raid casualties; one snap raid by a determined enemy pilot had clearly wreaked havoc across this tiny corner of North London. Amidst the groans of pain and sickly smell of ether and iodine, Amy reached Ernie's bed. She heard voices coming from behind the screens, and when she peered in, a doctor, assisted by a young nurse, was just completing a major examination of Ernie's condition. 'Can I come in?' said Amy, her voice barely audible. Both doctor and nurse turned with a start.

'Who are you?' asked the elderly doctor.

'I'm Mr Dodds's daughter,' replied Amy, anxiously.

'Come in, please,' called the doctor.

At the first sight of her dad lying prostrate in the bed, Amy felt her stomach churn over. But even though he seemed to have tubes wedged into various parts of his body, she was surprised to see very few apparent injuries. 'Wot's 'appened to 'im?' she asked nervously. ''E's not goin' ter die, is 'e?'

The doctor replied with no emotion, 'We don't know yet. At this stage it's impossible to assess the seriousness of his injuries.' He turned to look back at his patient. 'Apart from a few bruises,' he continued, 'it's a miracle how his body has managed to sustain the bomb blast. But he has a very severe concussion. We shan't know for some time whether he's suffered any brain damage.'

Amy clamped her hand over her mouth to stifle a shocked

gasp. Her face was racked with anguish as she looked at her dad's stone-like figure laid out before her. 'When will yer know!' she asked, terrified by what the answer might be.

The doctor, deep in thought, scratched his chin. 'Not until he comes out of this coma.'

''Ow long will that be?' asked Amy.

The doctor shrugged. 'A few hours,' he replied, 'days, weeks, months. There's never a way of knowing these things. All we can do is wait, I'm afraid.' He smiled as much as he was capable at her, then left to attend to other victims.

Once he had gone, the nurse turned to Amy and smiled sympathetically. Then she sighed, and took a resigned look at the poor creature she had just tucked in. 'I hate this war,' she said softly, leaving Amy alone with her father.

Amy drew closer to her dad and leaned down over him. As she looked at his motionless face, she tried to work out in her mind what exactly a coma was. As far as she could tell, her dad was just sleeping, just the same as she had seen him many a time at home. And yet, he had a far more distant look on his face than she had seen before, as though he was miles away in another place, another world. Where was he now, she wondered? Was he back with her mum, dancing a waltz round the Emmanuel church hall? Was he holding her tight, and telling her that he was sorry for all the unhappiness he'd caused her, and that he loved her and wanted her to come back home to him and the family again? Or was he in the arms of that woman, that slut of a woman outside who was determined to break up his marriage and his life? *Where are you now, Dad?* asked her tormented inner voice. She leaned as close as she could, so that she could just feel the short but rhythmical streams of breath filtering through his dry, parched lips.

'Dad,' she whispered. 'It's me, Ame – *your* Ame.' She took hold of his hand, and gently stroked it. 'You're goin' ter be all right, Dad,' she said. 'You're goin' ter wake up soon, an' when yer do, I'm goin' ter be 'ere waitin' for yer. I won't leave yer, Dad. I promise – I won't leave yer.'

Amy spent the night at his side, never once letting go of his hand. By the time she left hospital at daybreak, Ernie was still far away wherever he'd gone.

At first light the following morning, Aggs made her way to King's Cross. Ever since she had left home over a year before, this had become something of a ritual, for on Saturday mornings, the WVS had set up a mobile canteen for the emergency services, and anyone else who was in need of a hot cup of tea and a piece of toast. Situated in a quiet street near the gas works just behind the mainline railway station, the canteen never failed to draw not only the weary men and women of the fire, police, and ambulance services, but also every down-and-out in the district. Aggs usually got there about half-past eight, because by then the queue had thinned out a bit, which meant that she wouldn't have to stand in the freezing cold for longer than necessary. Most of the regulars knew her well, for the moment she arrived there were calls of 'Oy! Oy! 'Ere she comes – Churchill's secret weapon!' Aggs ignored them, of course, and once she'd collected her breakfast, she was off to the station concourse, where there was always a place to sit and enjoy her tea.

As always at this time of morning, the station was bristling with activity, for apart from the relentless brigades of out-of-town commuters, there were the miserable, tearful scenes of soldiers, sailors, and airmen taking leave of their wives and families, as they returned to what was looking like a hopeless, dark period of the war.

Aggs mingled with the crowds until she found somewhere to sit on a hard wooden bench alongside a pile of sandbags, which had been stacked up near the main entrance to the station. Just behind her on the wall was a huge, ominous poster which showed someone putting a finger to their lips, and apparently saying, 'Sssh! Careless Talk Costs Lives'. The figure trying to listen in the background of the picture was the old Führer himself, Adolf Hitler. Aggs started to sip her tea, which was still surprisingly quite hot, but she cursed when the driver of the train on Platform 2 suddenly pierced the air with the sound of the horn, causing Aggs nearly to jump out of her life, spilling hot tea on to her already well-stained raincoat. The moment she composed herself again, she was only too aware that someone was sitting beside her. Whether or not it was the smell of the person she recognised, she seemed to be totally unconcerned that he was someone she knew. Without turning to look, she asked irritably, 'Wot d'yer want, Jim?'

'It's Ernie,' said Jim Gibbons. 'He's been badly injured.'

Aggs swung a startled look at him. 'Wot yer talkin' about?' she asked, eyes wide with shock.

'He was in Tollington Road last night. This Jerry plane came over – he must've been a stray or something because there was no warning. He machine-gunned the whole road, then dumped a bomb not far from where Ernie was trying to get away. There was a massive explosion. The whole street took the blast. It's a miracle he wasn't killed outright.'

It took Aggs a moment to take it all in. ''Ow bad is 'e?'

'Touch and go.'

They were distracted by the muffled voice of a station announcer, booming out train departure details over the totally inadequate Tannoy system. Whilst it was going on, Aggs got up from the bench. When the announcement came to an end, she said, 'Wot d'yer expect me ter do about it?'

Jim got up. 'He's dying, Aggs,' he said, turning to face her. 'He may not last the night.'

Aggs's expression hardened. 'I said, wot d'yer expect me ter do about it?'

Jim was bewildered by her callousness. 'But – he's your husband.'

'Not any more, 'e's not,' said Aggs, dumping her paper cup into a litter bin. 'As far as I'm concerned, 'e's the past. In my book, 'e don't even exist no more.'

Jim watched her go in disbelief. Then he hurried after her. 'Look, Aggs,' he said, trying to keep up. 'I know how you feel about Ernie. I know how much he's hurt you, but you can't just dismiss him as though he's not there – because he *is* there.' He suddenly took her arm, and forced her to a halt. 'There must be something inside you that still feels *something* for him?'

For one brief moment, Aggs watched a distraught young woman by a platform gate nearby. Her face was crumpled up, and tears were streaming down her cheeks as she held on to what must have been her soldier husband, carrying a rifle, and with a kitbag strapped to his back, just about to take his leave of her.

'I don't care whevver Ernie Dodds lives or dies,' Aggs said, icily. 'I've shed too many tears about 'im in the past, but not any more. I just don't care.'

'And what about your kids, Aggs?' asked Jim, talking to

the side of her face. 'You upped and walked out on them over a year ago. Are you telling me that you don't care about them either?'

Aggs swung him a resentful look, then walked on.

Once again, he followed her.

Outside the station, passengers came streaming into the Euston Road, and made straight for taxi or bus queues. The sounds of motor and bus horns mixed with the frenzied shouts of news vendors: '*Star! News! Standard!* Stray bombs on London!' Aggs ignored them all, and started the long walk back to her pitch in Hyde Park.

'He's in the Royal Free,' called Jim, as he tailed Aggs.

Aggs stopped with a start, and turned back on him. 'It's no good, Jim!' she snapped. 'Ernie's the past. I only live fer terday.'

The crowd rushing past were irritated that their passage was hindered by two people having a conversation right near the station exit.

Undeterred by everyone's anger, Jim went to Aggs and faced up to her. 'Am I the past too, Aggs?' he asked. 'If so, why do you let us meet, when no one else can find you?'

Aggs tried to avoid his gaze.

Jim drew closer. 'I'll tell you why, Aggs,' he said, forcing her to look directly into his eyes. 'It's because the past isn't just the past. You *want* to know. You *want* to know about your kids. And because Ernie still means something to you, you *want* to know about him too.'

She was about to answer him, but in a split second, changed her mind. Without a word, she turned, and walked off, leaving Jim where he was, to be engulfed by a great tide of human impatience.

* * *

Amy spent most of the day at her dad's bedside in the hospital. Ernie still hadn't emerged from the coma, and, despite Amy's constant watch for any sign of life, he showed no signs of doing so. Her great support at this time was Tim, who had shown her such care and attention, proving to Amy that he was rapidly becoming the love of her life. The elderly doctor told Amy that as there was no way of knowing if and when her dad would ever regain consciousness, rather than sit around the hospital for long periods at a time, it would be far more sensible if she were to pay shorter visits, leaving the hospital to notify her if there were to be any marked change in her dad's condition – for better or worse.

'Is Dad goin' ter die?'

Even though the question was innocent enough coming from her five-year-old sister, to be greeted with it the moment she came through the front door sent a chill down Amy's spine. 'Don't ever let me 'ear you say such fings, Else!' she growled, as she closed the street door after her and Tim. 'Dad's goin' ter be all right. 'E's goin' ter get well.'

'When?'

This time Amy ignored the question. Ever since the small child had learned about her dad being injured in the bomb explosion the previous night, Amy had been bombarded with just this kind of question, not only from Elsie, but from Thelma and Arnold too.

'Go an' wash yer 'ands,' ordered Amy, gently shoving the child into the back parlour. 'I'm just goin' ter get yer tea ready.'

'Is 'e 'avin' tea wiv us?' asked Elsie, nodding towards Tim, as she led the way into the scullery.

'Yes,' replied Amy, exasperated. 'Now get a move on, Else!'

The back parlour stank of nail varnish.

'Thelma's been painting her nails again,' said Arnold, who was playing solo his favourite card game, 'Beat Your Neighbours at the Door', at the kitchen table. 'They look awful – bright red!'

Amy sighed. Thelma was determined to follow her own road. 'Go and wash your hands, Arn,' Amy said, to the boy. 'I'm just about ter get the tea.'

Arnold quickly gathered his playing cards together, and got up from the table. 'How's Dad?' he asked. The casual way he addressed the question could not disguise his concern.

Amy smiled unconvincingly. ''Bout the same,' she replied. ''E's still asleep.'

Arnold nodded his head without looking at her, then went out to join Elsie in the scullery.

As the scullery door opened, Elsie yelled out, 'Amy! Is Tim going ter kiss yer now?'

Amy clenched her teeth, and went to the scullery. 'Wash yerself!' she yelled back, then slammed the door shut.

As she turned back to Tim in embarrassment, she suddenly found herself wrapped in his arms, with his lips pressing hard against hers.

'G-got ter do wot yer little s-sister asks,' he said, as he withdrew his lips. 'Anyway, I've b-been wanting to do that.'

To Tim's delight, she replied, 'So 'ave I.'

They parted immediately as Thelma entered the room. 'Oh – sorry,' said the girl. 'Don't mind about me.'

To Amy's dismay, her younger sister was wearing make-up – only a suggestion of bright red lipstick to match her identically coloured nail varnish, but enough to make Amy's hackles rise.

'Wot's all this then?' she asked acidly.

'Wot's wot?' asked Thelma.

'Don't muck around wiv me, Thelm,' replied Amy. 'Wot've yer got all that paint on for?'

'I'm goin' round ter see Linda,' she said, shaking back her hair haughtily. 'She's got some new magazines from America she wants ter show me. I'm only goin' fer an hour.'

'So all this dollin' up is fer Linda, is it?' asked Amy, incredulously.

'I'm not dolled up!' Thelma snapped, resenting the embarrassment she was being subjected to in front of Amy's boyfriend. 'I don't say fings like that ter you when *you* put on lipstick, and paint yer legs wiv gravy powder!'

Amy ignored her remark, and started laying the table. 'You can ferget about Linda,' she said adamantly. 'You're comin' ter see Dad in 'ospital ternight.'

'No!' growled Thelma.

'Yes!' insisted Amy.

'Wot's the point?' asked Thelma, on the verge of throwing a tantrum. ''E won't be able ter see us if 'e's in a coma. 'E won't even know we're there.'

Amy exchanged a fleeting glance with Tim. 'Thelma,' she said, doing her best to remain calm. 'Just do as I say, an' go an' get that stuff off yer face. We're all goin' ter 'ave tea, an' then we're goin' off ter see Dad. Understood?'

Bursting with anger, Thelma glared at her sister with such venom that Tim was convinced she would hit Amy. But instead, she stormed out of the room, slamming the door so hard that the whole house shook.

After she had gone, Amy, in a state of total despair, flopped down into a chair at the table and covered her face with her hands.

Tim went to her, kneeled down beside her, and gently removed her hands from her face. To his dismay, he found tears streaming down her cheeks. 'C-come on now,' he said, with quiet affection. 'It's not as b-bad as all that.'

'Oh yes it is!' sobbed Amy. 'In fact it's worse.' She searched for a handkerchief in her dress pocket, but couldn't find one. 'It's out of control. This whole family's out of control – no muvver, an' now no farver. I can't go on like this much longer, Tim, I just can't.'

With the tips of his fingers, Tim tenderly wiped the tears from Amy's cheeks. 'You'll g-get through this, Amy,' he said. 'One day you'll w-wake up, and suddenly everything'll be d-different. W-when you start your new j-job, it'll give you the chance to meet new p-people, to see n-new things.'

Amy was shaking her head. 'I'm not goin' ter take the new job, Tim,' she said. ''Ow can I? If anyfin' 'appens ter Dad, 'ow can I keep my eyes on this family? It's wot Thelma wants. She can't wait for me ter be out of the way. She can't wait ter go 'er own way, an' do anyfin' she likes.'

'Now l-listen to me, Amy,' said Tim, standing up again. 'I'll h-help you. I'll b-be there whenever you need me. If you have s-someone to talk to, s-someone who can h-help you sort out a problem, then I p-promise you, you will b-be able to cope.' He stood behind her, and put his arms around her. 'B-but whatever happens, you m-mustn't let Thelma get you down. You m-mustn't let any of them get you down. This is a b-bad patch, that's all.' He leaned forward, and kissed the top of her head. 'If you'll l-let me, we'll f-face up to it – together.'

147

They kissed again. Amy felt the warmth of his cheeks against her own. His love and support raised her spirits so much. And yet, when their lips parted, and they stared into each other's eyes, she found it hard to believe that this was the same person who was so clearly possessed by another woman, his own mother.

It was late in the evening when Aggs entered the main entrance of the Royal Free Hospital in Gray's Inn Road. In normal circumstances someone as scruffy-looking as she would never have been allowed near any of the wards, but wartime was no normal circumstance, and the life-and-death atmosphere which pervaded the wards gave credence to anyone who needed to see a loved one for the last time.

'I'm sorry but you're far too late for visiting.' The night nurse on duty in the emergency casualty ward was adamant. Even though Ernie was still fighting for his life, she had no intention of allowing any old down-and-out to disturb the other poor creatures who were trying to recover from the trauma of the previous night's air raid. 'Come tomorrow afternoon,' she said, her voice no more than a whisper. 'This is not a good time.'

'An' wot 'appens if my bruvver dies before it *is* a good time?' asked Aggs tersely, her beady eyes glistening in the soft glow of a solitary overhead night lamp.

The nurse kept her distance; the smell of Aggs's sour breath was a bit too overpowering. 'Why didn't you come during regular visiting hours?' she asked.

'I came as soon as I 'eard,' replied Aggs. 'It's a long walk from the Mile End Road, y'know.'

The nurse's eyes widened. 'Walk?' she asked, taken aback.

'You – *walked* – right across London, all the way from the East End?'

Lying through her yellow-stained teeth, Aggs replied, ''Ad ter get 'ere some'ow, didn't I?'

The night nurse's whole attitude changed to one of admiration. 'You say you're Mr Dodds's sister?' she asked, with a sympathetic smile.

''S'right.'

The nurse hesitated a moment, then opened the ward door. 'Five minutes, please – not a moment longer. He's at the end of the ward, on the left.'

Aggs entered the darkened ward. There were groans, and an air of restlessness everywhere as critically ill patients tossed and turned in their beds. The drawn blackout curtains and the stench of freshly dressed wounds increased the feeling of claustrophobia. Aggs's plimsolls plodded along the highly polished linoleum floor, but as she went, she resisted the temptation to take in the rows of beds lined up against the walls on either side of her, for in her mind, she had quite enough suffering and pain of her own to cope with.

At the far end of the ward, it was easy for her to pick out the bed she was looking for. A thin ray of light from a dim bedside lamp was highlighting Ernie's immobile face, with the thin rubber tube from a saline drip protruding from his nose. The moment she saw him, she came to an abrupt halt. Suddenly, time seemed to stand still, for her past life with this man came flooding back to her. She had an urge to turn and walk away, but something inside prevented her. She gradually took the last few steps towards his bedside. When she finally got there, she became absolutely still, her eyes transfixed by the face she thought she had always known so well. Then she spoke to him, not with her lips, but with her mind. *Bleedin' fool*, she said, with what she thought was cool detachment. *See where it's landed yer? I warned yer, didn't I? Gord knows, I warned yer.* She leaned over him, so that her face was so close to his that she could feel short bursts of breath popping through his lips. *I gave yer too much, Ern,* she continued. *I gave yer far too much, more than yer ever deserved. Still, maybe yer couldn't 'elp yerself. I can see that now. Never was one ter see straight, was yer? Never was one to see 'ow easy it was ter destroy someone's life.* She sighed. *If only you could've said sorry, Ern – just once, just ter let me know that yer cared – just a bit.* She paused, and stared straight down at his closed eyelids. *But there's no point in lookin' back now. That was the past – this is the present. So don't you go an' die on me, Ern – not only for the kids' sake, but mine too. Fink of Amy – our own Amy. D'yer remember 'ow we always used ter say 'ow she alone was worf our weddin' day? Well, she is, and don't you forget it. Give 'er a break, Ern. Stop bein' a stupid git, an' get back 'ere! Just remember what yer used ter be, what yer could still be!*

She straightened up again, and after one last look at his face, she turned and hurried out of the ward.

A few hours later, the night nurse called the doctor urgently to Ernie, who had apparently shown the first real sign of movement, and had even partly opened his eyes.

CHAPTER 10

Amy was under no illusions about working at Lyons Corner House in Coventry Street. Not only were the hours long – sometimes as much as eight hours on her feet at a time – but the customers *were* different, just as had been intimated to her by Mr Pearson during her interview. Not that they were a different breed of person, for most of them were quite ordinary individuals from modest backgrounds, who had probably saved up for a long time to celebrate a birthday or some other kind of anniversary. In fact anniversaries were a speciality of the Corner Houses; no matter who or where the customer came from, they were made to feel very special, despite the fact that food rationing had made life so difficult for the catering business.

For the first couple of weeks, Amy found work as a nippy quite tough. It wasn't the rigours of the job – God knows, she needed superhuman stamina to look after her own sisters and brother – but learning how to deal with people who were actually interested in food, and who treated it as more than just something you cooked, ate, and forgot about as soon as possible. If trying to remember what was on the menu was bad enough, describing what some of the fancy dishes were made of was, for a meat-and-two-veg girl, an absolute nightmare. And then there was the business of laying the table with all the cutlery in the right place, and setting one glass for water and another for wine in exactly the right position, and when the customers had left, changing the tablecloth, and starting all over again for the next customer. Admittedly, she and Hilda had spent the first week being trained by one of the senior nippies, always under the watchful eye of Miss Fullerton, but it was an ordeal Amy had not foreseen. It was all so different to her customers back in the tea shop in Holloway Road, who popped in for a quick cuppa and one of Mrs Bramley's home-made sausage rolls. However, at least Amy had discovered what being a nippy really meant, for getting a move on at all times had been one of the key elements of her training.

By the end of the second week, Amy had settled down into the job enough to unwind, and start to enjoy the extraordinary atmosphere that had made Lyons Corner Houses so popular. On her first day, she couldn't believe that during evening meals, a four-piece orchestra played background music for the customers, with the players kitted out in black tie and dinner jackets. And even at lunch time, a pianist with dark greased-back hair, parted in the middle, played cosy tunes by Cole Porter, Noël Coward, and Jerome Kern, which always set the customers' feet tapping beneath their tables. To her surprise, Amy got on well with nearly all the other girls, many of whom came from similar backgrounds to her own. There was, however, one exception.

'Better watch out,' said Bertha Willets, as she and Amy waited in the ground-floor kitchen for their orders. Bertha was just a few months older than Amy, though a more archetypal nippy than Amy – tall, thin, immaculately turned out, with only the faintest suggestion of make-up. 'Your cap's crooked, and your collar's got a dirty fingermark on the back.'

Amy froze. She always did when Bertha made a comment like this; it made her feel even more self-conscious.

'If you take my advice,' continued Bertha, in her assumed West End voice, 'always look at yourself in the mirror before you come into the restaurant. Miss Fullerton's got her eyes on you. I'd hate to see you get hauled down to the office.'

Amy watched Bertha collect her order of mutton pie and vegetables, then make her way with her tray back into the restaurant. Once she had gone, Amy quickly adjusted her sparkling white cap and collar, and straightened her neat apron and black uniform dress. She really hated the way Bertha kept giving the impression that she was only trying to help her, when it was perfectly obvious that every time she spoke to her was to make her feel thoroughly uncomfortable.

'Take no notice of her at all,' said Hilda, as she hastily joined the small group of waitresses who were waiting for their orders. 'She has a mouth longer than the entire Piccadilly Line!'

'I can't understand why she's always on at me,' said Amy, anxiously inspecting her entire appearance. 'D'yer know wot she said ter me on our first day? She said, "I can't understand how someone like you got accepted into a job like this. I've always thought girls here have to be slim, and well turned out."'

'I'll tell you why you got the job, Amy,' growled Hilda, seething with indignation. 'You got it because of your personality. That's something *that* one wouldn't know about if she lived to be fifty – which she's probably already done twice over!'

'But she's got a point, 'Ild,' said Amy, gloomily. 'Yer don't see many fat gels servin' on the tables.'

'More's the pity!' growled Hilda. 'They should start a fashion!'

'One *agneau,* one *bombe surprise!*' called an assistant chef.

The two girls immediately collected their orders, and nipped off briskly back to the restaurant.

Amy's table, one of six she was waiting on, was occupied by an elderly retired-colonel-looking type, and a young, heavily made-up girl.

'Ah!' exclaimed the colonel, heartily, rubbing his hands with anticipation, and then adding in a somewhat suspicious French, 'The *agneau au Lyons!*'

Amy placed the tureen of mutton pie in the centre of the table, followed by two dishes of mixed fresh vegetables, and a small jug of brown gravy.

'Don't look like much *agneau* there,' sniffed the girl, haughtily. 'It's all powdered potato.'

'*Fresh* potato, madam,' Amy assured her courteously.

'Smells good to me, Sandra dear,' said the colonel, who from the moment he had sat down at the table had done his best to give the impression that the girl was his daughter. '*Agneau* is a real luxury these days.'

The girl shrugged her shoulders.

Amy served the pie and vegetables. Out of the corner of her eye, she observed and felt sorry for the girl. By her bored look, it was obvious that Sandra was only earning her living. After all, there *was* a war on. Times were hard.

On her way back to the kitchen, Amy stopped briefly at the next table to collect some of the empty dishes from a table occupied by three young women in WRNS uniform, and when she moved on from there, struggling with the heavy tray, a young RAF sergeant, clearly trying to make a hit with the three WRNS leaned back in his chair and called, ''Scuse me, miss! D'you serve whitebait here?' Amy positively yearned to answer, 'Yes, sir. We serve everybody,' but thought the old, well-worn gag might not go down too well with the head waiter, who was nearby, so she merely called back politely, ''Fraid not, sir.'

It was almost midnight when Amy and Hilda left by the rear door of the restaurant. The streets were not fully deserted, for the American military police, known as the 'Snowdrops' because of their white tin helmets, were patrolling the streets, on the lookout for any of their servicemen who might be causing trouble.

'It's hard to believe this is the same place, isn't it?' said Hilda, as she and Amy struggled by torchlight to pick their way across the pitch-dark of Piccadilly Circus. 'I remember before the war, it used to be so full of life, so full of neon signs flicking on and off across the buildings up there, lights, colour, people having a damn good time. And now look at it!'

The beams from their torches helped them across Regent Street, and once they'd taken a short cut through Air Street, they were only a few steps away from their bus stop in Piccadilly.

Despite a long and tiring day, when they got there, Hilda suddenly came to life. 'Oh God!' she cried. 'The day this bloody awful war comes to an end, I'm going to dance stark naked on a table in the Café de Paris!'

''Ilda!' protested Amy, horrified. 'That's filthy!'

'Oh, stop being such an old fuddy-duddy, Amy!' replied Hilda, her arms wrapped around the bus stop pole, hugging it as though she was making love to her latest boyfriend. 'I'm only joking.'

Amy breathed a sigh of relief.

'But I'm going to do it one day – not the table bit – but I do want to go inside the Café de Paris – preferably on the arm of some gorgeous, *rich* American army officer. It's a dream of mine, to be wined and dined in somewhere really famous. Life is for living, Amy! Oh, I do love London!' Her arms were flung wide high into the air, as though she was embracing the entire city.

'I prefer 'Olloway,' said Amy, uncompromisingly.

This immediately brought Hilda back down to earth. With a laugh she replied, 'Holloway *is* London, Amy.'

'Yes, I know,' conceded Amy, 'but it's kind of – different to uvver places. I feel more – at 'ome there.'

Hilda suddenly felt a surge of affection for her friend. 'You know, it's a funny thing,' she said, putting her arm round Amy's shoulders. 'When you're at home, you yearn to get away, but the moment you're not there, you pine. You've gone through so much, Amy.'

'Yes,' replied Amy, squinting in the beam of Hilda's torch. 'But fings are diff'rent now that Dad's back on his feet again. I never fawt the day would come when I'd 'ear 'im say that from now on 'e wants ter look after me an' the uvvers. When I first saw 'im in that 'ospital, I fawt we'd lost 'im. I fawt I'd never see 'im nor Mum ever again. But now I've got 'im back, I just *know* that Mum's still alive.'

Hilda turned off her torch. 'You really do believe it was her who went to see your dad in hospital that night?'

'She told the nurse she was dad's sister,' replied Amy. 'Dad doesn't have a sister.'

A few minutes later, the night bus arrived, and the two girls disappeared into the gloomy interior light on the lower deck, leaving a blacked-out Piccadilly Circus to another long, dismal winter's night.

It was raining cats and dogs in Enkel Street, not that any self-respecting cat or dog would have wanted to stay out in a downpour like that, for water was bucketing down on to the pavements and turning into a small, fast-flowing stream, as it raced along the kerb straight into the rapidly filling drains. Wet and freezing cold with it: a typical February day.

Uncle Jim was not amused to have been caught out in the sudden downpour. He had only just left the sorting office when the heavens opened so unexpectedly, and even though it was only a few minutes' walk back to number 16, he managed to get drenched to the skin. Once he'd opened the front street door, he quickly took off his trilby hat and Post Office topcoat, shook them out, and slowly made his way upstairs. As it was only the middle of the afternoon, the place was pretty quiet, for Amy had only just started her first day shift up at the Corner House, and the kids were not yet home from school. But as he reached the first floor, Ernie called out to him from his bedroom.

'That you, Jim?'

'Yes, Ern!' he called back. 'You OK?'

'Can yer spare a minute?'

A little concerned, Jim came to find the door of Ernie's

bedroom partly open. 'Wot's up?' he asked, as he went in.

Ernie was lying fully clothed on the double bed in which he had shared so many of his nights with Aggs. 'Nuffin' wrong, mate,' he said brightly. 'Gettin' better by the day. Just fawt you'd like a nip. Don't usually partake of the 'ard stuff meself, but Bert, my supervisor, brought me some. Black market, I reckon.' He stretched across to a small bedside cabinet and collected a quarter-bottle of whisky. 'This'll dry yer out!'

Jim wasn't a big drinker himself, but he was still shivering with the cold, and the prospect of something warm to bring him back to life was very inviting. 'Thanks, Ern. I won't say no.'

Ern sat up on the bed, collected a spare glass from the bedside cabinet, and poured Jim a small measure of whisky. Whilst he was doing so, Jim watched him closely. Ern looked so well. He had only been home for a few days, but already the colour had returned to his cheeks, and he seemed full of life. In fact, Jim reckoned he looked better than he had seen him for quite a long time.

'Aggs should be 'ere now,' said Ern, as he handed Jim the glass. 'She loved this stuff.'

'Wasn't always like that,' Jim reminded him. 'Only – during those last few months.'

'You're right,' said Ern, picking up his own glass, and taking a puff from his nearly finished dog-end. 'In fact you was always right about Aggs. I reckon you knew more about 'er than I ever did.'

Ernie's remark made Jim feel a bit uncomfortable. 'I wouldn't say that,' replied Jim, cautiously. 'She just liked a good old chinwag sometimes, that's all.'

Ernie grinned. 'Yer've bin a good mate ter this family, Jim,' said Ernie. 'There've bin times when I don't know wot we'd've done wivout yer. The kids fink the world of yer. Yer've bin like a second farver to them.' He gulped down a swig from his glass then looked across at Jim, who had now perched on the edge of the bed. 'As a matter of fact,' he continued, 'yer've bin more of a farver to them than I 'ave.'

Jim was embarrassed. Before answering, he took a sip from his own glass. Once he had felt the liquid warming first his windpipe and then his stomach, he said, 'That's not really true, Ern. There's only one father in any family.'

Glass in hand, Ernie got up from the bed, and stared out of the window. 'I need anuvver chance, Jim,' he said. 'I wanna be a farver ter my kids again.' He turned round and looked at him. 'But I can't do it wivout Aggs.'

Jim lowered his eyes. He didn't know what to say.

'Where is she, Jim?'

Jim's eyes flicked up with a start.

'You were the last one ter see 'er that night,' said Ernie. 'You were the only one who must've known wot she was goin' ter do, where she was goin'.'

Jim was shaking his head. 'No, Ernie,' he replied. 'All I knew was that Aggs was unhappy.'

'Did she ever tell you why?'

Jim thought hard before replying. When he eventually did, it was with great difficulty. 'She knew about – another woman in your life.'

Ernie hesitated a moment, then started to wander aimlessly around the dingy room, it's gloomy, dark varnished wallpaper peeling from the walls. 'All those years ago – when I first got married, I told myself it wasn't possible to love anyone but Aggs. Ter me, she was the best fing that could've 'appened in my life. She was the *only* fing.' He took one last puff of his dog-end, then stubbed it out in the saucer of a used teacup. 'But one day, someone looked at me in a certain way. I can't explain it, all I know is that it made me feel good. I felt I wasn't just someone who was married wiv kids ter provide for, but I was a man who someone actually fancied.' He turned and spoke directly to Jim. 'Blokes can be such vain sods, Jim,' he said, with a sigh. 'They fink they can do fings be'ind their woman's back, and just get away wiv it.' He came across to Jim, and stood by him. 'You wouldn't know, Jim,' he said. 'You've never loved anyone.'

Jim lowered his eyes again, avoiding Ernie's look.

'Or 'ave you?'

Jim quickly gulped down the last of his whisky, then got up. 'I'd better be goin',' he said, putting the glass down on to a small once-polished table. 'Thanks for the drink.' He turned, and made for the door.

'Jim.'

Jim stopped and turned.

'When I was lyin' in that 'ospital,' said Ernie, 'miles away from anywhere I'd ever known, I 'eard someone talkin' ter me. "*Stop bein' a stupid sod, an' get back 'ere!*" she said. '*Just remember wot yer used ter be, wot yer could still be!*"' He had a knowing smile on his face. 'I'd know that voice anywhere! The fing is, Jim, she was right. I do know wot I could still be. All I need is the chance to prove it. I've got a lot of decisions ter make, but I'm determined ter take them. I want my family back, Jim. I want Aggs back. So if you know where she is, yer've got ter tell me.'

On Friday afternoon, Thelma came out of school with little

Elsie soon after four o'clock. Elsie always hated having to wait behind for her big sister, for the juniors finished their school day at three, but Amy insisted that her youngest sister wait behind until Thelma could see her safely back home. However, today Thelma had other plans, for Kenny Silver was waiting for her just outside the school gates.

'Come on!' growled Kenny. 'If we're goin', let's go!'

Thelma snapped back angrily, 'Give us a chance, will yer? I've gotta get this one 'ome first!'

'Oh shit!' groaned Kenny. 'The picture starts at quarter-past.'

'Quarter-past!' protested Thelma. 'Yer told me 'alf-past!'

'Quarter-past!' Kenny barked. 'Why can't she go 'ome on 'er own?'

''Cos she's too young!' replied Thelma.

'I'm too young!' repeated Elsie, provocatively.

'Fer chrissake!' Kenny complained. 'It's only up the end of the road. Surely she can walk that bit on 'er own?'

'No, I can't!' snapped Elsie, her face crumpled with indignation.

'Oh yes, you can,' said Thelma. 'Yer should know 'ow ter get there blindfold by now!'

'I don't want ter be blindfold!' protested Elsie. 'If Amy finds out yer've gone ter the pittures an' left me on me own, she'll give yer 'ell! Why don't yer take me wiv yer? I 'aven't bin ter the pittures fer ages.'

'Go 'ome, Else!' snarled Thelma, angrily. 'Yer know the way. Arn's at 'ome. 'E'll let yer in.'

'I'll tell on yer!' replied Elsie, determined, as usual, to get her own way.

Thelma got back at her like a shot. 'If yer do, yer won't get

161

any of *my* sweet ration next week.' That said, all she had to do was point her finger in the direction of home.

Elsie loathed being outwitted, but she had no alternative than to do what her sister demanded, and make her own way up Roden Street and back home to Enkel Street. However, when she turned round to see Thelma and Kenny disappearing into the crowds of kids pouring out through the school gates, she decided to do her own thing, and go off in a totally different direction.

Amy didn't get home from her day shift at the Corner House until well after six. By then, of course, the blackout curtains had been drawn all along the streets, and it was pitch-dark everywhere. The first thing she did was to flop down in a chair at the kitchen table, and pull off her shoes. Her feet were killing her. To her relief, Arnold had already laid the table, so she could rest for a few minutes until she had to start peeling the potatoes. It wasn't until she heard the front door open in the passage outside, followed by anxious voices, that it even crossed her mind that the silence she'd been greeted with as she got home meant that something was wrong.

'Amy! Are yer 'ome?' Ernie's voice was calling from the passage outside.

'Dad!' Amy sprang up from the table, and rushed out. She was greeted by not only her father, but Arnold and Uncle Jim. All were carrying torches. 'Dad!' she cried. 'Wot's goin' on?'

'It's Elsie,' replied Ernie, grave-faced. 'We've been all over the place. Can't find 'er anywhere.'

Amy felt her blood turn to ice. 'Wot d'yer mean?' she asked, her voice cracking with anxiety.

'She didn't get back home from school, Amy,' said Uncle

Jim. 'I've been here all the afternoon, but there's bin no sign of her.'

'Christ!' gasped Amy. 'But where's Thelma? She was s'pposed ter collect 'er.' When the two men shook their heads, she immediately turned to her young brother. 'Arn! Wot's 'appened? Where's Thelm?'

Arnold shrugged his shoulders.

'Yer mean, she din't bring Elsie 'ome?'

Arnold shook his head.

Amy didn't seem to realise that she was shouting at the boy. 'Then where the bloody 'ell is she?'

Cowering from his eldest sister's rage, he replied. 'I think she was going to the pictures.'

'The—' Amy was about to explode. 'Which one?'

'I dunno.'

Waiting not a minute longer, Amy rushed back into the parlour, quickly put on her shoes, and collected her hat and coat, which she put on whilst she was charging into the passage again.

'Uncle Jim,' she said, with mounting urgency, 'could you check round the picture 'ouses – the Gaumont, Marlborough, Savoy, the Astoria – all of 'em. Ask at the box offices. If it's urgent they'll always flash a message on the screen or somefink. I'm goin' off to look for Else . . .'

'I'm comin' wiv yer,' said Ernie.

'No, Dad!' replied Amy, firmly. 'You're in no fit state ter go traipsing round the streets in your condition. Just look at yer. Yer look dreadful. Get back ter bed and leave this ter me. She can't be far.'

Just as she was about to rush out the front street door, Ernie took hold of her arm. 'Amy,' he said, trying to reassure her, 'she'll be all right. I know she will.'

As he spoke, the air-raid siren wailed out from Hornsey Road police station.

Amy stopped dead in her tracks, and turned to look back at her father and Uncle Jim. The expressions on their faces told it all. Now they really did have something to worry about.

CHAPTER 11

URGENT MESSAGE FOR THELMA DODDS
PLEASE GO TO MANAGER'S OFFICE

The moment Thelma saw her name flashed up on to the screen at the Marlborough cinema in Holloway Road, she nearly had a fit. Up until then she had been perfectly happy snogging with Kenny Silver in the back row of the circle, whilst John Wayne fought hostile Red Indians single-handed in *Stagecoach*.

'Blimey!' she cried in a cold panic, quickly disentangling herself from Kenny's arms, and springing up from her seat. 'That's me.'

A few minutes later, Thelma found herself downstairs in the cinema foyer where, to her horror, she came face to face with both her dad and Uncle Jim.

'Yer bloody little fool,' growled Ernie, who looked pale and drawn, and far too weak to be out of his sick bed. 'Where's yer sister, Thelm? Wot's 'appened ter Elsie?'

Thelma was completely nonplussed. 'W-wot yer talkin' about?' she replied, keeping well back from her dad, who looked as though he was about to give her a fourpenny one. 'She's gone 'ome, ain't she?'

165

'Elsie's missing, Thelma,' said Uncle Jim, doing his best not to undermine her father's authority. 'She hasn't been home since she went to school this morning.'

Thelma went as white as a sheet.

Ernie took off his flat cap and wiped the anxious sweat from his forehead. 'Wot're yer doin' at the pittures, Thelm?' he demanded, showing a rare display of anger. 'Yer was s'pposed to've waited for 'er. Yer was s'pposed to've brought 'er 'ome!'

'I *did* wait for 'er!' snapped Thelma. 'I watched 'er go down Roden Street. She *was* on 'er way 'ome.'

'Well, she din't arrive, did she?' growled Ernie, eyes glaring, voice raised. 'Don't yer care wot 'appens to 'er? You're 'er sister, fer chrissake! The least yer can do is ter keep an eye on 'er.'

'Why?' barked Thelma, defiantly. 'I'm not a bleedin' nanny! It's not my fault if the stupid little cow won't do as she's told!'

Ernie raised his hand as though he was about to hit her. But he resisted the temptation. 'Elsie's five years old, Thelm,' he replied calmly, and with restraint. 'If anyfin's 'appened to 'er, I'll never fergive yer.'

Amy was soaking wet. She had been searching the streets for nearly an hour in a slow and steady ice-cold drizzle – and with no sign of little Elsie, she was becoming desperate. As she strode frantically along one back street after another, the flickering yellow beam from her torch cutting through the pitch-dark air, her mind was consumed with guilt. How could she have been so stupid, she asked herself, as to trust Thelma? Thelma was a pain in the neck, who could see no further than her own selfish desires, someone who lived for having a good time, and who felt no sense of duty towards anyone but herself. As she struggled to adjust the woollen scarf she had pulled tightly over her head, her stomach felt like a dead weight, and by the time she had turned into Isledon Road, she thought she was going to be sick. She had no idea where she was going; all she knew was that she had to find Elsie, and she had to find her as soon as possible.

Isledon Road, usually a busy cut-through from the Finsbury Park area to Holloway, was as quiet as a graveyard. Amy hoped it would remain so, for the air-raid siren had wailed out some time before, suggesting an even greater threat to little Elsie's safety. As she struggled her way in the pitch-dark, rain streaking down her cold, red cheeks, she was imagining all the worst possible things that might have happened to the child.

Suppose someone had picked her up in the street, and kidnapped her? This war had turned so many people's minds that anyone was capable of doing harm to a small child. It didn't bear thinking about. Even if Elsie had lost her way, and was trying to keep warm in a secluded place somewhere, she would feel bitterly cold, troubled, and frightened. A rush of blood to her head sent Amy into a sudden fit of rage; she wanted to kill Thelma, she wanted to kill her stone dead. Oh God, she thought, why couldn't her mum be here to help her? It was at times like this that a mum was important to her children; a mum should be there to lean on, to advise, to comfort, to reassure . . .

At that moment, there was the sound of some kind of vehicle approaching from behind, and as the dimmed slatted lights drew closer, Amy realised that it was a Green Line bus making its laborious way in the blackout towards its next stop just a few yards on, outside the side entrance of the Astoria cinema. She quickly flagged it down and called up to the clippie, ''Ave yer seen a little kid on yer way?'

'Ain't seen no one, luv,' returned the middle-aged clippie. 'Why? Wot's up?'

Amy felt so low that she wanted to cry. 'She's my sister,' she replied, her face crumpled up with despair. 'She's got lost. We can't find 'er.'

'Blimey!' called the clippie. 'We'll keep an eye out for 'er.' She tapped on the driver's cabin to move on. She popped her head out just long enough to call, 'Poor little mite. Dangerous bein' out on a night like this – in the air raid.'

Amy watched the green single-decker bus disappear into the dark. Although the clippie had meant well, she had been no comfort at all. But it was true, there was an air raid on. She moved on from the Green Line bus stop, and decided to make her way back home along Seven Sisters Road.

She had gone only a few yards when she suddenly heard the distant rumble of anti-aircraft gunfire.

Little Elsie was furious. Up until a short while ago, she'd been having a marvellous time. Once Thelma had dumped her outside the school, and left her to go home on her own, she had made her way up to Finsbury Park, hoping to go to the lake her mum used to take her to, to see the ducks and all the other wild birds who had claimed the territory as their own. But as it was already getting dark, the park gates had been closed, and she had had to find an alternative way to enjoy her brief spell of freedom. This she soon accomplished, when she turned the corner from Seven Sisters Road, and found a queue of people waiting to get in to see a murder film outside the side entrance of the old Rink cinema in Stroud Green Road. To her delight, the queue was being entertained by a funny-looking old man wearing a top hat and a long black coat with tails, and who was not only playing a mouth organ which was fixed on a clamp on his chest, but he was also playing a drum with his hands, and clapping cymbals together, which were strapped to both his knees. Elsie thought he was hilarious, and stayed watching him in awed fascination until the queue eventually filed into the cinema, with only some of them willing to part with one or two of their spare coins.

Further down the road, she suddenly smelled the wonderful aroma of roast chestnuts. When she had finally managed to track down the source, she stood motionless in front of the old codger who was roasting the chestnuts on a coke brazier, waiting in hopeful anticipation.

'Sod off!' growled the old codger, waving her away with his hand.

'Sod off yerself!' Elsie snapped back. She didn't really care that she had used a rude swear-word as, since she had often heard both her mum and her dad use it, she knew it must be all right. But when she realised that the old chestnut codger had taken umbrage, and was coming round the brazier to give her a clout round the earhole, she ran for her life. She stopped only briefly to turn and put her tongue out at him, making quite sure, of course, that she was at a safe distance.

From there on, Elsie had no idea where she was wandering, for the back streets around Finsbury Park were now dark and forbidding, and when it started to drizzle, her only thought was to find somewhere to shelter from the cold.

She finally ended up huddled in the doorway of a kitchen utensils shop. And that's why she was furious. Not only was she cold, lost, and hungry but, knowing that the air-raid siren had sounded just a short time before, it was perfectly obvious that when she got home her sister Amy was going to give her hell. But then, she was only five years old, and the only thing a five-year-old could do at a time like this was to fall asleep.

The first explosion came from the direction of Stoke Newington. At least, that's what it looked like to Amy, who had once been over that way to visit her Aunt Flo and Uncle Sid, before they moved up north somewhere to get away from the bombing in London.

Amy was at the Nag's Head at the time, at the junction of Seven Sisters and Holloway Roads, with number 16 Enkel Street just round the corner. From where she was standing, she could see the red glow of an enormous fire spiralling up into the dark night sky, and she was now quite frantic with worry, for the barrage of ack-ack gunfire had gradually crescendoed into loud pops and bangs, which echoed around the streets, shaking the ground beneath her. She dreaded to think what had happened to Elsie; all she could see in her mind was a small, helpless child, wandering alone in the dark, tears streaming down her little face as the evening erupted with the sound of war. It was that thought, and that thought alone, that made her determined not to go home until she had found the child, even though it was now becoming inevitable that she report Elsie's disappearance to the police.

But just as she was on the point of heading off towards the police station in Hornsey Road, the dimmed, slatted headlights of a passing car suddenly picked out three figures just crossing the wide stretch of the main Holloway Road, in front of the Marlborough cinema. The moment she could see who they were, Amy went rushing to meet them.

'Dad!' she yelled, as loud as she could, over the deafening roar of anti-aircraft gunfire. 'Uncle Jim!' Only when she got closer could she pick out the person with them. 'Thelma!' she shouted at the top of her voice. 'Wot've yer done? Where is she? Where's Elsie?'

It took all Ernie's efforts to prevent Amy from launching into her sister. 'Calm down, Ame!' he shouted, shielding Thelma.

'If anyfin's 'appened to 'er, I'll kill yer!' shrieked Amy, directing the beam of her torch straight into Thelma's tear-stained face. 'Where is she?'

As she spoke, a profusion of shells burst in the sky above them, lighting up their traumatised faces, and causing them to cover their ears with their hands.

'We've got ter get 'ome, Ame!' insisted Ernie. 'There's no point in putting all our lives at risk in this! We've got ter get back ter the shelter.'

'We've *got* ter find 'er!' insisted Amy, who was beside herself with worry. Then, turning her torch beam on Thelma again, she yelled, 'You're a wicked little cow! 'Ow could yer do this to yer own sister? 'Ow could yer leave 'er ter go wanderin' off on 'er own in the middle of an air raid!'

'There's nothing we can do round here,' said Jim, trying to calm Amy down by putting his arm round her shoulders. 'Our only hope now is the police.'

As he spoke there was the terrifying, high-pitched sound of a bomb screeching down from an enemy aircraft directly overhead.

'Down!' yelled Jim, and everyone threw themselves on to their stomachs on the wet pavements.

Thelma screamed out hysterically as the bomb landed with a deafening explosion in the distance, the blast near enough to shatter the shop windows all around them.

For what seemed like an eternity, all three lay paralysed face downwards, Ernie desperately trying to protect both his daughters by hugging them close to his side. Above them, the sky was like a massive kaleidoscope, with shells bursting into thousands of tiny luminous white sparks, and searchlights crisscrossing the sky frantically, desperately trying to locate the intruder, but only managing to pick out the dull silver colour of the cigar-shaped barrage balloons.

Uncle Jim was first to recover and get to his feet. Then he helped the others up and collected their torches from the pavements.

'Christ Almighty!' gasped Ernie, his eyes turned up towards the flaming red sky. 'That was close!'

'Looks like it's somewhere up Finsbury Park way,' called Jim, above the shellfire.

By this time, Thelma had collapsed into hysterics, 'I wanna go 'ome!' she sobbed. And she screamed as a shell burst immediately above them.

'Come on!' yelled Ernie to them all. 'Let's get out of 'ere!'

But when he turned to Amy, she had already gone, heading off as fast as she could run in the direction of Finsbury Park.

The scene in Kirsty Street was one of utter devastation. When Amy got there, she found workers and volunteers from all the emergency services digging in the rubble of a row of completely flattened shops. Even at the height of the Blitz, she had never witnessed such a scene, for searchlights had illuminated the entire stricken area with dazzling white lights, and tracker dogs were trying to sniff out any poor souls who might be trapped under the wreckage. There were also the most powerful smells coming from where a chemist's shop had stood, an old tin bath buckled in two by falling debris, window frames torn out of their brickwork by the blast, the remains of tables, chairs, sofas, stone kitchen sinks and washday coppers, and even large chunks of lavatory basins. Perhaps even more poignant, however, was the twisted and dented collection of what had once been brand-new cooking utensils, all that remained of a neat little kitchenware shop.

Amy felt absolutely shattered as she stood there, watching the desperate race against time to rescue any survivors. A rope barrier had been hastily set up to prevent any unauthorised person from getting too close to the devastation, but from where she was standing, she could just see the mangled body of a white collie dog, which until a few hours before had clearly been a most treasured family pet. Amy's stomach retched; the smell of death all around, and the stifling smoke from the aftermath of the explosion was utterly unbearable.

'You shouldn't be 'ere, young lady,' called a gentle voice at her side. It was a St John Ambulance driver, one of the many who were waiting to convey the first casualties to hospital. 'It's not a pretty sight.'

'I'm lookin' fer my sister,' replied Amy, doing her best to keep down the sick that was rising from her stomach to her throat. 'She's five years old. She's not very big. She's got dark blue eyes, like me, like my mum.' She knew she was rambling, but she had to say what she needed to say. 'She's got a luvely little face. She's not very big. She's my sister . . .'

The driver, who was a caring, middle-aged woman, put a comforting arm round Amy's shoulders. 'It'll take some time,' she said, trying to be helpful. 'They've only got a few out so far.'

Amy steeled herself, and asked, 'Wos there a . . . ?'

'There *were* some children taken out,' the woman said, with much difficulty. 'They're in the temporary mortuary down the road.'

Amy took a deep breath. 'Whereabouts?' she asked.

'The church hall,' replied the woman. 'Just round the corner at the end.'

Amy nodded her thanks to the woman and moved on.

Her legs now felt so weak that she wasn't sure whether they would carry her more than a few yards, but with her usual resilience, she managed to reach the end of the road, where, just round the corner, she saw a whole lot of people with torches, milling outside a yellow-brick building adjoining what looked like an old Victorian church.

'Who are you looking for miss?'

The sombre-voiced man, wearing an ARP warden's tin helmet, was sitting at a small card table just inside the church doorway.

'My sister,' replied Amy, her throat and lips so dry she could hardly form the words. 'She's five years old.'

'Name, please?'

For one brief moment, Amy looked bewildered. 'Pardon?' she asked.

'The name of your sister?' said the elderly man.

'Oh – Elsie,' replied Amy. 'Elsie Dodds.'

The man checked a rapidly growing casualty list in front of him on the table. 'No . . . no one by that name here . . .'

Amy breathed a sigh of relief.

The man looked up from the list. 'I'm afraid we haven't identified most of the victims,' he said, apologetically, 'as yet.'

Amy bit her lip. 'Are there – any kids amongst them?' she asked, remembering what the ambulance driver had said.

'One or two,' replied the man, his voice barely audible. 'If you're up to it, this lady will take you in.'

He nodded to a young Red Cross nurse, who came forward and gave Amy a warm, reassuring smile. 'This way,' she said softly, opening the hall doors.

Amy was led into the hall, which, like the entrance lobby, was only dimly lit by the light of several paraffin lamps, which had been hastily brought in when the power throughout the neighbourhood had been cut by the bomb explosion. It wasn't a very big hall, which in happier times was used for church socials and Sunday school meetings. But the place was ice cold, which was all that could be expected, considering there were five bodies laid out on the floor, all lined up against a white distempered wall on one side, each one covered only by a blood-red ambulance blanket.

'How old did you say your sister was?' asked the nurse. Even though her voice was no more than a whisper, it echoed in the empty silence right up to the timber eaves of the high sloping ceiling.

Amy shuddered when she heard Elsie referred to in the past tense, but she took a deep breath before answering, 'She's five.'

The nurse's face tensed. 'I'm afraid we do have a little girl about that age,' she said with immense reluctance. 'She's up the end there.' She nodded her head towards a tiny covered figure in the far left-hand corner of the hall. 'Can you cope?'

Amy took another deep breath, then nodded.

The nurse put a comforting arm around Amy's waist, then led her slowly towards the far end of the hall. It was impossible for them to go quietly, for as they went, their shoes echoed on the hard parquet floor, adding to the already eerie atmosphere of that harrowing place. On the way, Amy's eyes couldn't avoid the bright collection of children's crayon drawings on the walls, a child's-eye view of dogs and cats, and houses, and caricatures of Hitler, who had brought so much trauma and destruction into their lives, and the images of war in the streets of London, a war they never asked for, a war in which they were targets just as much as their dads who were fighting somewhere on the battlefields, or at sea, or in the air.

When they finally reached the tiny covered figure they had come to see, an elderly man wearing Home Guard uniform was waiting for them. Amy was taken to the side of the covered figure, but paused whilst the nurse explained what was needed.

'Just an identification, that's all,' the nurse said softly. 'But you must be absolutely sure. Is that all right?'

Amy nodded. But in her heart of hearts she knew that the moment they removed that blanket, the face she would see would be her baby sister's. And in those few seconds that she was standing there, she could see little Elsie's life laid out before her. She could remember the day she was born – how, in the first few hours of her life, she had yelled the place down, so much so that Amy had told her mum that she should send the kid back where it came from. And she remembered the time when Elsie pulled a cat's tail and got a scratch on her nose for doing so. It was just one of so many funny moments she remembered about her little sister, a sister that Amy now felt so guilty about, guilty because she hadn't appreciated her enough, just like their own mum and dad.

The nurse nodded to the Home Guard man.

The blood-red blanket was removed just enough to reveal the face concealed beneath it.

Amy steeled herself, then looked down at the face of the small child lying there. She immediately clasped her hand to her mouth. What she was looking at were the perfectly formed features of a little girl whose eyes were shut, and whose face was like a valuable piece of porcelain, a beautiful face, precious, lovely, showing no visible sign at all of the injuries that had robbed her of her young life. It took Amy a moment to focus on the face, but when she did, all she could say over and over again in her mind was, *Elsie . . . Elsie . . . oh Elsie . . .* !' But it wasn't Elsie.

'Yes?' asked the nurse, tenderly.

Amy slowly shook her head.

'Certain? Absolutely certain?'

This time, Amy nodded her head vigorously.

The nurse signalled to the Home Guard man, who replaced the red blanket.

The All Clear siren wailed out just as Amy was coming out of the church hall. Emotionally drained, she slowly made her way back to the scene of the bomb explosion, quietly expecting the next batch of bodies they dug out of the wreckage to include that of little Elsie. On her way, she really thought that she must be going mad, for there seemed to be no logical reason why Elsie should have wandered this far from school in the dark. Why choose this direction? she asked herself. After all, the child might have made off to any part of the neighbourhood, got lost in the dark, and decided to stay where she was until daylight. By the time she had reached the devastated row of shops, the rescue operation was becoming more and more frenetic, the air pierced with the shrieks and wails of relatives who had waited in vain to find out that their loved ones had survived. It wasn't long before the grief felt by everyone started to affect Amy. Unable to control the fear and dread that was gradually rising within her, she suddenly fell to her knees, clasped her hands tightly together, and burst into tears. This time she let her feelings be known out loud.

'Oh God!' she called, looking up at the now restful night sky. 'Why Elsie? Why a poor little kid who ain't done nuffin' ter no one?' Tears were now rolling down her cheeks. 'Wot've yer got against the Dodds family, God? Wot've we done ter deserve all this? First yer take me mum, then yer 'ave a go at me dad, an' now my Elsie . . .' With the back of her hand she tried to rub away the tears from her eyes. 'We were chumps, God,' she continued out loud. 'We were chumps not to send Else, Arn, and Thelma away as soon as the war started. It was Mum an' Dad's fault. They should've let them be evacuated like every uvver kid, then none of this would've 'appened. I love my family, God! I really love 'em! So why d'yer 'ave ter do this to us? Why?'

'Come on now little lady,' said a special constable, who was suddenly standing over her. 'Yer can't 'elp anyone bein' like this.'

Amy allowed him to take her arm, and gently ease her to her feet. 'It's my sister,' she said in a daze. 'I'm waitin' fer my sister. She's in there somewhere. I know she is.'

The constable, his uniform covered in dust and mud, looked her straight in the eyes. 'Best ter wait down the rest centre,' he said. 'It'll take hours ter get them all out.'

The rest centre had been hastily set up in the ground-floor hall of a school built in the latter part of the Victorian era, which had been closed soon after the start of the war when most of its pupils had been evacuated. It was a great barn of a place, which had been stripped of all furniture with the exception of a few flip-top desks and chairs, left behind in some of the classrooms. By the time Amy had got there, however, the hall itself had been transformed, teeming with victims who had been bombed out of their homes, and the saintly voluntary services who had miraculously provided instant help with the provision of blankets and mattresses, hot drinks, and a great deal of psychological comfort and support.

From the moment Amy had set foot inside the hall, she had been approached by a quick succession of middle-aged voluntary workers who had done their best to give her comfort and advice that she didn't really want. God knows they were well-meaning enough, thought Amy, but in the state she was in, all she wanted was to be left alone, and to see the night through if necessary, waiting for news of little Elsie. 'No news is good news,' one kindly grey-haired WVS lady kept telling her. But although the woman, like all her colleagues, was nothing short of angelic, at present, her advice was of no help at all.

Amy's only real comfort turned out to be the cup of tea she had been given, taken from a large tea urn which had been placed on a trestle table in the centre of the hall. At least it was piping hot, and helped her to combat the cold and wet outside, and the haunting memory of that dead child's face she had just seen in the makeshift mortuary. All around her, people were huddled in groups, chatting together in hushed tones, waiting, like her, for the latest news of the desperate recovery operation taking place just a stone's throw away. The school hall was, in many ways, a cold and soulless place, for, in the absence of electric power, the only light and warmth available came from half a dozen paraffin lamps, the blue flames from their blackened wicks flickering in the dark. Thank God for the dear old paraffin lamp, thought Amy, as she warmed her hands around her cup of tea. How would they ever survive this war without them?

For several minutes or so, she just sat there, staring aimlessly out of the hall's tall windows, which were too numerous to black out. It was inevitable that her mind kept racing all the time, for the trauma of being in such a place only kept reminding her not only of what might have happened to Elsie, but of the whole futility of the war. Try as she may, she still couldn't believe why these sudden snap air raids came, and where from. But then she thought that, although during the past year or so there had been a great reduction in the number of enemy attacks on London, it was obvious now that everyone, including herself, had become complacent. The war was far from over; in fact, with the British now having to fight the Japanese as well as the Germans and the Italians, it was getting worse. Through the window, she was able to look up at the evening sky, which was now calm. She could even see a bright star battling to make its presence felt, as it popped out from time to time behind jealous black clouds. Somewhere behind her, she could hear a woman quietly sobbing, and one of those angelic figures trying over and over again to reassure her.

'Don't you worry, dearie,' said the angel's soothing voice.

'We'll get you another place of your own. You're going to be just fine, you'll see.'

Amy couldn't bear to listen to all this, nor any of the other false hopes that were being spread around the hall. As far as she was concerned, things were never going to be 'just fine'. Elsie was dead. The idea was now fixed firmly in her mind. There was no way they were going to find the kid alive. It was all over. Elsie was the past. From now on, she was going to be nothing more than a memory. Through the window, Amy watched the star lose its battle, and disappear behind the forbidding dark clouds. But as it did so, she gradually became aware of a sound in the background, somewhere behind her. It was a sound that confused her, for in some strange way or another, she seemed to recognise it. However, whatever it was, it immediately snapped her out of her lurid daydreams, for she found herself thinking: That's a bad cough yer' ve got there, Else. I'm goin' ter get you some cough mixture. Yes, it was a cough she was hearing, all right, not an ordinary cough, but a real hacking one, the sort you get when you've eaten your bread and marge too fast. Amy couldn't remember how many times she'd told little Elsie about doing just that . . .

The blood suddenly rushed straight to her head, and she swung back to look behind her. That cough, that hacking cough – it was coming from the other side of the hall. She suddenly caught sight of her. She was there – little Elsie. She was there, definitely there. Elsie! Elsie! The hard wooden bench she had been sitting on fell to the ground with a thud as she leaped up and, virtually throwing her empty teacup down on to the floor, rushed across to the other side of the hall, winding her way frantically through the groups of people huddled on the floor everywhere.

'Elsie!' she yelled, at the top of her voice.

A sea of faces turned to look at her, as she practically threw herself at Elsie, who was crouched in a dark corner, snuggled up in a blanket round her shoulders, and halfway through a hot cup of cocoa and a digestive biscuit.

'Elsie!' The moment she saw the child, she dropped to her knees, and threw her arms round her. 'Oh God, Elsie!' she cried, her heart pumping hard with relief. 'You're safe! You're safe!' Eyes streaming with tears, she looked upwards, where flickering shadows from the ever faithful old paraffin lamps were dancing across the ceiling. 'I din't mean all them fings I said to yer – 'onest I din't!'

Elsie was astonished by all the fuss her big sister was making. 'Wher've yer bin?' was all she could say, her mouth full of digestive biscuit. 'I'm starved!'

That only made her cough all over again.

CHAPTER 12

A few days later, Aggs arrived early for her morning job at The Turk's Head. After she had found her way into the back yard of the pub, and discovered the slaughtered pig in Charlie Ratner's shed, she had vowed never to set foot inside the place again, but since then, she had had a change of mind. Her first reaction had been to go straight back to the bluebottles, and tell them what she had found, for her young parkie mate, The Kid was the number-one suspect for something he hadn't done. But there were two things that had changed her mind. First, there was Ratner's daughter, Maureen, who had shown concern for Aggs's safety by warning her of the dire consequences of getting to know too much about her father's black-market activities. And then there was her determination to take revenge on Ratner. This she would do by keeping a close watch on what was going on at the pub, and exactly who was involved. Once she had managed to accumulate the hard evidence the law would require to charge Ratner, that would be the time when The Kid and her other parkie mates would no longer be suspected of nicking pigs from the park police compound.

'Mornin', Ma! An' how are you terday?'

Ratner was always up early enough to let Aggs in, but he

was never a one to be so bright and breezy with her. Her only response was to sniff and grunt.

'Wot about a cuppa tea, mate?' persisted Ratner. 'I've just made one fer the missus. All right fer some, eh?'

Now Aggs knew something was up, and she didn't like it. 'Never drink tea in the mornin's,' she said. 'Bad fer me figure.'

At least Ratner had the grace to laugh. Again, not like him. Aggs started to make her way to collect her bucket and brush from the cupboard in the side passage, but before she got there, Ratner called to her from behind the bar counter. 'Don't worry about cleanin' up in 'ere terday, Ma. Got a little job fer yer out the back.'

Aggs turned to look at him. He was holding the bar counter flap up for her. Reluctantly, she followed him through the door behind the counter.

In the back yard outside, everything looked much the same as the last time she had found her way out there, except that now there were a few crates of empties piled against the wall, some empty beer barrels, and a dustbin overloaded with household junk.

'You 'aven't been out 'ere before, 'ave yer, Ma?' said Ratner, not expecting an answer, as he made towards the shed. 'It's good ter 'ave one little bit of privacy to ourselves.'

Aggs followed him warily, and when they reached the shed, she waited whilst he undid the padlock. Her mind was racing. What was he up to now?

Ratner opened the shed door, then stood back to let Aggs in. 'Welcome to our humble abode,' he said with a flourish.

Aggs held back. She didn't like this. She didn't like it at all.

184

'Come on, Ma!' called Ratner, reassuringly. 'There's nothin' in 'ere ter bite yer.'

Reluctantly, Aggs went into the shed. Her shock was immediate. The place had been cleared, completely cleared of all the black-market booze and fags that had been piled there, to be replaced by empty beer barrels, old newspapers, and a newly erected Morrison air-raid shelter. Most important of all, however, was that there was no sign at all of the pig that had been slaughtered there. In fact, even the large hook that the poor creature had been hanging from had been removed, and the hole in the ceiling where the hook had been, filled in with cement painted over.

Ratner watched Aggs's reaction carefully. 'Bit of a shambles, eh, Ma?' he remarked. 'Wants a good old mop out. Can't bear places that aren't used enough. They always smell ter high heaven.'

Aggs didn't answer. She knew very well what he was talking about, for although he had been able to remove all evidence of his shady activities, the one thing he could not erase was the stench of dead pig.

'Oh, I was forgettin',' said Ratner. 'You've never been out 'ere, 'ave yer? Takes a bit of gettin' used to, I grant yer. 'Specially the rats. They're a real problem at times. That's why I don't encourage people ter come out 'ere. I wouldn't want them ter get hurt or anything. The rats, I mean.' He smiled. 'I'll get yer some carbolic,' he said. 'I'm sure you'll make a good job of cleanin' up the place.'

Aggs watched Ratner stride across the back yard and disappear through the back door of the pub.

He had delivered his warning.

* * *

Chief Inspector Rob Hanley waited patiently in the opulent front entrance of Lyons Corner House, smoking a cigarette, and doing his best to take in the grandeur of a place that was somewhat classier than his own police canteen back in Hornsey Road. It was not yet opening time, but already he could savour the enticing smells of roast chicken seeping up from the kitchens downstairs, which mixed uncomfortably with the pong of cleaners scrubbing the magnificent main marble staircase with carbolic. The receptionist, who had already announced the inspector's arrival to the staff changing rooms in the basement, watched disapprovingly as Hanley paced slowly up and down the hall, his shoes leaving wet footprints on the freshly polished floor tiles.

It was several minutes before Amy appeared, her tiny leather shoes clip-clopping on the stairs as she came up to join the inspector. The moment he set eyes on her, togged out in her Corner House cap, dress, and neatly laundered uniform his face brightened into a rare smile. 'Hello, Amy,' he said.

Amy, looking tired and drained after her ordeal with little Elsie a couple of nights before, limply shook his outstretched hand.

'You look very good in your uniform,' said Hanley. 'Pretty as a picture.'

Amy ignored his compliment. ''Ave yer found out anythin' yet about Mum?' she asked.

Embarrassed that, for the first time, he had actually said something nice to Amy – and had been put firmly in his place by her ignoring him – the expression on Hanley's face immediately reverted to its usual glum look of formality. 'We think we might have a lead,' he replied. 'Nothing definite, but we're following it up.' He looked round for somewhere to stub out the last of his cigarette, eventually getting rid of it in a tall, free-standing stone ashtray full of sand. 'We've had one or two sightings of a woman who might possibly be your mother.'

Amy's heart jumped. 'Where?' she asked, eagerly.

'Various places,' replied Hanley. 'One of our office people at Caledonian Road described seeing someone like her on King's Cross Station.'

'King's Cross?' said Amy, on tenterhooks. 'Wot's she doin' up there?'

Hanley shrugged. 'Difficult to tell,' he replied. 'We know there's a WVS canteen on emergency service there most mornings, but apparently they haven't seen her for a while.'

'But this woman,' pressed Amy. '*Is* it her? I mean, do they say she looks like Mum?'

'It's possible, Amy,' replied Hanley, trying to dampen too much of her enthusiasm. 'All they say is that by the look of the clothes she's wearing, she sleeps out rough.'

This took Amy aback. 'Wot d'yer mean, sleeps out rough?'

Hanley, who was a bit of a chain-smoker, was already feeling into his raincoat pocket for his packet of cigarettes. 'It means sleeping out rough on the streets, Amy, hiding out some place, living from hand to mouth each day, getting bits and pieces of grub wherever and whenever she can.'

Amy was truly shocked. 'But – it ain't possible,' she said. 'My mum's not a tramp. She needs a roof over 'er 'ead.'

'That may be so under normal circumstances,' said Hanley, taking a cigarette out of the packet. 'But in her present mental condition, she may be living a completely different life style.'

Amy was horrified. The idea of her mum living rough out on the streets seemed totally unnatural to her. But the inspector was right: these were not normal circumstances. Even Dr Ferguson had told her that. Her mum was ill, really ill. She was capable of doing anything. 'If somebody's seen 'er,' asked Amy, 'they must know where she is?'

'It's not as easy as that, I'm afraid,' replied Hanley. 'If she doesn't want to be found, chances are she's hiding out. Could be anywhere – a shop doorway, beneath the arches at Charing Cross, a bombed site, down the sewers – anywhere.'

Amy shuddered at the thought of her mum spending her nights down the sewers.

'And then again,' continued Hanley, lighting his latest cigarette, 'there are the parks.'

Amy was puzzled. 'The parks?'

'The parks all over London are full of down-and-outs,' he said, after inhaling smoke into his lungs. 'Because of the war, we tend to turn a blind eye to them.'

Amy thought about this for a moment, then asked, 'D'you fink my mum might be living out rough in a park?'

'No idea,' replied Hanley. 'But it's a possibility.'

'Which one?' asked Amy.

Hanley shook his head. 'Needle in a haystack. We just have to keep our people on their toes. She could be in any of the London parks, even right up here in the West End.'

'Well, why don't yer get your people out lookin' for 'er?'

The inspector sighed and, much to the disdain of the receptionist, flicked his ash on to the tiled floor. 'There's a war on, Amy,' he reminded her. 'We don't have nearly enough people to do all the things we ought to be doing. Your mum's just one person out of God knows how many who've been made homeless since the Blitz.'

'She may be one person to you,' replied Amy, scornfully,

'but ter me, she's me whole life.'

Hanley shrugged his shoulders. 'Oh well,' he said, with resignation, 'at least she's still alive. We can at least be grateful for that.'

A short while later, Hanley left, with a promise that he would not give up the search for Amy's mum. Watching him go from behind the partially opened door of the ground-floor restaurant, was Amy's pain-in-the-neck fellow nippy, Bertha Willets.

During the following week, Amy and her new, greatly cherished boyfriend, Tim, spent as much time as they could searching some of the parks in north and east London. As it was still only February, it was bitterly cold, and the parks themselves were pretty bleak places, especially in wartime, when flowerbeds had to give way to the growing of vegetables, and large open spaces were occupied by the RAF barrage balloon teams. But even in winter, nature has a way of making you feel how good it is to be alive, especially when the bare trees and limp perennial plants are covered with a thin layer of dazzling white frost. Unfortunately, however, no matter how beautiful it all looked, Amy and Tim found it a depressing experience to talk to the down-and-outs who roamed the parks by day, searching for scraps of food that would barely be enough to keep the sparrows alive.

In Finsbury Park, they stopped to talk to an elderly ex-soldier from the previous war, who was stretched out on a cold wooden bench, covered only by a few damp, soggy newspapers.

'A woman, yer say?' replied the old man, when asked by Amy whether he had ever come across anyone looking like her mum. 'We don't 'ave no females in this park,' he said, the row of military medals and ribbons still pinned to the chest of his grubby raincoat. 'Females is the ones who sit at 'ome an' wait fer their menfolk. The park's fer us cast-offs.'

And in Victoria Park, in the East End of London, they came across two more examples of their nation's gratitude – two former sailors, both with bushy, straggly beards, who spent most of their days whiling away their time together, deep in alcoholic stupors. Unfortunately, they too were unable to cast any light on Anges Dodds's whereabouts.

Although these traumatic encounters brought Amy nothing but disappointment, it did give her an insight into those many poor souls whose lives had been brought to a state of abject despair.

'Why *do* people just go ter pieces like that?' wondered Amy, as she and Tim strolled arm in arm across Hackney Marshes early one morning.

'The m-mind is a delicate thing, Amy,' Tim replied. 'It's like a m-machine. When it d-doesn't know how to w-work things out, it just gives up. There are t-times when I f-feel a bit like that m-myself. S-sometimes I get really angry when I c-can't get the words out.'

When she heard him say that, Amy hugged him. The more she got to know Tim, the more she realised not only how vulnerable he was, but how important he was becoming in her life.

Amy's first real break came early one morning, when, hours before she was needed at the Corner House, she took a bus to King's Cross, which is where Inspector Hanley had told her of a possible sighting of her mum at a WVS mobile canteen. When she eventually found where it was parked, workers and volunteers from the emergency services were already queuing up for their morning cuppas and hot toast with margarine.

'Old Ma, yer mean?' replied a bleary-eyed NFS fireman, who had been out on call most of the night. 'Oh yeah, I've seen 'er up the counter plenty of times. Right ol' character, that one.'

'Always good fer a laugh, though!' added his mate, who was just stuffing a bit of Spam roll into his mouth.

Some of the others in the queue joined in the laughter, as they exchanged brief comments about some of 'Ma's' antics.

Amy didn't take too kindly to their quips. Irritated, she suddenly raised her voice to make herself heard. 'She's my mum!' she bellowed.

The queue immediately came to order, almost as though a door had been closed on the rumpus they had been making.

'So if anyone knows where she is,' continued Amy, feeling a bit guilty that she had been so rude, 'I'd be – very grateful.'

She glanced along the queue, looking at one face after another. Most of the men, all of them looking rather sheepish, merely shook their heads. One or two others replied, 'Sorry, mate. No idea.'

Amy's spirits sank yet again. But when she turned to walk off, a middle-aged WVS woman, who had been washing up cups in a chipped enamel bowl behind the mobile canteen, came out to her. 'Have you tried the park, dear?' she asked sympathetically.

Amy turned with a start. 'The park?' she asked eagerly. 'Which one?'

'I'm not absolutely sure,' replied the woman, wiping her hands on a tea cloth, 'but I did see her once from the bus, up near the far end of Oxford Street, near Hyde Park. It was during the week, though. She usually only makes her way down here at the weekends. Poor woman. She looks as though she could do with a really good meal.'

'Hyde Park!' At last Amy had found someone who had actually seen her mum, and she couldn't wait to rush off. 'Fanks,' she said excitedly. 'Fanks very much.'

'Don't take it for gospel, my dear!' said the woman, aware that she may have raised Amy's hopes unnecessarily. 'It's only a guess, that's all.'

Guess or not, Amy was already racing off to catch a bus to Marble Arch.

In Hyde Park, Scrounger was pitched on his usual bench close to Park Lane. Just behind him, traffic rumbled by noisily in both directions, and, much to his irritation, a bunch of small kids were playing football, watched over by their adoring well-to-do mothers. When Amy approached him warily, he was trying to chew the remains of a jam sandwich he had retrieved from one of the litter bins. The sight of his long, straggly grey hair, and generally unkempt appearance unnerved her. 'Can yer 'elp me, mate?' she said, keeping her distance. 'I'm lookin' fer my mum.'

Scrounger didn't even glance at her. He merely finished chewing, then quickly popped the rest of the sandwich into his mouth.

'I've 'eard she might 'ang out round 'ere,' said Amy, undeterred.

Scrounger still didn't reply. His attention was focused on a small sparrow on the ground just to his right, that was gradually edging its way towards a crumb of bread he had unwittingly overlooked.

Amy persevered. 'I've got a snapshot of 'er,' she said, reaching into her topcoat pocket.

'Got any fags?'

The fact that Scrounger had suddenly found his voice took Amy by surprise. 'Sorry,' she said. 'I don't smoke.'

Scrounger grunted.

'You can 'ave this, though.' Amy opened her purse, and took out a threepenny piece. 'This'll buy yer a coupla fags.' Scrounger's eyes shot up, and he made a grab for the coin, but Amy immediately held on tight to it. 'This is my mum,' she said, holding up a snapshot of Aggs in happier times.

Scrounger was furious to be outwitted by the girl. But the coin was more important, so he reluctantly flicked his eyes at the snapshot. His scowl gradually turned into a grin, and that suddenly turned into a rip-roaring laugh, which sent the poor marauding sparrow fluttering off in panic back to the trees.

Amy quickly lowered the snapshot. 'Wot's so funny?' she asked, irritably.

The more Amy spoke, the more Scrounger fell about with laughter. 'Wot is it?' yelled Amy. 'Wot're yer laughin' at?'

Like a tap suddenly being turned off, Scrounger stopped laughing. 'Never seen 'er!' he growled. Then he got to his feet, and started to move off.

Amy immediately rushed in front of him, and barred his way. 'Yer *do* know 'er, don't yer? Yer *do*!'

Scrounger stared her out. There was a look of defiance on his face which for one brief moment frightened Amy. If he did know anything, it was clear that he was not going to budge. Amy gave up. She opened her hand and gave him the threepenny piece. Scrounger grabbed it, she moved out of his way and he shuffled off.

For some time, Amy just stood there watching him, as he slowly wound his way along the roughly hewn path, headed off past the posh kids playing football, finally to dissolve into a tiny figure on the other side of the wide-open space of the park. It was a revealing sight for Amy, for in some strange way, that pathetic old tramp represented a world that she never knew existed. She turned, and moved on. But as she did so, she found someone blocking her way. It was another down-and-out, a young bloke this time, wrapped up against the cold in an outsize threadbare overcoat, his face partly covered by a tight-fitting khaki balaclava.

'She ain't 'ere, miss,' said The Kid, with what seemed to be immense understanding. 'And even if she was, you wouldn't want ter see 'er.'

Amy wanted to say something to him but he prevented her by speaking again.

'We're a funny ol' lot out 'ere, miss,' continued The Kid. 'We come 'ere ter ferget, but we never do. There are lots of people like you're lookin' for. We're best left alone. It's the only way we can cope.'

With his hands tucked into his overcoat pockets, the boy turned and made off towards his pitch for the day – if he could find one.

CHAPTER 13

When Amy got home that night, the whole place smelled of DDT and floor soap. She didn't know what had hit her, for that was the kind of smell that only ever pervaded number 16 when she was the skivvy, which was generally every day of the week. But today, it was like walking into the Corner House, for the front passage not only smelled fresh and clean, but it was actually tidy.

The shock continued the moment she went into the back parlour. Elsie, Arnold, and even Thelma were sitting round the kitchen table having their cooked tea-time meal with their dad. 'Blimey!' was all Amy could say, as she watched the family tucking into fried slices of Spam, and big chunky chips fried in beef dripping, just the way both she and her mum had been used to doing it. 'Wot's all this then?'

'Dad made us tea!' proclaimed little Elsie, a huge fried chip gradually disappearing into her mouth. ''E cooked it all 'imself!'

Amy turned to look at her dad, who, on seeing her, got up from the table. 'Got yours in the oven,' he said. 'Sit yerself down an' take the weight off yer feet.'

Amy put down her shoulder bag, took off her coat, and watched in absolute astonishment as her dad disappeared into the scullery, and returned almost immediately carrying a hot plate of fried Spam and chips.

'The chips've gone a bit hard in the oven,' said Ernie. 'I shouldn't've cooked yours till yer got 'ome.'

Amy sat down in an empty chair between Elsie and Arnold. She took one sniff of the food in front of her, and, forgetting all about the fancy dishes she had been serving all day at the Corner House, thought she must be in heaven. 'I don't understand, Dad,' she said. 'I din't even know you could cook.'

'Neivver did I,' said Ernie, with a chuckle, as he took his place at the table again. 'But yer never know till yer try.' He looked across at Amy, and gave her a wink. 'Don't let it get cold.'

Soon after tea, Arnold and Elsie were packed off to bed and, much to her disdain, Thelma was told by her dad to go and do her homework in the front room. At seven o'clock, Amy and her dad listened to the news on the wireless. Everything sounded pretty grim, for apparently, the British forces in the Far East had had to surrender Singapore to the Japanese, and when Mr Churchill came on later to talk about it, he gave a solemn warning that it was a 'heavy blow to the nation'. Amy and her dad listened to the Prime Minister with gloomy expressions on their faces; by the sound of things, the end of the war was a long way off.

Whilst Ernie was washing up the tea-time dishes in the scullery, Amy helped by drying them for him. It also gave her one of her rare chances to talk with him alone. 'That was a wonderful treat yer gave us, Dad,' she said. 'I really appreciate it.'

Ernie, at the sink, flicked a quick, but warm smile back at

her. 'I reckon it's about time I started 'elpin' out around 'ere,' he said.

Amy smiled back at him. She wanted to pinch herself; it all seemed too good to be true.

'Oh, by the way,' said Ernie, 'I've applied for a job up the Post Office in Bovay Place. Jim upstairs says they've got vacancies in the transport division. I 'aven't driven since I was in the army soon after the last war, but if I put me mind to it, I reckon I could soon pick it up again.'

Amy couldn't believe what she was hearing. 'You're – lookin' fer anuvver job?' she asked. 'Yer mean, you're goin' ter leave the baths?'

'Why not?' Ernie replied, cagily. 'No prospects there, Ame. I've got a family ter keep. I want ter move on.'

Ernie's new sense of direction had been a long time coming, but now it had come, Amy was overjoyed. 'Get yerself well first, Dad,' she said. 'No need ter rush into fings.'

Ernie chuckled. 'The one fing I've never done fer this family, Ame, is ter rush into lookin' after 'em.'

Later on, Amy made up the fire in the stove, and she and her dad sat in front of it, chatting over all the things they needed, and needed to do, to bring the household back into good working order. Amy hadn't intended to mention her mum, but somehow, it just slipped out.

'I went ter Hyde Park this mornin',' she said, staring into the fire, the warm red glow from the chunks of coke reflected in her eyes. 'Somebody told me Mum might be hiding out up there. I talked to a lot of poor old tramps. They all said they didn't know anyfin' about Mum. They said there was no such fing as a female living out rough in the park. But I wasn't so sure. I just got this feelin' that Mum was there somewhere.'

She sighed. 'Anyway, it was worf a try.'

Ernie remained silent. He sat back in his chair, resting his hands on his knees, deep in thought.

Amy waited a moment, then turned to him. 'Will yer help me find 'er, Dad?'

Ernie stirred, but kept his eyes firmly focused on the glow from the fire, hands resting on his knees.

Amy was not deterred. Covering his hand with her own, she spoke quietly and tenderly. 'Let's bring 'er back 'ome, Dad,' she said. '*You* need 'er. We *all* need 'er. Let's bring 'er back an' make 'er well again.'

Ernie turned to her. There was such a pained expression in his eyes. He looked as though he wanted so desperately to say something, to tell her something, but the words just wouldn't come out. All he could say was, 'One step at a time, Ame. One step at a time.'

Amy pulled her chair closer to him, so that she was able to look directly into his eyes. 'But you've taken the first step, Dad,' she said, squeezing his hand reassuringly. '*You've* come back to us. Now we must do the same for Mum. She's ill, Dad. She's got everyfin' mixed up in 'er mind. It's this war, this bleedin' war. It chokes us up. We're so scared wot each day's goin' ter bring that we can't see straight. All Mum needs is a bit of love. When yer take someone fer granted fer so long, there comes a time when it ain't easy ter tell them that yer love them. But we all need ter be told. We all need ter be told that we're special.'

Ernie closed his eyes, then opened them again, to find Amy still staring into them.

'Let's get the family tergevver again, Dad,' she pleaded. 'Like it ought ter be. Like it always used ter be.'

Ernie managed to give her a weak, but tender smile. 'Give me time, Ame,' he said, gently. 'Just give me time.'

The last person in the world Aggs wanted to see that morning was Scrounger. She'd been awake half the night, her mind, as usual, dominated by images from her past, and now she felt as though she'd been dragged through a hedge backwards.

'Saw yer pitture yesterday,' croaked Scrounger, his chest bubbling with phlegm. 'Quite a good-looker in yer time, weren't yer?' For no apparent reason at all, he burst out laughing, until that was overtaken by a fit of coughing.

'Wot the 'ell you rabbitin' on about now?' growled Aggs, scratching her head with both hands.

Scrounger was enjoying this. 'This nice gel showed me a snapshot of yer,' he teased. 'Din't look a bit like yer now. You 'ad an 'at on!' This again sent him into fits of laughter.

'Get out of 'ere, yer silly ol' sod!' Aggs yelled, as she tried to free herself from beneath the comfort of her pile of old sacks and newspapers.

For once, Scrounger wasn't scared of her. 'She said she was yer daughter!' he said, quickly backing out of her way in case she stretched up and gave him a fourpenny one.

Aggs sat up with a start, and gave him a look to kill. 'Wot's that you said?' she growled.

'Yer daughter, Aggs,' teased Scrounger. 'You know, someone yer gave birf to!' He laughed again.

To his horror, Aggs was up on her feet and clinging on to his long, straggly beard. 'Wot d'yer mean, my daughter?' she barked. 'Tell me, yer stupid ol' git! Tell me!'

Scrounger wailed out in pain, and tried to pull away from her, but she had a vicelike grip on him. 'It's true, Aggs!' he whined. 'Swear ter Gord, she said she was yer daughter. She come lookin' fer yer. She 'ad this snapshot. I could tell it was you, Aggs, 'onest I could! But I never told 'er nuffin', Aggs – nuffin' at all! It's true, I tells yer! True!'

Reluctantly, Aggs let go of his beard. 'When was this?' she demanded.

'Yesterday mornin' – early!' retorted Scrounger, cowering from her at a distance. 'I was tryin' ter 'ave me breakfast.'

'Where?'

For some misguided reason, Scrounger now felt he was at a safe enough distance to be cocky with her. 'Ain't goin' ter tell yer!' he chided, spit darting out from his near toothless mouth as he spoke. 'Find out fer yerself!'

He should have known that he was far too slow and riddled with rheumatism to get away from Aggs, for she suddenly leaped at him, and brought him to the ground. 'See this!' she snarled, sitting on his stomach and threatening him with her clenched fist. 'Can yer see it?'

Scrounger's eyes crossed as he tried to focus on the clenched fist that was held against his face.

Aggs leaned in as close as she could to him. 'Now you tell me where yer saw this gel,' she warned, 'or I'm goin' ter knock out every bleedin' toof yer've got left!'

Scrounger could see the whites of her eyes, and that was always a danger sign. 'Park Lane side!' he replied, without hesitation.

Aggs thought hard for a moment, then lowered her fist. But for the time being, she remained where she was, squatting on his chest. 'Wot did she look like?'

'Like you!' replied Scrounger, quickly. Aggs had got more muscle than he, and he wasn't prepared to provoke her any longer. 'Round face, same nose . . . just like you. More flesh, though.'

Aggs thought hard again, then got up.

For a moment, Scrounger remained right where he was, flat on his back on the lakeside path. 'Yer've done me back in! I won't be able ter move. Me bleedin' back . . . !'

'Get out of 'ere!' yelled Aggs, turning on him.

Scrounger didn't have to be told twice. Rheumatism or no rheumatism, he was up on his feet in a flash, and on his way.

Aggs called after him, 'If you come diggin' round my pitch first fing in the mornin' again, I'll 'ave yer guts fer bleedin' garters.'

Scrounger had already put distance between them. But as soon as he was far enough away, he stopped just long enough to put two fingers up at her.

Aggs didn't bother to watch him go, for she had already turned back to her pitch. For a moment, she just stood there, looking at her bundle, the small collection of personal possessions that was all she had in the world. She felt strange, disoriented. What Scrounger had told her had unsettled her. This was the second time Amy had come looking for her, and it was beginning to worry her.

She went to the edge of the lake, and kneeled there, cupping her hands in the freezing cold water, and freshening her face with it. When she looked down again, the ripples on the surface seemed to form a distorted picture of Amy herself. Aggs watched it until the water had settled again, but when it had, she could still see Amy's round face and fringed forehead smiling sweetly up at her. She tried to compose herself by looking away, over to the small island in the middle of the Serpentine where the wild ducks, geese, and countless varieties of other birds were just emerging from their night's hibernation. But the image of Amy's face was still there, in her mind, as it had been night after night since Aggs had upped and left home over a year before. This time, however, it was different. This time the image was accompanied by an aching feeling inside, not in her stomach, but in her chest. It was more a yearning, a longing to know what was happening to Amy, to the family she had left behind. It was a feeling that had been growing for some time, and it just wouldn't go away. She looked all round her. On the far side of the lake, traffic was already hurrying at the start of the day's rush hour, and the streets of posh Knightsbridge were filling. As she stood there, deep in memories of the past, she quite unconsciously placed her hands over her breasts, feeling them pulsating with the lives of the four children she had suckled there. She closed her eyes and squeezed those two burning lumps beneath her shabby old raincoat. In the darkness, she could see the family there, *her* family – all of them, little Elsie, moaning and groaning about having to go to school; Arnold, kneeling on a chair at the kitchen table, lost in the world of a book about the stars; Thelma, pouting her lips in the mirror as she tried to emulate Lana Turner or Hedy Lamarr; and Amy, dear, straight-as-a-dye Amy, born to love and be loved.

But then there was Ernie. She could see him quite clearly there, rolling his own fag, and licking it together. She could see him lying beside her in bed at number 16, caressing her, holding her in his arms and whispering words of love, if that's what they really were. But that was a long time ago. Long before he stopped desiring her, long before his eyes wandered elsewhere. Oh, if only she could turn back the clock and start all over again, things would be different, so different. Or would they? How could she ever forgive him for the way he had betrayed her? How could she ever trust him again? How could she ever learn to *love* him again?

She collected her things together, and tucked her bundle into its usual hiding place beneath the landing-stage. A few minutes later she was on her way again, heading off towards the vast open space that led to Marble Arch. As she went, she had a lot of mulling over to do, some hard decisions to make. Like it or not, her past was gradually catching up with her. She wasn't sure if she wanted it to, but with Amy searching for her, she was going to have to decide which road she was going to take – the one back home to Holloway, or the endless road to nowhere.

Hilda Feathers was in her element. She had at last met the man of her dreams, even if he wasn't the soft-speaking sexy GI officer she had actually dreamed of. Her new beau was, in fact, an officer in the Grenadier Guards, a blond-haired man in his late forties, immaculate in his uniform, and, in Hilda's own words, 'with piercing blue eyes to die for!' He also had a cut-glass accent to match Hilda's, so much so that when they were together, Amy sometimes thought they were talking in a foreign language. Needless to say, they met when Major Harry Smethurst was Hilda's customer at the Corner House, and with Hilda's wholehearted encouragement, things developed somewhat from there on. However, Amy was certainly not expecting the kind of development Hilda had suddenly thrust upon her.

'Gettin' married!' Amy nearly laddered her regulation plain black stockings when she heard Hilda's news. 'But yer've only known 'im a fortnight!'

'Is it that long?' asked Hilda, who, like Amy was getting dressed in her nippy's uniform in the changing room, ready for the evening shift. 'I feel as though I've known him for a lifetime.'

The other girls who were also changing at the time made wry sounds when they heard that. But Bertha Willets remained silent, apparently uninterested.

'A fortnight's not a lifetime, 'Ild,' said Amy. 'Yer've got ter get ter know someone before yer spend yer whole life wiv them.'

Hilda pulled up one of her stockings, and attached it to a suspender. 'None of us know how long a lifetime can be, Amy,' she replied. 'You have to grab at opportunity whenever you can.'

To Amy, all this sounded absurd. 'Can yer really get to know someone, ter love them – in a fortnight?' she asked.

'In an hour,' replied Hilda. 'Harry's special. I knew that the moment I set eyes on him. And guess what,' she said, standing up to check that the seams of her stockings were straight. 'He wants to take me one night to the Café de Paris. Who said dreams never come true?'

'Dodds!'

Amy turned to find one of the other nippies calling to her from the door.

'Down the office right away!' yelled the girl. 'Miss Fullerton wants to see you.'

'*Me?*'

'I wouldn't keep her waiting if I was you,' called Bertha, with a knowing smile. 'You never know, it might be important.'

* * *

Miss Fullerton's office in the basement was much smaller than that of her boss, Mr Pearson. In fact it was not much bigger than a broom cupboard, and almost as dark. But even though she rarely had a need to use the place, she had done her best to brighten it up with a bowl of flowers which was changed every few days, and her small table lamp had a pretty little yellow shade which she had made herself. Most prominent in the room however, was a poster she had pinned to the wall which read: 'JESUS LOVES YOU', and to complement this, on the corner of the table she kept a modest-sized copy of the Bible.

When Amy came into the room, her supervisor was sitting at her table, fingering the row of simulated pearls around her neck. Amy thought Miss Fullerton's plain black dress made her look even more severe in such a bleak setting, and it made her nervous.

'Tell me, Amy,' she asked, peering through her tortoiseshell spectacles. 'Where do you usually go to when you've finished your night shift here in the restaurant?'

Amy was puzzled. 'Go to, miss?' she asked.

Miss Fullerton took off her spectacles and looked straight across at her. 'I mean, do you go straight home?' She knew she was asking a difficult question, and it made her feel awkward. 'Or do you have – any other place to stay?'

Amy, confused, screwed up her face. She had no idea what this woman was getting at. 'I go straight 'ome, miss.'

'*Every* night?'

'Course, miss,' replied Amy, a touch indignant. 'Me an' 'Ilda always catch the night bus down Piccadilly.'

Miss Fullerton thought for a moment, then said, 'I see,' and put her spectacles back on. 'Amy,' she continued, 'when you were accepted for your job here, why did you not opt to take up accommodation in the staff hostel?'

Again, Amy was puzzled by the question. 'It wouldn't've bin possible, miss. I 'ave ter get 'ome ter my bruvver an' sisters. I can't leave 'em on their own all night.'

'But you have parents, don't you?'

Amy wished she hadn't been asked that question, for until now she had done her best not to mention her problems at home. 'My mum don't live wiv us any more,' she replied cagily. 'An' my dad's bin ill.'

Stony-faced, Miss Fullerton again replied, 'I see.' This time, however, she sat back in her chair, and rested her elbows on its arms. 'I'll be perfectly frank with you, Amy,' she said disconcertingly. 'We've had a complaint that you've been seen late at night – how shall I put it – walking the streets behind Leicester Square.'

Amy's mouth dropped open. 'Miss?' She was so taken aback, it was the only response she could give.

'It's also been suggested,' continued Miss Fullerton, 'that you are sometimes accompanied by – a complete stranger.'

Amy looked at her as though she was mad.

'Is that true, Amy?' asked the supervisor.

'Of course it ain't true, miss!' she protested. 'I don't know who told yer such a fing, but it's a lie! It's a dirty rotten lie!'

'Now calm down, Amy—'

'Me an' 'Ilda go straight ter the bus stop every night regular,' she replied, refusing to be calmed. 'If yer don't believe me, then ask 'Ilda. *She'll* tell yer!'

Miss Fullerton leaned forward in her chair, and tried to pacify Amy by giving the faint suggestion of a sympathetic smile. 'I want you to know that I'm not accusing you of *anything*, Amy,' she said softly. 'That is, not until I get to the truth.' Amy tried to speak, but Miss Fullerton held up her hand to prevent her. 'This is why I asked to see you, Amy,' she continued. 'I wanted to hear your side of the story.'

'There ain't no *story*, miss!' insisted Amy, dogmatically. 'I ain't done nuffin' wrong!'

Miss Fullerton lowered her eyes, and sat back in her chair again. She had a strict look on her face. 'What is your idea of *wrong*, Amy?' she asked.

Amy couldn't believe she was having to go through this. Who *was* this woman, she asked herself, this Bible puncher with a mind as narrow as a tube platform? 'Wrong is doing fings that might upset uvver people,' she said, with her usual candour.

Although her eyes were still lowered, Miss Fullerton's mind was firmly on Amy, in whom she saw all the perils someone as vulnerable as this girl could face. She saw a young life in real danger, a life that could be ruined by misadventure. She saw foolishness and stupidity, an unguarded moment that would live with the girl for the rest of her life. She saw herself. 'Wrong,' she said, 'was giving in to weakness, in turning your back on everything you have been brought up to believe in. You know, Amy, men have a lot to answer for. You mustn't let them use you.'

Amy was so outraged, she could hardly speak 'I've *never* let a man *use* me!' she protested. 'Never once in my whole life.'

'Then why have you been interviewed by the police, Amy?'

Once again, one of Miss Fullerton's questions completely threw Amy. 'I don't follow you, miss,' she replied.

Miss Fullerton took a deep breath. She had that strict look

on her face again. 'I am told that you were recently interviewed by a police officer, and that he gave you a formal warning about – street walking.'

Now Amy was really angry. This was madness, absolute madness. Job or no job, she was not going to let this woman get away with that kind of accusation. 'I don't know who's been tellin' you these fings,' she said, 'but I can assure you—'

Miss Fullerton interrupted her. 'Did a police officer visit you here last week, Amy?' she asked.

Amy faltered. 'Yes, but—'

Miss Fullerton put up her hands, palms faced towards Amy. 'That's all I asked, Amy,' she said. 'There's no need for you to say anything more.' She got up from her chair, and, perhaps unconsciously, lightly touched the Bible with the tips of her fingers as she moved round the table to join Amy. 'You know, my dear,' she said tenderly, 'when you joined us, Mr Pearson had his doubts about whether someone with your type of appearance was a suitable choice for a nippy. But I was the one who persuaded him that it is what is inside that counts, not just physical attributes. I had faith in you, Amy. I still have faith in you. That's why I don't want to hear any more unpleasant stories about you.' She put a hand on Amy's head, and gently caressed her hair. 'As long as you're here, as long as I'm here to protect you, no harm will come to you. But don't let me down, Amy. Whatever you do, please don't ever let me down.'

When Amy left Miss Fullerton's room a few moments later, she was more convinced than ever that the whole world had gone stark raving mad.

CHAPTER 14

On the day Mr Churchill announced the formation of his new Cabinet to enhance the Government's war effort, Ernie Dodds started work at his new job for the Post Office at Bovay Place. The pay wasn't all that marvellous, but it was a darned sight better than the paltry wage he earned as an attendant at the public baths in Hornsey Road. Best of all, of course, was that he enjoyed the work, which not only involved helping with the maintenance of Post Office motorised vehicles, but also occasionally driving the vans on deliveries to other parts of London. But in one way he had been sad to leave the baths, for Bert Farrar, his supervisor there, had always been good to him, and even when Ernie went in to hand in his notice, Bert assured him that his move to a better-paid job was good for both him and his family. However, not everyone was quite so supportive.

'Yer could've told me first,' said Sylvie Temple, as she and Ernie had a drink together in a quiet corner of the Private Bar of The Enkel pub in Hertslet Road. Their change of venue had been forced upon them, for, prior to the injuries Ernie had suffered during the bomb explosion, tongues had started to wag, mainly on account of scandalmongers such as Gert Tibbett, who seemed to keep track of their every move.

'I didn't even know you'd handed in yer notice till a new bloke arrived ter take over your job.'

'I didn't get the chance ter tell yer,' replied Ernie, his eyes darting all round the bar to make sure no one was listening. 'This new job came out of the blue. I 'ad ter grab it while I could.'

'Yer should've told me, Ern,' insisted Sylvie, with just a hint of warning in her voice. 'I'm not just a bit of ol' rag that yer can use when yer want. I do 'ave some rights, yer know.'

Ernie was getting irritated with her. 'Fer chrissake, Sylve!' he complained. 'I can't spend the rest of me life cleanin' out uvver people's barfs. I wanna do somefin' that occupies my mind. An' in any case, I get far better money at the Post Office.'

'Well, that's somefin' I s'ppose,' replied Sylvie, eyeing him carefully as she downed a mouthful of light ale. 'P'raps I might get some of them back-payments yer owe me now.'

Sylvie's cryptic tone unsettled Ernie. He was not sure if her remark was a threat, or a plea. 'I'll be able ter give yer a bit more at the end of next week,' he promised. 'At least it'll tide yer over.'

'Not fer ever, Ern,' she replied. 'Not fer ever.'

Ernie sighed, and lowered his eyes. 'Sylve,' he said, without raising his eyes to look at her, 'I've got somefin' I want ter say to yer. It's not easy, but I've got ter get it off my chest.'

Sylvie eyed him warily.

Ernie looked up at her. 'We've got ter call it a day, Sylve.'

Sylvie froze.

'We've 'ad a good run,' he continued, 'but this fling can't go on any longer.'

Sylvie came back at him in a flash. 'Is that wot it is, Ern?'

she said icily. 'Is that *all* it's ever been – a fling?'

Ernie could have bitten off his tongue. 'That's not wot I meant, Sylve,' he said, quickly.

'Oh yes, it is, Ern,' replied Sylvie. 'In fact it's wot yer've always meant. I've always bin nuffin' more than your little bit of a "fling" in the back cupboard, waitin' ter be let out whenever it suits yer.'

'That's not fair, Sylve.'

'Fair!' Sylvie's voice suddenly erupted. 'Just 'ow fair would you say yer've bin ter *me* all these years, Ern? 'Ow many times 'ave you whispered sweet nuffin's in my ear, and then gone back like the good little hubby ter number 16 just ter tell the uvver woman in your life the same bloody fing?'

Aware that one or two people perched up against the counter had flicked them a quick, curious glance, Ernie leaned close, and covered Sylvie's hand gently with his own. 'Listen ter me, Sylve,' he pleaded. 'I've not bin fair ter you, I know that. I've made mistakes . . .'

'Ha!' grunted Sylvie.

'. . . but I want ter put fings right, Sylve,' he continued. 'I want ter be fair by yer, ter make sure that yer don't 'ave ter go on sufferin'.'

'How thoughtful of you,' replied Sylvie, with a sickly smile. Suddenly her stomach felt as though it was going to explode; she was so overwhelmed with bitterness that she couldn't see or think straight, and could only retort with the first thing that came into her head. 'After the best part of fifteen years, you want ter be fair by me!' She took a deep but anguished breath. 'I love you, Ern,' she said, with great pain. 'I've always loved you. That's been my problem.' When she tried to look him straight in the face, his eyes were lowered again. 'Do I take it, you don't feel the same way about me any more?'

Ernie briefly hesitated before finally looking up. As he stared into her violet, oval-shaped eyes, he saw all the pain, all the suffering he had caused her over the years. And he hated himself for it, he hated himself because he had used her, and never once considered her feelings and the heavy burden he had bequeathed her. 'I love my family, Sylve,' he said, his hand still covering hers. 'I love my family – *an*' my wife.'

Sylvie pulled her hand away from his before replying, 'Then that's *your* problem, Ern.' She got up from the table, and started to leave but, on an impulse, turned back just long enough to add, 'But I can't promise I'll make it easy for yer.'

It was just after four in the afternoon when the air-raid siren wailed out across Hyde Park. Fortunately, it was a false alarm, for the All Clear had sounded within just a few minutes, but even a false alarm was enough to agitate Aggs, for on two separate occasions in the past, she had only just managed to survive stray bombs that had been dropped in the park, one of which had nearly blown her straight into the Serpentine.

The real reason why Aggs was feeling so unsettled these days, however, was Uncle Jim. It had been several weeks now since he had made contact with her in the park, and she was beginning to wonder whether he would ever do so again. She didn't really understand why she felt this way, for Jim was the only link she now had left with the family, and for over a year she had convinced herself that she wanted to forget all about them, all about her former life at number 16 Enkel Street. There was, of course, another reason why she was so anxious to see Jim, for, after her anonymous night-time visit to see Ernie struggling for life in hospital, she had no idea if he was alive or dead. As usual then, her mind was being torn in two directions, but more so now than ever before. As she trudged her way laboriously alongside Rotten Row, she tried to fathom out why she had come to rely so much on a man who, after all, had only ever been her family's lodger. Or was he? It was a question she had asked herself many times before.

Jim Gibbons had always treated her as though she was a goddess or something; in some ways that was understandable after she had once shown him an immense act of kindness and support. But although she had appreciated Jim's fondness for her, her feelings for him had never been anything more than that of a close friend – or at least, that is what she'd told herself at the time. During this past year or so, she had often thought back to those last, unbearable months living at home, when Jim was the only person she had felt safe enough to confide in. Maybe it had something to do with the fact that he had been a bachelor all his life, looking after an elderly sister who gave him no mental stimulation, no room to breathe. Aggs had been his only lifeline; to him, kindness meant love, even if it wasn't reciprocated.

It was almost half an hour later when she finally saw him. At first sight he was not much more than a dot on the horizon, growing a little at a time as he wound his way across the vast muddy field from Marble Arch, gradually drawing closer and closer towards her down by the Serpentine. When he was within striking distance, she noticed for the first time that he was developing a slouch. Getting too fat, she said to herself. Still, to her surprise, his very appearance gave her a warm feeling inside, and made her want to greet him with a big smile. The moment he reached her, however, it was a different story.

'Wot you doin' 'ere?' she growled, with what appeared to be complete indifference.

'Sorry I couldn't get over,' said Jim, a bit po-faced. 'I've been a bit tied up just lately.'

Aggs grunted, turned and moved on.

Jim meekly followed her. 'So how are things?'

Aggs shrugged. 'Who cares?'

'*I* do,' he replied sadly. 'You know how it upsets me to see you like this.'

'Yer don't 'ave ter be upset about *me*,' she sniffed dismissively. 'I can take care of meself.'

'I'm not the only one who's worried about you, Aggs,' said Jim.

Aggs ignored that one, and walked on.

They paused briefly to allow Aggs to bend down and pick up a crust of bread which a couple of kids had earlier dropped whilst feeding the ducks. As she did so, however, a huge web-footed goose came rushing at her, wings outstretched aggressively, beak poised for the attack. But Aggs was no mean opponent; she quickly popped the bread crust into her mouth, and kicked out at the goose with her foot. 'Get out of it!' she yelled, mouth full. 'You're not the only 'ungry one round 'ere!'

Knowing it had met its match, the goose immediately retreated, and with an angry call of rebuke, took flight across the surface of the water.

'Ernie's fine now, Aggs,' said Jim, walking off with her again. 'Thanks to you.'

Aggs did an inward double take, but replied with disregard,

'Don't know wot yer're talkin' about.'

They moved on at a snail's pace, but when they reached one of the lakeside benches, Aggs brought the two of them to a halt, wiped the bench over with her hand as though it might dirty her shabby raincoat, and sat down.

Jim sat beside her, then, after a pause, continued where he had left off. 'Things have been happening at home, Aggs,' he said. 'You wouldn't recognise the family now.'

Aggs wiped her running nose with one finger, and turned to look in a different direction.

'Especially Ern,' continued Jim, refusing to drop the subject. 'He's a new man since he came out of hospital. He's been cleaning the place from top to bottom, and you should see how he's looking after the kids.'

Aggs suddenly turned on him. 'Look, Jim!' she snapped. 'I don't know why yer bovver ter come 'ere, if all yer can gab ter me about is Ern. Can't yer get it into your fick skull that I ain't interested in 'im no more?'

Jim felt put down. For one second, he couldn't understand how he had ever felt anything for this woman. But then, just as quickly, he remembered what she had once done for him. 'Ernie's a changed man, Aggs,' he persisted. 'He's left the baths, got a job with me up at the Post Office. He really cares for the kids. He talks to them, helps them. He's being a real father to them.'

'It's about time,' replied Aggs, acidly.

'Most important of all,' continued Jim, pointedly, 'is he's taken the load off Amy.'

This sudden mention of Amy's name seemed to jolt something in Aggs's mind. Amy. Once again Aggs could see her face, feel her presence, hear herself whispering 'G'night

Amy,' as she saw her girl down into the Anderson shelter. Aggs was feeling remorse, guilt, call it what you will, but whatever it was, her stomach felt quite empty. She was missing her girl, and the feeling was tearing her apart. Two minds, two worlds. What had she done to Amy, to her family? Where was she going? Where was this aimless wandering, this desperate attempt to forget, taking her? Two minds. Which one should she follow? Torment, confusion . . .

'Come home, Aggs.'

The sound of Jim's voice suddenly woke Aggs from what seemed like a deep sleep. 'Wot d'yer say?' she asked, bewildered.

'Come home, Aggs,' he repeated. 'Start over again. You won't regret it.'

Aggs paused, then got up from the bench. 'It's gettin' dark,' was all she could say.

Then she wandered off, not at all sure in which direction she was heading.

Amy and Hilda were rushed off their feet. Both of them had been drafted in for a one-off evening shift, helping to swell the number of nippies and general catering staff who had to deal with a private wedding reception in the main restaurant. In Hilda's opinion the whole thing had been a pretty rushed affair, for she was convinced that the bride was showing the early signs of pregnancy, thanks to a weedy young naval lieutenant, who, in her mind, looked totally incapable of achieving such a thing. None the less, the restaurant itself looked magnificent, showing no sign of austerity imposed by the war. The tables had been rearranged in such a way that they formed a perfect half-moon shape, with the top, central

ignored Amy, quickly picked up her tray of empty dishes, and started to walk off.

Amy was on her in a flash. 'Oh no you don't!' she bellowed, grabbing hold of the knot of Bertha's apron which was tied behind. 'I 'aven't finished wiv you, Willets!'

Bertha had to juggle frantically with her tray to keep her balance, her feet sliding around the tiled floor in madcap steps like someone straight out of a Charlie Chaplin film.

Amy continued to hold on to Bertha's apron, her face blood red with anger, one finger pointing menacingly straight at her face. 'You tried to get me the boot, din't yer?'

'I don't know what you're talking about!' spluttered Bertha, helplessly, her nippy's cap knocked skewwhiff.

'Don't yer?' barked Amy, at full throttle. 'Well, let me tell you somefin', little miss smart-arse. When someone does somefin' ter me wivout any rhyme nor reason, I see red. I ain't done nuffin' ter ruffle your fevvers, but ever since I come 'ere, yer've bin 'avin' a go at me. Wot I wanna know is – *why*?'

Bertha suddenly got her wind back. ''Cos I don't like yer, that's why!' she retorted defiantly, her true South London lingo giving her away. '*I* 'ad ter do six weeks' trainin' before I was allowed ter work 'ere. You come straight into the place after just two.'

Amy was taken aback. 'An' that's it, is it?' she said, in disbelief. 'That's wot this is all about? You're prepared ter go an' tell a bunch of lies about me, just becos I did less trainin' than you?'

Bertha gave her a haughty sneer, and tried to move off. But Amy hadn't finished with her.

''Ad it ever occurred ter you that there's a war on?' Amy

said, calmly. "As it ever occurred ter you that fings don't always run the same way as they did before the war? It may interest you ter know that I din't ask ter do this job, I was offered it. But now that I'm 'ere, no matter wot silly little trollops like you fink, I'm 'ere ter stay! Got it?'

In a desperate attempt to restore what dignity she had left, Bertha straightened herself up, and balanced her tray on one hand again. 'Try tellin' that to the law,' she said smugly. 'Unless my eyes deceived me, it was *you* that flatfoot came to see – wasn't it?'

Amy paused a moment, then slowly smiled at her. 'Oh – I see,' she said, everything gradually dawning. 'Put two an' two tergevver, did yer?'

Bertha turned her back on Amy, and marched off.

'Willets!' she called.

Bertha stopped, but didn't turn back to look.

'D'you really believe I've bin walkin' the streets each night?'

Bertha slowly turned. She had a sickly smile on her face. 'No,' she said, trying to assume her West End accent again. 'As a matter of fact, I don't. I just think you're the type, that's all.' Thoroughly satisfied with her own quick riposte, Bertha smiled broadly, and strode off. The moment she did so, however, her foot slipped on a lump of margarine stuck to the floor. With a resounding crash, both she and the tray of dirty dishes went tumbling to the floor.

To Amy's astonishment, the place suddenly echoed to the sound of wild applause and laughter. When she turned around, she found that a whole battalion of nippies and waiters had been watching her.

Hilda came hurrying forward, took hold of Amy's hand,

and held it up high. 'Ladies and gentlemen!' she announced triumphantly. 'I give you – Amy Dodds – the heavyweight champion of Piccadilly!'

The place erupted into laughs, cheers and applause.

CHAPTER 15

It was early Sunday morning, and Arnold was in his room when his dad came in to see him. The room was small and airless, with no window, and only just about big enough for an eight-year-old, but Arnold loved it, and called it his 'den', for it was the one place that he could get away from everything and everybody, particularly his sisters, and do all the things in private that he was interested in, like building model fighter and bomber planes, and dissecting worms in matchboxes. He also kept all the books there that Uncle Jim had passed on after he'd finished reading them, and even though he didn't much care for detective stories, and much preferred books about heroes and bloody wartime battles, they looked good on the shelf that Uncle Jim had fixed up on the wall for him.

'Feel like 'elping me do a job, son?' asked Ernie, from the open door. 'The back garden needs a bit of a tidy up. I wanna get it ready ter put some plants in come the good wevver.'

Arnold was squatting on his tiny bed, cutting his toenails at the time, but this sudden suggestion from his dad took him totally by surprise. His dad had never suggested they do anything together before; for the past couple of years or so, it had been Uncle Jim who had been the real dad to him. 'Can't do much in the garden while the Anderson's still there,' he said, awkwardly.

'Yer can make air-raid shelters look really good, if yer try 'ard enough,' replied Ernie. 'You've got imagination. I bet you'd 'ave one or two good ideas.'

Arnold thought about this. His dad was right. Maybe they *could* make the garden look good, like it used to look before the war. 'OK,' he said, getting up from the bed. 'Where do we start?'

The back garden was actually a back yard. What had once been a patch of rough grass with a small diamond-shaped rose bed in the centre, had now been completely overwhelmed by the Anderson shelter, a corrugated-iron contraption which had been dug into the ground, with only its arch shape protruding, and even that was covered with a foot or so of clay and soil. When Arnold came out from the back door with his dad, he took one look at the pile of litter and empty beer bottles and declared, 'Not much we can do with all this junk.'

'Wanna bet?' asked Ernie, who had already started to pick up bits of rubbish. 'Get it all cleaned up, and then we'll 'ave somefin' ter get started on.'

Sure enough, half an hour or so later, the rubbish had been collected and pushed into old cardboard boxes, leaving both Ernie and Arnold to start shovelling away the remnants of a recent snowfall around the outside of the shelter. But it was some time later before Ernie managed to find a convenient moment to have what he had planned as his 'man-to-man' talk with his son. The opportunity came when they worked together struggling to pull out some of the previous season's hollyhocks, which over the winter had been reduced to nothing more than sad, damp stalks, with melancholy drooping heads.

'Yer know, I reckon we should've asked yer sisters ter come out an' 'elp us,' said Ernie, as he wrestled with the remains of a dead hybrid rose. 'If we all mucked in tergevver, we'd knock this into shape in no time.'

Arnold grunted. 'Girls can't do this kind of work,' he complained, dismissively. 'They're not tough enough.'

'Don't you believe it, son,' replied Ernie, with more than a touch of irony. 'Women can be just as tough as us men – an' a bit more!' He waited a moment or so before continuing his build-up to the real point of his plan. 'Sorry yer mum an' I never gave yer a bruvver, Arn,' he said, throwing it in as casually as he could. 'Chances are, yer wouldn't've felt so put upon.'

The remark seemed to have passed right over Arnold's head, for he just carried on pulling up dead weeds.

Ernie persisted. 'Bet you'd've liked a bruvver, wouldn't yer?' he asked, as discreetly as he could.

'Wouldn't mind,' replied Arnold, with little or no interest.

Ernie waited another moment or so before pursuing the subject. 'Would yer've liked a younger or an' older?'

'Pardon?' asked Arnold, without any real reaction.

Ernie was becoming nervous. 'A bruvver, Arn,' he said, edging cautiously. 'Would yer 'ave preferred one younger than yerself, or older?'

'Don't care,' replied Arnold. 'As long as it wasn't anuvver sister.'

'Personally,' continued Ernie, 'I'd always prefer an older bruvver meself. Someone yer can look up to, who can give you advice, or 'elp yer out of a scrape.'

As he spoke, an ice-cold drizzle started to flitter down from a friendless grey sky. Some of the neighbours who had been idly watching them from the back windows of their own homes in Hertslet Road, quickly disappeared, leaving Ernie and Arnold to rush for cover in the air-raid shelter.

Once down there, Ernie brushed the freezing drizzle from his chunky pullover. Arnold quickly followed him, and the two of them perched side by side together on the edge on the lower bunk. Once they had settled, they shared a brief silence. The old blanket that covered over the entrance left the shelter in semi-darkness, but a few chinks of the dull Sunday morning light did manage to filter in down the sides, to cast narrow vertical patterns on their faces.

Whilst they sat there, Ernie kept churning over in his mind how he was going to reopen the conversation he had already started with Arnold. He took out the small tin of loose tobacco from his trouser pocket, which also contained some cigarette papers. When he finally spoke, his voice sounded flat as it bounced off the curved corrugated ceiling.

'You an' me 'ave never really got ter know each uvver, 'ave we, Arn? It's my fault, I know that. I always wanted a son, an' yet when you come along, I din't know 'ow ter deal wiv yer.' He started to fill, then roll himself a fag. 'Yer mum an' I often used ter talk about it, yer know,' he said.

Arnold turned to look at him. 'Talk about what?' he asked.

'You,' Ernie replied. 'Our boy. 'Ow rough it was goin' ter be for yer 'avin' two sisters. That's 'ow Elsie came along. We tried ter get a bruvver for yer, but it din't work out.'

Sitting there with nothing to do while he listened to his dad, it was gradually dawning on Arnold that he was being set up. The question was – why?

Ernie licked the ends of the fag paper, and stuck them

together. 'Of course, that don't mean ter say that we don't love yer sisters. They're good gels.'

Arnold grunted.

'Oh, they are, Arn,' insisted Ernie. 'It's just that they don't fink the same as boys.'

'Amy does,' said Arnold.

The boy's reply took Ernie by surprise. 'Is that right?'

'*She* talks to me,' said Arnold, perched on the edge of the bunk, swinging his legs back and forth aimlessly. 'She talks about lots of things, about what's on at the pittures, about the war. Sometimes she talks about you an' Mum.'

Ernie swung him an anxious look. 'Wot does she say?'

Arnold shrugged his shoulders. 'That Mum'll come back home one day, that you an' she'll get back together again, that you really miss Mum, an' that she only went away becos she's not well.'

Ernie listened carefully. Until this moment, it had never really occurred to him how much his break-up with Aggs had affected his kids. As they sat there, he felt closer to his son than ever before, as though a real bond was beginning to develop between them. Not that he didn't love his daughters – especially Amy, who, for the past year or so had struggled to keep the rest of the family together. It was just that, for one reason or another, dads had more to relate to with sons, and daughters felt more comfortable confiding in their mums. Tentatively, he slipped his arm affectionately around the boy's shoulders. He had never done such a thing before. It felt strange, but good. ''Ow'd'yer like ter come out fer a ride wiv me in the Post Office van one day?' he asked, quite suddenly.

Arnold turned with a start. 'D'yer mean it? D'yer really mean it?'

Ernie smiled. 'We're not s'pposed to,' he replied. 'But I reckon if we keep quiet about it, we could 'ave a go.'

Utterly overcome with excitement, the boy threw his arms round his dad and hugged him. It was the first time he also had ever done such a thing. All he could say over and over again was, 'When can we go, Dad? When can we go?'

As he and his boy hugged each other, Ernie had a broad, happy grin on his face. Deep down, he reckoned he had quite a lot to thank Amy for, and that if he wanted to be a real father to his family, she was the only person who could help him.

As far as Arnold was concerned, however, totally immersed in the prospect of a ride in a Post Office van, he was no longer bothered what his dad had been trying to tell him.

As it was Sunday morning, Amy had her first real lie-in for ages. In fact, when she eventually woke up and discovered that it was already past nine o'clock, and that both Thelma and Elsie's beds were empty, she leaped out of her own in a panic, anxious that the family would all be waiting for their breakfast. However, when she got downstairs, she was astonished to find that the breakfast table had already been cleared, except for her place, where she found a pot of tea waiting, together with half a loaf, the margarine, and a jar of strawberry jam which had clearly been assailed by Elsie.

'Where *is* everyone?' asked Amy, as her youngest sister came in from the scullery.

Elsie was, as usual, in a petulant mood. 'Thelm's gone ice-skatin' wiv 'er gang up 'Arringay,' she said, clearly tetchy that she hadn't been taken along with them.

'Wot about Dad and Arn?' asked Amy.

'Down the shelter,' replied Elsie.

Amy pulled a face. 'Wot're they doin' down there?'

''Cos it's rainin'!' Elsie came back cheekily, before sweeping grandly out of the room.

Amy went out into the kitchen, and looked out of the window. No sign of her dad or Arnold. But the sky was heavy with rain, which meant that yet another winter Sunday was going to be a bit of a washout.

It was much the same in Hyde Park. The usual Sunday morning crowd at Speakers' Corner had been somewhat diminished by the heavy drizzle that was freezing almost as it touched the ground. But there was still a hardcore of tub-thumpers there, together with their admirers and fierce opponents. The hecklers were also out in force, doggedly braving the elements with coat collars turned up, hands sunk deep into their pockets to keep warm, and flat caps and trilby hats dripping with rain. Aggs was amongst them, having chosen to harass a thick-set bible-punching preacher who was gloomily prophesying the end of the world. As usual, her shrieked comments brought ripples of laughter from the crowd. 'Beware!' bellowed the preacher. 'The Lord is nigh!' Aggs responded with, 'Not till you get out the boozer, mate!' Not everyone was so amused, however, especially two swarthy-looking types who mingled with the crowd. During the entire proceedings, their eyes were constantly focused on Aggs.

Once the ritual arguing and bickering had come to an end, and the speakers had carried off their wooden box platforms until the same time the following week, Aggs shuffled off in the direction of the Bayswater Road side of the park. She hadn't gone very far when The Kid hurried to catch her up. 'Got some news for yer, Ma,' he said, his eyes flicking all around him as he talked.

Aggs carried on shuffling. 'News don't int'rest me,' she sniffed, without turning.

'*This* news will!' insisted The Kid, his face only barely visible behind his balaclava. 'It's about your mate down The Turk's 'Ead.'

Aggs swung him a piercing look, and brought them both to a sudden stop.

'That's right,' continued The Kid. 'Charlie Ratner. The flatties 'ave 'ad 'im in fer questioning. Seems they raided his place, lookin' fer that pig of theirs that was nicked.'

Aggs expression was like stone. 'Where d'yer 'ear all this?' she asked warily.

'A pub up by Paddin'ton Station,' replied The Kid, adding pointedly, 'They say it all came from a tip-off.'

'Wot's that s'pposed ter mean?' growled Aggs.

The Kid drew close to her. 'It means that someone close to Ratner squealed on 'im. Someone in the know. Someone who knew wot's bin goin' on up there.'

Aggs ground her teeth together so hard, the muscles in her cheeks became fixed. 'Wot's 'appened ter Ratner?' she asked apprehensively.

'Back 'ome again,' said The Kid. 'Nuffin' found, no charge. But I tell yer this much: I wouldn't like ter be in the shoes of whoever it was put the flatties up to it.'

Aggs ignored him, and shuffled on.

'I don't wanna poke my nose into your business, Ma,' persisted The Kid, keeping up with her, 'but you better be careful.'

'Don't know wot you're goin' on about!' snapped Aggs, eyes fixed firmly ahead of her.

'You've bin workin' at that pub, Ma,' said The Kid. 'You probably know more than anyone wot's bin goin' on there.'

Aggs barked back at him, 'I don't know nuffin' about nuffin'!'

'Ratner's got a reputation,' insisted The Kid. 'He's as mean an' rough as an undertaker's bog'ouse!'

Aggs quickened her pace. 'I ain't scared of no undertaker,' she barked, 'an' I certainly ain't scared of Charlie Ratner!'

'Your life's in danger, Ma.'

The Kid's stark warning brought Aggs to an abrupt halt. 'Wot make's yer so sure?' she asked.

'No questions asked,' replied The Kid. 'Just believe me.'

For a moment, they both stood there, just staring at each other, ice-cold drizzle streaming down their cheeks.

'Anyway, wot's so special about life?' asked Aggs. 'One moment you're 'ere, the next – you're gone. Who cares if I catch one?'

'*I* do.'

The Kid's reply took Aggs off guard. 'Look, sonny Jim,' she said, 'I'm old enough not ter care a monkey's fer scum like Ratner. If 'e wants ter get rid of me, let 'im go right ahead.'

The Kid paused a moment, then replied, 'Not while *I'm* around, 'e won't.'

On the opposite side of the road, the two swarthy figures from Speakers' Corner passed by without looking in any particular direction. Only when they were at a safe distance did they turn to gaze over their shoulder at the old hag they were interested in.

* * *

Sunday morning had turned out to be a pretty dismal time in Chapel Market. On this day of the week, the place was usually brimming with shoppers, winding in and out of the colourful stalls which nestled side by side along the bustling, popular back street close to the Angel, Islington. But today, the crowds had kept away, for the ice-cold drizzle had been relentless from early in the morning. But, as always, the die-hard barrow boys were undeterred. Second-hand clothes were kept dry beneath sheets of glass, newspapers, tarpaulins, or anything else the stallholders could lay their hands on; budgerigars for sale were protected from the cold by being kept in cardboard boxes wrapped up in old blankets; and bargain stalls – which carried everything from soap powder, nail scissors, babies' dummies and aluminium buckets, to jars of home-made jam, tins of corned beef, and sacks of loose haricot beans – struggled bravely to look enticing to the dwindling army of shoppers. But the coke braziers were still there, doggedly roasting chestnuts, pork trimmings, and mouth-watering sausages stuffed with a minimum of minced meat and a surfeit of breadcrumbs.

The only two people who seemed to be completely oblivious to the weather were Amy and Tim, who were relishing one of their rare opportunities to walk out alone together, away from the prying eyes of little Elsie. Amy was so secure in Tim's company. Despite the fact that there were times when she felt as though she was a rival to his mother for his affections, the one thing she was sure of was that in times of stress, he was the one person she could rely on. But it was more than just that. She was in love with him. For the first time in her life she was in love, and the feeling of being wanted was something she had only ever dreamed of. Strolling hand in hand in the rain, with Tim clumsily trying to hold up an umbrella over both of them, she pulling up her coat collar with one hand to keep her neck warm, they ambled along, stopping at one stall, and then another. The patter of the tradesmen followed them wherever they went: 'Come on, darlin' – give 'im a scrub wiv some good carbolic soap! Goin' cheap, only tuppence ha'penny a bar!' 'Right, sir! I can see you're a man after me own 'eart! Wot about a good fag case to impress the little lady?' The barbed humour was all good fun, and both Amy and Tim had smiles on their faces.

Just before midday, most of the traders started to shut up shop. All along the market, shutters were being fixed back into position, other stalls were dismantled, and some of the permanent ones covered over completely with large tarpaulins. Just before the market closed, however, Amy and Tim stopped at a stall selling imitation jewellery, where nothing cost more than a few bob. None the less, Amy was over the moon when Tim bought her a small brooch in the shape of a cat, set with mock garnet stones, which, although costing only one shilling and sixpence, was, as far as she was concerned, the most valuable thing she had ever been given in her whole life.

Further down the road, they took a short cut through a narrow back alley which would eventually lead them into Pentonville Road. There was no one in the alley but themselves, and when they were halfway along, Tim suddenly lowered the umbrella, brought them to a halt, pinned Amy against the wall, and kissed her long and hard. It was a quick, impetuous moment, and Amy gave herself willingly to it. They stayed like that for several minutes, locked in each other's arms, the cold drizzle soaking the scarf over Amy's head and Tim's flat cap, and the warm blood flowing through their veins pulsating with excitement. After that, they wandered aimlessly around the back streets, totally absorbed in each other's company, oblivious to anyone else. They only noticed the rest of the world again when they were just passing a pub called The Penny Farthing. Tim suggested they have a drink, so they quickly shook the rain off their coats, and went in.

The Public Bar was full and lively, clearly a favourite haunt for Sunday morning Chapel Market barrow boys and servicemen. The air was choked with the smell of fag smoke and draught beer, and some of the customers were getting high and playing darts simultaneously. Tim managed to find a place for Amy at a table close to the open fire, but she had to share it with three old dears, clearly regulars, who were all wearing curlers covered over with cotton scarves, and, in direct competition with the men, downing pint glasses of stout. Whilst Tim went to order their drinks at the counter, Amy took the opportunity to have a good look round, and her immediate impression was that the pub was also a haunt for some of the local street girls who were out to make a bob or two amongst the male clientele.

'Sorry about this,' said Tim, as he returned with the drinks. 'I realise now that this is no place for decent girls like you.'

Amy smiled at his lovely, protective remark. 'Don't 'ave ter worry about me, Tim,' she replied. 'I've seen worse than this in me time. In a way I feel sorry for gels like them. They must be pretty desperate ter do it.'

They suddenly noticed that the three old dears had stopped chatting amongst themselves, and were all sizing them up suspiciously. Before continuing what he was saying, Tim, deliberately leaned towards Amy as close as he could, and lowered his voice. 'I've got an idea about your mum,' he said.

'D'you still reckon she might be hiding out somewhere in Hyde Park?'

At the mention of her mum, all Amy's worries came flooding back to her. 'I just don't know, Tim,' she sighed. 'When I was up there the uvver day, I had this strong feelin' that I was close to 'er. But the more I fink about it, the more I'm sure it was no more than that. Let's face it,' she sighed again, 'she could be anywhere.'

'Well, there's one way we *could* find out for sure,' said Tim. 'We could go and ask the police in the park itself? They must keep tabs on all the down-and-outs who sleep rough out there.'

Amy slowly shook her head. 'I doubt it,' she said reluctantly. 'Mum's been on the Missing Persons list ever since she left home. Every police station must 'ave a pitture of 'er somewhere. Let's face it, Mr 'Anley does 'is best. The police've got quite enough on their 'ands without goin' lookin' fer Mum.'

'I know,' said Tim. 'With all the people who've been bombed out, it must be one hell of a job.'

'It's not just that,' said Amy. Then she also realised that the three old dears were straining to hear their every word, so she leaned closer to Tim, and lowered her voice even more. 'The problem is, if Mum's had some kind of a nervous breakdown, chances are she doesn't *want* to be—' She suddenly stopped what she was saying. Her eyes were riveted to something on the far side of the bar.

'Amy?' Tim asked anxiously. 'What is it?'

Amy didn't reply. Astonished, the three old dears had to hold on to their glasses, as she leaped up from the table, and rushed off.

Tim got up quickly and followed, calling after her, 'Amy!'

Amy frantically pushed her way through the crush of customers, until she finally reached that end of the counter which was partly concealed from the rest of the bar. Before she got there, she bellowed out at the top of her voice, 'Thelma!'

Thelma, dolled up in a short skirt, revealing sweater, high-heeled shoes, her hair swept up on top of her head, and her face covered in thick make-up, was snogging quite openly at the counter with a young army private. 'Christ!' she gasped, as she turned with a start to find her sister rampaging towards her. Immediately breaking loose from the soldier, she tried to make a bolt for it.

Amy was on her in a flash, and launched straight into her. 'You . . . dirty little . . . !' she growled, grabbing hold of Thelma's sweater and dragging her back.

'Leave me alone!' screeched Thelma, struggling desperately to release Amy's grip from her sweater. 'Leave me alone . . . !'

Amy held firm. In a fit of uncontrollable temper, she slapped the girl across the face with the back of her hand, yelling, 'Dirty little bitch! Dirty! Dirty! Dirty . . . !'

'No, Amy!' cried Tim, as he caught up with her.

Amy was too incensed to listen to him, and refused to let him pull her away from the girl.

'Get off, yer stupid cow!' barked the young soldier, who was engaged in his own tug of war battle with Amy. 'Who the bleedin' 'ell d'yer fink you are – fat arse!'

'Who am I?' yelled Amy, still holding Thelma in a vicelike grip. 'I'll tell yer who I am, mate! I'm 'er sister, I'm 'er muvver, I'm every bleedin' fing!'

'Oy!' Angered by the commotion being caused in his bar, the pub landlord came rushing at them from behind the counter. 'I want none of that 'ere!'

'Oh no?' asked Amy, provocatively. 'Don't want no trouble, is that it? Then yer'd better be careful who you allow on your premises. The law don't take kindly to pubs admittin' fourteen-year-olds!'

'Fourteen!' The soldier darted a quick look at Thelma, then suddenly realised what he'd got himself into. 'Christ!' He was out of the pub in a flash.

'Get 'er out of 'ere!' growled the landlord, pointing to the door. 'All of yer, get out of 'ere!'

Thelma used the distraction to free herself from Amy. 'Cow!' she yelled back, as she pushed her way through the crowd.

'Thelma!'

Amy immediately tried to go after her, but was restrained by Tim. 'No, Amy,' he pleaded, trying to pacify her. 'Let her go.'

By seven o'clock that evening, Thelma had still not come home. Amy and her dad sat in the dark, one each side of the front parlour windows, eyes glued to the street outside. With every minute that passed, Amy feared the worst. What had she done? Had she driven Thelma away, just like her dad had done to their mum? She felt crushed, defeated. What she had done in that pub earlier in the day had been wrong. She had no right to humiliate her own sister like that, in front of all those people. She wasn't Thelma's mother. She wasn't her keeper. Thelma was no different to any other girl of her age – perhaps a bit wilder; she was exploring, experimenting with life. What she needed was guidance, not scorn. Amy's mind was racing. Oh God! What *had* she done? She was haunted by all the possibilities. Had she really driven Thelma away from her own home? Would they ever see her again?

'Yer mustn't blame yerself, Ame.' Ernie's voice, soft and low, broke the anxious silence of the dark room. 'This 'ad ter 'appen sooner or later. It was *bound* ter 'appen.'

Amy got up and went to sit with him. He slipped his arm around her shoulders, and she rested her head against his.

'It's so easy ter go off the rails, Ame,' said Ernie, the dim glow from his rolled up fag glowing in the dark. 'At that age, when someone tells yer yer can't do somefin', it grates. Yer want ter get up and do the opposite, make yer own decisions, make an impression on yer mates, make 'em fink you're a big shot. I was the same. I did what I fawt was all the right fings. I 'ad gels – plenty of 'em. They made me feel good. They made me feel like I was really somebody. But it was a mug's game really. When it comes down to it, walkin' a straight line is the only one that counts.' He drew on his fag, inhaled deeply to take most of it down into his lungs, then released the residue. 'It's 'ard growin' up, Ame,' he said. 'It's pretty 'ard *bein'* grown up.'

At that moment, they heard the front yard gate open and close. Amy immediately leaped to her feet, but Ernie took hold of her gently. 'No, Ame,' he said softly. 'Leave this to me.' He released her, and stood up. 'I'm 'er dad. I've got ter start somewhere.'

In the passage outside, Ernie turned off the light, and waited for the key to go into the street door lock. Then, as soon as he heard the door open and close, he turned on the light again.

When Thelma saw her father, she started to sob. It was

clearly not the first time she had done so that evening, for her exaggerated make-up had streaked down her cheeks.

For a brief moment, Ernie made no movement towards her. 'Are yer hurt, Thelm?' he asked in a calm but firm voice. ''As anybody 'urt yer?'

Thelma shook her head.

'Sure?'

Thelma nodded.

Ernie opened his arms out wide and Thelma rushed into them.

'I want my mum!' she sobbed. 'I want my mum . . . !'

CHAPTER 16

With the fall of Singapore the month before, and the apparent inability of the British army to stem the advance of General Rommel's Afrika Korps in North Africa, at the beginning of March feelings were running high around the country that the Government was not doing enough to bring the war to an end. Some misguided radicals even called for the resignation of Mr Churchill and his entire wartime cabinet, accusing his Foreign Secretary, Anthony Eden, of being totally ineffectual in the face of the superior enemy war machine. The accusations were, of course, spurious, but they did have an adverse effect on the morale of at least some of the more sceptical Londoners. Others, however, had more important matters to think about.

'I think I'll go for the powder blue,' chirped Hilda, confidently. She was in her element as Amy helped her to try on a selection of two-piece suits for her forthcoming marriage to Major Harry Smethurst of the Grenadier Guards.

As expected, Hilda had chosen Dickins & Jones, one of the more fashionable West End department stores, to buy her wedding outfit. Her family had readily given their blessing to her 'quickie' wedding, mainly because her father, like her future husband, had once been a senior army officer.

'Why've yer got this fing about blue?' asked Amy, as she watched her mate trying on her ninth outfit to date. 'That was a smashin' lilac one yer tried on.'

'No, no, no,' insisted Hilda. With the help of a weary women's department assistant, she was busily inspecting herself in a full-length mirror. 'Blue is very important to me. I want to match Harry's eyes. They're absolutely gorgeous. Then, of course, there's Her Majesty the Queen.'

Amy looked bewildered. 'The Queen?'

'I met her just before the war,' replied Hilda, talking to Amy's reflection, which was behind her own, in the mirror. 'It was at an afternoon tea party at the Grosvenor House Hotel for girls who were coming out.' She turned back to look at Amy. 'Oh, Amy, she looked so lovely in powder blue. In fact every time I've seen her, she always seems to be wearing the same colour. It suits her so well.'

Amy was wide-eyed. 'Yer mean ter say – yer've actually *met* the Queen? In person?'

Hilda was looking at herself in the mirror again. 'Of course, darling! I've met her several times. Daddy got invited to a reception at Buckingham Palace once, and as Mummy had flu at the time, I went with him. She was so – gracious, so nice to everyone. Thank goodness we didn't have that awful Duchess of Windsor on the throne. If our dear Queen lives to be a hundred, she could never be as calculating as that!'

'How do we feel about this one, madam?' asked the assistant, rapidly becoming impatient.

'I'm not sure yet,' replied Hilda, pinching in the material at her waistline. 'Not quite right here, I think . . .'

'It suits madam admirably.'

'Does it?'

'Absolutely.'

'Wot do *you* think, Amy?'

Amy stared in awe at the costume. 'They all look smashin' ter me,' she replied.

'Hmm . . . not bad,' said Hilda, engrossed in her own reflection. 'Not bad at all. A little bit of alteration here and there perhaps. Yes . . . I like it . . .'

A look of intense relief came over the assistant. 'Then you'll take it?' she asked, eagerly.

Hilda shot her a look of surprise. 'Take it? Oh goodness, no. I haven't seen the others yet.'

A short while later, Amy was carrying out the same duties as she watched Hilda trying on hats in the millinery department. Every shape and size was stuck on Hilda's head – wild creations with wax eggs at the front, large wide-brimmed monstrosities made out of basket-weave, and even a hat made in the shape of a horseshoe, with a long brown chicken's feather stuck down the side. Amy roared with laughter at Hilda's antics as she tried on everything she could lay her hands on, but when she looked at some of the price labels on the hats, she nearly had a fit.

'Blimey, 'Ild!' she gulped. 'If yer can afford prices like this, why d'yer bovver ter keep on workin'?'

Hilda was studying herself in a small hand-mirror. 'Mummy's idea really,' she replied, cocking from side to side a natty little hat with a navy-blue veil. 'She was a shop girl in Streatham when she met Daddy.'

Amy was shocked. 'Your mum?'

'Why not?' replied Hilda. 'We're not all born with silver spoons in our mouths. Anyway, Daddy says it's only right and proper that we earn our living. After all, it's the only way to meet all kinds of people. Just think, if I hadn't, I'd never have met you.' She turned back to give Amy a warm, affectionate smile, adding, 'I wouldn't have missed that for the world.'

Amy gave her a similar warm smile.

Hilda finally chose what she was looking for – a powder-blue, military style pillbox hat, which delighted both of them. 'It's funny, isn't it?' she remarked, as she watched the assistant pack her hat in a box. 'I've always dreamed of getting married in a church, white flowing wedding dress, walking down the aisle on Daddy's arm, organ playing, you know – the full works. But here I am, doing it all in a boring old registry office, just because I'm head over heels for the man I've been dreaming of. But what does it matter? After all, powder blue means just as much to me as virgin white!'

Amy laughed, got up from her seat, and hugged her mate. She was more convinced than ever that being an official witness at Hilda's wedding was going to be one of the happiest moments of her life.

In Hyde Park, the band was playing. These days it wasn't a very familiar sight, for the military had more important things to do. But it was a ray of sunshine during those dying days of a particularly harsh winter, for despite the potholes in the grass nearby, caused by discarded enemy incendiary bombs, the defiant old bandstand had so far withstood the worst excesses of the air raids.

Defying the cold early March afternoon, a small crowd had gathered to listen to a selection of military marches from all the armed services, together with popular tunes of the day. The kids in the crowd particularly liked the rousing, 'The

British Grenadiers', because it gave them the chance to salute and march in time to the music. But everyone else seemed to prefer best songs like, 'There's Something about a Soldier', and 'The White Cliffs of Dover' – in fact anything that gave them the opportunity to join in, and tap their toes. Aggs was there too, and despite the fact that she knew the words of all the songs, she resisted the urge to sing or, like all the other onlookers, to sway in time to the rhythm. It reminded her too much of the past.

Before the band entertainment had come to an end, Aggs left the crowd, and went in search of something to eat. The moment she had heard from The Kid that Charlie Ratner had been taken in for questioning about the theft of the police station pig, she had not returned to her job at The Turk's Head, which meant that she needed to find other ways of filling her stomach each day. The crowd around the bandstand hadn't been very helpful, for every time she asked for a penny for a cup of tea, she was either met by a disdainful shake of the head, or a refusal to even acknowledge her presence. So, for the time being, her only hope were the litter bins, and for that, her best bet was on the south side of the park along the path just behind the Albert Memorial.

To her dismay, however, there was little to be found in her favourite bins; it was clear that both the squirrels and her parkie rivals had already picked them clean. Reluctantly, she moved on, and stopped more than a dozen times to sift through every bin she could find. She even searched under the park bench, where visitors would idly drop whatever leftovers they had in their hands.

As it was early March, there were now clear signs that the nights were beginning to draw out, and by the time Aggs had reached the wide open spaces of Kensington Gardens, the sun had only just dipped behind the red-brick grandeur of Kensington Palace, leaving behind a landscape shimmering with a rich, scarlet glow. Exhausted, she sat down on a bench on the edge of the gardens, watching the last of the day's visitors ambling their way slowly out of the park towards Kensington Road. In the distance she could just see a bunch of kids playing tag with each other, their shrieks of laughter echoing across the vast open field. For one split second, they reminded her of her own kids, years before, doing much the same thing when she foolishly took them along to Finsbury Park to feed the ducks, and how they played her merry hell when she tried to get them to come home. By this time, the early evening cold was beginning to bite, no more so than in her feet, so she bent down, pulled off one of her well-worn plimsolls, and rubbed and squeezed her frozen foot back into life. Only then did she notice the one litter bin that she had missed. It was situated back on the path on which she had just come, and was partly concealed behind a bench that was too broken to be used. Quickly replacing her plimsoll, Aggs got up, went straight to the bin, and immediately found it promising.

Picking through it meticulously, she felt something she recognised, hidden away at the bottom of the bin beneath a pile of soggy newspaper, empty ginger beer bottles, and half-chewed pickled onions. When she eventually succeeded in retrieving it, she was delighted to find that there were still some crisps left in their bag, so she dipped in, and started to gorge herself for the first time since finishing off a discarded Spam sandwich that morning.

But her moment of ecstasy was not to last long, for, without warning, from behind, a hand suddenly clamped over her mouth, leaving her to choke on the partly chewed crisps. Simultaneously, a man's arm tightened around her throat; her eyes were popping out of her head. She dropped the crisp bag to the ground, and struggled to free herself, but her calls for help were stifled by the hand that was preventing her from drawing breath. Then she felt a blow to the face. Her eye felt as though it had been split wide open, and her cheekbone as though it had cracked. She suddenly succeeded in freeing her mouth by biting the hand that was clamped over it, but before she could cry out, she was winded by another blow, this time to her stomach. The pain was too much to take, so she crumpled up, and slowly fell to her knees.

'Bastards . . . !'

The voice seemed to come from nowhere. But Aggs could just hear it, descending like a crazed animal on what she now realised were two assailants.

For the next few moments, she lay crumpled up on the ground, a searing pain tearing her stomach apart. Somewhere behind her she could hear The Kid's voice, yelling every obscenity he could muster at the two men he had taken on single-handed. The scuffle sounded rough and boisterous. It only ended when she heard a man's voice gasping in pain after a bottle came down on his head with a thud, and then smashed to smithereens on the ground. That was followed by another man's voice calling. 'Out of 'ere! Come on, Ron! Go! Go! Go!' It was only the sound of feet running off along the path that finally brought the roughhouse to an end.

The next voice Aggs heard was that of The Kid. 'Ma! Are yer all right, Ma! Jesus – wot have they done to yer?'

Aggs could only just feel him trying to turn her over, but

the moment she got a blurred glimpse of his frantic young face, everything turned black.

That evening, Amy got off the bus at the Nag's Head pub at about seven. The sky was quite clear, and with a crescent-shaped moon and dazzling bright stars, she was only too glad that, for the present time at least, there were no air raids.

As she passed the pub, which was on the corner of Holloway and Seven Sisters Road, she could hear the usual rowdy crowd of dart-players inside, and the sound of Paddy O'Reilly thumping out 'When Irish Eyes are Smiling' on the old joanna. When she turned into Enkel Street she found it was bathed in a brilliant luminous glow, which gave her a perfect view right to the end of Roden Street. On the opposite side to where she was walking, she hardly noticed the back doors of Woolworths, Marks and Spencer, and her beloved Lyons Tea Shop, which were firmly locked up for the night. But the silence along the street was, as usual, shattered by the sound of the Dolly Sisters' wireless, blaring out the week's edition of *ITMA*.

It was not until she was further down the street that she suddenly noticed someone perched on the coping stone of number 16. For a time, it was impossible to identify the person, but as she drew closer she saw that it was a woman. Eventually, the bright moonlight picked out the face of Sylvie Temple.

'Wot you doin' 'ere?' snapped Amy. 'Ain't yer got no 'ome of yer own ter go to?'

'My 'ome,' replied Sylvie, cuttingly, getting up to meet her, 'is my business. I came 'ere ter 'ave a civil conversation wiv yer, so the least I expect is a bit of respect.'

'Respect! For you?'

Sylvie was determined not to be riled. 'Listen, Amy,' she said calmly. 'I know you don't like me, and ter be 'onest wiv you, I don't much care fer you eivver. But even though you're a good bit younger than me, we're both of an age to discuss fings wivout gettin' worked up.'

Amy went through her front yard gate, closed it behind her, and stood there defiantly. 'I would've fawt it was my dad you needed ter 'ave words wiv, not me.'

'Talkin' ter your dad in't easy, Amy,' replied Sylvie, her fair complexion bathed in moonshine. ''E's 'ad nuffin' sensible ter say ter me in a long time.'

Amy crossed her arms. ''E probably finks the same about you.'

'Yes – probably,' replied Sylvie, with a sigh. 'But the fact is, we need ter talk. Your dad has – responsibilities, Amy. He can't just run away from them.'

Amy flinched. 'Wot "responsibilities"?'

'That's up ter 'im to tell you,' replied Sylvie. 'That's the only reason why I've come round ter see yer. I want 'im ter tell yer about – 'im an' me. I want him ter be fair an' straight wiv you, wiv yer family, *an'* me. It's somefin' 'e should've done a long time ago.'

Although bursting to know what she was talking about, Amy turned away haughtily, and started to make her way to the front door.

Sylvie stopped her by calling, 'I've 'eard so much about you, Amy.'

Amy didn't turn.

'I've 'eard 'ow yer've been a tower of strength to yer family, 'ow yer've looked after them since yer mum went away.'

Amy stopped dead and swung round. 'Wot I do for my family is none of your business, Mrs Temple! You're a divorced woman. You gave up your rights to a family a long time ago.'

Sylvie felt stung. 'That's not only a cruel fing ter say, Amy,' she said, 'but it's also not true. I 'ave every right to a family, just like anyone else, just like – your mum.'

Amy turned, and made for the door.

'No, Amy!' pleaded Sylvie. 'Please don't go. Please let's talk, let's at least try ter get ter know each uvver.'

Amy already had the key in the lock. 'I don't *want* ter get ter know you, Mrs Temple,' she called over her shoulder. 'I only talk ter people who don't go round breakin' up uvver people's lives.'

'Then yer 'ave a lot ter learn, Amy,' said Sylvie. 'If you're not prepared ter listen, there won't be many people left ter talk to.'

Amy ignored her, went into the house, and slammed the front door behind her.

The first thing Aggs saw when she opened her eyes were two dark figures. She couldn't tell who they were because she felt so weak from the blows she had received to her face and her stomach. Her entire body ached from head to toe, and even if she wanted to, the way she felt at the moment, there was no way she was going to try. Nervous that the two figures crouched over her might be the thugs who had attacked her, she quickly closed her eyes again, and listened. Only when she heard the familiar voice of The Kid talking to old Scrounger did she feel confident enough to open them again.

'Wos goin' on?' she croaked.

The Kid immediately drew closer. 'Ma!' he called softly. ''Ow yer doin' then, mate?'

Aggs swallowed hard, then responded with, 'Feel like doin' a tango!'

Both The Kid and Scrounger laughed with relief. 'I've got Scrounger 'ere, Ma,' The Kid said.

'Now I feel worse!' came her reply.

The Kid laughed and Scrounger snorted.

'Looks like someone don't like yer very much, Aggs,' sniffed Scrounger, mischievously. 'Wot yer bin up to then?'

'You tell me!' replied Aggs.

She struggled to sit up, so The Kid helped her. Only then did she realise that she had been leaning her head on her own bundle, back in her pad down by the boathouse.

'Yer've got a real shiner, Ma,' said The Kid. 'They roughed yer up good an' proper. I fink we oughta get yer down the 'ospital.'

Aggs sat bolt upright. 'You're not takin' me ter no 'ospital!' she growled, angrily. 'If yer do, I'll tell 'em you was the one that did me over!'

The Kid smiled. Despite the pain and discomfort she must be in, he thought, she was clearly back on form. 'I warned yer about this, Ma,' he said quietly, at her side. 'I did warn yer. Those two shits've bin followin' yer fer days. I tried ter tell yer, but you're so bleedin' obstinate.'

Aggs tried to move her jaw, but it hurt. She also felt a huge swelling on her left cheek. 'I'll get Ratner fer this,' she said, fiercely. 'I'll 'ave 'is bleedin' guts fer garters!'

'Leave 'im ter the flatties, Ma,' advised The Kid. 'They've still got their eyes on 'im. They won't let 'im go just like that. They won't rest till they get their pig back – dead *or* alive!'

'I always knew yer'd catch it one of these days, Aggs,' said Scrounger. He knew he would be provoking her, so he moved back, and kept his distance. 'Yer should pack up and git yerself back 'ome. The park's no place fer gels.'

'It's no place fer stupid old gits like you, eivver!' snapped Aggs, ungratefully.

Scrounger was hurt by her remark. 'Fanks a lot,' he sniffed indignantly. 'The next time yer get done over, don't ask me ter come runnin'.'

Aggs watched him slowly disappear into the dark. For one rare moment, she actually regretted what she had said to him. But she was suddenly distracted by a pungent smell.

'Come on, Ma,' said The Kid, holding a miniature bottle of brandy under her nostrils. ''Ave a swig er this, gel. It'll get yer blood workin' again.'

Aggs hated spirits, but her head was thumping, so she reluctantly took a sip. 'Bin nickin' again, 'ave yer?' she asked.

'Needs must,' replied The Kid, with a knowing chuckle.

For the next few moments they sat there, staring out at the cold calm waters of the lake, the reflection of the crescent-shaped moon shimmering across the surface as a slight, icy breeze occasionally drifted in from the south side of the park. They were both miles away, living in worlds far apart, but close in spirit, closer than they could ever realise, Aggs washing little Amy in a large enamel bowl when she was just a few months old, The Kid sharing a fag with his mates on the beach at Dunkirk just prior to being rescued by a flotilla of small civilian boats from England. In their individual ways, they were tormented souls, both on the run, both trying hard not to look back, but never quite succeeding. Neither knew what they were searching for, neither knew how they were going to untangle the mess they had got themselves into. But they both possessed one saving grace: the need to be wanted.

''E's right, Ma.'

The Kid's voice immediately brought Aggs back to reality.

'Old Scrounger,' he continued. ''E's not such an ol' fool as 'e looks.' He turned round to face her in the dark. 'This is no place fer someone like you. Yer really should go 'ome.'

'This *is* my 'ome,' she replied, unconvincingly. 'This is where I am, an' this is where I stay.'

She couldn't see him, but he was slowly shaking his head. 'Some people was born inter this kind of life, Ma. But not you. You was born to care fer people, for yer kids, for yer family, for yer ol' man.'

Aggs tried to object, but he stopped her.

'No, Ma,' he continued. 'It's time yer faced up to yerself, faced up ter the truth. You know as well as I do, what you're doin' out 'ere don't come natural to yer. You've got ter be true to yerself. You're somebody's mum, in every kind of way.'

Aggs didn't snap back, for her thoughts were too preoccupied mulling over what he had said. She eventually responded, 'An' wot about you? If you know so much, 'ow come *you're* still out 'ere?'

'Me?' The Kid smiled to himself. 'No, Ma,' he said wryly. 'I won't go 'ome. Not now. Not never.' Then, with no trace of self-pity, he added, 'After all, yer can't get blood out of a stone. If someone don't ever bovver ter find out wevver you're dead or alive, wot's the point?'

CHAPTER 17

Uncle Jim was in a dilemma. For over a year now he had kept Aggs's secret of her whereabouts, and because of his devoted loyalty to her, he had not revealed to the rest of the family that she was alive, nor that he was in contact with her. But things were now different. During the past few weeks Ernie had set about becoming the father to his family that he had never been. Whatever it was that had happened to him in hospital on the night Aggs visited him, it was now obvious to Jim that Ernie Dodds was a changed man. For the first time in his life, Ernie was actually spending time with his family, helping Amy to prepare meals for them, chatting to them, and, when he was not on duty at the post office, even picking them up from school. For Jim, however, the real change was in the way Ernie had been developing a close personal relationship with each individual member of his family. It seemed incredible that in so short a time Arnold had come to adore his dad, so much so that he actually went looking for him when he wasn't around. Elsie too was showing signs of being tamed; she wasn't nearly so lippy these days, even if she did still have a mind of her own. But it was with Thelma that Jim had seen the greatest change, for on the night she came home in tears from her wild day out with a serviceman up at Chapel Market, it had been Ernie who had taken on the responsibility of talking to her about the dangers of growing up before her time. There was no flaming row, no shouting or hollering, just a plain, homely chat about the difficulties of being a girl of her age during wartime. Thelma had never been shown this kind of attention before, not even by her mum, but it helped. In some quite extraordinary way, it helped her not only to cope with her own boredom, but also to know that she was cared for.

Jim watched all these developments with intense interest, and he agonised over whether he had the right to keep the family from their own mother. His divided loyalties had given him many sleepless nights, and he knew this was a situation that couldn't go on for ever. With this in mind, he resolved to tell Amy where to find her mum. The only question was how and when.

His first opportunity came early one evening when, coming down the stairs on his way out to go to work, he overheard a tense but intimate conversation between Amy and her dad in the front parlour. Jim had always been a bit of an old eavesdropper, so when he heard Amy say, 'I saw that woman the uvver day. 'Er at the baths,' he stopped dead in the passage outside and listened.

There was no response from Ernie, so Amy asked, 'Are yer still seein' 'er, Dad?'

'Please, Ame,' said Ernie, clearly ill at ease, 'I don't want to talk about it.'

'Yer've got to sooner or later,' persisted Amy. 'Fings are never goin' ter get better till yer do.'

Ernie hesitated before replying. 'Much as I love yer, Ame,' he said, 'there are some fings I can't discuss wiv yer.'

'She was waitin' outside fer me the uvver night, when I come 'ome from work.'

When Jim in the passage outside heard Amy say that, he could almost *see* the shocked expression on Ernie's face. 'Wot're yer talkin' about?' Ernie asked.

'She wanted ter talk ter me. About you, about you and 'er. She said somefin' about you 'avin responsibilities towards 'er. I asked 'er wot she meant, but she said the only person who can tell me that is you.'

Ernie went silent again. But Amy was not prepared to let the subject drop. 'Yer know, Dad,' she continued, 'this family's gone frough a hell of a lot since Mum left 'ome. None of us were ever told that she was ill – mentally ill, I mean. None of us knew wot 'appened between you an' 'er, an' *why* it 'appened. This is somefin' you owe ter us, ter all of us. There should never be any secrets between people who love each uvver.'

Jim's ear was now flat against the passage side of the door. Ernie's mind was clearly in a state of absolute turmoil, and he was unable to answer until after a lengthy silence.

'It 'appened a long time ago,' he said, his voice barely audible. 'I first met Sylvie – Mrs Temple – when she got her job at the barf'ouse. She was a real good-looker, an' I s'ppose I just took a shine to 'er.'

Amy broke in. 'More like *she* took a shine ter you?'

'No, Ame,' said Ernie, frankly. 'It wasn't like that. It wasn't like that at all. As a matter of fact, she was walkin' out wiv someone else at the time, an' she 'ardly noticed me. But I wanted 'er. I wanted 'er bad.'

Outside, Jim could hear Amy groan, 'Oh, Dad . . . !'

'I know, Ame,' said Ernie, his voice full of remorse and

guilt. 'I do know wot yer must fink of me. But when somefin' like that 'appens to yer, believe me, yer just can't 'elp yerself.'

'But you was a married man. Din't yer care about Mum?'

'Yes, Ame. I *did* care about Mum. In fact I've never stopped carin' about 'er.'

'But did yer stop – *lovin'* 'er?'

Ernie paused. 'No, Ame,' he replied. 'I've never stopped lovin' yer mum.'

'Then – why?'

In the passage outside, Jim could hear Ernie striking a match to light his fag end.

'When somefin' like this 'appens, Ame,' said Ernie, 'when someone lights a match an' burns yer up inside, yer never stop ter ask why. It's a case of do first, then fink later. That's 'ow it was wiv me. I couldn't see furver than the nose on me face.'

After a silence that to Jim seemed an eternity, Amy asked, 'Is this the reason why Mum went away? Was it becos yer told 'er about you an' – this woman?'

Ernie sighed. 'Yer mum knew what was goin' on a long time ago, before Elsie was born. I told 'er it was all over, that I wasn't goin' ter see Sylvie again. For a time, I fawt she believed me, but then she started drinkin' an' goin' ter pieces. We never stopped rowin' an' quarrellin'. You 'eard us, you knew wot was goin' on. You all knew. There was nuffin' I could say to 'er, nuffin' I could do ter make 'er believe me.'

'Then why didn't she?'

There was another long pause. ''Cos I was lyin' to 'er.'

In the passage outside, Jim felt his whole body tense.

'Yer – lied?' asked Amy, who was doing her best to contain the distress she felt. 'Yer was still carryin' on?'

Ernie hesitated. For him, this was the worst part. 'It was more than that, Ame,' he replied. 'The day before yer mum went off, she found out somefin' which I'd tried ter keep from 'er since before Thelma was born. It's me own fault. At the time, I 'adn't given 'er any cash terwards the rent, so when I was out she went thru my trouser pockets in the wardrobe, looking fer some loose change. She found this letter. It was from Sylvie, askin' fer some back payments.'

Amy was puzzled. 'Back payments?'

Ernie hesitated before answering. This was going to be the most painful admission in his entire life. 'For the upkeep of 'er son, Ame – 'er son, an' mine.'

Amy walked the streets for what seemed like hours. It was, in fact only twenty minutes or so, but she had to do it, she had to be alone, she had to try to come to terms with what had been one of the most traumatic evenings of her life. Her mind was in absolute turmoil, dominated by the realisation that she had a fifteen-year-old half-brother, named Joe, conceived by her own dad and a woman that she couldn't bear. She wandered aimlessly, in a daze, unaware of which street she had turned into, or in which direction she was heading. At her every step, all she could see along the darkened pavements was the expression on her dad's face at the moment when he had told her how he had lied to her mum for all those years. How could he do it? she asked herself over and over again. How could he keep a secret so dark from his own wife for fourteen whole years? How could he have lived such a lie for so long?

She crept into bed just after midnight. Thelma and little Elsie were asleep, and both they and Arnold were on Amy's mind. How would she tell *them* that they had a half-brother?

How would she explain that their dad had deceived them all for so many years, and that the bulk of his earnings that should have been spent on keeping his own family going, was being spent on someone they didn't even know? The very thought of what her dad had done filled her with a mixture of revulsion and sympathy. She found it hard to believe that he could have done such a thing, hard to believe that he could have lived such a lie for so many years. And then she thought about her mum.

Lying there in the dark, she turned on one side, and closed her eyes. But there was very little chance of sleep; her mum was too close for that. She could see the poor woman over the years, washing and scrubbing the floors, getting the kids ready for school, queuing up for meat at Dorners the butchers, cooking their meals, work, work, work. And she could picture what her mum's face looked like on the night she was told that the man she had been married to for so many years had given another woman a child. As she lay there, tears began to well in her closed eyes. She felt she was a child again. She wanted her mum. She wanted her so desperately. She wanted to tell her that, however much she had been deceived by Ernie Dodds, she, Amy, still loved her, would always, always, always love her. 'Where are yer, Mum?' she asked, over and over again. 'Dear God, bring her back home. Tell her it's all right. Tell her, tell her . . .'

Dissolving into tears, Amy suddenly felt someone creep into bed beside her. Then a thin, scrawny arm wrapped itself round her waist, and hugged her. 'Don't cry, Ame,' said Thelma, gently. 'Yer don't 'ave ter worry. We heard. We know.'

As Amy turned on to her back, someone else squeezed into the bed beside her. 'Don't cry, Ame,' said little Elsie, also wrapping her arm round her big sister. 'I promise I won't give yer any more trouble – 'onest!'

Aggs shuffled her way across the park, heading out towards Marble Arch. As she went, the park's early crop of daffodils, practically the only flowers to survive the wartime rape of the flowerbeds, swayed in a gentle breeze, their golden petals smiling up mischievously at the bright midday sun. Although Aggs had always considered daffodils her favourite flowers, today she hardly noticed them. She had important things to do.

The traffic at Marble Arch was quite busy, and the queue outside the Regal Cinema to see the day's early showing of Tyrone Power and Betty Grable in *A Yank In The RAF* stretched from the Oxford Street entrance right round the corner into Cumberland Place. Along Edgware Road, Aggs took a passing glance at each litter bin, just in case there was anything worth taking, and if there wasn't, watched by bemused passers-by, she grunted her disapproval, and shuffled on. She wasn't at all concerned that the beating-up she had received at the hands of Ratner's henchmen several nights before had left her face bruised, cut and battered.

Earlier that morning, she'd woken with a thick head, partly because she'd been on the binge with a bottle of stout the night before, but mostly because of Ernie Dodds. All night long she had dreamed about him – him and the brat he'd brought into the world. Ever since he had told her about the secret he'd kept from her all those years, she had often imagined what his bastard offspring looked like, but, for some unknown reason, last night, at least three different versions had appeared to her. The first one looked like that slut Ernie had opened up, the second looked like a cut-down Ernie himself, complete with a fag end behind his ear, but the third – the third one had worried her, because in some extraordinary kind of way, it resembled Amy. The thought repulsed her so much that she forced herself to wake up and pull herself together.

Trundling across the wet grass had left her plimsolls even muddier than usual, and by the time she had reached the park police station, her threadbare socks were soaking wet. As her visit was no more than a courtesy call, once she had made quite sure that her Missing Persons picture was not adorning the walls, she stayed only a few minutes. Just enough time, in fact, to have a little chat with Sid and Roy, her two special constable mates. That was The Kid's idea. He had put her up to it.

Once she had turned the corner into Praed Street, it didn't take her very long to reach The Turks' Head. As it was nearly one o'clock, the Public Bar was, as usual, crammed with all the rough and tough of Paddington. Aggs was pleased about that. She wanted to make sure that her performance was going to be appreciated by as many of Charlie Ratner's pals as possible.

When Aggs suddenly appeared, Ratner himself was at the counter, drawing up some draught bitter into a pint glass. As soon as he saw her approaching, his face lit up into a broad smirk.

'Well, well,' he called loudly for the amusement of his customers. 'An' wot do we owe for the 'onour of *your* company – madam?'

Aggs grinned back, but more to herself than to him. 'Missed me, 'ave yer, boss?'

'Understatement of the year, my good woman!'

Aggs waited for the roars of laughter around her to die down, then said, 'I've missed you too. But at least I 'ad a couple of your mates ter keep me company. Din't I?'

Ratner's smile became fixed, his eyes quickly darting back and forth discreetly to his customers. At the same time, his daughter, Maureen, came out from behind the curtain masking the back yard door.

'I just came ter fank yer fer the message yer sent me,' Aggs continued, her voice also intended for the customers around her, having brought the place to a rare moment of silence. 'But I can assure yer, it wasn't necessary. Yer see, my mates over the yard – you know, the one in the park – they said they'd be prepared to listen ter anyfin' I 'ad ter tell 'em. So I did.'

'Ma!' called Ratner's girl. 'Don't! I beg yer!'

Aggs refused to respond to Maureen's pleas.

Ratner was feeling uncomfortable. 'OK, everyone!' he bellowed. 'Entertainment's over!'

'Not quite!' bellowed Aggs, overriding him.

The bar remained silent and tense.

'The fing is, Mr Ratner, sir,' continued Aggs, beginning to enjoy herself, 'my mates, the flatties, 'ave taken a very great int'rest in you. It seems they've lost somefin' that belongs ter them, somefin' they miss a great deal.'

Ratner was glaring hard at her.

Provoking him even more, Aggs picked up the pint glass of bitter he had just drawn and took a gulp of it. He made as if to go for her, but his daughter prevented him.

'Pigs!' scowled Aggs, a rim of foam around her lips. 'Can't bear 'em meself. Nasty, smelly fings.' She flicked Ratner a sly look. 'Still, the flatties like 'em, that's fer sure. They don't take kindly to arse'oles who nick 'em from their own personal sty!'

There was an immediate rumble of concern from around the bar. But Ratner remained impassive.

'Fact is, boss,' continued Aggs, 'if it 'adn't've bin for your "message", I'd never've opened my gob – about wot I saw that time – in that backyard hut of yours.'

More excited rumbles of shock from the customers.

'Sorry, Ma,' Ratner said, finally ending his silence. 'I can't fink wot you're talkin' about.'

Aggs smiled. 'No, I don't expect you can, Mr Ratner.'

Determined to regain the initiative, Ratner snatched the glass of bitter back from Aggs, and poured it down the sink behind his counter. 'Bluff can get folk inter trouble, yer know,' he said menacingly, but with an ingratiating smile. ''Speshully dangerous bluff.'

Aggs smiled back at him. 'You wouldn't know bluff from a monkey's arse!' she taunted.

There was laughter and uproar in the bar. But the rumpus disappeared immediately at the sound of a police car skidding to a halt outside the front entrance of the pub.

'Wot's that?' someone called out in panic.

'Wos goin' on?' called another.

'Don't fret yerselves!' said Aggs. 'It's only some mates of mine. It's only a bit of bluff!'

A few moments later, Ratner was taken into custody, and led out of the pub by Aggs's two special constable mates, Sid and Roy. As he went, she called, 'The next time yer want ter get a message to me, boss, make sure yer send it by post!'

* * *

That night, Uncle Jim must have sorted through nearly one thousand letters. Despite the war – or maybe because of it – people wrote to each other more than ever – servicemen sending as much news as their censored airmail photo-letters permitted; elderly correspondents worried about their relatives living in dangerous air-raid-prone cities. But tonight, Jim was not concentrating too much on his job at the sorting office, for during the past twenty-four hours he had been turning over in his mind what to do about the Dodds family.

Although feeling guilty about listening in to the intimate conversation between Amy and her dad a couple of nights before, what he had heard had convinced him that there was now a genuine desire on Ernie's part to bring his family back together again. The trouble, however, was still Aggs herself. After the indifferent way in which she had treated him on his last few visits to her, Jim was not sure how he would convince her that Ernie really did want her back, and that, in Jim's own opinion, it definitely *would* be possible for them to make a fresh start in their marriage. Anyone could tell that it wasn't going to be easy, not with an illegitimate fifteen-year-old boy to contend with.

Jim left the sorting office in Bovay Place shortly before five in the morning. By then, most of the letters and parcels had been assigned their various collection points, and within hours would be delivered to their destinations. Although it was still bitterly cold outside, Jim could sense the oncoming signs of spring. He didn't exactly know why, for he was wrapped up so warm he looked like an Eskimo. But somehow, there was hope in the air, a feeling that perhaps warm days and nights were not too far away after all.

During the few minutes he took to get home, he wrestled

with all kinds of options about how he would eventually tell Amy where to find her mother. But when he sized up every aspect of the situation, he had to accept that once he had told her, nothing could ever be the same between him and the Dodds family again. After all, if they had been deceived by their father, then they had also been deceived by him, Jim Gibbons. Only now did he realise that he had been wrong to keep Aggs's secret, for, in protecting her, he had also prevented her from getting the medical attention she so clearly required.

By the time he reached the front yard gate of number 16 Enkel Street, he had convinced himself to say absolutely nothing, and let the family sort out their own monumental problems. Even so, he still had his doubts.

It was just as difficult to open that damned front door as it was to open the creaking old gate. Number 16 was not a place that could be entered without waking the entire household. But he went in as quietly as he could. As usual, the moment he had closed the front door behind him, he turned on his Post Office torch he always used in the blackout, then removed his shoes and started to carry them up the stairs. But he was suddenly taken off guard by Ernie calling to him from the back parlour.

'In 'ere, Jim.'

The place was in complete darkness, but when he directed his torch on to the parlour door, he found it half open.

Inside the parlour, he picked out Ernie in the torch beam, sitting alone in front of the dying coke embers of the oven range.

'Ern!' Jim whispered, as softly as he could. 'What are you doing up at this hour? Can't you sleep?'

Ernie squinted at him in the torchlight. 'Where is she, Jim?'

he asked, his voice cracking and his eyes red from lack of sleep. ''Ow many times do I 'ave ter ask yer? 'Ow many times do I 'ave ter beg yer ter 'elp me get Aggs back? I can't go on like this much longer, Jim. It's tearin' me apart, d'yer 'ear. It's tearin' me apart . . .'

CHAPTER 18

Hilda's big day was approaching fast. In fact she was in such a tizzy about it that in recent days, whilst collecting dirty dishes in the main restaurant, she had dropped three plates to the floor and broken them. Fortunately, an understanding Lyons management hadn't taken the cost of the plates out of her wages, but one of the head waiters did give her a warning that she must not let her personal life interfere with her work.

The better Amy got to know Hilda's future husband, the better she liked him. Harry Smethurst was much more down to earth than most of the army officers she'd waited on at table in her time. Despite his public school accent, in her eyes he was just 'one of the boys', which meant that he could mix with anyone, no matter what their class. That certainly included Amy, and every time she met him, she was not only completely bowled over by how warm and friendly he was to her, but how genuinely concerned he was with all the traumatic things that were happening in her life. He was also extremely good-looking, the archetypal rugged, blue-eyed blond, and although he wasn't her type, she could see why her best mate had fallen for him on sight.

However, as the big day drew closer, Amy started to get worried about some of the questions Hilda was asking, such as, 'Amy, d'you believe in sex before marriage?'

The two girls were serving lunch in private upper-floor rooms at the time, and when they met fleetingly with their trays in the corridor outside, Amy was totally nonplussed to be asked something so intimate. "Ild!' she protested, voice lowered to a shocked hush in case they were being overheard. 'Yer shouldn't say such fings!'

'Why not?' asked Hilda, puzzled by her friend's response. 'There's nothing wrong with sex. It's part of nature.'

Amy was having palpitations. 'Stop it, 'Ild!' she hissed, acutely embarrassed.

They went off with their customers' orders into adjoining rooms. When they both reappeared, Hilda said, 'I'm giving it serious thought.'

'Wot?' asked Amy, puzzled.

'Sex,' replied Hilda. 'I think I should sleep with Harry before we get married next week.'

"Ild!' Amy nearly had a fit.

'Oh, don't be so old-fashioned, Amy!' scolded Hilda. 'I mean, what's the difference between now, and sleeping with a man only when you've got a ring and a piece of paper in your hand? If you love each other, you should grab the moment.'

Amy took another quick look around to see that nobody was coming. 'Marriage ain't just about a ring an' a piece of paper, 'Ild,' she said, voice as low as she could manage. 'It's about *till death do us part*.'

At the mention of Amy's familiar quotation from the wedding vows, Hilda's mood changed. 'I know,' she replied, for the first time serious. 'That's what I'm thinking about.'

Amy was puzzled.

'Harry's a soldier, Amy,' said Hilda. 'Every time I say goodbye to him, I never know if I'll ever see him again. This bloody war has no respect for marriage.'

Only then did Amy realise how insensitive she's been. 'But – if yer did it –' she said, fumbling awkwardly for words – 'I mean, if yer did it – before yer got married – wot would yer do if—'

'If I got pregnant?' asked Hilda, completing the question for Amy. She smiled inwardly. 'I'd be a proud woman,' she replied. 'Anyway,' she continued, brightening up again, 'what about you? I bet you've done it with that boy of yours.'

Amy was outraged. 'I have *not*!' she asserted, firmly.

'But I thought you told me you loved him?'

'I do.'

'Then what's the problem?'

Amy sighed and steeled herself. 'You'd know the problem, 'Ilda,' she replied, 'if yer came from a family like mine.'

Remembering what Amy had just been told by her dad, Hilda could have bitten off her tongue. But before she had the chance to put things right, they were both distracted by Bertha Willets, who suddenly came rushing down the corridor in tears.

'Hope you're satisfied!' she sobbed, as she reached the two girls.

Amy and Hilda exchanged puzzled but wary looks.

'What are you talking about, darling?' Hilda asked, with little or no interest.

Bertha nodded directly towards Amy. 'Ask 'er!' she bellowed contemptuously, abandoning any trace of her assumed posh accent. 'Got wot yer asked for, din't yer? Got wot I deserved – is that it? Is it?'

271

Amy growled back at her. 'I 'aven't the foggiest wot you're goin' on about!'

'Oh no,' sneered Bertha. 'Of course yer 'aven't. Butter wouldn't melt in that pretty, spiteful little mouf – would it?'

'Stop it!' snapped Hilda, angrily. 'Now just calm down and tell us what this is all about.

'*She* knows!' sobbed Bertha, one finger pointing straight at Amy. 'Madam 'ere's got me the push, ain't she? Opened 'er big mouf an' got me the boot. Couldn't wait, could yer? Couldn't wait ter get yer own back. Cow! That's wot yer are – a vicious, mean-minded cow!'

Hilda slapped Bertha's face.

Bertha shrieked.

'Now pull yourself together, you stupid girl!' barked Hilda, grabbing hold of the girl's shoulders and shaking her.

The rumpus brought both customers and staff rushing into the corridor.

Bertha was crying profusely, and Amy tried to pacify her. 'Berfa, listen ter me,' she said calmly. 'Just tell me wot this is all about. *Who* gave yer the push?'

Bertha wiped her streaming nose on the back of her hand. 'Ask your mate down in Admin,' she sobbed. 'She won't 'ear a word against you – oh no! Little Miss Bright Eyes, ain't yer? Teacher's pet! Go on – ask 'er! She'll tell yer *all* yer want ter know!'

Miss Fullerton was at her desk when Amy knocked on her door. It had been a wretched morning for the poor woman, what with a disagreement with Mr Pearson about the change in the staff roster, followed by a complaint from a regular Lyons customer about dirty linen on her table, and to cap it all, the unpleasant task of having to dismiss Bertha Willets for spreading scurrilous rumours about another member of the nippy staff. She'd put it off, tried to avoid making the decision, but knew it was her duty and responsibility to sack the girl immediately.

'Come in!' she called out wearily, towards the door.

Amy entered. 'Can I see yer fer a moment, please, miss?' she asked.

Miss Fullerton got up immediately to greet her. 'Of course, my dear. Come and sit down. What can I do for you?'

Amy remained standing. 'It's about Berfa Willets.'

Miss Fullerton's smile dissolved into a false expression of sadness. 'Yes,' she sighed, lowering herself into her chair again. 'Such a foolish girl.'

Amy came forward to the desk. As she did so, she sensed a faint smell of brandy. 'Is it true yer sacked 'er?' she asked.

Miss Fullerton nodded slowly. 'I'm afraid there could be no other decision. Lying about fellow members of the staff is not something we can take lightly.'

'But she din't mean it,' insisted Amy, her body pressed against the edge of the desk. 'Berfa's a stupid person, really stupid, but it isn't right ter punish 'er just fer that.'

'Isn't right?' asked Miss Fullerton, taking off her spectacles and staring at Amy in astonishment. 'Do you realise that girl accused you of something quite outrageous? She has a thoroughly nasty mind. She could have ruined your entire future at this Corner House.'

'Everyone makes mistakes, miss,' said Amy, fervently. 'Berfa's trouble is she's all wind and no sails. She finks everyone's out to do one on 'er.'

'Her trouble is that she's a troublemaker.'

Amy shook her head. 'No, miss,' she said. 'She's afraid.'

'Afraid? Afraid of what?'

'Of not bein' noticed. That's why she tried ter do the dirt on me. She fawt I was some kind of threat. I've met a lot of people like 'er in my time. The only way they can draw attention ter themselves is ter make trouble.' Amy leaned both hands on the edge of the desk. 'I'd be really grateful if yer could overlook wot she's done.'

'Overlook?' Miss Fullerton put on her spectacles again, focusing more closely on Amy. 'My dear child, how can you possibly ask that after what she's done to you?'

'Becos Berfa needs anuvver chance,' replied Amy. 'If I can fergive 'er, I fink you should too.'

Miss Fullerton sat back in her chair. 'You know, Amy,' she said, after a pause, 'there are times when you amaze me. Why should you care a fig about what happens to a girl who falsely accused you of the most terrible things, who set out to destroy the excellent reputation you have with all of us?'

Amy thought about this for a moment, then replied, 'Becos I feel sorry for 'er.'

Miss Fullerton started to tap her fingernails on the top of her desk, the first sign that she was becoming irritated. 'I'm sorry too, Amy,' she said. 'Trust is important to me, to every member of the staff. If we can't trust the people we work with, life for us – and our customers – becomes intolerable.'

Amy stood her ground. 'Berfa won't do it again,' she said. 'I know she won't.'

'*How* do you know?'

'Becos she's learned 'er lesson. That's why I fink you should give 'er anuvver chance. Give 'er a chance to prove it.'

Miss Fullerton shook her head. 'I'm sorry, Amy,' she said.

'If I gave Bertha Willets another chance, I'd be betraying all the other nippies who work with her.'

'But she didn't do it to any of the uvvers,' Amy replied, adamantly. 'She did it ter me. Berfa loves her job 'ere. It's 'er life – probably the only fing in 'er whole life she cares for. I don't want 'er ter be kicked out becos of me. I don't want ter be the one who ruins that life.'

For a brief moment, Miss Fullerton sized her up. Then, with a glimmer of an admiring smile, she eased herself from her chair, and went to Amy. 'You're a good person, Amy,' she said. Then, raising Amy's chin gently with her hand, she stared into her eyes, and said, with a hesitant, intimate smile, 'Your mother was very fortunate to have a daughter like you. But remember – ' with her fingers, she gently traced the line of Amy's fringe – 'I did this for you.'

As Miss Fullerton spoke, Amy could again detect the smell of brandy on the woman's breath. She tactfully eased herself away.

Embarrassed, Miss Fullerton discreetly retreated back behind her desk. 'I'm sorry, Amy,' she said. 'I would be completely out of order if I allowed this girl to remain on the staff, I'm afraid there's no way I can reverse my decision now. She has to go.'

With a pained expression on her face, Amy replied, 'Thank you, miss.' Then she turned, and made for the door. When she got there, however, she stopped and briefly looked back at Miss Fullerton. 'In which case,' she said, formally, 'if Berfa goes, I'll go too.' She turned again, and left the room.

Tim was waiting for Amy outside the entrance of the former Del Monico's hotel, which had been closed down for some time, and now seemed to be undergoing a major reconstruction, to become, it was rumoured, a vast new club for American servicemen. Tim felt that that building, situated on the corner of Shaftesbury Avenue and Piccadilly Circus, was a more discreet place to meet Amy from work, rather than the adjoining Lyons Corner House, mainly because some of the nippies, who knew that he was Amy's boyfriend, giggled as they came out. He never understood why.

When Amy did finally appear, she was in a glum mood. She told Tim that, following her meeting with Miss Fullerton, she had to accept that her so-called career at Lyons was over. But when Tim questioned whether it was wise to sacrifice a good job for somebody who had tried to blacken her name, all she would reply was, 'It's the principle that counts, Tim.'

A little later, they strolled arm in arm towards Piccadilly Circus, which looked quite naked without its much-loved statue, Eros, god of love. As it was now well into blackout time, they had to use their torches to look at the billboards outside the London Pavilion where they were advertising a film of John Steinbeck's famous novel *The Grapes of Wrath*. Tim had set his heart on seeing the film, but with Amy feeling the way she did, they both decided it would be better to go along to the New Gallery Cinema in Regent Street, to see Betty Grable and Carmen Miranda in a happy musical film called *Down Argentine Way*.

They were halfway down Regent Street before they changed their minds again. It was only too clear that Amy was too downcast to take in a picture; all she wanted to do was to take the weight of her feet somewhere, and just be with Tim. Wandering off aimlessly, they eventually found a bench seat down the Mall. It seemed so unnatural to see the place plunged into such pitch darkness, for in peace time this majestic, wide avenue, with at one end Buckingham Palace and at the other Admiralty Arch, was the centrepiece of so many royal ceremonial occasions in London. But this was wartime, and this part of London was, inevitably, a major target for enemy bombers, a fact made acutely aware to Tim when an air raid warden yelled out to him, 'Keep that light down!' Tim obeyed immediately; in such a place, even the flickering beam from a hand torch, carelessly pointing up towards a dark night sky, could be misconstrued as an act of sabotage.

As soon as they had settled down on the bench, Tim undid the buttons of his overcoat, and wrapped half of it round Amy. She responded by snuggling up to him, and leaning her head against his shoulder.

'Oh, Tim,' she sighed, as she felt his arm wind round her shoulders. 'I don't know wot's wrong wiv me these days. When Dad first told me about this half-brother we're s'pposed to 'ave 'ad all these years, I was so angry, I felt like yelling straight into 'is face. But then, when I got ter finkin – it was Mum I was really angry wiv. I said ter meself, "Yes, Ame. It's a terrible fing Dad's done, an' 'e should be ashamed of the way 'e's deceived us all. But in some ways, Mum's just as much ter blame. I mean, I know 'ow she must've felt when Dad told 'er about this kid, but why did she 'ave ter go an' take it out on us – the whole family? It wasn't our fault. We din't know wot was goin' on".'

Tim slid his other arm round her waist, and hugged her to him. He was so aware of the despair she was feeling, her vulnerability, and the struggle she was having within herself. In many ways he felt as though he was living through his own traumatic life all over again – a life where he had no father, only a selfish, domineering mother, who had suppressed him in everything he had ever done. It was no wonder he had grown up to be nervous and unsure of himself.

''Ow could she do it, Tim?'

Tim turned briefly, and kissed her gently on the forehead. 'D-do what, dear?' he murmured, lovingly.

'Go off an' leave 'er kids, leave us to look after ourselves. No matter 'ow she felt, she should've fawt about us.'

Tim could feel the warmth from her body merging with his own. 'When a b-bomb drops,' he said, 'it's n-not always easy to think about anything b-but yourself.'

After a brief silence, Amy continued, 'Mum should come 'ome, Tim. She should come 'ome an' face up ter fings, ter 'elp 'er kids cope wiv the very same fing that sent 'er 'round the bend.' Although she couldn't see him in the dark, she looked up towards his face. 'It ain't easy for us ter be told suddenly that we've got a half-bruvver we don't know anyfin' about. I mean, we don't even know wot 'e looks like.'

'C-can't be easy f-for him, either,' said Tim.

'Who?'

'For your half-brother – Joe.'

Amy was silent again.

Suddenly there was a flurry of activity, as one of the royal cars passed quickly by, flanked on either side by four motorcycle outriders. Although Amy and Tim became just as excited as everyone else, because of the dark, they were unable actually to see whether the occupants of the car were in fact the King and Queen.

Once all the excitement was over, Amy and Tim settled

back together on the bench again. 'Oh Tim,' Amy asked, with a wistful sigh, 'wot *can* I do?'

'About what?' he returned

'About Joe. We can't just ignore 'im as though 'e don't even exist.'

Tim thought about it for a moment. 'I would've thought the least you c-could do,' he said, 'is to meet him.'

Astonished, Amy sat bolt upright. '*Meet* 'im!'

'You'll never find out what he looks like until you do.'

For the first time since they had met, Amy was suddenly irritated with him. 'That's a stupid idea, Tim!' she snapped. ''E's *er* kid! Why should we want ter meet a kid that's come inter this world just becos of my dad's fling?'

Tim hesitated, then answered, 'Because he's part of *your* flesh and blood too, Amy. He's your half-brother – remember?'

It was no secret that Aggs had never much cared for poor old Scrounger. It wasn't just that she found him a nosy old bugger, or that he ponged of stale beer all day and would sooner die than go down the men's toilets in Oxford Street to have a good wash. No. Her problem with him was merely that he was always going on about how healthy he was, and how good he was for his age. It was clearly untrue, of course, for, apart from the fact that his eyesight was so poor he could only see everything by squinting, the skin on his face and hands was loose and shrivelling, his feet were riddled with arthritis, and he had a frequent hacking cough that could be heard on the other side of the park. Aggs had no idea if he *was* good for his age, for he had solidly refused to reveal his years to anyone, but by the looks of him, Aggs was convinced that once his present pair of lice-ridden army surplus socks had worn out, he wouldn't be needing any more. Little did she know that her prediction was in danger of coming true.

'I ain't goin' to no 'ospital, an' that's final!'

Scrounger, stretched out on a park bench, was recovering from what he called one of his usual attacks of indigestion. He was attended on by a group of his parkie mates, who all seemed to be waiting patiently to see if this time he really was going to snuff it.

'Wot's up wiv 'im this time?' growled Aggs, as she pushed her way through the group. 'Stupid ol' sod. Bin stuffin' too much caviar again, 'ave yer?'

Everyone laughed, except Scrounger. He was not amused.

'I ain't goin' ter no 'ospital!' he croaked again, a large dewdrop about to drip from the end of his nose.

''E come down up by the bridge,' said Flapper, who got his nickname because of the size of his ears. 'Pain in 'is chest, an' right down 'is arm.'

Hooter chimed in, 'Couldn't move when I found 'im.' *His* nickname was a reflection of the excessive size of his nose. 'Groanin' like a stuffed bull, 'e was!'

Scrounger swung him a real angry scowl, and repeated adamantly, 'I ain't goin' ter no 'ospital!'

'That's all right, mate,' said Aggs. 'They can take yer ter the mortuary instead. Yer'd look good laid out wiv a dafferdil stuck between yer 'ands!'

To Scrounger's intense irritation, this provoked howls of laughter from the other parkies.

From behind, The Kid whispered into Aggs's ear, 'Can I 'ave a quick word wiv yer, Ma?'

Aggs let him take her to one side, making quite sure that

they couldn't be overheard by the others.

''E's not too good,' said The Kid. 'This time, I fink it's fer real. We've sent fer the ambulance.'

''Ow come?' asked Aggs.

'If yer look at 'is mouf, it's all blue. I saw my grandad like that before 'e died. I reckon 'e's 'ad a bit of an 'eart attack.'

Despite her feelings for Scrounger, Aggs looked grim. 'Well, if that's the case,' she said, 'there's not much we can do.'

''Cept fer one fing.'

Aggs gave him a puzzled look. 'Wot?'

'Wot about 'is family?'

'Family? 'As 'e got one?'

For a few rare moments, The Kid had removed his khaki woollen balaclava. 'No idea. But I did once 'ear 'im say somefin' about 'is daughter.'

'Din't know 'e was married.'

'Nor me. But I fink we ought ter do *somefin'* about it. I mean, if 'e snuffs it, someone'd 'ave ter identify him.'

Aggs sniffed disdainfully. 'I don't see why. If they ain't come lookin' fer 'im before now, 'e'd probably prefer if 'e goes out wivout a name. I know *I* would.'

The Kid lowered his eyes. He wasn't going to say it, but that's how he felt too.

The early morning air was suddenly pierced by the clanging of an ambulance bell.

'I ain't goin' in no ambulance!'

Despite his frailty, Scrounger's voice boomed out in repeated protest.

'Don't worry, Scrounger,' riled Hooter, cradling the old boy's head between his hands. 'It'll be the best ride yer've 'ad since yer slept wiv yer ol' woman!'

'Wot about yer daughter?'

Scrounger turned with a start to see Aggs advancing on him.

'Yer might as well own up, 'cos we all know about 'er,' she growled, bossily. 'Where'd she live?'

Scrounger glared at her, and refused to answer.

Flapper butted in, 'Come on, Scrounger! If you're goin' ter snuff it, 'ow we goin' ter know where ter claim yer fortune?'

The others laughed.

Everyone turned to watch the white-coloured LCC ambulance, as it sped along the park road leading to the Serpentine. The moment it arrived, the driver leaped out, quickly followed by a nurse, who went straight to the group round Scrounger.

'Well now,' she said, immediately kneeling beside the old boy, and taking hold of his wrist, 'and what have you been up to, Dad?'

Scrounger abruptly pulled his hand away, and croaked angrily, 'I ain't your dad, and I ain't goin' ter no 'ospital!'

The nurse smiled. She'd seen it all before. 'What happened?' she asked the others.

Flapper repeated his account. 'Come down by the bridge,' he said. 'Pain in 'is chest, an' right down 'is arm.'

The nurse's smile disappeared. She had noticed the color of Scrounger's lips. 'How are you feeling now?' she asked.

'All the worst fer seein' you!' he growled. The moment he spoke however, a sudden sharp pain in his chest caused him to double up and start fighting for breath.

'Get back!' the nurse demanded with great urgency.

The ambulance driver was there in a flash, handing her a red blanket. With a nod from his companion, he rushed straight back to the ambulance.

By this time, Scrounger was groaning, and there was a nasty crackling sound emanating from his throat.

'Wot is it?' called Hooter.

'Is 'e croakin' it?' asked Flapper.

Aggs exchanged looks of foreboding with The Kid.

Using the palms of both her hands, the nurse was frantically applying pressure to Scrounger's chest in a desperate effort to resuscitate him. 'Somebody give us a hand!' she called to the others, as the driver returned quickly with a stretcher.

Aggs remained motionless as she watched the parkies help the nurse and the driver to get Scrounger on to the stretcher. A few moments later, the old boy was laid out inside the ambulance with an oxygen mask strapped to his face. He was now unconscious.

'Who's coming with him?' called the driver, waiting to close the back doors of the ambulance.

No one volunteered.

The Kid turned to Aggs. The look in her eyes told him what he must do.

A moment later, the ambulance was on its way, emergency bell clanging loudly as it headed off across the park. In the back of the vehicle, doing his best to help Scrounger's desperate struggle to survive, was The Kid.

Grim-faced, Aggs watched them go, convinced that that was the last time she would ever see Scrounger alive.

CHAPTER 19

When Arnold was told that he had a half-brother named Joe, he thought it was the best news he'd ever had. He couldn't remember a time when he didn't have to put up with harassment from Thelma and Elsie, and now there was another boy in the family, there would be no more ganging up on him. Amy had insisted that her dad tell Arnold what the others already knew, about Ernie's 'friendship' with Mrs Temple, and Joe, and the reasons why Mum had so suddenly run off and left them. To Ernie's surprise, Arnold took all this in his stride, at the same time expressing the hope that it wouldn't be too long before he had the chance to meet his half-brother. Ernie balked at the idea; after all these years of successfully keeping the secret of his relationship with Sylvie Temple, he had decided that the two families should be kept apart. However, Arnold had his own ideas about that.

After years of service, Sylvie had given up her job at the Hornsey Road Baths and taken a better-paid position as a lathe worker in a munitions shop up near Highbury, which was closer to the top-floor two-bedroomed flat she shared with Joe. Shrewd and inquisitive as ever, Arnold connived to find out the address of his half-brother, and on Saturday afternoon, he set off to look him up. Unfortunately, just as he was on his way to the bus stop in Holloway Road, three air-raid sirens wailed out from different police stations around the area. Although taken by surprise, Arnold refused to be deterred from his mission, and he ploughed on stoically. After all, since the start of the year there had only been spasmodic air raids on London, and even when they came, they usually turned out to be either a stray enemy raider, or a false alarm. Today, however, Arnold decided quite categorically that it was the latter.

Despite the air-raid alert, Holloway Road was still bristling with Saturday afternoon shoppers. Jones Brothers department store was particularly busy, for their windows were sporting large posters announcing their 'SECOND WARTIME SPRING SALE'. Arnold hurried past, disinterested in such mundane matters, but by the time he had got to the bus stop, he groaned to see the length of the queue, and secretly wished that they would all stay at home. To make matters worse, it started to rain, and as there was never any shelter at the bus stops for the poor traveller, he had to rely on his Pakeman Street school cap for protection. This annoyed him, for he had specially spruced himself up to meet his half-brother, even cleaning his shoes with Cherry Blossom shoe polish, a task practically unheard of at number 16 Enkel Street. But whilst he was waiting in the queue, he at least had time to speculate on, not only what his half-brother, Joe, might look like, but also what kind of person he would turn out to be. Arnold imagined someone who was a cross between his father and Mrs Temple. But he hoped he was more like his father, because Mrs Temple wasn't nearly as nice-looking as his own mum. Several trams, buses and trolley buses arrived full, and it was almost twenty minutes before he was finally able to get on to a 609 trolley bus, whose final destination was Moorgate.

It was only a five- or six-minute journey up to Highbury Corner, but as there were no seats available, Arnold had to stand, which for someone of his height was none too easy, for no one had thought about providing straps that were low enough for an eight-year-old to hold on to. So he just allowed his mind to drift away from his discomfort, and think of nothing else but the great adventure awaiting him. Even if Joe *was* only his half-brother, it was going to be a major event to have an elder brother who would stand up for him against the two monster girls of the family. A big brother of his own! It was almost too wonderful to be true!

When the bus stopped briefly at Drayton Park, most of the passengers got off to go down Holloway Road tube station, just across the road. This left Arnold with a place on the bench seat near the conductor, who had so far been too busy to collect his fare. By the time the bus moved on again, Arnold's heart was already pumping with anticipation, so much so that he didn't notice the bus slowing down as it reached the junction of Holloway and Liverpool Roads. Then, quite by chance, he looked out of the window, where to his horror he saw that everyone in the street had flopped face down on to the pavements.

The bus skidded to an abrupt halt.

'Everyone off!'

The bus conductor's frantic shout brought the few remaining passengers on the lower deck to their feet, followed by a mad scramble as they all tried to get off the bus. Arnold didn't know what was going on. He leaped up from his seat, but got jammed in the rush of people hurrying down the stairs from the upper deck.

Suddenly there came the deafening roar of a plane as it zoomed down from the sky, then a loud explosion on the road nearby, which shook the trolley bus from top to bottom and disconnected its poles from the electric wires overhead. This was followed by the sound of police and ARP whistles piercing the air, and people rushing about all over the place in a panic. Arnold, wedged between the passengers on the bus platform, was now really scared, especially when a stifling pall of thick black smoke forced him back, trapping him and the few remaining passengers on the bus platform.

A few seconds later, the entire trolley bus was engulfed in a wall of flame.

Amy wasn't too worried about Arnold. Even though the boy was only eight years old, he was very responsible, and if he ever found himself caught out in the street during an air raid, he would almost certainly take cover. At least that's what Amy had always told him and his sisters to do; that's what all children were told to do during wartime. In any case, she told herself, this was Saturday afternoon, a time when Arnold loved to go off on his own, either to search through books about reptiles, one of his favourite subjects, in the public library down the road in Manor Gardens, or to go train spotting at Finsbury Park Station, where, with a bunch of other lunatics of his age, he would buy a penny platform ticket and spend hours jotting down the numbers of every train engine that stopped there. Amy had long since accepted that Arnold was a bit of a loner, and if he was caught out in an air raid, she knew that he would be quite sensible and safe.

When the siren wailed out on this particular Saturday

afternoon air raid, the rest of the family went straight down into the Anderson shelter in the back yard. They knew it wouldn't last very long, for these days, if any stray enemy bomber was mad enough to break through the clusters of barrage balloons that filled the skies, it would be only a matter of minutes before it was brought down, either by the army's defence system of anti-aircraft fire, or by one of the determined Spitfire pilots of the RAF.

To pass the time during the unexpected air raid, Ernie read his *Daily Herald*, which carried endless depressing reports about the 'other war', the equally dreadful one raging out in the Far East. Things were not looking good out there, he said to himself, fearing what was happening to the hordes of British soldiers who were being forced to surrender to the invading Japanese marauders in Malaya. Amy spent her time perched on the edge of the lower bunk, sewing one of Elsie's socks on a darning-stool, whilst Thelma and Elsie were left squatting on the top bunk, where they were playing Snap, Elsie's favourite card game.

Amy's attention, however, was not entirely engrossed in Elsie's socks, for, quite out of the blue, she asked, 'Dad, when're we goin' ter meet Joe?'

Ernie, taken completely off guard, abruptly lowered his newspaper. 'Please, Ame,' he replied, with a sigh. He had already had to endure a session with Arnold on the same question, and it was unnerving him. 'Do we 'ave ter talk about that now?'

'Yes, Dad,' replied Amy, looking up from her darning. 'I fink we should.'

They paid little or no attention to the distant sound of fire-engine bells, which indicated that there was trouble somewhere, following the explosion they had heard a short while before.

'We can't go on avoidin' it,' Amy continued, once the frantic sound of fire engines had passed. 'We've all bin talkin' about it. If this boy's our bruvver – even our 'alf-bruvver – we fink we've got a right ter see 'im.'

'Amy's right, Dad,' Thelma chimed in. ''E ought ter get ter know us too.'

'*Snap!*' Elsie used the distraction to plonk her matching card down triumphantly over Thelma's.

Amy put down her darning. 'I can't believe 'e's not curious,' she said. 'I know *I* would be if I was in 'is shoes.'

'*If* 'e's bin told about us,' added Thelma, darkly.

'That's a point,' said Amy. '*Does* 'e know about us, Dad?'

'Ferget about it,' snapped Ernie, fidgeting with his newspaper. 'It ain't goin' ter 'appen – so ferget it!'

In the brief silence that followed, Amy returned to her darning, and Thelma to her card game. Despite Ernie's efforts, however, Amy was determined not to let the subject drop.

'Wot's 'e like, Dad?' she asked, recklessly.

Ernie, immersed behind his newspaper again, pretended he hadn't heard her.

'I mean, yer do see 'im – do yer?'

This time Ernie slammed down the newspaper on to his lap. 'Amy,' he said, forcefully, 'it don't matter wevver I see 'im or not.'

'It does to us,' she replied, with just a flick up of her eyes.

Ernie was getting anxious that he had now got himself into a tight corner. Suddenly aware that Thelma and Elsie had abandoned their card game and were studying him, and that Amy had once again put down her darning, he spluttered,

'Now listen, all of you. Sylvie – Mrs Temple – don't want any of this family ter make contact wiv the boy. D'yer understand?'

'Don't want us?' protested Thelma, in disbelief.

'Wot's *she* got ter do wiv it?' demanded Elsie, pulling an outraged face.

'Remember, Else, Joe's 'er son,' replied Ernie.

Elsie came back quick as a flash, 'An' yor 'is dad – ain't yer?'

Ernie scratched his head in frustration. 'Look,' he said, 'if I took yer along ter see 'im, 'is mum wouldn't even let yer inside the 'ouse.'

'Wot about Joe, Dad?'

Ernie turned back to Amy. She was the one he was going to have the most trouble to convince.

'By my reckonin', 'e must be about fifteen years old. Don't 'e 'ave some say in the matter?'

Ernie sighed deeply. 'It won't work, Ame,' he insisted. 'It just won't work. Sylve's got a mind of 'er own. She'll never let yer meet 'im.'

'I bet she won't stop Arn,' said Elsie.

The others swung her a surprised look.

'Wot d'yer mean, Else?' asked Amy, alarmed.

''E's gone up ter see 'im,' replied Elsie. 'Din't yer know?'

A few moments later, the All Clear sounded, but as the family started to climb out of the shelter, they were startled to hear their next-door neighbours, the Dolly Sisters, calling to them from a first-floor window.

'They've got one down 'Olloway Road!' yelled Doris, waving frantically.

Mabel echoed her, 'Just near Drayton Park! It's terrible!'

'Terrible!' repeated Doris. 'Direct 'it!'

The family were shocked. ''Ave yer 'eard wot's bin 'it?' Amy called.

'They say it's a trolley!' yelled Mabel. 'Set on fire!'

'Burned ter pieces,' added Doris. 'The 'ole bus.'

'Christ!' Ernie said to himself.

'Anyone 'urt?' asked Amy.

'By the sound of fings,' replied Doris, 'it must be bad!'

Having revelled in the drama of being the first to break the news, the two sisters disappeared back inside, slamming down the window behind them.

Amy was first out of the house. Behind her were Ernie, Thelma, and Elsie. Amidst sudden panic, there followed a mad rush to take the shortest cut to Drayton Park via the Hertslet, Tollington, and Holloway Roads. Amy feared the worst. If Elsie was telling the truth, and Arnold was making his way up to Highbury to meet his half-brother, then he would have had to have taken the bus.

A few minutes later Amy was practically running off towards the railway bridge alongside Holloway Road underground station. Her heart was pumping hard when, in the distance, she could see thick palls of smoke spiralling up in the sky from the middle of the road just past Drayton Park. When she finally got to the scene of the incendiary bomb attack, the fire brigade had, mercifully, put out the fire, leaving the bus no more than a black, smouldering metal skeleton. All around the wreck, shopkeepers were using their stirrup pumps to dowse the smaller, subsidiary fires which had been set off by fragments of metal from the Molotov cocktail incendiary bombs, and spread out on the pavements were passers-by who had either been injured by the blast, or were suffering from shock.

Amy began a frantic search for Arnold. However, there seemed to be no one who had any information about who the casualties were, or even where they had been taken. She was in a state of despair and anger until, wandering in and out of the crowd of helpers and onlookers, she suddenly caught a glimpse of a young boy being led across the road by an elderly ARP warden.

'Arn!' she yelled at the top of her voice.

Arnold stopped dead in his tracks, and the moment he saw his sister rushing across to meet him, he broke into a broad smile.

'Arn!' bellowed Amy, as she threw her arms round him in relief. 'Wot the 'ell are yer doin' 'ere? Are yer 'urt? Oh God, Arn, yer scared the livin' daylights out of me . . .'

Arnold gawped at her in astonishment. He couldn't understand why his big sister was in such a state. 'It was t'rrific!' he said, chattering excitedly. 'You should've seen it, Ame. I couldn't see anythin' but fire – fire all round me. I jumped off the bus right through the flames! It was t'rrific!'

Amy's panic suddenly turned to anger. 'Yer stupid little sod!' she snapped, shaking him. 'Where've yer bin, fer chrissake?'

Arnold looked hurt, and pulled away from her. 'What's up?' he gabbled. 'I was only going to see Joe. I've got a right to see my own brother – 'aven't I?'

Behind him stood his dad, who was only now realising that this was a question he could no longer avoid.

The random incendiary bomb attack on the trolley bus, which, miraculously, had resulted in no fatalities, was condemned in the national newspapers as 'a barbarous attack on innocent civilians'. The land and aerial defence system around London was also criticised as being totally inadequate to cope with such stray and isolated attacks. However, whatever the truth of such criticism, the young Luftwaffe rebel pilot, who had perpetrated the trolley bus outrage, paid the penalty for his callousness when his aircraft was brought down by the electric wires of a barrage balloon over Hackney Marshes within minutes of releasing his bombs.

On Sunday, Amy felt absolutely drained by the knowledge that Arnold had been so close to death, and even though the boy had emerged unscathed from the horrifying incident, after her family's all-too-frequent brushes with death, from now on, she was determined never to let them go out on their own again.

The way she was feeling, Amy had no wish to turn up for work. But, following her remark to Miss Fullerton that if Bertha Willets was sacked, she would go too, she arrived for lunch-time service at the Corner House in the knowledge that today would be her last as a West End nippy.

When she went into the changing room, she found the place empty, as most of the other girls had clocked in early, and were already upstairs, preparing the various restaurants for the lunch-time customers. It was unlike Amy to be late; ever since her first day's work at the tea shop in Holloway Road, she had been conscientious about punctuality. But today was different. By the end of the day, she would be out of a job, and after all she had gone through during the past twenty-four hours, she felt that Lyons could afford to allow her to be just a few minutes late.

Amy was just slipping into her nippy's dress when she

heard the door open and close behind her. It took a moment for her to see who had come in, for her dress had got stuck over her head, and it was a bit of a struggle to squeeze through. When she did finally succeed, she was surprised to find Bertha Willets there, standing with her back to the door, just watching her. Amy ignored her, and carried on dressing. The way she felt, she had no stomach for a row with anyone on her final day of work.

'Amy.'

Amy looked up. Bertha had come over to her. 'Wot?' she asked, brusquely.

To her astonishment, Bertha's hand was held out to her.

Amy looked suspiciously first at the hand, then directly at Bertha herself.

Bertha's face was pallid and expressionless. 'I want ter fank you,' she said, with difficulty.

Amy was puzzled.

'I heard wot yer said ter Miss Fullerton. She told me 'ow you'd stood up fer me.'

Amy stiffened. 'She 'ad no right—'

'She's given me back me job,' Bertha said, adding caustically, 'real teacher's pet, ain't yer?'

Amy's expression hardened. 'I don't know wot you're talkin' about.'

Bertha grinned knowingly. 'No – course not,' she said. 'Anyway, fanks.' She was still holding out her hand to Amy.

Amy hesitated before reluctantly taking it.

'I've bin a silly cow,' Bertha said, finding it hard to swallow her pride. 'I'm sorry fer wot I did to yer.'

'Yer don't 'ave ter apologise, Bertha,' Amy said. 'These fings 'appen.'

Bertha made a half-hearted attempt to smile. But this was never easy for her. 'Yer see, all me life I've bin so scared,' she said awkwardly. 'Scared of my mum, my dad, you – everyone. I've always fawt of people as a kind of – threat – as though they wanted ter do the dirt on me or somefin'. I don't know why. Maybe it's 'cos I don't really like meself. When I come ter fink about it, I don't fink I ever have.'

Amy smiled tenderly at her. 'It's over now, Bertha,' she repeated. 'Time to ferget.'

'Oh, I won't ferget,' replied Bertha. 'You're the only person in the world who's ever stood up fer me. No, I won't ferget.'

Amy's resistance waned. She smiled comfortingly, went to Bertha and gently hugged her. 'Time ter move on,' she said softly.

The door opened. It was Hilda. 'My goodness!' she said brightly, mischievously. 'Hope I haven't interrupted anything!'

Embarrassed, Bertha quickly left the room. Once she'd gone, Amy said, 'She's got 'er job back.'

'Yes, so I've heard,' said Hilda, acidly. 'It's more than she deserves. I've always said you're a saint!' Then she quickly changed the subject. 'Oh, Amy, I've got some wonderful news! Harry's taking me to the Café de Paris.'

Amy's face at last lit up. 'Oh, 'Ild,' she replied, excitedly, 'that's t'rrific! I'm so 'appy for yer.'

'But that's not all!' returned Hilda, taking hold of Amy's hands. 'He's going to take you too – you and Tim.'

Amy nearly had a fit. 'Wot!'

'Oh, it was *his* idea – not mine. He's so thoughtful. He knows how much you mean to me. Anyway, he's booked a table for the night before the wedding. Normally the bride and groom shouldn't meet until the actual day they get married, but – phooey, who cares! Oh, Amy, it'll be so wonderful, so utterly divine!'

Amy gently eased Hilda away and stared at her in horror. ''Ild!' she gasped. 'I can't go ter no posh place like that. It's a night club. All the toffs 'ang out there.'

'Amy Dodds!' chided Hilda. 'You may not believe it, but you're a toff too! So is Tim. It'll be wonderful. It'll make that awful mother of his absolutely livid with envy!'

Amy was frantically shaking her head. 'No, no, no, 'Ild!' she insisted. 'I can't go, I just can't! Besides, yer need a long dress fer a place like that.'

Hilda raised the palms of her hands to silence her. 'You have it!' she announced, triumphantly. 'My sister's coming to the rescue again. She's got just the thing, a beautiful midnight-blue organza with a lovely shaped bodice. It's long too, and it'll suit you perfectly.'

Amy was shaking from head to foot. 'No, 'Ilda,' she insisted, shaking her head vigorously. 'I can't keep borrowin' yer sister's clovves like this just becos she's my size.'

'Why not?' protested Hilda, staring her out in disbelief. 'She's worn it at several parties, and in any case she always looked terrible in it. But you – you'll look a million dollars.'

Amy tried to say something, to protest – anything. But Hilda would have none of it. 'This is *my* night, Amy,' she said, her stomach churning with excitement. 'My night and my Harry's. And there's no one in the whole wide world I'd sooner share it with more than my own best mate!'

CHAPTER 20

Relations between Amy and Uncle Jim had become somewhat cool. Ever since the night when she had gone up to his attic room and discovered a snapshot of him and her mum arm in arm, she couldn't get over the nagging feeling that he had abused the trust the Dodds family had always had in him. Amy hated people keeping secrets, especially secrets that affected people's lives. In some ways, Jim himself felt the same way. The past year or so had been a hell on earth for him. Despite the fact that everything he had done had been with the best intentions, trying to retain the confidence of both sides of the family had put an enormous strain on the genuine affection he had for them all. These days, he had no choice but to avoid them. It pained him to do so, but now that Ernie had finally taken on the task of being a responsible father, it seemed that the Doddses' interest in him had diminished.

These days, he kept himself to himself, creeping upstairs whenever he got home from work after a day or night shift, and staying there until it was absolutely necessary to go out again. In fact there were times when he was sitting alone, shut away in his own private kingdom on the top floor, that he thought about giving up his lodgings and moving on.

Perhaps he had been there long enough? Perhaps he had become too involved in matters that didn't concern him? Perhaps he had outlived his welcome? On top of that, Ernie's heartfelt pleas for him to help get Aggs back home had torn him apart with guilt. It was an intolerable situation. Something had to be done. It had to be done quickly. By Monday morning, he had made up his mind what to do.

Monday was Amy's day off. She needed it, for she had worked all day Sunday, and, because one of the nippies had succumbed to the latest flu epidemic, she had had to work overtime. Consequently, she hadn't arrived home until late that evening, which meant missing her usual Sunday date with Tim. Despite all that, however, she was up bright and early on Monday morning, for this was the week in which Hilda was getting married, and that involved preparing herself not only for the big day itself, but also for the nerve-racking ordeal of a night out at the Café de Paris on the evening before.

Once she had packed the kids off to school, the first thing she did was to go and make an appointment to have her hair done at Astrid's Ladies' Hairdressers in Seven Sisters Road. Usually, she did her own hair, washing it first with bath soap, then trimming her fringe with a pair of tailor's scissors that her mum had bought in Woolworths for threepence just before the war. But this was a special occasion, which needed a professional touch. The last thing she wanted to do was to let Hilda down.

After that, she crossed over the road to the North London Drapery Stores, where she browsed around the ladies' clothes department for nearly half an hour. She was desperate for a new pair of knickers, which she hadn't had since the start of rationing the year before, for even though they wouldn't be seen, something new would help to make her feel just that little bit special.

Her next stop was the Gas, Light, and Coke Company just along the road, where she wanted to buy a new mantle for the gas fire in her dad's bedroom, but, predictably, they had run out of them, and as with so many other shortages during wartime, there was very little chance of the stock being replenished for quite some time. As she turned to leave the showroom, however, she was surprised to see Uncle Jim waiting for her outside.

'Thought I saw you through the window,' he said. 'Long time no see. How are you, Amy?'

Amy stiffened. She didn't know why, but she couldn't help it. 'I'm OK, fanks, Uncle Jim,' she replied, rather formally. She wasn't to know that he had been tailing her since she left the house first thing that morning.

The early spring sunshine seemed to have persuaded Jim to abandon his overcoat, but it was still quite cold, so he kept his hands in his pockets. 'I've been wondering how you're all getting on,' he said. 'Don't see any of you very much these days.'

Amy attempted a smile, but what emerged wasn't very convincing; that snapshot was still too fresh in her mind. 'We've bin quite busy up the Corner 'Ouse,' she replied, awkwardly.

Jim also tried a smile. 'Of course,' he said quickly. 'I quite understand. Still I wouldn't mind catching up on all the news some time.'

Amy gave a polite nod. 'Well – better be gettin' on,' she said, making a move to go.

'Fancy a cup of tea, Amy?'

Jim's sudden invitation unnerved her. 'I – I don't fink I can now, Uncle Jim,' she spluttered, falteringly. 'I've got the rest of me shopping ter do, an'—'

Uncle Jim cut in, 'I need to talk to you, Amy. It's about your mum.'

Amy suddenly found her eyes meeting his. She was unsure of him.

'It's important,' he said, holding her look.

A few minutes later, they were sipping tea in the Lyons Tea Shop in Holloway Road. The moment Amy had come through the door, she was treated like royalty for, even though she had popped in to see them from time to time, both Marge Jackson and Mrs Bramley missed her terribly, and wished that she and Hilda were back in their old jobs instead of the two girls who had replaced them. But it wasn't easy for Amy to be sitting there, face to face with Uncle Jim. She didn't know why, for over the years, he more than anyone else in the whole wide world had supported the Dodds family through thick and thin, and it was surely ungrateful of her now to treat him as though he was a stranger just because of what might easily have been a perfectly innocent snapshot she had found of him and her mum.

'There are a lot of things you don't know about me, Amy,' said Jim, who found it agonising to look this courageous girl straight in the eye and tell her that he, like her dad, had been keeping so much from her. 'Just before the war, your mum saved my life.'

Amy did a double take.

Jim avoided her look by stirring his tea. 'I got into trouble with the police. I was depressed at the time, really depressed. It was when my sister, Lil, was still alive. As you know, she was housebound, stuck in a chair with her polio all those years. I went through this period when I thought I was going mad. I felt like a prisoner, trapped in somebody else's world. I couldn't cope.' He hesitated, and took a quick, nervous sip of his tea. 'I nicked something,' he continued. 'Nothing very much. It was in Jones Brothers. I saw this tie. I wanted it – at least, for that one stupid moment, I wanted it – I *had* to have it. In some kind of way, I was doing it as a protest, as though I wanted to prove that I could do something for me, just me alone.' He sighed. 'Anyway, I shoved it in my pocket. Then I suddenly came to, panicked, and quickly put it back on the tie rack again. But just as I was making for the door, this bloke stopped me, made me go into the manager's office. They called the police.'

Amy watched him in silence, and despair.

'The long and short of it was, they sent me up the Magistrates' Court. It was an open-and-shut case. I didn't have a chance.' His eyes flicked up. 'Not until your mum heard about it. She told them all about me, about what an honest man I was, and how I couldn't ever get married because I had to look after my elderly sister.' He lowered his eyes again. He was finding the emotion difficult to contain. 'They let me off with a fine, and a warning. They wouldn't have done, if it hadn't been for Aggs – for your mum.' His eyes looked up again. 'I loved her, Amy. I still love her. And she loves me.'

Amy's face hardened. She avoided his look.

'No, Amy,' insisted Jim, stretching across the table to cover her hand with his own. 'It's not like that, not the way you think. I love your mum, because she knew what I was going through, knew that if somebody didn't stand up for me, I'd fall down good and proper. And when I say she loves me, I don't mean in the physical sense, I mean – up here.' With one finger, he pointed to his head. 'The love she had to offer was to protect me. You see, Amy, there are some women in this world who are born to protect, to understand people like me. Your mum is one of those people. All her life she's given far more than she takes. Unfortunately, the only one she's never been able to protect is herself.' He squeezed her hand, and stared hard at her. 'I think you're old enough to understand what I'm talking about, Amy,' he said. 'Am I right?'

Amy felt a great lump in her throat. Lowering her eyes, she gently nodded.

'Then I hope you'll also understand why I've never told you where she's been hiding since she left home.'

Amy looked up with a start. As she did so, Marge Jackson came across with a Chelsea bun for each of them. 'Compliments of the 'ouse,' she said with a radiant smile. 'Mrs B's put real butter on them.' She put a finger to her lips, a plea for them to keep it to themselves, then quickly scurried off.

Amy didn't respond. She was too shocked by what Uncle Jim had just told her. 'Yer mean – yer know where she is?' she asked in disbelief. 'Yer've known where Mum's bin all this time – an' yer've never told us?'

'It was your mum's wish, Amy,' replied Jim. 'She made me promise. After all she's done for me, I had a duty to protect her. She trusted me. I couldn't let her down.'

Amy couldn't get over it. Her hand was clasped against her mouth in sheer disbelief. 'Where is she?' she asked. 'How d'yer find 'er?'

'She's hiding out in Hyde Park, Amy,' he replied. 'I saw her quite by chance. She was amongst the usual rough-and-tumble lot up at Speakers' Corner –' he smiled faintly, to himself – 'giving the soap-box brigade a hard time.'

Amy was now eager for information. 'So wot did she say when she saw yer?' she pressed. ''Ow did she look? Did she say anyfin' about us, about Dad an' the kids?'

'She was shocked, Amy,' said Jim. 'At first, she tried to make a break for it, but I caught up with her. I told her not to be afraid.'

'Afraid?'

'Someone who tries to run away from life, Amy,' replied Jim, 'is really trying to run away from theirself. That's what your mum's done. The moment she saw me, she saw her entire past coming back to haunt her, like a bad dream. It took me ages to get her to trust me. When someone feels betrayed, it takes a long time for the pain to heal.'

Amy was troubled and confused. She desperately wanted to know so much. She wanted to get up and go straight to Hyde Park and tell her mum to come home, that everything was all right, and that from now on, she, Amy, would take care of her, and that she'd never let her be hurt again. But then she suddenly realised that hope is not reality.

''Ow is she?' she asked, urgently. 'Is she ill? I mean, wot state is she in? 'Ow does she look?'

'She's a parkie, Amy,' replied Jim. 'She's become just another of the destitutes who roam the park and streets, begging, and looking for any scraps they can find that'll keep them alive. All I can say is that she looks awful. She won't even allow me to bring her a sandwich. I'm too close to the past.'

Tears were welling up in Amy's eyes. 'Wot can I do?' she pleaded.

'You can talk to her.'

Amy's eyes widened. Swallowing harder, she asked, 'Will you take me to her?'

Jim nodded. 'Yes, I'll take you to her, Amy,' he said. 'But if I do, I'll be betraying the trust she has in me. But it's a risk I have to take. What I have to decide is, do I keep that trust, by leaving her out there, to rot away in the cold, without any real friends, without even one good meal a day inside her stomach, or do I just turn my back on her and walk away, swapping the love I have for her, so that she can return to the love and warmth of her own family?' He clasped his hands together on the table in front of him, lowered his eyes, and quickly raised them again. 'Yes, Amy. It's a risk. But it's a risk I'm prepared to take.'

Sylvie Temple came out of the munitions shop for her midday meal break at about twelve thirty. She could have gone to the canteen to eat, but the other girls there were always so noisy, chattering and listening to *Workers' Playtime* piped through on the Tannoy speakers, that she preferred to go home and make herself a sandwich and a cup of tea. She was disappointed that her son, Joe, never joined her, for although he had won a free place at Highbury Grammar School, just round the corner from home, he usually opted to have a school meal, followed by a quick game of football with his mates across the road in Highbury Fields.

It was only a few minutes' walk from the munitions shop to Sylvie's new flat in Balls Pond Road, but after being shut away all morning in an atmosphere choked with the smell of oil, grease, and explosives powder, she relished the opportunity to take in some fresh air. She had grown to love the neighbourhood she and Joe had just moved to, for, in her mind, it was a real cut above the dump they had been living in. As she made her way down Wallace Road, she had to battle against a stiff breeze which had sprung up during the morning and was now threatening to turn into a real March wind. Luckily, she had a cotton scarf tied over her head, which helped to keep her home perm in place, but because she was walking directly against the heavy breeze, she had to bend the upper part of her body forward to keep her balance. The going got easier once she had turned into Balls Pond Road, which was shielded from the wind by the tall rows of Edwardian houses, and as it was now only a short distance to her own front door, she was finally able to straighten up and increase her speed. But the moment she looked up, she came to an abrupt halt; someone she recognised was strolling towards her. The moment she saw him, she glared.

''Allo, Sylve,' said Ernie, as he joined her.

Unlike on previous occasions, neither made a move to embrace.

Sylvie gave him a surly look. 'Wot're *you* doin' 'ere,' she asked, raising her voice to a high pitch to combat the sound of the swelling breeze.

'Fawt we ought ter talk fings over,' he replied. 'About where we go from 'ere.'

Sylvie responded coldly. 'There's nuffin' *to* talk about,' she said. 'Not now. Not any more.'

'I've told the family everyfin', Sylve,' Ernie said. 'Everyfin' about you an' me. It's all out in the open.'

'My word,' she replied, sarcastically, 'we *'ave* become brave all of a sudden, ain't we?'

'Sylve,' he said outright, 'the kids want ter meet Joe.'

'No!' she snapped. But as she tried to move on past him, he blocked her way.

'Please, Sylve,' he pleaded. 'Let's at least talk about it. We can't just leave fings as they are.'

'Never!' she barked. 'Not as long as there's breff left in my body!'

She pushed past him and went on her way.

Ernie, watching her go, hesitated a moment, then pursued her.

On the other side of the road, a sudden gust of wind had removed the tattered flat cap of a builder's navvy, who was on his way to the pub nearby. Sylvie and Ernie were too preoccupied to notice the farce taking place, as the poor man ran after his cap, leaped on it with one foot, only to lose it for a second time, before finally retrieving it from a vast puddle in the gutter, left from a brief shower first thing that morning.

'Sylve!' Ernie called. He had caught up with her just as she was passing a discarded brick-built public air-raid shelter, just a stone's throw from her front door. She ignored his calls, and walked on. But once he'd caught up with her, he grabbed hold of her arm, and forced her to stop. '*Please*, Sylve!' he begged.

'No!' she growled, turning her back on him. 'I'll never let them meet. Joe's *my* son. I'll never let you take him away from me! Never!'

'Fer chrissake, Sylve!' retorted Ernie. 'I'm not tryin' ter take Joe away from yer. But 'e's my son too!'

Sylvie's response was harsh and direct. 'The talkin's over, Ern,' she said. 'It's over, it's finished!'

Aware that passers-by were giving them inquisitive looks, Ernie gently led her into the open doorway of the brick shelter, where, as usual with such places, the smell of cat and dog urine seeping from inside was overpowering. Sylvie struggled to break loose, but he had her pinned against the wall.

'Look, Sylve,' he said, trying to calm her. 'Wot we did all those years ago was wrong – we both know that. But we can't take it out on the kids – none of the kids. Wevver we like it or not, Joe's a part of the family – yours an' mine. If we don't let 'em meet, they'll never stop askin' questions. My lot want ter know, they want ter know about their 'alf-bruvver, an' wot 'e looks like. They want ter get ter know 'im, Sylve. An' I'll bet yer any money in the world, Joe wants ter know them too.'

For one brief moment, Sylvie stared him out without replying. Then she pushed him away, saying, 'You're wastin' yer time, Ern. I want nuffin' ter do wiv your family. An' neivver does Joe.' She moved off, but before leaving called, 'If you or any of your woman's lot ever try ter see 'im, I swear ter God yer'll live to regret it.' With that, she went back out into the street, and disappeared.

Ernie watched her go. She had left him in a state of hopeless frustration, and abject despair.

The trees in Hyde Park were bending in the wind. The stiff breeze that had swept through during the morning had now become bombastic and angry, flattening the massive yellow carpet of spring daffodils, and playing havoc with the vegetable plots. Within the past hour or so, the fierce, gusting winds had brought down dead branches from the trees, leaving the new buds vulnerable and unsure if they had the stamina to survive the onslaught. On an afternoon like this, few people ventured into the park. Even the wild geese, ducks, and other forms of bird life had taken cover, and were sheltering in any nook around the lake that they could find. The Serpentine itself was also not immune to the raging intruder, for the surface of the water had been churned up so much that ripples had turned into a swell that rose up, and overlapped the embankment paths.

Uncle Jim had tried to persuade Amy not to come to the park today. For the reunion with her mum that she had so longed for, he had suggested that they wait until the weather was more clement. But for Amy, the urge was too strong. She had waited long enough for this day, and no wind nor high water was going to keep her parted from her mum for one more minute.

The wind was at its most severe as they approached the old bandstand. Here, they had to struggle really hard to keep their balance, for what was now virtually a gale was huffing and puffing across the lake from the south side of the park, which meant that, as they reached the water's edge, they were in danger of getting their feet wet.

'Are you sure this is the place?' Amy had to yell to be heard.

'She always beds down behind the boathouse!' he called, one arm wrapped round Amy's shoulders to support her. 'But during the day she could be anywhere!' They reached the old, dilapidated boathouse and, as Jim had expected, found Aggs's usual haunt deserted. 'If she has any sense,' he yelled, 'she's taken cover somewhere.'

Amy looked in despair at the pathetic little cubbyhole Aggs had taken over for herself, and her heart sank at the thought of her own mum spending night after bitterly cold winter's night in such a terrible, exposed place.

Unperturbed, they moved on, heading in the direction of the old horse path known as North Ride.

The wind was now whistling through the trees, and a scattering of dead wood had even blown into the lake, where it floated on the surface like a gathering of prehistoric reptiles, and was dragged away on the oncoming surge. Above them, the puffy white clouds rushed past in such a hurry, it seemed as though they had a train to catch, and the cold air swirling around their legs was biting and relentless.

When they had reached the old path itself, Jim raised his voice as much as he could, and called out, 'We'll never find her in this! Needle in a haystack.'

Amy's response was to shake her head uncompromisingly, indicating that she was not prepared to abandon the search.

They moved on slowly again, bending their bodies against the wind, Jim holding on to Amy with one hand, and his flat cap with the other. They looked incongruous in such hostile weather conditions, two grim but determined human shapes matched against the equally determined forces of nature.

Their first ray of hope came as they were about to cross over the bridge leading to the Alexandra Gate. Just ahead of them in the centre of the bridge itself, they could see the silhouette of a solitary, dark figure, standing firm in the wind, hands tucked deep into his raincoat pockets, and a stance that looked as though he was waiting for them. As they approached, he blocked their path.

'Yor wastin' yer time,' called The Kid, his voice competing against the wind. 'Yer won't find 'er round 'ere.'

For a brief moment, Amy stared at the boy's face. Although it was barely visible beneath his khaki balaclava, she could see that the eyes meeting her own were determined but kind, as though they were trying to tell her something.

'Where is she?' she pleaded, trustingly. 'Please tell me.'

The Kid sized her up before answering. His face carried a faint smile of recognition; he'd seen those features before – even if they were an older version. 'Try the Pan,' he replied. Then he walked straight past them, and hurried off back in the direction from which they had just come.

Amy immediately turned to Uncle Jim. 'Wot does 'e mean?' she asked. 'Wot's "the Pan"?'

After finding their way down to the extension of the Serpentine known as the Long Water, they eventually reached the site of the Peter Pan statue, celebrating Sir James Barrie's much-loved children's fictional character, which in happier times overlooked the vast expanse of Kensington Gardens. Only now did the wind show the first signs of blowing itself out, which came as a great relief, for it at last enabled Amy and Jim to keep on the move without too much hindrance. The statue itself had, like its mythical counterpart in Piccadilly Circus, long been removed to a safer location as a precaution against bomb blast, and it was a poignant sight to see its solid plinth support left behind to face the lonely vigil of war.

In the area between the Peter Pan plinth and Marlborough Gate, they searched everywhere, behind trees and bushes, the yard at the back of the public toilets, even down an uncovered crater which had once contained an unexploded enemy bomb.

Amy was becoming desperate. Although the sky had begun to brighten after the storm, in less than an hour the light would begin to fade. 'Where is she?' asked Amy, her eyes scanning the desolate surroundings. Her heart was pumping with hope and anticipation.

Jim shook his head. He was pessimistic. But as they moved slowly past the great ornamental fountains near the Marlborough Gate exit, he noticed what appeared to be an abandoned timber builders' shack, which was nestled into thick foliage well back from the path. It would have escaped his attention completely if it hadn't been for the sudden movement behind the half-broken glass of the window. Jim's mood changed immediately. 'Over there,' he said quietly, confidently, to Amy.

Amy turned a questioning look towards the shack, then back again to Jim.

Jim responded with a comforting nod.

Amy, with trepidation, slowly approached the shack door. Then she gently pushed it open. 'Mum?' she called, trying to peer inside. 'Mum?' she called again. 'It's me – Amy. Are yer in here?'

Receiving no reply, she went in. The place was in semi-darkness, for the only light that was available came through the small window with the broken pane of glass. The shack, which was not much bigger than a back yard shed, smelled of stale sweat and rotting timber, and for a few seconds Amy had to strain her eyes to accustom them to the dark. To help her do this, she slowly pushed the door open as wide as it would go, and the moment she did so, a shaft of light immediately picked out the tiny figure of Aggs, crunched up on the floor in the corner.

'Mum!' Amy gasped, rushing to her.

'Go away!' rasped Aggs, shielding her eyes from the light with her hands. 'Leave me alone, will yer?'

Amy dropped to her knees in front of her. 'Oh, Mum!' she said, close to tears. 'I've missed yer so much . . .' But as she stretched out to touch her, Aggs flinched back from her. Amy stared in horror, as she got her first real glimpse of her mum's face – pale, drawn, cheekbones protruding through her flesh, and long straggly, unkempt hair that just hung straight down over her shoulders. 'Oh, Mum,' said Amy, distraught. 'Just look at yer.'

'Yer shouldn't have come,' said Aggs, staring into her own lap, her back pressed hard against the shack wall behind her. 'Yer've got no right ter come.'

'But it's me, Mum,' said Amy, doing her best to get a closer look at Aggs's face. 'It's your Amy.'

Aggs shook her head. 'Yer shouldn't've come,' she repeated, her voice sounding like a sulky child. 'I din't ask yer ter come.'

Amy tentatively stretched her hand forward. As she did so, Aggs covered. But Amy persevered. Gently putting her hand beneath Aggs's chin, she slowly raised it. 'There's nuffin' ter be afraid of, Mum,' she said, quietly.

On hearing these words, Aggs gradually felt confident enough to look up slowly, straight into her daughter's eyes. In one rapid flash of memory, her whole life came flooding back to her. Amy. Yes it was *her* Amy all right, the same cherubic face with the fringe trimmed neatly across her forehead, the same large, dark blue eyes, and the same sweet smile that she'd got from her loving girl every day of her life. '*G'night Amy.*' Those words had echoed through her mind so many times as she lay night after night in her cold and friendless cubbyhole behind the boathouse. So many times she had seen that face gazing out at her, and smiling radiantly

314

at her in her dreams. Yes, this *was* her, this *was* her, Amy, and although she, Aggs, had very little to thank God for, she thanked Him now, thanked Him for letting her look upon that loving young face again. A rare flow of warmth gushed through her veins. But it was not to last long, for she suddenly snapped, harshly, 'Yer shouldn't've come!' The warmth had frozen up again. The dream had gone.

'I've come ter take yer 'ome,' replied Amy. Then, taking hold of Aggs's hands, she added tenderly, 'Where yer belong.'

Aggs quickly pulled her hands away. '*This* is where I belong. This is my 'ome. This is where I stay.'

'No, Mum, no!' Amy pleaded, shaking her head. 'Oh, why did yer leave us?' she asked, reaching out for her mum's hands again. 'Why did yer 'ave ter go away an' leave us, when we all love yer so much?'

Aggs came back at her. 'Love comes in small doses,' she growled cynically. 'It don't ever last.'

'That's not true, Mum,' insisted Amy, passionately. 'I've never ever stopped loving you.'

Aggs flicked a look at her. But it was a puzzled, confused look, full of doubt and suspicion. None the less, it prompted her to raise her hand falteringly, as though she was about to stroke Amy's head. But once again, the impulse failed her, and she quickly withdrew. 'You're only one person,' she replied bitterly. 'It takes more than one ter make a family.'

Amy, still on her knees, moved as close as she possibly could towards the poor, hapless woman. She was deeply pained to see the state her mum was in, a mum who had devoted so much of her life to bringing up her kids, a mum who only gave and never took. It was so wrong to see her like this, wrong to see such a proud and courageous woman reduced to living in the depth of despair. 'Mum,' she said brightly, in an attempt to relax them both, 'd'yer remember that time before the war, when Aunt Midge asked us all over ter tea at Walfamstow? Do yer?'

Aggs didn't respond. Ernie's Aunt Midge, meant nothing to her – nor did any of the two families who had, over the years, stolidly kept their distance.

Amy continued, regardless, 'D'yer remember 'ow 'ouse-proud she was, 'ow she wanted us ter take our shoes off at the front door before we came in? An' d'yer remember 'ow Dad told 'er that 'e wouldn't let us do any such fing, an' 'ow 'e threatened to take us all back 'ome. D'yer remember that time, Mum? Do yer?'

Aggs remained silent and impassive.

''E was right, Mum, wasn't 'e?' continued Amy, persisting. 'Wot 'e said was right, becos an 'ouse is not an 'ome if the doormat ain't 'ad feet on it, and the tea table ain't got at least one burn mark from a hot cuppa on it. An 'ouse is about people, not fings. Ain't that right, Mum?'

Aggs remained stubbornly silent.

'Wot I'm tryin' ter say, Mum,' said Amy, cautiously feeling for Aggs's hands again, 'is that Dad was right. An 'ouse is not a 'ome wivout people, an' people are not the same wivout a family – our family, everyone's family.' Aggs had allowed her gently to take hold of her hands, and Amy could feel the blood pumping through the poor woman's veins. 'Our family should be tergevver, Mum,' Amy continued. 'We don't exist wivout you, wivout the one person who can 'old us all tergevver.' She pressed closer. 'We want yer back, Mum,' she pleaded, a great lump in her throat. 'We all want yer back. We can't do wivout yer – me, Thelma, Arnold, Elsie – *and* Dad.'

At the mention of Ernie's name, Aggs pulled her hands away again.

'Yes, Mum!' insisted Amy. 'Dad as well. 'E loves yer. Believe me, 'e really does love yer.' Aggs struggled to get up, but Amy gently held her down. 'Listen ter me, Mum!' she begged. 'Just listen ter me. Wotever Dad did in the past, wotever pain 'e's caused you, 'e wants ter put fings right. I swear ter God, Mum, 'e's not the man yer knew. 'E's not the man who caused yer all that pain. Dad's come back 'ome again, to us, to all of us. Ter *you*. Especially ter you.'

Regardless of Amy's heartfelt plea, Aggs pulled herself up. 'Wants me back, does 'e?' she rasped. 'Wants me back in the fold again, just like the good ol' days, just like the times when me eyes were closed an' 'e could go off an' 'ave as many flings wiv 'is women as 'e wanted. Well, I can tell yer somefin'. It won't 'appen. I'm out of it, I'm out of it fer good. *My* family's out 'ere now. Out 'ere, where I can be meself, where I can ferget wot it's like ter be let down by a man who doesn't care.' She turned, and made for the open door. 'Loves me, does 'e? Wants me ter come 'ome, does 'e? Well, tell that to *'er*. Tell that to 'is whore. Tell it to their son!'

With that, she was gone, leaving Amy still kneeling on the floor, dazed and devastated.

Outside, Aggs stopped just long enough to confront Jim with an angry, hurt glare. 'I'll never fergive yer fer this,' she said with icy disdain. 'Never.'

With guilt and silence, Jim watched her go, until she had disappeared back into the windswept spaces of her muddled world.

CHAPTER 21

Tim Gudgeon felt most uncomfortable. It was bad enough having to wear a black tie and dinner jacket for his forthcoming night out with Amy, Hilda, and Hilda's husband-to-be, but when he looked at himself in the full-length mirror in Amy's bedroom, Elsie reckoned he looked more like a penguin she'd seen in a Mickey Mouse cartoon at the pictures. What's more, he only hoped that his mother wouldn't find out that it had cost him practically half a week's wages to hire the damned outfit from Jay's Dress Hire in Camden High Street.

The only trouble now was Amy herself. The shock of finding her mum living out rough in Hyde Park had deeply distressed her, and the fact that she had been unable to persuade the poor woman to come back home had only made matters worse. Her dad was also devastated by the news that Aggs had been found, but when Amy recklessly tried to get him to go straight to the park to beg her mum's forgiveness and tell her that he had never stopped loving her, and that what he'd done had been cruel to both her and the family, Tim warned that, in her present state of mind, Aggs might see such a move as a threat, which could send her away for ever.

In desperation, they turned once again to Chief Inspector Rob Hanley.

'If you take my advice,' Hanley said, sizing up Amy, her dad and Tim from behind his desk, 'you'll leave well alone – at least for the time being. Let's give her time to take in that you know where she is. She's been out there in that park for over a year now. It must have been quite a shock for her to see you again.'

'But couldn't yer just send your people after 'er?' asked Amy, who was sitting with her dad, facing Hanley. 'Couldn't yer just tell 'em ter pick 'er up, and bring 'er back 'ome?'

Hanley exhaled smoke from the cigarette he had just lit. 'Yes, I could do that, Amy,' he replied. 'But if I did, I couldn't be held responsible for the consequences.'

'Consequences?' asked Ernie, with trepidation.

'If the doctor does think she's had some kind of a nervous breakdown, taking her into custody could do more harm than good.'

'The inspector's r-right,' said Tim, who was standing behind Amy, his hands resting gently on her shoulders. 'She m-might make a break for it, then we'd never f-find her.'

'With a bit of luck, that won't happen,' said Hanley. 'We have a couple of special constables in the park who'll keep a close watch on her. As a matter of fact, we've been doing so for some time now.'

Amy and her dad exchanged looks of shock. 'You – *wot*?' she asked in disbelief. 'Are you tellin' us yer *knew* all the time that Mum's bin 'idin' out in 'Yde Park?'

Hanley hesitated before replying. 'Yes, Amy,' he admitted. 'We knew.'

'Christ!' Amy gasped. 'I don't believe this! I just don't believe it!'

'Why?' Ernie demanded.

'Yes – *why*?' Amy growled, angrily. ''Ow can yer sit there an' tell us that after all the times I've bin ter see you, yer couldn't once tell me that you'd found Mum, that you were prepared ter let us go frough over a year of agony wivout lettin' on that you'd actually found 'er? *Why*, Mr 'Anley? *Why*?'

In an attempt to calm her, Hanley gently raised the palm of his hand. 'Hold on a moment now, please, Amy,' he said, defensively. Without finishing his cigarette, he stubbed it out in his ashtray. 'In a sense, I did tell you – or at least, I tried to – that morning when I came to see you up at the Corner House. D'you remember?'

Amy glared at him. 'I don't know wot you're talkin' about,' she replied, defiantly. 'All I remember is you tellin' me that you suspected Mum might be livin' out rough in one of the parks, and that 'Yde Park was a possibility. Yer never once told me that—'

'There were reasons,' said Hanley, interrupting her.

'Reasons that can't be shared with 'er own family?' asked Ernie, in disbelief.

'Yes, Mr Dodds,' replied Hanley. 'Let me try to explain. You see, this war has been responsible for turning the minds of so many people. It's hardly surprising, when you think what we've had to go through – rationing, sons and fathers dragged off into the army, their wives and families left behind to cope on their own with the most appalling hardships, bombs falling on them night after night, air-raid shelters, very little food, no luxuries, kids evacuated – it's all a nightmare.' He got up from his desk and stood with his back to the window. 'When some people are so desperate that they don't know which way to turn, they resort to extreme measures. Most times, they're not aware what they're doing, there's no logic, no sense, just a feeling that they want to get away – away anywhere, as long as they can forget what it is that's driven them to the point of despair.' He turned his look towards Ernie. 'It takes just one moment to reach that point of despair, to turn the mind of someone who in every other way has always seemed so normal. You've no idea how many poor souls I see like that in here, day after day, all of them trying to get away from something or somebody. I've seen it amongst my own people right here. When this station was bombed last year, we lost six men, six good men, all of them with families of their own, all of them carrying out their duties not only to arrest criminals, but to help people like your mum.'

Amy lowered her head, and stared into her lap.

Hanley continued, 'Whatever it was that happened that night which sent Mrs Dodds running away from herself, she can't be blamed. There are plenty more like her, whether they're hiding out in the parks, or in the bombed-out ruins of their own homes. You can't treat them as though they're animals. They need help and understanding. They need time to bring their lives back into focus again.' He paused, then turned to Amy. 'That's why we left her there, Amy,' he said. 'It was my decision, but I think it was the right one. I could have taken her in, had her locked up in some hospital or mental home, but if I had done that I think it would have killed her.'

Tim had to comfort Amy, who was shaking. 'But will she *ever* come 'ome?' she asked, tearfully.

Hanley went to her. 'Oh yes,' he replied, with a comforting smile. 'But not before she's good and ready.' He flicked a quick, knowing glance at Ernie. 'Not until she's sure that the past can be put together again.'

Ernie, his hand shielding his eyes, remained solemn, and silent.

Anyone in the park who knew Aggs could tell that she was on the warpath. It was the way she walked, with purpose instead of her usual shuffle; the way her chin jutted out menacingly as she quickened her pace along the south bank of the Serpentine. She hadn't slept a wink since the moment when Amy had suddenly appeared in that workmen's shack in Kensington Gardens. She hadn't slept because she'd been betrayed, betrayed by people she thought she could trust. It was bad enough with Jim, but there was also someone else she was going to give a piece of her mind to, and a lot more if she got the chance. The Kid's betrayal, of course, was not the real reason she was so worked up. Oh yes, she could use him as the scapegoat all right, but it went far deeper than that. It was the fact that she had set eyes on Amy again that had so unsettled her, the first time she had seen her since she, Aggs, had left home. The sight of her girl's face was like a breath of fresh spring air. It was filled with hope, eagerness, and compassion. Why then, Aggs asked herself, did she greet her with such unbridled hostility? Surely she had been dreaming night after night of that face, that gentle face, and the longing inside her to see and to cherish it again. Now that she had time to think of what she had done, she was ashamed of herself, ashamed because Amy had never done her any harm, and had always been the one person who had supported her through thick and thin. Chances like the reunion Amy had sought only come once in a lifetime, said her other self. Miss them, and there's no turning back.

'Wotcha, Ma!'

Aggs hardly recognised him. From the first time she had ever set eyes on him, The Kid had worn the same old threadbare army-issue overcoat, and the same woollen balaclava pulled down tight over his face. In fact, she had never once seen him without his trademark clothes, summer or winter; it was almost as though they had been stuck to his body with glue. But here he was, bouncing cockily towards her along Rotten Row, practically naked as far as she was concerned, for the glorious spring sunshine had persuaded him to discard his winter wear, and expose his face to the elements for the first time. 'Pleased wiv yerself then?' she snapped, the moment they came face to face. 'All in a day's work, is it?'

The Kid knew what she was going on about; he'd been expecting it. But he was not going to let on. 'Wos up now then?' he replied, cheekily. 'That cat pissed on yer again last night, did 'e?'

'Why d'yer do it?' she growled, ignoring his jibe.

'Do wot?'

'*You* know wot, yer little tyke! Give me away, din't yer? 'Ad ter open yer big mouf, an' let me in the dung. Why d'er do it, eh? Why d'er give me away ter my daughter? Tell me!'

The Kid did a double take. Even though it was a false one, he thought he'd better go through the motions. 'Yor – daughter, did yer say?' he asked, with wide-eyed innocence. 'Wos that yor – daughter?' Gradually his face lit up, as though the fact had just dawned on him. 'Blimey!' he gasped. 'I fawt at the time that she was like someone I knew. Gotta give it ter yer, Ma. Real good-looker, that one. Cleans 'er teef more than you, though!'

Aggs was not in the mood for his mischievous wit. 'Yer

told 'er where ter find me. I know it was you, 'cos no one else knows I shack down in that shed when the wevver's rough. Own up, yer git! Own up!'

'Tut, tut, Ma!' he replied, with a broad, scampish grin. 'That's no way for a lady to talk.'

Aggs raised a hand as though she was about to wallop him. 'I'll show yer wot a lady I am . . . !'

The Kid quickly dodged out of striking distance.

'Why d'yer do it? *Why*?'

''Cos I 'ad to.'

Aggs's hand became frozen in mid-blow.

The Kid's expression had suddenly become serious. 'Becos I *wanted* to.'

Despite the sound of distant traffic, you could have heard a pin drop between them.

Aggs slowly lowered her hand. 'Yer – wanted – ter give me away?' she asked, staring at him incredulously.

'Yes, Ma,' he replied, with hidden feeling.

'Why?'

''Cos I like you. 'Cos I fink yer deserve better than all this.'

Aggs screwed up her face. She always unconsciously did that when she didn't understand something. 'Who're you ter—'

'Go 'ome, Ma,' interrupted The Kid, implacably, 'That's where yer belong, not 'ere, not in this dump. You're diff'rent ter the rest of us. You're someone who 'as a lot ter give, someone who cares about people, all sorts of people – even me.' Aggs tried to interrupt again, but he wouldn't let her. 'You was born ter love, Ma,' he continued. 'You was born ter *be* loved. There ain't many people around like that,' he said.

'I'm tellin' yer – I know.' Prepared to combat any fury she might still feel towards him, he ventured closer. 'Do yerself a favour, mate,' he said, with gentle warmth. 'Get out while yer can. Go back an' find yerself. It's fer the best – believe me.'

To Aggs's astonishment, he leaned tentatively towards her. For a moment, she flinched. Then, without really knowing why, she let him kiss her gently on the cheek.

With one last smile, he moved on. He stopped only briefly to call back cheekily, 'Oh, by the way, I'll miss yer!'

By late in the afternoon, Amy was a near wreck. It was the night of Hilda and Harry's 'bash' up at the Café de Paris, and, despite Tim's assurance that she had nothing to worry about, Amy's stomach never stopped making the most disgusting rumbling sounds. Hilda herself had been over at number 16 during the day, helping Amy to make last-minute alterations to the long evening dress she had borrowed from Hilda's sister, and giving Amy a lesson in how to make up discreetly. 'You don't have to overdo the lipstick to send them wild, dear,' Hilda had told her. 'Believe me, suggestion is the key to conquest!'

When Tim turned up at about five o'clock, Thelma was helping Amy put the finishing touches to her hair. Amy was still wrapped up in a towel and Tim thought she looked like she'd just stepped out of an advert for bath salts. He couldn't take his eyes off her. Amy also couldn't take her eyes of Tim, for, despite his moans and groans about having to dress up like a penguin, he looked so handsome in his dinner suit, white shirt, and black bow tie.

At about six o'clock, Amy got dressed, and when she came

down the stairs into the passage swathed in the long dress of midnight-blue organza, her hair glistening from her trip to Astrid's, there were gasps of astonishment and delight from Tim, Ernie, and all the family. Even little Elsie was impressed. 'Don't ferget ter get back before midnight,' she warned. 'Yer might turn into a pumpkin.'

'Yer look smashin',' commented her dad. 'I just wish yer mum could see yer.'

The fact that her mum was not there to see her had not been lost on Amy. The past few days had been traumatic for her. It was difficult to accept that there was very little any of them could do to get the poor woman back home until she herself was ready to come of her own free will. Amy couldn't bear to think of her mum wandering aimlessly around the park, alone with her thoughts, living from hand to mouth, and with no roof over her head. But Amy's despair had gradually given way to reality. Time was the healer, she kept telling herself, time – and patience.

By six fifteen, Amy had made up her mind. 'I'm not goin',' she announced, flopping down exhausted into a chair in front of the oven grate. 'It's no use kiddin' meself. I'm not Hedy Lamarr. I've got no 'ips, 'air that looks as though it's bin stuck on wiv glue, a double chin, and a voice that'll tell everyone I come from Enkel Street.'

'Wot's wrong wiv Enkel Street?' queried a puzzled Elsie.

'There's nothing wrong with Enkel Street,' insisted Tim. 'Enkel Street or anywhere else.' Then putting a reassuring arm round Amy's waist, he added, 'It's *w-what* you are that c-counts, not who. I'd choose you any time to s-some of the crowd we'll see tonight.' In full view, he kissed her gently on her cheek.

327

'Well, I fink yer look lovely,' said Thelma, also putting an arm round her sister's waist. 'In fact I've never seen anyone look so lovely in my whole life,' she added.

Arnold was sick of all this girl-talk. 'I reckon you look the best, Tim,' he said, without actually looking up from stacking his cigarette card collection on the parlour table. 'Girls in dresses only look good when they're with a man.'

This remark provoked howls of indignation from both Thelma and Elsie, but laughter from the others.

'I don't care wot any of yer say,' insisted Amy, beginning to ease off the matching shoes that were pinching her toes, 'I'm not goin' ter that club ternight. I'm just not cut out for it.'

'An' wot about 'Ilda?' asked Ernie, reprovingly. 'If she's your best mate, don't yer fink yer owe it to 'er ter 'elp 'er 'ave a good time on the night before she gets married?'

Amy flopped back into the chair, and sighed. Her dad was right; she was being thoroughly ungrateful, and only thinking of herself. This was Hilda's night, not hers. Ever since they'd met, Hilda had been a wonderful mate to her, kind, generous, and supportive, so the very least she could do to repay her best mate was to help Hilda's dream of a night out at the Café de Paris come true, although she hoped that Hilda would not dance naked on the table, as she had once threatened. To sighs of relief all round, she asked, 'OK then. So wot time is this taxi pickin' us up?'

The Café de Paris was packed with officers on leave from all the armed forces. Most of their dates were from the cream of London's high society and, despite the austerity of wartime clothes rationing, they looked it. And so did the famous night club in Coventry Street itself, with its stylish twin staircases, winding down each side of the bandstand from the street above, and its glittering chandelier, which every so often swayed gently in the smoky atmosphere, sending small globes of light racing up and down the elegant walls.

Hilda arrived on Harry's arm and, whilst she was being led regally down the floral carpeted staircase, she flushed with joy at the thought that this, at last, was her dream come true. And when the manager, Martin Poulsen, led them to their table across the crowded dance floor, she felt importance such as she had never known before, as though every eye was turned towards her, and her alone. As well she might, for she looked absolutely radiant in a black, off-the-shoulder, tight-fitting evening dress, and an oval-shaped black suede and diamanté evening bag and shoes to match, all of which set off the magnificence of her bright ginger curls to perfection.

Once they had settled down and Harry had ordered some drinks, Hilda met his eyes, and lovingly said, 'If I were to tell you that this is the happiest night of my life, would you believe me?'

Harry leaned across, and, taking her hand, replied, 'And if I was to tell you that I am the luckiest man in the whole wide world, would *you* believe *me*?'

A few minutes later, they were out on the dance floor, doing a quickstep to the music of Cole Porter, and smooching shamelessly to the rhythms of Ken 'Snakehips' Johnson and his Caribbean band. When they returned to their table, a waiter brought them a chilled bottle of champagne, a real luxury for wartime. Then they linked arms, stared into each other's eyes, and made a toast.

'Here's to the future Mrs Smethurst,' said Harry, raising his glass to Hilda.

'Here's to my future husband,' she returned, touching his glass gently with her own. But the moment they took the first sip Hilda suddenly looked at her wristwatch. 'They're late,' she said, anxiously. 'Amy and Tim. They should be here by now. Where are they?'

Amy and Tim were indeed late. The taxi Harry had sent to collect them turned up a good ten minutes later than it was supposed to, without so much as an explanation as to why from the driver. However, the moment it arrived, they were off, heading briskly down Hertslet Road towards the junction with Tollington and Holloway Roads. They hadn't even reached the Mayfair Cinema in Caledonian Road when the air-raid siren wailed out from the top of the police station there.

'D'yer wanna carry on?' called the driver, over his shoulder.

Tim turned to Amy. 'What do you think?' he asked.

Despite the fact that she would relish any excuse not to go ahead with her ordeal, Amy declared, 'Might as well. It can't last long.'

However, by the time they reached Euston Road, the whole sky was bursting with anti-aircraft shells, lighting up the darkened streets almost as much as during the height of the Blitz. The decision was finally made for them when the taxi was suddenly rocked by an explosion which seemed to come from somewhere along Tottenham Court Road just ahead of them.

'That's it!' yelled the driver, skidding the vehicle to an abrupt halt. 'That's as far as I go!'

Tim quickly helped Amy out of the taxi, and with all hell breaking loose in the sky above them, they both made a run for it, rushing straight for Euston underground station on the other side of the road.

They looked an incongruous sight in their evening clothes as they hurried down the stairs of the escalator, which had been turned off, allowing as many people as possible to take cover on the station platforms below. Like the handful of stray air raids that had taken place during the previous year, this one had taken everyone by complete surprise. Consequently, pandemonium had broken out along the passages leading to the tube platform itself, with babies crying, older folk struggling to keep up with the moving tide, and a group of drunken youngsters squabbling about who got to which vacant plot first along the platform.

'You goin' ter give us a singsong then, little lady?' jibed one elderly, overhearty man, on seeing Amy all togged up in her long dress.

'If I sing,' countered Amy, 'everyone'd sooner take their chances up top!'

The laughter this provoked all round came to an abrupt halt as an explosion from the street above sent shock waves all through the rail tunnel and along the platform.

'Oh God!' Amy gasped. 'Poor Hilda!'

Tim hugged her close. 'D-Don't worry,' he said, trying to reassure her. 'They say that r-restaurant's one of the safest in London.'

In the Café de Paris, way down in the depths beneath the Rialto Cinema, nobody even noticed there was an air raid on. The atmosphere was happy and glamorous, and by the time

'Snakehips' had lined up his band for a rousing chorus of 'Oh, Johnny', no one seemed to have a care in the world.

Although Hilda was deeply disappointed that Amy and Tim hadn't turned up for her final celebration before getting married the following morning, she knew there must have been a good reason. Amy would never have let her down intentionally, she kept telling herself. But there was no doubt that she did miss her. Amy was her best friend, and in her books, there was no one quite like her. As she and Harry joined in the boisterous chorus with everyone else, they smiled at each other, and sneaked a quick, but passionate kiss.

And then the whole place shuddered.

The All Clear siren seemed as though it would never come, and even when it did, it took Amy and Tim the best part of twenty minutes to disentangle themselves from the hordes of people who were straining to push their way free from the claustrophobic atmosphere of the tube platform.

Once out in the open, Amy and Tim wiped the sweat from their faces, but the brisk night air was no longer fresh, for during the past few hours it had been contaminated by the pungent fumes of burning fires and exploding ack-ack shells. The pavement outside was littered with jagged lumps of shrapnel, and over the rooftops in the direction of the West End, a great pall of smoke spiralled up into the dark March sky, which was now lit up with a soft red glow.

With fear in her eyes, Amy looked out at the fires which had broken out in the distance. 'Oh Christ, Tim!' she said, apprehensively. 'It looks like the West End's got it. Please, God, don't let it be Hilda.'

Tim put a comforting arm around her. 'No,' he assured

her. 'Looks f-further on to me. Probably d-down by the Embankment somewhere.'

Amy was now in complete disarray. 'Wot're we goin' ter do?' she asked fearfully 'It's after 'alf-past ten. We're over two 'ours late.'

'Stop w-worrying, Amy,' Tim replied, kissing her gently on the forehead. 'At a place like that, you can never turn up too l-late.'

A fleet of ambulances and fire engines were lined up outside the Rialto Cinema in Coventry Street. Although the fire in the building had now been put out, smoke was still billowing out through the upper-floor windows, the auditorium, and up from the Café de Paris restaurant in the bowels below.

When Amy and Tim arrived on the scene, they were horrified by what they could see. The whole area from Leicester Square to Piccadilly Circus was littered with broken glass and debris, and an endless snake of fire hoses was still trying to dampen down the excessive smoke and heat from two bombs that had penetrated the roof of the cinema. Although only one of the bombs had exploded, the damage and loss of life it had caused was, in the words of one of the countless emergency service workers, 'a bloody tragedy'. Even the adjoining Corner House had not escaped unscathed, for although its large street windows were heavily protected by sticky tape, they had virtually collapsed from the blast of the explosion, leaving the majestic restaurant wide open to the chaos outside.

Amy and Tim were allowed no closer than a rope barrier which had been set up on the corner of Leicester Square and Leicester Street. All around them, people were either crying, or just looking on in sheer disbelief. They may not have had anyone they knew inside the wreckage of the building before them, but the sheer tragedy of the disaster that had taken everyone by surprise completely overwhelmed them.

Amy herself was devastated. As she and Tim watched the endless procession of lifeless bodies brought out of the building on stretchers covered with red blankets, she felt as though her limbs were paralysed. Quite impulsively, she suddenly called out to one of the waiters who had somehow survived the blast, and was now being helped out through the front entrance of the Café by a nurse and a St John Ambulance driver.

'Please!' she yelled. 'Please – did yer see a gel in there? Her name's 'Ilda. She was wearin' a black dress. She was wiv 'er 'usband – I mean 'er friend. 'Is name's 'Arry, 'Arry Smethurst.'

The cut and bleeding waiter was too shocked to be able to give her more than a passing glance before being bustled off into a waiting ambulance.

'Please!' Amy yelled again. 'Please – somebody tell me!'

Tim only just managed to stop her from breaking through the cordon. 'D-Don't, Amy!' he pleaded, holding and hugging her. 'There's n-nothing we can do – nothing.'

Amy pressed her head into Tim's chest, and dissolved into tears. ''Ilda!' she sobbed. 'Please God, don't let it be 'Ilda.'

Behind them the pavement was now strewn with the remains of personal possessions which had been taken from the restaurant below. There was expensive jewellery, both men and women's shoes, and wallets and evening bags.

One bag was oval-shaped, made of black suede, and adorned with sparkling diamanté.

Thirty-four people had lost their lives in the Café de Paris that night. Amongst them were 'Snakehips' Johnson and another member of his band, together with staff and customers alike. It was a tragedy that no one was ever likely to forget. Least of all Amy herself.

CHAPTER 22

It had been the worst week of her life for Amy. The death of her dear best mate on the eve of her wedding had completely devastated her, and she was inconsolable. The bomb on the Café de Paris had taken not only the lives of harmless, innocent people, but it had also destroyed a bond, a close personal friendship between two girls who meant a great deal to one another. At Hilda's funeral, followed by the burial in the Brompton Cemetery, Amy met Hilda's family for the first time. It was a strange, poignant meeting, for Hilda's mother was the living image of her eldest daughter, with hair, although now streaked with grey, just as bright as Hilda's. Tim was there with Amy at the graveside, holding her, supporting her through her ordeal. Amy thought her heart would break, as she watched Hilda's coffin being lowered into the grave. It was a loss for Amy that perhaps many would not understand, a bonding between two young women, a meeting of two young minds that went beyond the bounds of plain devotion. Theirs had been a relationship based on mutual trust and togetherness.

Despite the damage it had sustained from the Café de Paris bomb, Lyons Corner House was open for business again within a few days. The street windows were replaced, plaster restored to damaged walls, and glass fragments removed from

337

furniture. Like the rest of the staff, the nippies rose to the challenge magnificently, helping to sweep, scrub, polish, and tidy every one of the restaurants in the building. It was an astonishing effort.

For Amy, however, it was somewhat different. After Hilda's death, there was no way in which she could bring herself to go anywhere near the place in which they had laughed and toiled together during those precious last few weeks. Fortunately, both Mr Pearson and Miss Fullerton were sensitive enough to understand how Amy felt, for they too had been shocked by the tragic death of one of their own staff. They were therefore not too surprised when Amy wrote giving in her notice.

From that time on, the days seemed long and bleak for Amy, and if it hadn't been for Tim, she would have gone downhill fast. He alone seemed to know how much she now needed her mum, how much she needed her help to break free from the loss of her special close friend. But her mum just wasn't there, and there was still no sign that she was prepared to give up her aimless existence in the park.

To make matters worse, Thelma, Arnold, and Elsie were now harping on daily about wanting to meet their half-brother, Joe. Amy knew how they felt, but unless their dad was able to convince Sylvie Temple to allow that meeting to take place, there was nothing she could do. It was finally Tim who came up with at least an option, one day when they were walking home from Chapel Market. 'If you c-can't get your d-dad to talk to this woman,' he suggested, 'why d-don't we have a go ourselves?'

'Talk ter Sylvie Temple?' protested Amy, in disbelief. '*Me!*'

'S-Someone has to do it, Amy,' insisted Tim. 'You can't

338

go on like this forever, otherwise you'll all b-be strangers for the r-rest of your lives.'

'Never!' snapped Amy, angrily. The mere suggestion had clearly repulsed her, for she immediately turned her back on him, and walked away. But then, after thinking about it for a moment, she stopped and turned. 'Even if we did go ter see 'er,' she warned, ''ow do we know she'd even talk to us?'

'We d-don't,' replied Tim, going to her. 'But it's worth a t-try.'

Sylvie Temple, arms crossed stubbornly, was waiting for Amy and Tim at her street door. A few minutes before, she had caught a glimpse of them, turning the corner into Balls Pond Road, and making straight for her place, so after making quite sure that Joe kept to his bedroom, she came down to meet them.

'Yes?' she growled, curtly. 'Wot d'yer want?'

The very sight of Sylvie in the doorway reduced Amy to silence, so it was left to Tim to open the conversation. 'C-Could you spare a few m-minutes to have a chat with us, please, Mrs T-Temple?'

'Wot about?'

With no support coming from Amy, Tim replied, 'About your s-son, Joe. Amy and her brothers and sisters would like to m-meet him.'

'Would they now?' she replied, cuttingly, her look directed towards Amy rather than Tim. 'Well, the answer's – no.'

Amy at last spoke up. 'Why not?'

'Ah!' said Sylvie, sarcastically. 'So the cat's got a tongue after all, 'as she? Well, I'll tell yer, miss. My Joe's got nuffin' ter do wiv you, nor your bruvver an' sisters. Joe's my boy. I say who 'e gets ter meet, not none of the Doddses.'

'Be reasonable, Mrs T-Temple,' pleaded Tim. 'Amy only wants to talk to him. After all, he is r-related – in a sense.'

'Ha!' Sylvie threw back her head with a dismissive laugh. 'Related?' she quipped. 'Well, that's a laugh, that is!'

'But you can't k-keep them apart for ever.' insisted Tim.

'Oh yes she can,' snapped Amy. 'That's exactly wot she *can* do, wot she *wants* ter do. She's a spiteful, vindictive woman . . .'

'Amy!' Tim chided.

Sylvie was already closing the door in their faces.

Tim immediately put his hand against the door and held it back. 'Please, Mrs T-Temple!' he pleaded. 'Amy's upset. She didn't m-mean what she just said.'

'Oh yes, I did,' barked Amy, preparing to go.

'Why can't we t-talk about this sensibly?' asked Tim, holding on to Amy with one hand, and Sylvie's street door with his other. 'All you're doing, is m-making yourselves unhappy.'

'I told yer we'd be wastin' our time,' Amy snapped. 'I told yer she wouldn't budge!'

'We d-don't know that, Amy!' Tim scolded, displaying rare irritation with her. Then he turned to Sylvie. 'Why *won't* you change your mind, Mrs T-Temple?' he asked, with calm reason. 'Why can't you let Joe meet his family?

Sylvie came on to the doorstep. 'Joe 'as only one family, an' that's me. For fifteen years I've brought 'im up single-'anded, strugglin' ter keep 'im fed an' clothed, no 'elp from any sod, not even 'is own farver – espeshally 'is own farver!'

Tim sympathised with her. 'I know how you f-feel Mrs T—'

'Do you?' she snapped back. 'Do you really? I doubt that. I doubt that very much indeed. It's all right fer you lot. Yer've got a good 'ome, an' a family ter support yer. But not me. All I've got is a kid I never wanted, and a man who ran away and buried 'is 'ead in the sand like a bloody ostrich!' She took a deep breath, and looked away wistfully. 'My mistake was ter fall in love wiv somebody who never loved me.'

Amy waited a moment, then asked, 'Wot do yer want, Mrs Temple? 'Ow much more blood do we 'ave ter shed before you're satisfied?'

Sylvie swung her a look of cold disdain. 'Wot do I want?' she asked, wryly. 'I want an 'usband, a farver for my kid, a man who's willin' to cope wiv wot 'e's done, ter take on the responsibility for wot 'e's done. Is that too much ter ask? Is it? It takes two ter make a party, Amy,' she said, trying to illicit at least some understanding. 'One of these days, you'll *know* wot I mean.'

Aggs knew she was being watched. Nothing too sinister, just her two special constable mates, Sid and Roy, who, these days, never seemed to be too far away. She blamed it all on both Jim and The Kid, of course. If it hadn't been for them, Amy would never have found her, and she could have gone on living her life the way she wanted. On one occasion, she had thought about giving Sid and Roy a piece of her mind by telling them to bugger off and leave her alone. But she soon decided against doing anything so rash, for Sid and Roy had been good to her over this past year. Without them, her survival in the park would have become very precarious. But there were times when the two of them got on her nerves; they were like a double act.

'Wotcha, Ma!'

'How's our Betty Grable today, then?'

It always irritated her when they turned up unannounced like that. 'Wot am I up for this time then?' she growled. 'Dangerous drivin'?'

Sid and Roy laughed at her jibe. To them, Ma was always good for a laugh. Except when she was in trouble.

'Haven't seen you around for a bit,' said Sid, the older, taller and leaner of the two men. 'Where you been hiding then?'

Aggs, stretched out on her favourite park bench facing the Serpentine, snorted dismissively. 'Who you kiddin'? You're like Laurel an' bleedin' 'Ardy – can't keep yer eyes off me. Wos it all about?'

'Don't know what you're talkin' about, Ma,' said Roy, whose tin helmet threw a dark shadow over his boyish looks. 'We're just protecting your interests, that's all.'

'Wot interests?' blurbed Aggs 'Wot d'yer fink I am – Lord Rothschild?'

Both men laughed again, but it was pretty false. Then they did something that they had never done before. Once Aggs had sat upright on the bench, they joined her, one each side.

Aggs was now getting suspicious. 'Wos this all about?' she asked.

Both men took off their helmets, Sid first, then his partner. 'You may not be able to stick it out here much longer,' said Sid, lowering his voice absurdly, as though somebody was listening over his shoulder. 'Things are on the move.'

'Wot yer talkin' about?'

'It's the local council, Ma,' said Roy, who had a pasty face and an unruly flock of brown hair which flopped over his right eye. 'They're on the warpath.'

Sid leaned towards her again. 'They had a meeting last week,' he sniffed, wiping his nose on the handkerchief he'd just taken out of his tunic pocket. 'They want to clean up the park.'

'Which park?' Aggs asked, warily.

'This one,' said Sid.

Roy continued, 'They reckon there're too many sleeping out rough, gives the park a bad name. They want us lot to take action.'

'Wot d'yer mean "take action"?'

'Get rid of you, Ma,' said Sid, wiping his forehead with the same handkerchief. 'You and all your mates.'

Once it had sunk in, Aggs exploded. 'Who do they fink they are?' she barked. 'They got no right ter push us around like that. I pay my taxes – well, I used to. I'm stayin' right 'ere, an' if they try ter move me, I'll just come back again.'

'No, Ma,' said Sid, shaking his head.

'Wot d'yer mean "no"?' croaked Aggs.

'I mean, the council can do anything they want. If you try and resist, they'll take you up before the Magistrates.'

'Good bleedin' riddance!'

'No, Ma,' warned Roy. 'This is serious business.'

Although there were quite a few lunch-time strollers in the park, Aggs suddenly caught sight of The Kid, ambling along in his usual cocky way, heading straight towards her from the Long Water end of the lake. She immediately sprang to her feet and yelled out, 'Oy! Over 'ere! Come an' listen ter this.'

The Kid waved back, but the moment he did so, a military vehicle suddenly screeched to a halt alongside him, and before he had a chance to realise what was happening, two burly military policemen leaped out, and pounced on him.

Aggs was horrified. 'Hey!' she bellowed, at the top of her voice. 'Leave 'im alone!' But two pairs of hands suddenly took hold of her arms, and quickly pulled her back down on to the bench. 'Wot yer doin'?' she protested, struggling to get free. 'Get off, will yer? Get off!'

'Leave him, Ma!' said Sid, one arm round her shoulders, pinning her down. 'You can't help him now.'

'Nobody can help him,' added Roy.

Further along the road, a group of passers-by had stopped to watch the fierce struggle that was taking place, as The Kid took on the two MPs, using his bare fists to keep them away.

For Aggs, it was a pretty gruelling sight, and the more helpless she was as she looked on, the more distressed she became. 'Let 'im go . . . !' she kept yelling at the top of her voice.

The angry shouts, and the sight of fists flying all over the place, kept the passers-by well away from The Kid's determined battle to break loose from his two assailants. Quite unexpectedly, he did finally manage to do just that, which left him free to sprint at an amazing speed along the path straight in Aggs's direction.

As he approached, Aggs yelled her support: 'Go! Go! Go!'

The Kid's spectacular getaway was not to last for long, however, for no sooner had he reached the main path leading across the fields to Marble Arch, than another military vehicle headed him off, and he was trapped between that and the two MPs pursuing him close behind.

Aggs screamed out so loud in anguish that the flock of wild geese who were gathered along the embankment, took immediate flight, and made straight for the sanctuary of their island home in the middle of the lake.

The Kid was finally trundled into one of the two military vehicles, but not before he managed to flash one last knowing look back at Aggs.

The two vehicles disappeared as quickly as they had arrived. Constables Sid and Roy waited until they had completely disappeared before finally releasing their vicelike grip on Aggs's arms.

Aggs raised herself up from the bench, then turned to look at her so-called mates. There were tears of pain and anger in her eyes, but she had no words to describe how she felt about them. So she spat at their faces, and walked on.

Arnold's ninth birthday party was a pretty glum affair. It had no need to be, of course, but Arnold was a pretty glum sort of boy, and he never took kindly to sharing his birthdays with outsiders. The fact of the matter was that Arnold much preferred his own company, which is why he had very few mates, so in some ways, agreeing to have a party at all was really his way of humouring his family.

Much to everyone's despair, Amy had cooked their brother's favourite meal for his birthday, which was Spam fritters and chips, but as a concession for the others, she made a mutton stew, and although the meat was a little on the tough side, it tasted absolutely delicious, for it was cooked in two tins of oxtail soup, some carrots, turnips, swedes, potatoes, salt, and plenty of pepper. For 'afters' she'd made a fruit trifle, which turned out to be very popular with Elsie, who devoured two portions before anyone even had a look in.

Arnold's present from his dad was ten bob in cash, which

went down a treat, for it gave him the freedom to buy whatever he wished. Back in her day, their mum had encouraged all her kids to buy something for each other at Christmas and on their birthdays, no matter how small, and that tradition had not wavered. Therefore, Thelma bought Arnold a tin full of coloured pencils, and even little Elsie grudgingly bought him tuppence worth of liquorice and sherbet powder. Arnold's favourite present, however, was from Amy, who bought him a photo album from Woolworths, something he had hinted at repeatedly over the previous few weeks, for, unlike other collectors of cigarette cards, he wanted to put them on permanent display, so that he could use them for research for when he eventually wrote his memoirs.

That evening, Tim came by, and joined the family round the parlour table to play a game of Monopoly. This was a very risky thing to attempt, for on previous occasions it had all ended in tears when Elsie accused everyone of buying up property that she herself had eyes on. However, all went well, mainly because Amy, who had been voted Banker, allowed her youngest sister to get away with murder – and a wad of unearned artificial bank notes. Once the game was over, everyone sang 'Happy Birthday to You' to Arnold, who was then bumped on the floor on his bottom nine times by the others, in a family tradition which he had always detested.

It was late into the evening before the younger members of the family were finally packed off to bed, leaving Amy, Tim and Ernie to have a quiet drink on their own.

Amy waited for the right moment before asking, 'Dad, wot're we goin' ter do about Joe?'

For a brief moment, Ernie looked up from rolling his fag.

'Now we're not goin' ter start that all over again,' he replied tersely.

'The kids are restless, Dad,' warned Amy. 'If we don't do somefin' about it soon, we'll 'ave Arn makin' anuvver attempt to do it 'imself.'

Ernie put down his unrolled cigarette and sighed. 'I've told yer over an' over again, Ame,' he said. 'It won't work. It just won't work. Sylvie's never goin' ter let them meet.'

'I'm well aware of that,' scoffed Amy, contemptuously. 'She said as much when we saw 'er this morning.'

Ernie looked up with a start. 'You went ter see Sylvie?'

'It was m-my idea, Mr Dodds,' intervened Tim. 'I thought we c-could persuade her to change her m-mind.'

'Well, it was a bad idea!' Ernie snapped. 'Yer should've told me you was goin' up there. You 'ad no right ter go wivout tellin' me first.'

'You're wrong, Dad,' Amy assured him. 'As a matter of fact, we had every right. If we leave it ter you, we may never get the chance ter meet Joe. As a matter of fact, there were times I was quite sorry for her – that woman, I mean.'

Ernie looked warily at her.

'She's obviously 'ad quite a struggle ter bring up 'er boy. She says you 'aven't 'elped 'er.'

Ernie stiffened. 'Well, she would, wouldn't she?' he replied.

'She also loves yer.'

Ernie refused to meet her eyes.

'Do you love 'er, Dad?' Amy asked, point-blank.

Ernie remained silent for quite a few moments before answering. 'I thought I did – once,' he said, with difficulty. 'But it was just make-believe. I was lookin' fer somefin' that

347

I din't really need, din't really want. But it was there, starin' me in the eyes.' He looked up at her. 'No, Ame. There's only one person I've *ever* loved, but when yer've done wot I've done, when yer've hurt like I've hurt, it's too late to fergive.'

Amy got up and went to him. 'Never's a long time, Dad,' she told him quietly, tenderly. 'But yer 'ave ter go on tryin'.'

A few minutes later, Ernie went up to bed, leaving Amy and Tim alone together. They decided to go out into the back yard, where a solitary puff of night cloud was slowly undulating across a three-quarter moon, flooding the rooftops with an ethereal light. As they stood there, leaning against the back wall of the house, condensation was funnelling out through their noses as they breathed. The silence between them said a great deal; each knew what the other was thinking, and it prompted each to feel for the other's hand. Above them, they could see the reflection of the moon in the windows of the houses which backed on to Enkel Street. Sleep came early to this tiny corner of human life; the air was charged with peace, the peace seemed almost universal. Venus dominated. Jupiter smiled. Orion observed and approved. They were all there, high above, watching and waiting.

Tim went to Amy. He placed both his hands on her hair, and gently stroked it. Then his lips felt for hers. They kissed, hard, with a surge of warmth and passion. No words, only recognition.

'D'you think there's life after d-death, Amy?' Tim asked, softly.

'I 'ope so,' she replied.

'If there is,' he said, kissing her again, 'I hope they n-never part us.'

They remained there for several minutes, listening to the

sounds of the night, cats wailing at each other on the tiles of the sloping roof above them, the distant rumble of a train in the shunting yard behind Isledon Road, and the even more distant sound of the usual stragglers on the pavement outside the Enkel pub at closing time.

'If there is someone up there,' Amy said softly, suddenly, 'I hope 'E looks after Mum.'

'Don't worry. He will.'

''Ow do we know?'

'B-because you l-love her.'

They both stirred as Ernie, voice low, called from the back door. 'Amy? Amy, are you out there?'

'Dad?' she called anxiously, immediately going to him. 'Wot is it? Wot's wrong?'

'Yer mum,' he replied, urgently. 'Somefin's 'appened to 'er. Inspector 'Anley's 'ere. She's done a bunk.'

'Wot?' Amy gasped. 'Wot's 'appened to 'er? Where's she gone?'

'Nobody knows. She's just done a bunk. They've bin lookin' all evenin', but they can't find 'er anywhere.'

CHAPTER 23

The police station in Hyde Park smelled to high heaven. No reflection on its occupants, of course, but the pig sty they'd built in their back yard did hum quite a bit across the park, especially when the wind was blowing in the wrong direction. The pig club was the brainchild of the police officers who worked there, and was one of many that had been set up in the London parks as part of their own personal war effort, and since they had all contributed to the purchase of the pigs they were none too pleased when one of the much-prized animals was nicked by Charlie Ratner and his pals.

When Amy, her dad, and Tim arrived, the pigs were fast asleep, dreaming no doubt of the next feed of swill. But the police officers themselves were very much awake.

'She just disappeared from right under our noses,' complained Special Constable Sid Mullard. 'One minute she was there, kipping in her usual pitch down by the boathouse, and then all of a sudden – she was gone.'

Amy turned on Hanley. 'You said your people never took their eyes off 'er.'

Hanley shrugged his shoulders, and looked to the two specials for the explanation.

'Got a mind of her own, your mum,' grumbled Constable Sid.

'Especially when she's upset,' added Constable Roy.

'Upset?' asked Ernie.

The two constables exchanged a shifty look. 'There was a bit of a problem earlier on,' said Constable Sid. 'This young bloke, real layabout, army deserter – they caught up wiv him down by the Serpentine.'

'She saw it happen,' added the younger constable, Roy. 'This bloke was a bit of a mate of hers.'

'She tried to help him.'

'We had ter stop her.'

Amy exchanged an anxious look, first with Tim, then with her dad.

In the background, one of the regular drunks, who had just been brought in, was carrying on like mad, swiping out at anyone who tried to restrain him, and shouting abuse at two highly painted park girls, who'd been nicked for soliciting, and who were now engaged in a real slanging match with him. The station sergeant finally lost his patience, and yelled out, 'Shut up, the lot of yer!'

'Anyway,' continued Constable Sid, 'when the army carted off this bloke, Ma took it out on us, got real ratty.'

''Ardly surprisin'?' suggested Amy, wryly.

The two constables moved uncomfortably from one foot to another.

Hanley intervened. 'The point is, where is she now? Any ideas?'

The older constable shrugged his shoulders. 'She could be anywhere, sir, unless, of course, she's done a flit.'

'Wot d'yer mean?' asked Ernie, irritated with their stonewalling.

The two constables looked uncomfortable. 'We checked her pitch,' said Sid.

'She took her bundle.'

Amy didn't know what they meant.

'Her bits and pieces,' explained Roy. 'Everything she has in the world – I imagine.'

Behind them, a door opened, and an elderly man was bustled in in the custody of two police officers, one of them a woman in civilian clothes. 'Friend of ours!' she called triumphantly as her colleague drew the blackout curtain over the door behind them.

'Oh no!' sighed the station sergeant, shaking his head in exasperation. 'Not you again, Flasher.' The old offender was crying and too distressed to look him in the face, so after a signal from the station sergeant, he was led off to a cell.

'Right,' said Hanley, taking command of the situation. 'Where's your sub tonight?'

The station sergeant answered immediately. ''E's checkin' out a brawl sir. Down Bayswater Road.'

'How many do you have on duty?'

'Eight, sir.'

'How many can you spare?'

The station sergeant pulled a face. 'Not many, sir. It's a busy night.'

Hanley thought for a moment, then turned to Amy. 'Not much we can do till morning, I'm afraid. We'll try again at first light.'

In the background, the drunk was having another boisterous barney with the two park girls.

Day and night, there was never a dull moment in Hyde Park. Even the pigs were now wide awake.

Aggs wasn't used to being out this late. Most nights at this time of year she was back in her pitch behind the boathouse by nine, and kipping her heart out before half-past. But tonight was different. She'd been out on the streets since soon after dark, roaming aimlessly from one litter bin to another along Park Lane, then cutting round the posh back streets of Mayfair where she stopped from time to time to search through the pig swill bins on each corner, just in case the local hotels might have discarded something that might still be fit for human consumption. But she was out of luck, for the swillmen from the lousy local council had clearly been round on collection during the day, emptying the bins, and even clearing up the spillage after them. She cursed the lot of them, and moved on.

By the time she reached Piccadilly Circus, her bundle was beginning to weigh her down. It was a long walk from Hyde Park, and the rope she'd fixed around the rolled-up blanket was cutting into her shoulders. Like the rest of London, the nightly blackout had plunged the Circus into darkness, and as it was well after midnight, the only traffic around was the occasional late night bus or taxi, and a brewer's horse-cart on its way to a pub down Jermyn Street. She stopped to rest for a while on the steps of the plinth, which before the Blitz had supported the famous statue of Eros, but as the statue had been removed to a safe exile out in the country somewhere, the plinth was now protected with massive timber billboards, which made it look like a giant shuttlecock. Aggs took the weight off her feet by squatting on one of the steps at the base of the shuttlecock, where during the day a cockney flowerseller did a roaring trade with visitors to the 'old town'. Aggs took off her plimsolls and rubbed her toes. She didn't quite know what she was doing there; her departure from her pitch in the park had been so rushed, so irrational. All she could remember now was that she had had to get away from the place, as far away as she possibly could. She hated the place, everything about it – the trees, the vegetable plots, the usual nutcases strolling hand in hand down by her neck of the woods alongside the lake, the birds, the geese, the ducks – stupid things! But the moment her mind stopped racing, she took a deep breath, and wondered why. Why *did* she have to run away? Why was she *always* running away? And then she thought about The Kid.

All the way down the Haymarket, she couldn't get him out of her mind. She could see his face, his cheeky grin, his cocky walk. She could see the lack of confidence behind that mask, the fixed grin, those vacant eyes. She would never forget that final wave. The more she could see it, the more she felt as though a knife was being plunged into her chest. Her bitterness became intense. If there *was* such a thing as a God, she hoped He'd strike them all down – yes, the whole ruddy lot of them!

Trafalgar Square offered little comfort, so she shuffled her way across as fast as her poor sore feet would carry her. She didn't bother to stop at the ornamental fountains, for the water had long been cut off, and, much to the disapproval of the bronze lions at the bottom of each corner of Nelson's Column, several layabouts were using the large stone basins as a dosshouse. There were sandbags piled up high outside the entrances of all the grand buildings – Admiralty Arch, South Africa House, Canada House – God knows what it must be like up Whitehall, she thought. At the back of her mind, Aggs knew where she was making for. It was a place where she would be amongst her own kind, somewhere where she could be free of the shackles of park regulations and petty-minded bobbies who were lower than the lowest sewer in town.

At the far end of Northumberland Avenue she reached what she was looking for, the railway arch beneath Hungerford Bridge. Here she found plenty of her own kind, in fact there were more than a dozen or so of them, all of them barely recognisable as members of the human race, huddled up beneath any form of protection they could find – blankets, two or three layers of old overcoats or raincoats, newspapers. This was the other face of Britain at war. Some of them were old soldiers – the forgotten ones – and others who had simply opted out of a life they didn't know how to cope with. And they were all men.

Aggs looked around for a spare place to kip down, but the moment she found a spot by the curved brick wall, she was met with an angry chorus of abuse: 'Piss off !' 'No skirts 'ere!' 'Cow face!' Angry with them all, she gave a two-fingered salute, and moved on.

During the daylight hours, the Victoria Embankment was bright and bustling, the perfect place for a stroll in the sun, with excellent views of Big Ben and the Houses of Parliament, and on the other side of the wide stretch of river, the majestic County Hall, home to the London County Council. Aggs had always liked this part of town. When she was a small kid, her granddad had taken her on a horse-bus ride, where, from the top deck, she could see the whole stretch of the River Thames laid out before her. This was the place to be, she decided, the place to kip down for the night; the river was certainly more welcoming.

'That's *my* boudoir, yer know.'

Aggs had hardly settled herself down on the empty bench

overlooking the river, when the croaky old voice came at her from nowhere.

'You don't 'ave ter move, mind,' said the tall, willowy man in a bright red tunic coat, who suddenly appeared at her side. 'Yer can share it wiv me if yer like.'

Aggs glared at him suspiciously, then put down her bundle and reluctantly moved to allow him to sit beside her.

'My name's Charlie,' he said, offering his hand, which Aggs declined to shake. ''Aven't seen you down this way before. I know all the faces, all the regulars. If it's not a rude question, can I ask *your* name?'

Aggs snapped back immediately, 'No!'

Old Charlie smiled. 'No, you're quite right,' he replied, placidly. 'We shouldn't 'ave names, should we? Once yer live like we do, we've given up our names. Right?'

Aggs didn't quite know how to react to this odd character. Although she was wary of him, he didn't scare her. But she was certainly intrigued by his appearance, his head a bald crown surrounded by a thick flock of long, straight hair which flowed down over the shoulders of his bright red tunic adorned with shining brass buttons.

'Nice jacket, eh?' he said, noticing her interest. 'Pensioner,' he whispered, leaning in to her. 'Chelsea, no less.'

Aggs was puzzled. 'Wot yer doin' out 'ere?' she asked.

'Same as you, I s'ppose,' came the reply. 'Don't like bedrooms. They keep me awake.' He laughed to himself. 'They're always pickin' me up an' takin' me back, but I never stay long. It's not that I'm ungrateful, you understand. They look after yer well up there, that's for sure. But I've got too many memories, yer see. The ones who got left be'ind.'

Aggs hesitated a moment, then started to collect her bundle.

'No, don't go,' said Charlie, placing his hand gently on her arm. 'I don't mean no 'arm. I don't get the chance ter speak ter many people, espeshully ladies like you.'

It had been a long time since Aggs had heard herself referred to as a lady. It persuaded her to put her bundle down again.

For a moment or so, the two of them sat side by side in silence, staring out towards the river, two solitary figures in the dim light from a moon that was struggling to break through the dark night clouds.

'I miss 'ome, though,' Charlie said. 'My real 'ome, that is. Wot about you? Got any family, 'ave yer?'

'No.'

'Everyone 'as a family. *I've* got one. My missus died, but I've got two luvely daughters.'

'Then wot yer doin' out 'ere?' asked Aggs.

Charlie hesitated before answering. 'I often ask meself that,' he replied. Then he thought about it for a moment. 'I think it's because they took me fer granted.'

''Ow come?'

'They never come ter see me,' he said. 'In the 'ome, I mean. Ol' soldiers are very proud, yer know. We don't like ter be ignored. It was all 'cos of my eldest. She ran off wiv this man twice 'er age. She 'ad 'is baby, and then 'e left 'er. I was angry wiv 'er, told 'er she was bonkers. She got upset, said she never wanted ter set eyes on me again. I was wrong. Anyone can make a mistake. It's the puttin' it right that ain't so easy.' He gradually eased himself up from the bench. 'Well, I'll be off. You stay as long as you want. I ain't tired tonight. Got too many things ter do.' He started to move off, but stopped briefly, and turned. 'I wouldn't stay out 'ere too long,' he said. 'This is no place for a lady like you.'

Aggs watched him go. In the pale glow of a filtered moon, she watched the red tunicked frame as it gradually disappeared into the first signs of an early spring mist. Inside her, something stirred. She didn't know why, all she knew was that, for the first time since leaving home, she was wide awake.

It was almost midday when Amy and Tim got off the train at Holloway Road underground station. Together with Amy's dad, they had been searching all morning in the park for Aggs, but without success. Amy was beside herself with worry. She'd known instinctively that sooner or later her mum was going to do something like this.

'I told 'Anley it was a bad idea,' she complained bitterly. 'I told 'im they should've just picked Mum up an' brought 'er straight back 'ome. This is wot 'appens. People fink they know so much, an' yet they don't know nuffin'.'

'I still think he was r-right,' said Tim. 'Somebody who's had a nervous breakdown has to be treated with the utmost care.'

Amy suddenly stopped on the edge of the pavement, and turned on him. 'Who said she's 'ad a nervous breakdown?' she snapped. 'Every time somebody's depressed, they call it a nervous breakdown. It's all a load of old rubbish – just words, words, words.'

Tim did not rise to her tension. 'No, Amy,' he replied, calm but adamant. 'Your m-mum's condition isn't just about words. She's b-been – very ill.'

'Oh really?' Amy called back over her shoulder, as they hurried to cross the main road. ''Ow come you're such an expert on these matters?'

'C-come on now, Amy!' he protested.

When they finally reached the pavement on the other side of the road, Amy walked briskly ahead, leaving Tim to catch her up.

'L-Look,' he complained, 'I'm only t-trying to help.'

Amy came to an abrupt halt. 'She's *my* mum, Tim,' she said, eyes blazing. 'I should know my own mum after all these years. An' I'm tellin' yer, she ain't 'ad no so-called nervous breakdown.'

Tim shook his head in despair. He was beginning to lose patience with her. 'How c-can you say such a thing, Amy?' he asked. 'Your mum left home, her f-family, everything she ever knew about a stable f-family life.'

'D'yer blame her?' Amy asked. 'Wot would you do if after twenty-odd years of married life, yer suddenly discovered that not only was your uvver 'alf 'avin' an affair wiv someone else, but that there was also a kid?'

Tim hesitated. 'I'd be devastated,' he replied, gently taking her hands to try to comfort her. 'But I'd t-try not to go to p-pieces.'

'Oh yes?' snapped Amy, eyes blazing, pulling away from him. 'An' just 'ow would *you* deal wiv it, I wonder? Ask yer precious muvver?' She turned, and started to go.

Tim was stung by her outburst. It was the first time she had ever spoken to him in such a way. He called after her, 'That's n-not fair, Amy.'

Amy came to an abrupt halt, and swung round. 'Wot d'yer expect me ter say then?' she called. 'That 'Anley was right, and that we should leave Mum ter rot away in some lousy flea-ridden park?'

Tim had turned ashen-white. 'I m-mean what you said about m-my m-mother,' he said, thoroughly chastened. 'It's just n-not fair. All I w-was trying to say was that you've come this f-far, you shouldn't let your f-feelings get the b-better of you.'

Amy snapped back, 'Wot would you know about *my* feelings?'

Tim was hurt, and he showed it. 'I l-love you,' he replied. 'So I m-must know something.'

'Well, I'm not like you,' she snapped back, without thinking. 'All me life I've 'ad ter be strong. I couldn't live any uvver way.'

Tim's face crumpled up. He felt crushed. 'You know, Amy,' he said, trying to compose himself, 'I w-wish I knew your m-mum better. If I d-did, I think I m-might understand you m-more.' With that, he turned and went.

Simultaneously, Amy walked off in the opposite direction. But she had gone no more than a few yards, when it suddenly dawned on her what she had done. She stopped, and turned. 'Tim!' she called out frantically.

But it was too late. He had already gone.

Aggs got back to her pitch in Hyde Park early in the afternoon. She hadn't intended to return, and when she caught a glimpse of Constables Sid and Roy watching her from the distance, she wished she hadn't. But if there was one thing she had learned from her night's experience down on the Embankment, it was that, although you can run away from a former life, you can't run away from yourself.

When she got to the old boathouse, she had to wait a while before she could dump her bundle back into her pitch, for the boathouse itself had been opened up for business for the after-noon, and the first customers of the season were already hiring out rowing boats for a quiet flit round the lake. To pass the time, she searched the footpath for any spare lumps of bread that might have been overlooked by the wildlife residents of the park, but she was out of luck there, for once the people feeding them saw what she was up to, they packed up and moved on.

By twilight, it was beginning to get cold again, mainly because a thin film of freezing mist had descended on to the surface of the water, so once the boathouse was closed up again for the night, Aggs moved back into her pitch. She didn't bother to unpack, for she was far too tired after her exhausting day, and once she had stretched out, and leaned her head on her bundle, her eyes soon closed. It wasn't long before she started seeing 'pictures' again. The Kid was there, and, of course, Amy. But the real surprise was that she could see the faces of the other kids, her own kids – Thelma, Arnold, Elsie. They were all there, exactly as she had remembered them, clear as a bell. It was the first time she had laid eyes on them since she had left home. But there was still one face missing, hardly surprising, when she remembered how much he had done to hurt her. No, that was one face that she had erased from her thoughts and her memories, and her dreams. There could be no turning back now.

Just then, she felt a movement on the boathouse platform above her. Her eyes sprang open with a start. There was someone standing over her. She had long ago lost her only pair of glasses, so for a split second, she couldn't see who it was. But when she gradually did manage to focus, there was no mistaking the face, that same face she had rejected in her dreams so many times.

It was Ernie.

CHAPTER 24

Bernie's mobile snack bar was a gem. Nobody could remember how many years he'd been parking it every night on the waste ground more often used by the soap brigade at Speakers' Corner, but it was certainly a long time. At the height of the Blitz he had been invaluable, for he had joined the voluntary services in dishing out hot cups of char and meat-paste sandwiches to just about everyone who was involved in the fight to put out fires and pull people out of the wreckage of bombed-out buildings. These nights his customers tended to be shift workers, such as milkmen, post and newspaper van drivers, girls on the game, and even police officers on patrol. The odd thing, however, was that although Bernie was a British citizen, he had been born in Italy, so it was fortunate that he had escaped internment when his mother country so foolishly entered the war on the side of its dubious new ally, the German Third Reich. But it was not surprising, for from the moment he had left Italy during the poisonous years of *il Duce* Mussolini, he had been a staunch supporter of everything that was so typically British, and that included Aggs.

Tonight, Aggs was grateful for her free cup of Bernie's tea; it made such a change from the bottle of stout she usually turned in with each night. But what she found difficult to understand was why she had agreed to come here at all, in the middle of the night, in the company of the man she had vowed never to set eyes on again. But there was no doubt that the events of the last twenty-four hours had given her much to think over.

'I want yer back, Aggs,' Ernie said, watching over her whilst she sipped her tea. 'We all want yer back – Ame, Thelm, Arn, Else – we've missed yer so much.'

Aggs listened in silence. Standing with her back to him, the outline of her body only just visible against the thin veil of light coming from Bernie's van, she stared out towards Marble Arch, where the Edgware and Bayswater Roads joined up effortlessly with Oxford Street.

Ernie tried again. 'There's so much I want ter tell yer, Aggs,' he said, 'so much to explain. I know I've 'urt yer, I know wot I've done 'as been cruel an' unfair . . .'

'Unfair!' Aggs turned to face him in the dim light. 'Yer rob me of the only bit of self-respect I 'ave left in the world, an' all yer can tell me is – it's unfair? Yer waited best part of fourteen years before yer told me about – that boy. Yer let us live our lives tergevver, yet let us sleep in the same bed tergevver, knowin' that our marriage wasn't worf the paper it was written on.'

'I tried ter tell yer, Aggs. I swear ter God I did try ter tell yer – I don't know 'ow many times.'

'But yer never did.'

Ernie shook his head in anguish. 'I couldn't,' he said. 'Every time I told meself I *'ad* ter do it – I just couldn't.'

'An' if I 'adn't found out,' she replied wryly, 'yer'd never've told me?'

Ernie hesitated before answering. 'Aggs, I went frough fourteen years of 'ell.'

'An' wot d'yer fink *I* went frough, knowin' that three of our own kids 'ad come *after* that woman's boy was born. Is it any wonder that I—' She stopped, and clutched her forehead as if in pain. 'Our marriage was a sham, Ern. Why din't yer tell me years ago that there was nuffin' left between us any more? Why din't yer tell me that yer just din't love me?'

'Becos it wouldn't've bin true, Aggs,' he replied strongly. 'It still isn't true.' He moved closer to her in the dark. 'Wot 'appened between me an' Sylvie Temple was one stupid mistake.'

'A mistake that went on fer fourteen years.'

He took hold of her arms and held them tight. 'I never loved 'er Aggs – not ever. But once I knew 'ow involved I'd become, I just couldn't dump 'er an' leave 'er ter cope wiv a kid all on 'er own.'

'An' wot about me?' asked Aggs. 'You was quite prepared ter leave *me* ter cope on me own.'

'That's not quite true,' he replied. 'At least you 'ad Amy.'

'Amy's not me 'usband, Ern – any more than you are.'

Ernie was stung by that. But he continued, 'I'm not the only one ter blame, yer know. I made my mistake, an' I've admitted it. But it's *you* the kids've always turned to, an' it was *you* who let them down.'

Aggs tried to turn away, but he held on to her.

'It's true, Aggs,' he said. 'Whatever 'appened between you an' me, it was unfair of yer ter take it out on the rest of the family. 'Ow could yer just walk out on 'em, an' leave Ame to cope all on 'er own?'

Aggs pulled away from him. 'I needed ter breave,' she

replied. 'I needed to get away from everyfin' that 'ad anyfin' ter do wiv you.'

'An' fer wot, Aggs?' he asked, with compassion. 'A life like this? A life of wanderin' around all over the place, in all sorts of wevver, livin' 'an' ter mouf, not knowin' if or where yer next meal's comin' from? Wot sort of a life is that, Aggs? Tell me?'

'It's a life wivout lies!' she snapped, fiercely. Then she moved away a little, before turning back to face him. 'Wot sort of a life is it?' she asked, uncertainly. 'Well, I'll tell yer. It's a life where I expect nuffin' from nobody. It's all about me an' me alone. If I do somefin' wrong, I've only got meself ter blame. But at least I don't 'ave ter rely on anybody. At least I don't 'ave ter worry about being cheated, or lied to. Out 'ere, I'm nobody. I don't 'ave ter take, an' I don't 'ave ter give. I'm free as the air.'

'Are yer, Aggs?' asked Ernie. 'Are yer really free, or are yer just like me – runnin' away wiv yer eyes closed? We've made a lot of mistakes, Aggs – boaf you an' me. But we owe it to our kids – your kids an' mine – ter make up for it. I'm sorry fer wot I've done, I'll always be sorry. I never meant ter cheat on yer, I never meant ter break your will ter live.' He paused briefly to take a deep breath. 'I love you, Aggs. Whatever you fink about me, about wot I've done, I promise yer, I've never stopped lovin' yer. All I can do is ter ask yer ter fergive me – an' beg yer ter come back 'ome.'

Amy had decided to clean up the house. It was something she had wanted to do for a long time, and now that she had given up her job at the Corner House and had a lot of spare time on her hands, it was a job she was determined to get on with.

Housework, however, was Amy's way of coping with stress, and after all she'd been through just lately, for her, it was the ideal solution.

She heard the front street door open and close just as she had finished cleaning out the oven grate in the front parlour. Thinking it was her dad returning home from joining the police search for her mum in the park, she rushed out into the hall. But it wasn't Ernie at all.

'Oh,' she said, taken by surprise. 'Din't know it was you, Uncle Jim.'

'Hello, Amy,' he replied, rather awkwardly. 'How are things?'

''Bout the same,' said Amy. 'Dad's out lookin' for Mum. She went missin' last night.'

Jim was shocked. 'Oh no,' he said, only too aware that it had been he who had betrayed Aggs's confidence by taking Amy to the park to see her. He lowered his eyes guiltily. 'I'm sorry. Let me know if there's anything I can do.'

Amy smiled weakly, but as he started to walk up the stairs, she called, 'It's not your fault, Uncle Jim. Mum's so mixed up. Yer mustn't blame yourself.'

Jim smiled back, then went upstairs.

Amy watched him go, consumed with guilt that she had unjustly accused him of having a relationship with her mum. It was a stupid, childish conclusion to have drawn, and she deeply regretted it. With this is mind, she waited until she had heard his door close, and then followed him up.

'Come in!' called Jim, as he heard Amy tapping on his back room door.

Amy peered in. 'I came ter say sorry,' she said.

Jim was puzzled. 'Wot are you talking about, Amy?'

'For the way I've treated you,' Amy replied, coming into the room. 'For the way we've *all* treated you. Yer've always bin so good to this family. I'm ashamed of us.'

'My dear Amy,' said Jim, 'there's no need to feel like that. These have been hard times for all of you.'

'I thought all the wrong fings about you an' Mum,' she said. 'For some stupid reason, I put one an' one tergevver, but it didn't add up. If it 'adn't been fer that photo . . .'

Jim put his hand under Amy's chin, slowly raised it, and smiled reassuringly at her. 'I do understand – honest.'

Amy felt confident enough to smile back. But whilst she was doing so, she suddenly became aware that there was something different about the room. It looked bare, and in the corner of the room there was a tea chest containing cooking utensils.

'Wot's 'appening?' she asked, nodding towards the household items stacked up against the walls.

'Oh – all this stuff, you mean? Just a bit of spring-cleaning, that's all.' He was clearly hedging. 'Got to keep up with you, you know.'

For the time being, Amy thought no more about it. But she was curious. On the way down the stairs again, she heard the front street door open and close. This time it was Ernie.

'Did they find 'er?' she asked urgently, eagerly.

Ernie nodded. 'She's going ter be OK, Ame.'

'Wot d'yer mean?' she asked. 'They did find 'er, din't they?'

'Yes, Ame,' Ern replied, as he hung up his cap on a hook in the passage. 'They found 'er.'

'But did yer see 'er?' she persisted, following him into the back parlour. 'Did yer 'ave a chance ter talk to 'er?'

'Yes, Ame,' he said, searching for one of his fag ends on the mantelpiece. 'I talked to 'er.'

Amy's face immediately lit up. 'Oh, Dad – that's wonderful! Wot did she say? Did yer put fings right? Is she comin' 'ome.'

He swung a look at her. 'No, Ame,' he replied, quickly, firmly. 'Mum's not comin' 'ome. She needs time.'

'Time? Time fer wot?'

'Ter fink fings over.' He found a dog-end, and put it between his lips. 'She needs ter find a way to adjust. It's been a long time, yer know.'

Amy was not convinced. 'But she can do that 'ere,' she insisted, 'in the comfort of 'er own 'ome.'

'I'm not sure it's comfort she's lookin' for,' he replied, lighting his fag end. 'She can only work fings out in 'er *own* time, and in 'er own way.'

Amy then realised how tired and drawn he was looking. So she went to him. 'When will that be, Dad?' she asked, apprehensively. 'Is Mum *ever* goin' ter come 'ome?'

Ernie looked up at her. His face told a story. 'I 'ope so, Ame,' he replied with a sigh. 'Please God, I do 'ope so.'

Thane Villas was a cut above most of the back streets around Seven Sisters Road. For a start, the houses were Edwardian, semi-detached, and set on either three or four floors. In the surrounding neighbourhood, the Villas was known as the 'select' area, not because they were particularly posh, but because most of the folk who lived there were just that little bit better off. However, that wasn't quite so true of Tim Gudgeon and his mother.

Even though Thane Villas was no more than a stone's

throw from Enkel Street, Amy had never once set foot in the place, so it came as a bit of a shock to know that Tim lived in such well-placed surroundings. Amy had also never met Tim's mother, and, after some of the things she had said about her, she was dreading it. It was therefore with some trepidation that she rang the doorbell on the wall of the grand-looking three-storey house with the white window frames. Whilst she was waiting there, she tried to picture in her mind what this monster-woman would look like. How she hated her for keeping her son under her thumb for so long. How would she ever be able to tell Tim that with all her heart and soul she loved him, and that she would never forgive herself for all the cruel things she had said to him. But she had to do it, she had to do it before it was too late. With butterflies in her stomach, Amy prayed that the woman she so despised might not be at home. But when the door was finally opened, she was surprised by what she saw.

'Hello,' said the slim, middle-aged woman peering out. 'Can I help you?'

Amy bit her lip anxiously. 'Mrs Gudgeon?' she asked, tentatively.

'Yes?'

'I'm Amy,' she croaked, tentatively. 'Amy Dodds. I'm a friend of Tim's.'

The woman's face lit up. 'My dear!' she beamed, enthusiastically. 'Come in! Come in!'

Amy smiled bravely. 'Fanks,' she said.

The moment she walked in, she could smell furniture polish.

'You've caught me at just the right time,' Mrs Gudgeon

said, closing the door behind her. 'I've been looking for an excuse to stop doing chores and have a cup of tea. Now let me have a good look at you.' She brought them to a halt in the hall. 'Oh yes,' she beamed, as she looked Amy up and down. 'You're exactly as Tim described. Pretty as a picture.'

This was not at all what Amy had expected, and she suddenly felt quite self-conscious as Mrs Gudgeon led her into the large front parlour, which had an open fireplace, and antique furniture that was so highly polished she could see her face in it.

'I don't get too many visitors these days,' said Mrs Gudgeon, fluttering around excitedly. 'Except my mother on a Thursday afternoon. That usually means battle stations! Now you sit yourself down, and I'll go and put on the kettle.'

'Fanks all the same, Mrs Gudgeon,' said Amy apologetically, 'but I can't stay long. I've got ter get back ter collect me little sister from school.'

'Oh dear,' said Mrs G, disappointed. 'That's a shame.'

'I just came ter 'ave a few words wiv Tim. Is 'e around?'

Mrs G shook her head. Somehow, her face didn't match up to Tim's description of how dominant and possessive she was. Even so, Amy wasn't all that sure, for despite the woman's fixed smile, she had dark, flashing eyes which revealed an inquisitiveness that was really quite sinister. 'I'm afraid he's out, my dear,' she replied. 'He's at the hospital this afternoon, having his jab.'

Amy was puzzled. 'Jab?' she asked.

Mrs G looked surprised. 'Insulin, my dear,' she replied. 'Tim's a diabetic. Didn't he tell you?'

Amy was unmoved. 'Yes,' she said, squarely. 'He told me.'

'Poor boy,' continued Mrs G, her fixed smile momentarily

replaced by one of pity. 'It's such a burden for him to have to bear. It's really quite alarming at times, especially when you see him in a coma. Mind you, he doesn't get it from my side. It was his father, you see. Poor man, he died of it.'

Amy knew she was lying. Tim had already told her about the father who had disappeared before Tim was born. Despite the smiles, the cosy accent, and the warm, hospitable welcome, Amy didn't trust this woman one little bit. 'Well, when yer see 'im,' she said, 'could yer tell 'im I called?'

'Certainly, my dear,' replied Mrs G, as she led the way back out into the hall again, and opened the front door. 'I'm so glad Tim's found such a sweet little thing like you.'

Amy stepped out on to the doorstep.

'If you ask me,' continued Mrs G, 'he's a very lucky young man. He has few enough friends as it is. Too much of a risk. I mean, it's not easy to deal with someone whose life is always in such danger – is it?' She offered her hand to Amy. 'It's been so nice meeting you, my dear,' she said, with that smile again. 'I'm sure we shall be seeing quite a lot of each other from now on.'

Reluctantly, Amy allowed Mrs G to shake her hand. It felt like a piece of wet fish. 'G'bye, Mrs Gudgeon,' she said. Then without waiting for the woman to close her door, she turned, walked down the steps, and hurried on her way.

Right to the end of the road, she could still feel the woman's eyes looking straight through her.

Although winter still hadn't been officially left behind, along Seven Sisters Road, there were definite signs that spring was at last making real headway. The pavements were crowded with the usual afternoon window shoppers, mainly women who were out looking for something different to buy for their family's tea, or old-age pensioners passing the time idly chatting to their neighbours. As ever, Hicks the greengrocers was doing a roaring trade, especially in King Edwards, which, for some reason, always seemed to be the favourite spud amongst the people of Holloway. Being a family business, Hicks was very popular in the district, mainly because they could be trusted not to overcharge. During the summer months, Arnold particularly liked their fresh strawberries and cherries.

Making her way briskly through the afternoon crowds, Amy didn't have much time for window shopping today. After her first unpalatable meeting with Tim's mum, the only person she wanted to see now was Tim himself. How she pitied him, being brought up by such a conniving, dominating mother like that, who was clearly intent on keeping a hold on him for as long as she could. She could still hear that voice ringing in her ears: *Too much of a risk. I mean, it's not easy to deal with someone whose life is always in such danger – is it?* Risk! Her own son! God protect anyone who had to rely on a woman like that!

She was so angry, she hadn't noticed that she was practically running, dodging in and out of the crowds, cursing everyone who got in her way. To make matters worse, it took her ages to get across the road at the Nag's Head, for the traffic lights were stuck and everyone seemed too paralysed with fear to step off the pavement. When she did manage to get into Holloway Road, it was only a few minutes' walk to the Royal Northern Hospital in Manor Gardens, so she slowed down her pace, and tried to be calm. After her encounter with the formidable Mrs Gudgeon, her mind was full of things she wanted to say to Tim, things that would make him forgive her for the awful way she had talked to him. Over and over again she blamed herself for being so absorbed in her own problems that she was incapable of understanding the type of life Tim had had to endure with a mother who was clearly absolutely determined to keep a hold on him. No, things had to change. Remorse, guilt was not enough. From now on, she had to start thinking about *him*, about how she could give him the same loving support that he was always giving her. She came to an abrupt halt. A horrifying thought had suddenly occurred to her. What if Tim never wanted to see her again?

'Amy?'

In her panic, she hadn't noticed that Tim was standing before her.

'Tim!' she gasped, immediately throwing her arms around him.

'What are you doing here?'

'I was coming to meet yer,' she replied, quickly.

Tim was puzzled. 'How did you know where I was?'

She hesitated. 'Yer muvver told me,' she replied, awkwardly.

'My m-mother?' he asked, warily.

'I went ter see 'er. I was lookin' fer you. She told yer'd gone ter the 'ospital – ter 'ave your jab.'

Tim tensed. 'I see,' he said, gently releasing his arms from round her waist.

Amy was concerned by his change of mood. 'Yer didn't mind, did yer?' she asked, anxiously.

'What did you want to see me about?'

'I wanted ter apologise.'

'What for?'

'I wasn't very nice to yer this mornin'. I shouldn't've talked ter yer the way I did.'

Tim was embarrassed. 'It doesn't m-matter, Amy,' he replied. 'You were very upset about w-what happened in the park last night. It's perfectly n-natural. You need your m-mum, j-just as m-much as you think I n-need m-my m-mother.'

Amy felt terrible. His remark proved what she had feared, that she had hurt him terribly. 'I didn't mean what I said, Tim,' she tried to explain. 'It was just that, well, every time you've ever talked about your muvver, you've always sounded kind of – bitter.'

'Then I only have m-myself to blame,' he replied. 'I shouldn't have talked about her like that. In m-many ways, my m-mother's been very good to m-me. She brought m-me up, fed and clothed m-me, gave m-me anything I wanted. It can't've b-been easy for her. I shouldn't have talked about her l-like that.'

As they were standing in the path of busy passers-by, he placed his hand behind her back, and gently led her to the corner of a quiet mews known as Bowman's Place.

'All I wanted ter say,' said Amy, struggling for words, 'all I *ever* wanted ter say, was that there comes a time when everyone 'as ter leave 'ome, and get on wiv their own life.'

Tim lowered his eyes. 'W-what you implied,' he said with difficulty, 'was that I was w-weak.'

Amy was shocked. 'No, Tim! That's not true,' she said.

'You said that you w-were strong. Which m-means that *I'm* weak.'

Amy put her hand under his chin and gently raised it. 'I could never think that of you, Tim,' she said, her voice cracking. 'Anyone who has so much love ter offer as you, is strong – not weak.'

Tim found it difficult to meet her eyes. 'I can't l-leave her, Amy,' he said. 'I d-don't know why, but I just can't leave her. N-not yet.'

Amy stood back. After a pause, she asked, 'So where does that leave us?'

'I l-love you, Amy,' he replied. 'I d-don't think I could ever stop loving you. But what can I d-do if you find m-my mother a threat.'

Amy looked up with a start. 'She ain't a threat ter me, Tim,' she said almost resentfully. 'But she is ter you.'

'You d-don't understand her, Amy,' he replied. 'M-Mother's overprotective, that's all. She's had a hard l-life. She just d-doesn't want m-me to m-make the same m-mistakes that she's made.'

Amy thought hard about that. For one fleeting moment, she almost felt as though his mother was right. Perhaps she, Amy herself, had no right to be part of those mistakes. 'I understand, Tim,' she said, unconvincingly. 'I'm sorry if I've interfered.' She smiled bravely, turned, and started to go.

Tim immediately went to her. 'D-don't say things like that, Amy,' he pleaded. 'I r-respect everything you've said.'

'Do yer, Tim?' she asked, wryly. 'So where does that leave us now?'

Tim's face crumpled up in anguish. 'I don't want to lose you, Amy,' he said. 'I don't ever want to lose you. But it's up to you. It's your decision, not mine.'

CHAPTER 25

The four thirty train from Hatfield arrived late at Finsbury Park. There was nothing unusual about that, of course, because Sunday afternoon was more often than not the time when they carried out work on the tracks just outside Brookman's Park station, which, since the start of the war, had suffered intermittent attacks by rogue enemy aircraft. Sylvie Temple always took this same train back every week after visiting her elder sister, Vera, who lived with her husband in a comfortable semi in Green Lanes, Hatfield, an attractive rural area dominated by the de Havilland aircraft factory nearby. For Sylvie, it was a real breath of fresh air to get away once a week from the smoke and grime of the munitions shop in Highbury, and it also gave Joe the chance to enjoy at least one day a week without his mum constantly breathing down his neck.

The journey had been a tedious one, and Sylvie was even more irritated when she stepped out on to the platform to find soot marks from the carriage door all over her camelhair topcoat. Cursing, and only making the marks worse by brushing them with her hand, she joined the other passengers making their way down the bleak stone steps beneath the station platforms, and headed off towards the exit.

The roads outside the station were crowded with people just coming out from a Sunday afternoon matinée performance at the Rink Cinema, and Sylvie thought it was like bedlam as she was pushed and jostled crossing the Seven Sisters Road. Knowing that there would be long queues at the bus stop, she decided to walk back home to Highbury, taking a short cut through St Thomas's Road, and then along the main Blackstock Road. On the way, she stopped briefly to take a look at the billboards outside the Finsbury Park Empire, which were advertising the coming week's programme featuring 'Two Ton' Tessie O'Shea. It was almost blackout time, and, as her glasses were in her handbag, she had to strain to be able to see the photos on display there. To make matters worse, it started to rain, so she had to take shelter for a few minutes beneath the cover of the theatre's entrance canopy. With the noise of the raindrops pelting down on the pavement just in front of her, it took a moment or so for it to sink in that someone was talking to her.

'Mrs Temple?'

Sylvie hesitated briefly, then swung a look to the small figure standing next to her.

''Allo, Mrs Temple. It's me, Thelma.'

Sylvie had a look of thunder on her face.

'Yer know me, don't yer?' persisted the slender young girl, wrapped up in a warm topcoat, woollen headscarf and gloves. 'I'm Amy's sister.'

'I *know* who you are, thank you,' Sylvie replied, coldly. 'Wot d'yer want?'

Thelma shrugged her shoulders innocently. 'I saw yer crossin' the road,' she replied. 'I've bin ter the pittures wiv my friend, Pauline.'

Sylvie looked up helplessly at the heavy downpour. She felt trapped.

'D'yer mind if I ask yer somefin'?' Thelma turned round to face her. 'Why don't yer want us ter meet our 'alf-bruvver?'

Sylvie sighed deeply. 'If yer don't mind,' she replied, haughtily, 'I don't wish ter discuss such fings wiv you.'

'Why not?'

Sylvie was angry and exasperated with the girl's pushiness. 'Wot I'm tryin' ter tell yer, young lady,' she growled, 'is that I'm not obliged to discuss the matter wiv you. So will yer please stop askin' questions, and mind your own business.'

'Wot're yer afraid of, Mrs Temple?' Thelma asked, calm and reasonable. 'Joe's our 'alf-bruvver. It's not 'is fault, an' it's not ours. But yer can't deny that it's a fact. So wot's the 'arm in us all gettin' tergevver? I'm sure 'e'd like ter meet us just as much as we'd like ter meet 'im.'

'Then you'd be mistaken,' insisted Sylvie, staring out at the rain. ''E doesn't even know about yer.'

Thelma found this difficult to believe. 'Is that fair?' she asked, daringly.

Sylvie swung her an angry look.

'It don't seem right that innocent people should be kept apart when they ain't done nuffin' wrong,' said Thelma, and then added wistfully, 'Dad told us about Joe. 'E said 'e was a smashin' boy, that we'd get on well wiv 'im – if we ever got the chance.'

Sylvie wanted to snap back, but she didn't. In fact, for the first time there was a pained expression in her eyes, which she instantly revealed by focusing them back towards the rain.

'I don't 'old nuffin' against yer, Mrs Temple,' continued Thelma, with something more than just childlike simplicity.

379

'Neivver do my bruvver an' sisters. I know 'ow yer must feel 'cos of wot Amy's said to yer, but she don't mean it – 'onest she don't. She's 'ad a 'ard time since Mum went away. It ain't bin easy for 'er, 'avin' ter look after us. But in 'er 'eart of 'earts, she knows that wotever 'appened between you an' our dad, ain't just your fault. But yer shouldn't take it out on us. Yer shouldn't take it out on Joe. We're 'is family, an' we want 'im ter know that we care about 'im.'

Sylvie's eyes were moist. She had to close them. When she opened them again, the rain had stopped. She waited a moment, then slowly turned to look at Thelma. But she was gone.

Amy felt as though all the stuffing had been knocked out of her. It had been bad enough sacrificing her mum to a life of living out rough in the park, but to lose Tim to his possessive mother was just too much to take. The problem was, she loved him, and she knew only too well that he loved her too, so what could she do to win him back? In desperation, she turned to her old chum Marge Jackson at the tea shop in Holloway Road.

'If yer take my advice,' said Marge, sitting with Amy at the usual staff table at the back of the shop, 'yer'll hang on ter that boy of yours. If yer love him, then 'e's worth fightin' for.'

'Well, I tell yer wot I'd do,' chipped in Mrs Bramley. 'If I came across a woman like that, I'd push one of me custard tarts right in her face.'

The old cook's comment brought a glimmer of a smile to Amy's face. 'Waste of a good custard tart, Mrs B,' she said.

'I don't think we need to be quite as extreme as that, Dora,' said Marge. 'But it's not a bad idea!'

She and Amy chuckled together.

'Seriously though, Amy,' said Marge, once their expressions had changed. 'Wot *are* yer goin' ter do? Yer *do* love Tim, don't yer?'

Amy sighed and nodded.

'Then yer must 'ave it out with 'im.'

'We've said all we can say to each uvver, Marge,' replied Amy. 'What *I* 'ave ter decide is wevver I can take that woman breavin' down my throat fer the rest of me life.'

'Well – can yer?' asked Marge.

Amy sighed. 'I don't know, Marge,' she replied. 'I don't even know if I should.'

'Depends.'

'On wot?'

'On wevver yer love this boy of yours enough?' Marge looked at Amy's forlorn face, and smiled. 'Stupid question, I know.'

'Sounds ter me like 'e's a bit of a muvver's boy,' sniffed Mrs Bramley, lighting herself a fag. 'If 'e was one of mine, I'd tell 'im ter sling 'is 'ook an' get on wiv 'is own life.'

'Easier said than done, Dora,' said Marge. 'Especially when you're an only child. Leavin' 'ome is a big wrench fer a youngster.'

'It wouldn't be so complicated if 'is muvver still 'ad 'er 'usband,' said Amy. 'In a sense, Tim's taken 'is farver's place. It's really sad.'

Mrs Bramley grunted. 'Sad fer who, I'd like ter know!'

Despite Mrs Bramley's rough judgement, there was something inside Amy that made her feel sorry for Tim's mother. Possessive, overprotective, call it what you will, she told herself, Tim's mother was, after all, a human being, with human failings. Loneliness was a terrible thing. The fear that she was going to be left alone was a very real problem that she would find hard to face up to. As Amy looked around her at the other customers at their tables, she could almost hear her old mate Hilda saying flippantly, '*Just look at them, darling. Every face tells a story.*' Hilda was right. Every face around her *did* tell a story. And for some the story was about being lonely, about never hearing someone but themselves open and close the front door again, about lying awake at night knowing that the house was no longer throbbing with the sound of someone they loved in the next room. But was Tim's mother really like that, Amy asked herself? Was her problem really about being lonely, or was it something far more complicated, like unconsciously locking up her son's mind so that he could never think clearly for himself? And despite the fact that Tim was the one man Amy would want to spend the rest of her life with, how would she be able to unlock that mind, and help him to think for himself, to make his own decisions.

After Mrs Bramley had excused herself, and gone back to her kitchen, Marge said, 'I'll tell yer somethin', Amy. This same sort of thing 'appened ter me years ago.'

'It did?' asked Amy, intrigued.

'Oh yes,' said Marge, who linked her fingers together, and rested her hands on the table in front of her. 'It wasn't quite the same situation, but it was the same thing – really. It was Ben – my 'usband – it was when 'e got me ter 'elp 'im tell 'is mum an' dad that 'e was goin' off ter fight the Falangists in Spain. Ben was their only child, yer see. 'E was the apple of their eye. They nearly died when they 'eard wot 'e was doin'. They didn't understand anyfin' about fightin' a just cause, or standin' up fer principles. All they could see was their son who was goin off ter put 'is life in danger, their son who they might never see again. But like all those kids at the time, Ben was passionate about what he wanted ter do. All 'e knew was that people were being killed and maimed just becos they didn't believe in wot one man was tryin' ter drum into 'em. Although his mind was all mixed up, the one thing 'e knew was that 'e just 'ad ter go.' Marge now had the faint suggestion of a smile on her face. But it was a painful, wry smile. ''Is mum an' dad blamed me, of course – I was the one who persuaded 'im, I was the one who'd turned 'is mind. But it wasn't me. It wasn't me at all. It was somethin' 'e 'ad ter do, an' that's all there was to it. If only they could've understood that; if only they could've realised that their son 'ad a mind of 'is own.' She sat up in her chair, put her arms in her lap, and turned to look at Amy. 'The trouble is,' she said, with great poignancy, 'is that no matter 'ow much yer love someone, there are times when yer just 'ave ter let go.'

Aggs scowled at every flatfoot who came anywhere near her. She knew they were keeping their beady eyes on her, watching her wherever she went, and she was just as determined to keep them at a distance. None the less, it was obvious that the pressure was beginning to get her down. Why was it everyone had to keep harassing her, she asked herself? If she'd wanted to go home, she'd have done so a long time ago. Despite Amy and Ernie's assurances that everything would be all right, and that Aggs would be able to start a whole new life again with the family that loved her, she still wasn't convinced. Treachery took a long time to forget. She wasn't going to kid herself that it would be easy to turn back the clock and learn how to trust people all over again. And yet . . . and yet, something *was* stirring within her, something that was nagging, not only through the night, but during all her waking hours. There were times when she thought it was because she still hadn't got over the shock of seeing her young mate, The Kid, being bundled off into the back of an army van; her stomach retched every time she thought about that last, lingering, desperate look on the boy's face, and her complete inability to be able to help him. And what about Jim? How could she ever trust *him* again when he had quite deliberately betrayed her confidence? Everything was so mixed up in her mind. She couldn't go home; there was no reason for doing so. Nothing had changed, nothing – except that, for the first time, there was now a yearning, an aching feeling inside her stomach.

Monday afternoons along Oxford Street were never very profitable for Aggs. Most of the weekend shoppers had been and gone, and all that was now left were the people who worked in the many shops and department stores there. But even though she had almost gone through all that had been left over from her wages at The Turk's Head, today she was not really worried too much about begging with an outstretched hand for the odd penny or two. At the present moment, all she wanted to do was look. And, despite the austerity of war, there was still plenty to look at. For the past year or so, she had always walked straight past shop windows without so much as a glance. Even when she was at home, clothes had never really interested her; for her, they were only a necessity, and she couldn't care less *what* she looked like. But today, Selfridges shop windows seemed to take on a life that she hadn't noticed before. The models there, were, in her opinion, nothing but skinny lumps, but, scornful though she was, some of the clothes they were wearing did catch her eye, for, without realising it, her nose was pressed up hard against the window.

'Got enough coupons, 'ave yer?'

Aggs jumped with a start. When she swung round to see who was talking to her, she was faced with an elderly man, white hair greased right back, and immaculately togged out in a navy-blue three-piece suit and a smart tie and shirt. But the real shock came when she gradually focused on the hairless, well-scrubbed face, and the ribbon of medals pinned to his jacket. It was Scrounger.

'Blimey!' was all she could say.

'Wotcha, mate,' returned Scrounger, with a broad smile that revealed a wonderful new set of gleaming white false teeth.

'I fawt you was dead!' exclaimed Aggs.

'Not me, mate,' said Scrounger, with a cheeky grin. 'Can't keep a good man down, yer know. Mind you, it come pretty close. When they took me off in that am'blance, I fawt I was a gonna. It was me 'eart, yer see. When they stretched me out in the 'ospital, I could 'ear this geezer sayin', "Waste a time, this one." Well, that's wot I fink 'e said. But – 'ere I am, Aggs!' He drew close to her. ''Ere,' he said, his breath reeking of whisky. 'Feel peckish, do yer? Come on. I'll buy yer a slap-up.'

Aggs, too shocked to protest, followed him obediently as he led her off to a café just round the corner.

The other customers gave them a wide berth as they sat down, for although Aggs had probably had just as good a wash that morning as any of them, her tattered raincoat and crushed felt hat was a bit off-putting. Once they'd settled, Scrounger sent for a beer for himself, and a stout for Aggs. Then he sent the rather flustered waiter off to get them both a mince and vegetable pie, steamed parsley cauliflower, and potato pancakes, and at the same time he ordered the 'afters', which today was Bakewell tart and custard. Aggs didn't know she was living, and for a time she couldn't keep her eyes off all the different selections of food that were being served to the other customers in the rather posh-looking café.

Aggs waited until she had taken her first gulp of stout before asking, 'So wot's all this then? Won the pools or somefin'?'

Scrounger downed some of his beer, then gave her a mischievous wink. 'Not bad, eh?' he said, showing off his stylish togs. 'My family always said it pays me ter dress up. 'Ansome devil, ain't I?'

Aggs sniffed dismissively.

'Don't worry, I ain't nicked nuffin'. This is all mine. So's the lolly. I've always 'ad plenty of it.'

Aggs eyed him warily. 'Wot yer talkin' about?'

'I used ter 'ave me own business – second-'and furniture, that sort of fing. My firm was one of the best in the business. Made a packet, I can tell yer.'

'Yer lyin' old bugger!' grunted Aggs, wiping the rim of stout from her lips with the back of her hand. 'You told me you was a soldier in the last war.'

'So I was!' returned Scrounger, sitting up erect and proudly patting his medals. 'I'm talkin' about *before* the war. They was good days, I can tell yer. It was when I come back 'ome that – fings changed.' He started to cough, then quickly pulled out a clean white handkerchief from his jacket pocket to spit out some phlegm. Aggs could see that not everything about him had changed. 'It was my daughter, yer see. Ever since my missus died, she an' 'er 'usband 'ad their eyes on my pile. In some ways, I fink they'd've bin more 'appy if I 'adn't come 'ome from the front.' He blew his nose, and put his handkerchief away. 'Anyway,' he continued, 'they was out of luck, weren't they?' He touched the side of his nose with one finger, and again winked at her. 'Stashed it away, din't I? Somewhere where they couldn't get their greasy little fingers on it.'

They paused a moment whilst the waiter served them with their main course. It seemed to take forever, but as Aggs hadn't had a decent meal in months, she wasn't complaining. But she was completely bowled over by everything Scrounger was telling her, and as she watched him tuck into his minced beef pie, she couldn't believe that she was sitting opposite the same old codger who had plagued the daylights out of her from the first day she had ever set foot inside the park. This wasn't the Scrounger *she* knew. This was a complete stranger.

'Trouble is,' continued Scrounger, cutting up his crispy potato pancakes, 'when I come back from the war, fings 'ad som'ow changed. I couldn't settle, I couldn't get inter the swing of fings. Of course, my daughter was no 'elp at all. As far as she was concerned, I was nuffin' but a bleedin' pain in the neck, a hindrance, an interruption to 'er own plans – wotever *they* were. Anyway – ' Before continuing, he took another gulp from his glass of beer – 'all I wanted ter do was ter up an' get out of it. No matter 'ow 'ard I tried, I couldn't get my mates out of me mind. The ones who came back wiv me, and – ' he stopped briefly, eyes staring at the plate in front of him – 'and the one's who didn't.' He hesitated.

'Nuffin' I'd ever 'ad seemed important ter me any more.' He looked across at her. 'Know wot I mean, Aggs?'

Aggs shrugged her shoulders noncommittally.

Scrounger accepted her response, then wiped his lips with a paper napkin, and leaned back in his chair. 'Did I ever tell yer 'ow long I stuck it out in the park?'

Aggs nodded whilst she ate.

'Twelve years,' he continued. 'Soon after I come back from the war, I knocked around just about every street in London – one night in a shop doorway, anuvver kippin' out in the meat market up Smiffield, Rowton kip'ouse, a bench down the Embankment – anywhere, as long as I didn't 'ave ter rely on anyone. It's funny, ain't it? I mean, I could've gone 'ome any time I wanted, 'ad a good life – sleepin' in me own bed, three good tuck-ins a day wivout any problems at all – an' yet, an' yet, it's not wot I wanted – not then, not till I knew wot it was I *really* wanted.'

'Don't know why you're tellin' me all this,' Aggs said, curtly.

Scrounger smiled, and leaned across the table towards her. 'I'm tellin' yer becos it took a bleedin' 'eart attack ter tell me just exactly wot it was that I *did* want.'

Aggs looked back at him, but tried to appear as though she wasn't really interested.

'I wanted peace of mind, Aggs,' he said.

Aggs swallowed a piece of cauliflower. 'An' yer've found it, 'ave yer?' she asked, caustically.

Scrounger held back a moment before replying. 'Yes, Aggs,' he said, leaning back in his chair again. 'I've found it all right – but only just in time.'

Later that afternoon, Scrounger walked to the park with

Aggs. It had been a beautiful March day, and it wasn't hard to see that thin layer of fresh green grass that began to herald the start of a brand-new season. As they slowly made their way towards the Serpentine lake from Cumberland Gate, there was an invigorating feeling of spring in the air. In the distance beyond Notting Hill Gate, the familiar sight of barrage balloons could still be seen bobbing up and down in the sky high above the rooftops, and the sound of an ambulance pierced the air as it raced at speed to an emergency, bell clanging, along the Edgware Road.

'It's a mug's game, yer know, Aggs,' said Scrounger, as they went. ''Angin' round this place till the end of yer days. I mean, is it *really* worf it?'

'*You* clearly don't fink so,' replied Aggs, hands in raincoat pockets, her collar pulled up tight around her neck.

'I used ter,' said Scrounger. 'I used ter, right up ter that day when they carted me off in that am'blance. Ter me, this park was the way ter get away from meself. But when I thought I was gaspin' me last breff, I found meself askin' why I *want* ter get away. It took me a long time ter work it out that, wotever time I've got left, I ought ter make the best of it. After all, it's no use goin' ter yer box windin' on about 'ow many mistakes yer've made.' They came to a halt at the lake's edge. 'I've wasted a lot of my time, Aggs,' he said, wistfully. 'Now I'm goin' ter take wot I can before it's too late.'

Aggs grunted. 'Is that wot you call "peace of mind"?' she asked, with something less than her usual cynicism.

Scrounger smiled to himself. 'Somefin' like that,' he replied. His grey old eyes were reflecting the deepening rays of the late afternoon sun, which were beginning to send minute rainbow-coloured stars rippling across the surface of the water.

Then he turned to her, and said, 'It don't come easy, Aggs. But when it does, it's worf waitin' for.'

A few minutes later, he was gone. Aggs watched this transformed figure of a man shuffling his way back towards the tube station at Hyde Park Corner. He hadn't changed that much at all. Despite his fancy togs, and his way with words, he was still the same old bag of wind who'd fussed her so much over the past year or so. But one impression he had firmly left with her was that not only would this be the last time that she would see him, but that he was bequeathing to her a sense of direction that she just couldn't ignore.

CHAPTER 26

With the evenings gradually drawing out again, the people of Holloway used the extra hour or so of daylight to stand at their front doors and chat to their next-door neighbours. It had become a quaint custom, for up until the start of the war, back street Londoners, unlike their northern counterparts, kept themselves to themselves. The chat was, invariably, about the progress – or lack of progress – of the war itself. It was clear that, after the occasional one-off attacks by dare-devil enemy aircraft, no one was taking anything for granted. Only recently, Mr Churchill had warned that the end of the war was still a long way off, and the likelihood of an air raid containing gas bombs, or even the constant threat of an enemy invasion, was not to be ignored. This had alarmed many people, including Thelma, who had left her gas mask on the top of a number 14 bus months before.

One of the places where neighbours were still not too disposed to talk to one another, however, was Thane Villas. Here, the lace curtains remained drawn during the day, and only fluttered when there was something or someone in the street who was worth spying on. Amy was only too aware of that, when, the moment she turned into the quiet back street from Seven Sisters Road, she caught a middle-aged, smartly dressed woman chasing a stray brown and white mongrel dog who had dared to lift his leg against one of the timber posts of her newly erected front gate.

Amy could hardly believe that she was once again standing on Mrs Gudgeon's doorstep. The last time she had been there, she had vowed never to return, but here she was, ready to eat humble pie and swallow her pride, all in the name of love. Her instinct was to turn round and go straight back home, but she resisted the temptation because she had come to realise that making an effort for someone she loved was just as important as sticking to principles. Some way or another, she had to put things right with Tim's mother; she had to make the woman like her. It wasn't going to be easy, she knew that, but she had to make the effort. None the less, she was dreading the moment when that door was opened and the woman herself was standing there, that same fixed smile cutting right through her.

'Amy!'

Amy's face lit up when the door was finally opened, and she saw Tim standing there.

''Allo, Tim.'

'Come in!' he said eagerly, opening the door to let her in.

Amy was hesitant. 'Are yer sure it's all right?' she asked.

Tim came out, and led her straight into the hall. After he'd closed the door behind them, he turned to her with a wistful smile. 'It's g-good to see you,' he said.

Amy smiled back, but she was clearly ill at ease. 'Tim,' she said awkwardly, 'I came ter see yer muvver.'

Tim's expression changed. 'Oh, Amy.'

'Yer said the decision was now mine,' she said. 'Well – I've decided. If we're goin' ter 'ave any chance of a future tergevver, then I 'ave ter get ter know your muvver.'

Tim sighed. 'That's not wot I m-meant, Amy,' he replied. 'You have every r-right to feel the way you d-do. But you d-don't have to m-make friends with her. All I'm asking you to d-do, is to t-try and understand her.'

'I'll do me best, Tim,' said Amy. 'As long as yer don't expect me ter be a rival.'

'Amy!' Tim's mother entered the room, face beaming in her usual fixed smile. 'What a pleasant surprise. Tim! Why didn't you tell me you had a visitor?' She went straight to Amy and pecked her lightly on the cheek. 'Do you have time for tea today, my dear?' she asked. 'Or is this just another short visit?'

'Fanks, Mrs Gudgeon,' Amy said, sitting down on the sofa. 'I'd love a cup of tea.'

'Excellent!' exclaimed Mrs G, with apparent delight. 'Tim can do the honours whilst we girls get to know each other.'

Tim flicked Amy an anxious glance. But she returned a reassuring one, which gave him the confidence to go off to the kitchen and leave his mother alone with her.

'As you can see,' said Mrs G, as she sat beside Amy on the sofa, 'I've got him well trained.'

Amy smiled back weakly.

'He's a good boy,' said Mrs G, turning to face Amy. 'I don't know what I'd had done without him all these years. I'm very lucky to have a son like him.'

'I'm lucky too,' said Amy, directly.

Mrs G took the point. But her consistent smile was reduced to one of inquisitiveness. 'Are you in love with my son, Amy?' she asked.

Without flinching, Amy replied, 'Yes, I am.'

Mrs G reached for Amy's hand and gently squeezed it. 'I'm very happy for you, my dear,' she said. 'From what I hear, the feeling is mutual. I remember him talking about you years ago, when you were both children at Pakeman Street School.'

Amy felt a warm glow.

'Love is such an extraordinary thing, isn't it? One can never tell which form it will take. You love Tim because there is some kind of physical attraction between you. I love him for quite different reasons, because I remember him when I held him as a small baby in my arms, when I realised for the first time that I'd created something of my own that came from right down deep inside me, something that would remain a part of me for ever. I love him because he's my son.'

Amy very gently withdrew her hand. 'I fink yer've got the wrong idea about me, Mrs Gudgeon,' she said, solidly. 'I don't love Tim for the way 'e looks. I love 'im fer wot 'e is, fer the kind, warm person 'e is, someone who cares fer me, cares who I am an' not where I come from.'

'Yes, Tim's like that,' replied Mrs G. 'He's always had a way of making people feel better about themselves.'

Amy's look hardened. 'Wot d'yer mean?' she asked, curiously.

'Oh, you know what I mean,' replied Mrs G. 'If you think about it, we all lack a certain amount of confidence about ourselves. With me, I've always been self-conscious about the shape of my face, the pale complexion, the colour of my hair. But Tim will have none of it. Right from when he was a small child, he's been telling me that I shouldn't be thinking those things about myself, that he likes the way I look. I know he's wrong, of course, but he's such a wonderful confidence-builder.' She smiled sweetly at Amy. 'You must feel the same way?' she asked, with false sympathy.

Amy knew what she was trying to suggest – that Tim was only interested in her because he felt sorry for the way she looked. But she was determined not to rise to that kind of bait. 'Everyone needs confidence, Mrs Gudgeon,' she said. 'Even Tim.'

'Oh – you mean because of the stammer?' Mrs G got up from the sofa, and made her way towards the window. 'I think I can say that Tim has me to thank for helping him to cope with that.' She stopped at the window, to peer out briefly, then turned to look back at Amy. 'He used to be much worse, you know. It took him ages to utter even a few simple words. He was a bundle of nerves. Just like his father. All he needed was love. Thank God I was there to give it to him.'

Amy smiled wryly to herself.

Behind her, Mrs G's silhouette was framed against the bright morning sunshine which was flooding through the tall lace-curtained windows. 'Of course, you've not exactly had an easy life yourself, have you, my dear?'

Amy shrugged.

'It can't have been easy looking after your brother and sisters. Your parents are very lucky to have a daughter like you.'

'I'm very lucky ter 'ave *them*.'

'Despite everything?'

'They're me own flesh an' blood.'

'Flesh and blood is not always enough,' Mrs G replied, obliquely, as she came back to the sofa and sat with Amy again. 'Tim has part of *my* flesh and blood, but I know only too well that one of these days, I'm going to lose him.'

Amy looked directly at her. 'Does that scare you?' she asked.

'Scare me?' Mrs G hesitated. 'Yes, in some ways it does scare me. I suppose it's a fear of the unknown.'

Amy was puzzled. 'I don't foller yer.'

'Tim and I have been together a long time, Amy,' Mrs G replied. 'I know everything about him, the way he walks, talks, the food he likes or dislikes, the people he mixes with. I know about his habits, his irritation at being given advice. I know about the way he thinks. Oh, I suppose you could call me overprotective, but when you bring a child into this world you have to be sure that when they're finally ready to leave you, they make the right decisions. You see, throughout my life, that's something I've never done, and I regret it. I don't want the same thing to happen to Tim.'

Amy, with her hands neatly crossed on her lap, wavered only briefly before answering. 'I reckon we all make mistakes in this world from time ter time, Mrs Gudgeon,' she said. 'I know I 'ave, so 'as my mum, so as my dad. But one fing I 'ave learned is that yer can't 'old on ter people yer love for ever, 'cos if yer do, they're bound ter turn against yer.'

For the first time, Mrs G's persistent smile faded. 'What makes you think you're right for my son, Amy?' she asked, directly.

'I don't,' replied Amy, frankly. 'All I know is that I love 'im, and I fink 'e loves me.'

Despite all she had been saying, Mrs G's eyes showed that she was full of self-doubt. 'Is that enough?' she asked. 'Is loving someone – really enough?'

'No,' replied Amy. 'But it's a start.'

In the hall outside, Tim moved away from the parlour door,

where he had been listening to everything. After a moment of deliberation, he slowly made his way off to the kitchen.

The following morning, Aggs got up quite late. It was unusual for her, because most nights she slept quite soundly, and always woke up the moment the first army of ducks and geese came hurtling across the surface of the lake towards the bankside path. But last night had been pretty laborious, and it was well into the early hours before she could close her eyes and dissolve the face of old Scrounger from her consciousness. It would take a long time for her to forget that final, unlikely reunion with him in Oxford Street, and even longer to erase all the things he had told her. In any case, getting up late today of all days wasn't such a bad idea, considering that this would be the last time she would spend a night in her pitch behind the old boathouse.

Washing herself today also took longer than usual, for she needed to get rid of as many of the smells she had picked up in the park as possible. Not that the park was a dirty place to live in – far from it – but having a good wash down soon after getting up in the morning and before going to bed at night wasn't exactly an easy task, despite the fact that once a week she managed to carry out more thorough ablutions in the ladies' public toilets up near the Edgware Road exit. She was also quite methodical in the way she packed up her bundle. Every tatty old thing was carefully folded up and layered into a neat pile, scraps of soap taken from the public toilets wrapped up in strips of old newspaper, and even two clean empty Spam tins were thrown in for good measure, just in case they were needed. She left out a large chunk of bread she'd cadged off a small boy who'd been feeding the ducks the previous afternoon, for she needed something to eat for breakfast. When all those tasks were completed, she tied up the bundle, and threw it over her shoulder. With one last, lingering look at the boathouse, she turned and moved off.

On her way along the edge of the lake, she found the usual gang of water birds fluttering around one solitary woman who came into the park every day at this time laden with a huge bag of bread and bacon rinds. The noise the birds made always annoyed Aggs, for the way they carried on over a few crumbs of bread made them appear like a pack of thugs, who were not averse to attacking any of the seagulls who tried to swoop down and nip a bacon rind from beneath their snouts. And yet she was going to miss even them, for they, like the park itself, had become such a part of her life over this past year or so. As she passed, she took one last bite of her own precious chunk of bread, and, as a parting gift, threw the rest of it to the gaggle, who pounced on it from every direction.

She saw three recumbent figures stretched out on the steps of the bandstand. All three were still fast asleep, and their combined, high-pitched snores made them sound like a gramophone record of the Andrews Sisters at their worst. Flapper, Hooter, and Tiny Tim had never really been her best mates, but, like herself, they were parkies, and what they lacked in wealth, they made up for with a kind of inner dignity that was never given a chance to manifest. She quietly approached them, removed the bundle from her shoulder, and carefully laid it at the bottom of the steps just beneath them. Then she moved on.

Crossing the fields to the Cumberland Gate exit was a strange experience for Aggs, for she had decided that this was the last time she would ever do it. All around her she could feel the invigorating fresh air of a spring morning. Dogs of all shapes and sizes were being walked by their weary owners, babies were being given a mid-morning outing by their mothers and nannies, and the same elderly figures as usual took their morning stroll in the sun, as if to prove that there were still plenty of tomorrows to look forward to. For Aggs, the park had been a ritual. But it had never been a home.

Amy joined the queue for jellied brawn at ten thirty. After nearly forty-five minutes, she was still there, waiting as patiently as she was capable behind at least thirty other hopeful shoppers. Since the start of the war, endless queuing had become such a part of life that if you didn't conform, you would go without. Amy did conform, and was eventually rewarded with half a pound of the best pork brawn, freshly jellied by Sainsbury's in the Seven Sisters Road. By the time she finally left the queue, her legs were fit to drop, but at least she had something decent for her dad's tea.

On the way home, she stopped only once, to pop a coin into the hand of Pip the monkey, who was tethered by a long chain to Mickey Murphy's barrel organ, which was drowning out the sound of the passing traffic with a tinkling version of 'Me and My Girl'. Although she hated the sight of the poor furry creature being tied up like a prisoner, the music was like a breath of fresh air, and clearly lifted the spirits of the ration-weary shoppers.

On her way home, she crossed Hertslet Road quickly, mainly to avoid being caught for some idle chat with her neighbours, the Dolly Sisters, who were engaged in some highly animated group gossip just outside Barratts shoe shop. She didn't even bother to look in through the window of Lavell's sweet shop, for she knew that it contained it's usual dismal notice: SORRY. NO CHOCOLATE TODAY. Once she'd turned the corner into Enkel Street, she despaired at the sight of the pig-swill bins that had clearly been raided by stray cats and dogs during the night, leaving a trail of rotten fruit and vegetables right the way long the pavement. Her concentration was so firmly distracted, that she hadn't noticed the slim figure of Tim, who was sitting on the coping stone outside her own house.

'Hello, Amy,' he said, standing up to greet her.

Amy was taken aback.

'N-now it's my turn to s-say sorry.'

Amy rested her shopping bag on the coping stone. She was bewildered to find him there. 'Why've yer come, Tim?' she asked, tentatively.

Tim gently reached for her hands. 'I'm l-leaving home, Amy,' he said.

Amy was shocked. 'Wot!'

'It's the r-right thing to d-do, Amy. I should have d-done it a long time ago. It's b-better for me, and b-better for my m-mother.'

'But – what did she say?' asked Amy, astonished by Tim's sudden show of initiative. 'Is she goin' ter let yer go – just like that?'

'She wasn't v-very happy,' replied Tim. 'But I c-can't help it, Amy. I'm not a k-kid any more. My m-mother will have to g-get used to l-living on her own. She has to l-let me g-get on with my own l-life, to m-make up my own m-mind about things.'

Amy stared at him, tears of happiness welling in her eyes.

He pulled her back to him, and kissed her. From an upstairs window next door, curtains fluttered, as the Dolly Sisters got more than their money's worth.

'I'm m-moving in with Jack Billings,' said Tim, the moment his lips parted from Amy's. 'He's got a p-place over Stagnells, the baker's shop down Seven Sisters R-Road. He said I can stay until I find a p-place of my own.'

'I'm so glad fer yer, Tim,' Amy said. 'It's a new start.'

Tim felt for her lips again, and kissed her. Amy closed her eyes. When she opened them again, something distracted her. It was a figure gradually making its way towards them from the far end of the street.

Tim suddenly realised that her attention had strayed. 'Amy?' he asked, with concern. 'What is it?'

'Oh God!' exclaimed Amy. 'Oh God . . . !'

As she broke away from him, Tim swung round to see where she was going.

Amy was running as fast as she could along the street, straight towards the slow-moving figure who was gradually advancing upon her. As she went, she felt as though she was floating on air. 'Mum . . . !' she called, as she flew, her voice echoing along the deserted street with discarded cabbage leaves whirling in a gathering breeze. 'Mum . . . !'

Aggs came to a halt, and with outstretched arms, waited to be embraced.

The moment they met, Amy threw herself into the arms of the pint-sized woman in the felt hat and dirty raincoat. 'Oh God!' was all she could say, over and over again. 'Fank you, God! Fank you . . . !'

They stood there for as long as it took. Nothing mattered

now. They were together again. It was not just a reunion. It was, they both hoped, the start of a new era for the Dodds family.

CHAPTER 27

'Where've yer bin? Can we 'ave chips fer tea?'

Elsie's somewhat direct style of greeting may not have been quite the welcome her mum had expected, but at least it confirmed to Aggs that she was well and truly back home with her family again.

The moment Aggs threw her arms round Amy in the street, it was as though time had stood still. She could feel the warmth of Amy's body against her own, the flow of her blood – the same blood as her own – and the emotional quiver as she sobbed unashamedly. Once inside the house, she immediately tasted the cramped atmosphere of the narrow passage, the lingering smell of fried bread left over from breakfast, and the unmistakable smell of black oven polish in the back parlour. Everything was the same, nothing had changed. This is what she remembered, this is what she had sacrificed for her lonely vigil in the park. And when Thelma came rushing down the stairs in tears to hug her, shrieking, 'Mum! Mum!' and Elsie and Amy joined in, it was almost too much for Aggs to bear. For several minutes they all just stood there, unable to speak, hugging and kissing, and swaying back and forth together in unison, as though they were moulded into one disjointed shape. It was an extraordinary moment of loving reunion, which sapped away the lost months of despair.

Arnold's reaction on seeing his mum, however, was somewhat different. Coming in from the back garden, where he had been spending that last morning of the school holiday helping his dad to pump stagnant water from the Anderson shelter, his face was like stone. 'What're you wearin' those clothes for?' was his only comment. With some trepidation, Aggs put her arms round him, but his whole body remained limp and unresponsive. It was clear that Arnold was going to be no pushover; Aggs knew only too well that she was going to have to do everything in her power to help her son to forgive her.

'Welcome 'ome , Aggs.'

All eyes turned towards Ernie, who had followed Arnold in from the scullery. His face was ashen white, his expression sensitive and uncertain.

The others moved aside as he slowly came to her. Aggs watched him approach impassively. 'Welcome 'ome dear,' he said, with a desperate look of hope, as their eyes met. ''S good ter see yer.'

There was a moment of fear and apprehension, as everyone waited for Aggs's response. Then, without saying a word, she leaned forward, and gently kissed Ernie on the cheek. Overwhelmed with relief, both responded by throwing their arms round each other.

Amy and Thelma, tears streaming down their faces, quickly collected Arnold and Elsie, and shuffled them out of the room, leaving their mum and dad locked in a silent, tight hug.

At tea-time, Amy prepared the slap-up meal she had been planning to cook when her mum came home. It was Aggs's favourite – shepherd's pie, carrots, and tinned peas, and to keep Elsie quiet she even fried up some potatoes in the chip pan. Amy purred with delight as she watched all the family seated round the parlour table together, just like the old days, she thought, just like nothing had ever happened. But something *had* happened; despite her initial fears, her mum and dad were together again, and from now on, nothing in the whole wide world mattered any more. The past was the past. Tonight was no time for recriminations. It was a time for the family to get to know again the woman who had walked out on their lives, time to let minds heal, to recall what being together as one was all about.

After tea, Amy went with her mum to the bedroom that Aggs had for so long shared with her husband, Ernie. It was an extraordinary experience for her – so many painful memories of the distance that had grown between them, so many anguished memories of bitterness and blazing rows. For several moments Aggs found it impossible even to look at the double bed with the brass knobs, preferring instead to let Amy help her sort through the wardrobe, where her modest collection of clothes had remained intact since the day she had left.

The main problem, however, could not be avoided. It came when everyone was turning in for the night, when Aggs had to make up her mind whether she would return to that bedroom of so many unhappy memories. To Amy's despair, however, despite the fact that her mum and dad had carried on a reasonably normal conversation during the tea-time meal, and despite the fact that Ernie had offered to move in with Arnold for the night, Aggs decided that, for the time being at least, she would prefer to sleep alone on the 'Put-u-up' in the front parlour.

* * *

Sylvie Temple was on night shifts. This meant that she started work at the munitions shop at ten in the evenings, and didn't usually get home until after eight the following morning. By then, of course, she was whacked out, and all she wanted to do was to kick off her shoes, make her cup of tea, get breakfast for Joe, make sure he got off to school in time, then get to bed. This morning, however, was different, for by the time she got back home, young Joe had already left for school, which was not particularly unusual, for it was something the boy often did when he wanted to play a quick game of pre-school football with his mates on Highbury Fields. Unfortunately, he took after his mum for being untidy. When she got home, she found the place littered with discarded rubbish which he hadn't bothered to put in the bin out in the scullery, the usual dirty plate and cutlery that he never washed up, and folded-back copies of the latest issues of the *Champion* and *Radio Fun* left open on the table exactly where he had read them during his previous night's meal. She sighed, and went into his bedroom.

Things weren't any better there. The walls were plastered with newspaper cut-outs of football players. Worn underpants, socks, a grubby white school shirt were scattered around the floor, and his small table by the window piled high with school books intended for homework, but which looked very underused. She sighed again. What *was* she going to do about this boy? He needed a firm hand, but there was no one there to give it to him.

In a half-hearted attempt to clear up the place, she wearily went around the room picking up clothes and bits of junk, then crossed to his table to take a casual glance at what he might or might not have been up to. To her surprise, she found a couple of exercise books there that did at least show some semblance of effort. The maths book looked a bit of a shambles, with pages of unfathomable equations and geometric sketches, but as she hadn't got on her glasses, she had to squint to read the adverse comments from his maths teacher, who had simply scrawled, '6/10 See me.' There seemed to be more encouraging news in the second exercise book, where Joe had written a composition with the title 'Schoolboy at War'. Although she only read the first paragraph, Sylvie was impressed, for it turned out to be an account of his own experiences in an air raid during the Blitz. At least he can put pen to paper, she thought, which is more than she could say for herself. And for a fifteen-year-old, he had good, clear handwriting too. She was about to close the book, however, when, quite by chance, she came across what looked like a letter Joe had written on the last page. Her first inclination was to ignore it, but when she squinted hard enough, and managed to read the words 'Dear Dad', she immediately dropped to the floor the bundle of clothes and junk she was holding, picked up the exercise book, and hurried back out into the parlour. The moment she had retrieved her glasses from her handbag, she sat at the table to read what Joe had written:

Dear Dad,
Thanks for the ten bob you gave me last week. I know you can't afford it, but I'm going to put it towards a dynamo for the lights on my bike. Most of the batteries these days are dud even before you use them.

I was thinking about the pocket money you give me when we meet. Do you give the same to every one of the 'other side of the family'? If so, no wonder you're always stony broke! It's a pity I don't know any of my half-brothers and sisters (that *is* what you call them, isn't it?) cos if I did, we maybe could pool what you give us and make it cheaper for you.

At this point, Sylvie took off her spectacles and put down the letter. For a moment or so, she sat at the table, deep in thought. It was the first time she had known that Ernie Dodds had been discussing 'the other side of the family' with their son. Her immediate reaction was anger – anger that things were being said without her knowledge, behind her back. Ernie was the lowest of the low, she told herself. She wasn't going to let him get away with this. But then, she remembered meeting young Thelma Dodds outside the Finsbury Park Empire just a day or so before, and it all came back to her: '*Wot're yer afraid of, Mrs Temple?*' The girl's heartfelt pleas were ringing in her ears. '*Joe's our 'alf-bruvver. It's not 'is fault, an' it's not ours . . .*' She picked up her glasses, and continued to read Joe's note:

Dad, I'd like to meet my half-brother and sisters. I mean, I don't even know what they look like.

Again, Sylvie could hear that girl's pleading voice. '*I'm sure 'e'd like ter meet us just as much as we'd like ter meet 'im.*'

It would be really good if you could fix it so that we could all meet up somewhere. You've told me so much about Amy, Arnold, Thelma, and Elsie. D'you think we'd get on?

'Dad told us about Joe. 'E said 'e was a smashin' boy, that we'd get on well wiv im – if we ever got the chance.'

Sylvie could read no more. She closed the book, took off her glasses, and put them down on to the table in front of her. For the next few minutes, she just sat there, chin resting on her fist, staring down at Joe's exercise book as if in a trance. When she came to, she got up, picked up the book again, and took it back into Joe's room. Carefully, she rearranged the books on the small table, and placed the book back where she had found it. She paused a moment, to take a last look at it.

Only then did she realise that her eyes were filled with tears.

When Amy got up the following morning, she found her mum down on her hands and knees, scrubbing out the scullery. It had been Amy's intention to give her mum the luxury of a lie-in followed by a cooked breakfast. But Aggs would have none of it.

'I've got a lot er time ter make up,' she said, busily. 'I reckon you've done more than your fair share of work for this family.'

Amy was amazed how much her mum had softened since the time she had seen her sheltering in that builders' hut in the park. It was true that her small, round face was now heavily lined, but the dark blue eyes showed no sign of the stress and strain of the life she had now abandoned. It was also good to see her mum's hair combed and shining again, all the richer for the shampoo Amy had given her the night before. It all seemed too good to be true. But would it last, or would Amy wake one morning to find her mum gone again?

After Aggs had helped Amy to give the family breakfast, they wandered out into the back yard together. Although there was plenty of cloud around, there were, as the saying goes, enough blue patches to make a pair of sailor's trousers, and it brought one of those rare smiles to Aggs's face that showed a real sense of hope. Once she had checked the bucket of shrapnel that Arnold had collected on the streets at the height of the Blitz, she and Amy went down into the Anderson shelter, which was now drying out with a paraffin heater. The only light available came from the entrance with the curtain drawn back.

'So, 'ow's the war doin' then?' Aggs asked. 'Are we winnin' yet?'

Amy hadn't realised how out of touch her mum had been. 'I don't fink there's much chance of that,' she said, with a despondent sigh. 'Churchill says 'Itler could invade at any time.'

'So we can't get rid of the ol' Anderson then?'

Amy nodded. 'Not yet.'

'That's OK,' said Aggs. 'I'm quite fond of it.'

Amy looked astonished. 'This dump – an 'ole in the ground?'

'It's the only place that ever cheered me up,' she recalled, flashing Amy a quick smile. 'Sayin' g'night ter you every night.'

Amy threw her arms around her mum. 'Oh, Mum,' she said, tenderly. 'I can't tell yer 'ow many times I've prayed fer this moment. We all 'ave – includin' Dad.' She gently pulled away. 'He needs you so much, Mum. Wot will it take for 'im ter put fings right?'

'I don't know, Ame,' replied Aggs. 'When I finally decided ter do this, ter come back 'ome, it was a question I kept askin' meself over an' over again. But every time I even thought about it, all I could see was that woman; all I could see was the two of 'em – tergevver.'

''E doesn't love 'er,' Amy said. 'I don't fink 'e ever 'as. 'E was just stupid. It was all just a stupid mistake.'

Aggs smiled wryly. 'I know,' she said. 'That's wot 'e told me. But she 'as 'is son. That's somefin' yer can't change.'

'No, Mum, yer can't change anyfin',' said Amy, her face flooded with light, as she looked up through the entrance to the sky above. 'But yer can fergive. Wot's the use of livin' in the past? It's terday and termorrow that counts.'

Aggs perched on the entrance step, and breathed in the morning air. 'I used ter lay awake so many nights finkin' about 'im,' she said. 'I kept turnin' over in me mind all the fings I'd done wrong, all the fings I'd done ter turn 'im against me. For a long time, I blamed meself. When yer reach my age, Ame, you'll know wot I mean. Wot yer dad did was *my* fault, I know that now. I was so busy bringin' up kids, that I forgot about bein' a woman. Men like ter stay young. They like ter be admired. They like ter get as much out er life as they can. It ain't easy ter keep up wiv 'em.' She put her hands in her apron pocket to keep them warm. 'That's why I went ter pieces. I couldn't see straight. I boozed, I cried, I yelled at the top of me voice every time I thought about fings. I 'ad this thumpin' in me 'ead, everyfin' in me mind got muddled up. I didn't know where ter go, wot ter do, I couldn't even walk a straight line after six every night. Me life came to a stop the moment

I knew that yer dad couldn't bear ter set his eyes on me any more.'

'That's not true, Mum,' Amy said, putting a comforting arm around Aggs's shoulders. 'I don't believe that Dad's ever stopped lovin' you.'

Aggs briefly looked up at her. ''Ow do I know, Ame?' she asked. ''Ow can any woman *ever* know?'

Amy loved Tim's new room he had taken in the flat he was about to share with his old mate from school, Jack Billings. The smell of bread baking in the basement of the shop below seemed to be a million miles away from the smell of furniture polish in Mrs Gudgeon's house in Thane Villas, but what it lacked in antique furniture and heavy velvet curtains, it made up for in brightness and comfort. 'At least I won't s-starve,' he joked. 'They m-might give me a free loaf of hot bread for breakfast every m-morning!'

Tim had been overjoyed to witness Amy's reunion with her mum. He had worked so hard to help Amy find Aggs, and was only too grateful that this great gap in her life had at last been filled.

'She's dying ter get ter know yer,' Amy said, excitedly. 'I've told 'er all about yer, and she said I must be somefin' quite special to find someone like you.'

Tim took her in his arms. 'Your mum'll n-never know *how* special,' he replied, kissing her firmly. 'I w-wonder wot she'd say if I asked you to m-move in with me?'

Amy immediately pushed him away. 'Tim!' she gasped, incredulously. ''Ow can yer say such a fing?'

'Why n-not?' he countered. 'We're g-grown up, aren't we?'

'People don't live tergevver till they're married,' she

protested. 'Can yer imagine wot the neighbours would say?'

Tim suddenly fell back on to his bed, roaring with laughter.

'Wotcha laughin' at?' she yelled. 'It's true, ain't it?'

'D-Dear Amy . . . !' He grabbed hold of her hand, and pulled her down on to the bed beside him. 'Times are ch-changing,' he said, turning on one side to look at her. 'One d-day people won't have to get m-married to live with each other.' Amy tried to get up, but he held her down. 'That's not to say that I d-don't *want* to marry you.' He wrapped his arms round her, and slowly kissed her.

When their lips finally separated, Amy's eyes were like saucers. 'Did you say – *marry*?' she asked, in astonishment.

'Yes.'

'*Me* – marry *you*?'

'Well, don't m-make it sound so incredible!' he replied. 'I d-don't mean now, of course. But the m-moment I can get a decent job, the m-moment I can stand on m-my own two feet . . .' He stopped in mid-sentence. Amy had sat up, and was perched on the edge of the bed. 'W-what's wrong, Amy?' he asked, anxiously.

Amy paused before answering. 'What about yer muvver?' she asked. ''Ow will she feel about us after?'

Tim pulled himself up and perched beside her. 'This is *m-my* life, Amy,' he said. 'She t-told me to make m-my own decisions, and that's w-what I'm going t-to do. I've g-got to keep away from her.'

'It isn't as easy as that, Tim,' she said. 'I never thought about it until Mum came back home yesterday, but, you know, in some ways our two muvvers are alike.'

413

Tim couldn't believe he was hearing right. 'W-wot are you t-talking about?'

'Oh, I don't mean in the same way – they're chalk an' cheese really. But when yer fink about it, they both 'ave problems they can't cope wiv. There's my mum, lookin' back at 'er whole life as if it's a failure, and your muvver tryin' ter 'old on ter you out of some kind of spite becos 'er man walked out on 'er.'

Tim lowered his head. 'It goes f-far deeper than that, Amy,' he said, 'believe me.'

'Yes, I know,' Amy replied, leaning her head against his shoulder. 'But whatever 'er reasons, she is after all yer muvver. Yer owe 'er somefin', even if it's only understandin'.' She looked up at him. 'Wot I'm tryin' ter say, Tim, is yer mustn't turn yer back on 'er – not completely, not for always. If there's one fing I've learned from me own family over this past year, it's that life is too short ter make mistakes. People don't live for ever.'

Tim, confused, thought hard for a moment. 'I d-don't know what you're trying t-to say, Amy,' he replied.

'Look, Tim,' Amy said, meeting his eyes. 'A minute ago yer said yer wanted ter marry me. Is that right?'

'You kn-know it is,' he replied, anxiously. 'You're not turning me d-down, are you?'

'Of course I'm not! All I'm sayin' is that I don't want us ter go frough married life wiv this stone wall up between us an' your muvver. Now you've decided ter break loose an' make yer own decisions, yer've got ter show that you're bigger than 'er; yer've got to let 'er see that there's no reason why yer can't be on good terms wiv 'er, as long as she keeps 'er distance. If yer don't, she'll be left all bitter an' twisted

– an' so will you.' She put her arm around his waist. 'You can't get away from the fact, Tim. Your muvver's goin' ter be around fer a long time. You've got ter find a way ter get on wiv 'er – an' so 'ave I.'

Tim stared hard at her for a moment. It was easy for him to see why he had always been so deeply in love with her. Slowly, tenderly, he cupped her face in his hands, and kissed her. Then they rolled back on the bed, and he slightly pulled down her sweater so that he could kiss her neck and her shoulder. She responded, and they were soon fondling each other all over.

When they came up for air, Amy said breathlessly, 'I fink it's time I went 'ome – before I ferget meself!'

On the way back home, Amy felt as though she was walking on air. She couldn't believe how her life had changed so dramatically in just twenty-four hours – her mum coming back home, and a proposal of marriage from Tim. It had been such a long time since she'd had a perpetual smile on her face; life was certainly on the up and up for her.

In Roden Street, however, her high spirits were nearly dashed when she caught sight of old Gert Tibbett, hair in curlers as usual, waiting impatiently for her at the gate outside her house. Fortunately, Amy suddenly noticed Letty Hobbs cleaning her windows at number 13 on the other side of the road, so she quickly crossed over, which gave her the perfect excuse to bypass the fate that awaited just a few doors along.

'Amy! How are you, dear?'

Amy always felt so much better when she saw Letty, for she was a woman who had borne her own share of tragedy over the years, after her husband, Oliver, had lost his leg in the last war. ''Allo, Mrs 'Obbs,' she called, always impressed at how spick and span Letty kept the front of her house. 'Still at it, I see.'

'Just tryin' ter keep on top,' returned Letty, coming over to meet her. 'I'm so pleased ter hear about your mum,' she said, beaming. 'What a relief!' Then she added tactfully, 'Is – everything all right?'

Amy shrugged. 'I 'ope so,' she replied with a smile. 'Time will tell.'

Letty gave Amy's hand a reassuring squeeze. 'I wouldn't worry too much,' she said. 'What I know of your mum, she's a fighter. It won't be long before she gets on top again.'

'D'yer fink so?' asked Amy.

'I *know* so!' Letty replied. 'I remember once, before she went away, she stopped and talked ter me about her problems. It wasn't a grumble. It was a cry for help. I've often felt guilty that I never did more ter help her. Trouble is, if yer don't know, how can you put right? But I'll tell yer this, though.' She leaned forward, lowering her voice, her bright blue eyes twinkling in the morning sun. 'I don't know what happened between her and yer dad, but she thinks the world of him.'

Fortunately, once Amy had taken her leave of Letty, old Gert Tibbett had given up waiting, and had retreated back to the safety of her favourite vantage point behind the curtains of her front window. On the way, Amy thought a great deal about Letty, and how shrewd, but caring she was. What she had told Amy about Aggs's feelings for Ernie, had given her a real sense of hope, and something to work on.

In Enkel Street, Amy was puzzled to see a large van parked outside number 16, and when she approached, she found Uncle Jim helping another man to carry his bed out through the front door. On seeing this, she broke into a trot, calling as she went, 'Uncle Jim! Wot's goin' on?'

Jim helped the man to lift the bed into the van, then came out to meet her. 'I'm moving on, Ame,' he said, with a wistful smile. 'It's long overdue.'

Amy couldn't believe this was happening. 'Wot're yer talkin' about?' she said. 'Where're yer goin' to? Why?'

Before answering her, Jim waited for the other man to go back inside the house. 'It's time to move on, Amy,' he said, quietly. 'I always told myself that the moment you and the family got on your feet again, this is what I'd do. I'm getting stale. I need freshening up.'

Amy was in a two-and-eight. 'But – where're yer goin'? Wot about yer job up the post office?'

'I've got a transfer, Amy,' he said. 'Up to Mount Pleasant, the main sorting office. I found a couple of rooms just round the corner in Farringdon Road – over a grocer's shop. Not a bad little place. Not as nice as . . .' He turned to look up at the top floor of number 16. 'Still, beggars can't be choosers, can they?'

'Yer don't 'ave ter go, Uncle Jim,' said Amy, close to tears. 'We'll be lost wivout yer.'

Jim gently lifted her chin with one hand. 'Don't you believe it,' he replied, tenderly. Then with a passing glance at Thelma, Arnold, and Elsie who were watching from the parlour window, he added, 'You've got a lot of catching up to do.'

A short while later, all the family, with the exception of Arnold, had gathered around the van, which was now fully loaded with Jim's possessions. Jim went up to each of them to say his farewell.

'Be good,' he said to Elsie, lifting her up to give her a peck on the cheek. Thelma was crying, so he gave her a quick hug. 'You've come a long way, Thelma,' he said. 'Keep up the good work.' Thelma hugged him back, then quickly rushed into her mum's arms to be consoled.

Ernie offered his hand. 'I'll never be able ter fank yer enough, mate,' he said, emotionally. 'I won't ferget it.'

Jim smiled and squeezed Ernie's hand. 'I'll keep in touch,' he replied.

When Jim finally came to Aggs, her eyes were lowered. 'Welcome home, Aggs,' he said, offering her his hand. 'You've got a family in a million.'

Aggs slowly raised her hand, and Jim shook it. But just as he was about to take his leave of her, she held on to him, leaned up, and kissed him gently on his cheek. 'G'bye, Jim,' she said, softly. Then she met his eyes, and smiled, a smile that told Jim everything he wanted to know.

Amy, quiet but desolate, sat waiting on the coping stone for him. When he came to her, she got up. 'It's funny, ain't it,' she said, 'the way we've always called yer *Uncle* Jim? I mean, you're not related to us, not really. An' yet, I feel as though yer really *are* my uncle. I wonder 'ow many people 'ave someone around like that? Must be loads. The're worf their weight in gold.'

Uncle Jim smiled, leaned forward, and kissed her gently on the cheek. 'Goodbye, dear Amy,' he said. 'You're one in a million.'

As he went round to climb into the passenger seat in the front of the van, Amy joined the rest of the family, who were now huddled together on the pavement.

'Uncle Jim!'

At the sound of Arnold's voice, Jim halted before getting into the van.

Arnold came running up to him. 'You forgot this!'

Taken by surprise, Jim looked at the object the boy had thrust into his hand. It was a pack of miniature playing cards. He looked up for an explanation.

'I've got two packs,' said Arnold. 'This one's for you.'

Jim squeezed them in his left hand. He wanted to hug the boy, but he knew it would only embarrass him, and so, with his other hand, he did a mock punch on Arnold's chin. Then, with one last wave to the others, he got into the van. The driver turned on the engine, and they moved off.

As the van drove away, Jim craned his neck to see the Dodds family reflected in the driver's wing mirror. They were still huddled together, all comforting each other, and waving madly at someone they could no longer see. Jim smiled to himself, and swallowed hard, but the lump in his throat was not going to go down that easily.

As the van turned the corner and disappeared for the last time into Seven Sisters Road, he squeezed hard the small pack of playing cards he was clutching in his hand. During those few parting moments, he felt as though it was one of the most precious things he had been given in his whole life.

CHAPTER 28

As the days passed, Aggs gradually thawed back into life again with her family. Amy watched her carefully, always on the lookout for signs that her mum's morale was in danger of a relapse, always making sure that she never pushed her too far, and at too fast a pace. Aggs's new-found peace of mind was fragile, and Amy was determined to give her every chance to return to a normal daily routine in her own good time. During the time since she had returned home, the two of them had shopped together, shared the household chores, and listened to all Aggs's favourite programmes on the wireless: *Workers' Playtime*, *ITMA*, *Band Waggon*, and Vera Lynn's popular musical show for the armed forces, *Sincerely Yours*.

Although there was no doubt that Aggs was slowly losing that tough façade she had developed to defend herself in the park, her reconciliation with Ernie was still a long way off. Despite Amy's pleas, she continued to sleep on her own in the front parlour, and whenever there was a time when she and Ernie were left alone together, she invariably found some excuse to leave the room. The sticking point was, of course, the son he had had by Sylvie Temple. Amy was wise enough not to mention the boy's name for fear that it would trigger some crisis in her mum's mind, but when the time was right, she was determined to clear the air about the subject. The question was – how?

As Easter approached, Amy discussed with her dad the possibility of throwing a party to celebrate Aggs's return home, a kind of family get-together with some of the neighbours, a few drinks, a singsong and, with a bit of luck, a good old knees-up. At first Ernie, worried that Aggs might find too much attention a bit of a strain, wasn't keen on the idea, but when Amy assured him that this might be a way of getting her mum to let her hair down, he relented.

On Good Friday, three days before the party to be held on Easter Monday, Amy persuaded Tim to take her to the Emmanuel Church in Hornsey Road. He thought she'd gone out of her mind, for, until now, she had never indicated that she was even remotely interested in religion, let alone actually going to church. But, whether or not it was because of all she had been through, or because right through the previous week the wireless had been pumping out the story and music of Easter itself, she felt the need to experience something she had not done since she was a small girl.

When they got there, and took their places in a rear pew, the church was, predictably, filled with worshippers. War had taken its toll on so many of the local parishioners, and the Easter services, with their bowls of daffodils and colourful spring flowers adorning the altar, were clearly a worthy healing process for so many. Unfortunately, the service itself turned out to be a dull affair, with the vicar spending most of his time reading out passages from the Bible, instead of addressing his congregation as though they were human beings who were living through a dark age. None the less, despite the fact that, during the hymn singing, Tim enjoyed more than anything else watching several small children chasing each other up and down the central aisle, Amy was surprised to find things that she could relate to, especially the building itself, with its high timber eaves, and stone sculptures. But this moving commemoration of the Crucifixion of Christ seemed to convey to Amy something more than tragedy. It conveyed a message of forgiveness.

'I'm going up there ter see Joe,' Amy said decisively, as she and Tim left the church after the service. 'She can't lock 'im away fer the rest of 'is life. The only way Mum is going ter be able ter fergive Dad is for 'er ter come face ter face wiv 'im.'

'B-but Sylvie Temple's never going to l-let it happen,' insisted Tim. 'R-Remember the last t-time we tried?'

'I know that, Tim,' replied Amy. 'But I've got ter try again. If I give up now, Mum an' Dad are goin' ter live separate lives till God knows when.'

She took his arm, and they started to walk home via Hornsey and Arthur Roads. 'W-what happens if she says n-no again?' Tim asked.

'I just won't take no fer an answer,' replied Amy, adamantly. 'Wot she's doin' is unnatural. I bet if we took 'er ter court, she wouldn't 'ave a leg ter stand on.'

Tim sighed. 'Under the c-circumstances, I'm n-not so sure. Sylvie's the m-mother, remember.'

'Yes,' said Amy. 'An Dad's 'is farver.' At the corner of Arthur Road, she suddenly brought them to a halt. 'Tim!' she said, robustly. 'Will yer come wiv me ter see 'er? I asked the bloke Dad used ter work wiv round the baths. 'E said Sylvie Temple's moved. 'E told me the number.'

'Amy,' he said, taken aback by her swift decision. 'I'll d-do anything I can t-to help you, you know that . . .'

'I mean now – this minute.'

'Now!'

'It's Good Friday. She's bound ter be at 'ome. Let's give it a shot. Let's see if we can get it done over the weekend.'

Tim, utterly bewildered, scratched his head. He'd known Amy long enough to be aware that when she had made up her mind to do something, nothing in the world would stop her. 'OK,' he replied, reluctantly. 'B-but I hope you kn-know what you're doing.'

When the front doorbell rang twice, Sylvie Temple was doing her ironing, for, Bank Holiday or not, the chores had to be done. 'Joe!' she yelled. 'Can yer get that!'

From Joe's room, the sound of the madcap Spike Jones and his City Slickers on a gramophone record completely drowned Sylvie's voice.

With a frustrated sigh, Sylvie put down her iron. 'Lazy little sod!' she said to herself, making for the door. Halfway down the stairs, the bell rang twice again. 'All right! All right!' she yelled. 'Give us a chance, will yer?' By the time she had got to the front door, one of the woollen bobbles on her carpet slipper had dropped off. 'Bugger!' she cursed, quickly picking it up, and popping it into her dressing gown pocket. This put her in an even worse mood than she was already in, so that when she opened the door and saw who was standing there, the mood immediately turned to anger. 'Go away!' she growled. 'If yer come 'ere again, I'll get the law on yer.'

'No, Mrs Temple,' begged Amy, as the door was about to be shut in her face. 'Please don't shut me out. I don't want ter upset yer. I only want ter talk to yer.'

Sylvie opened the door just enough to peer round. 'Don't you ever give up?' she snapped. 'I tried talkin' ter *you* once – remember?'

'*Please*, Mrs Temple.'

Sylvie hesitated, then opened the door a little more. 'If it's about Joe—'

'My muvver's come 'ome, Mrs Temple,' said Amy, who was encouraged by Tim's supporting presence.

Again, Sylvie hesitated. 'Oh yes,' she replied. 'An' wot am *I* s'pposed ter do about it? 'Ang out the bleedin' flags?'

Amy refused to be intimidated. 'She's bin very ill. We're tryin' ter look after 'er. It's not easy.'

'Wot about yer farver?' Sylvie asked, acidly. ''E should be in 'is element now 'e's got 'er back again.'

Amy hesitated. 'It isn't workin', Mrs Temple,' she said, with difficulty. 'I mean, between Mum and Dad. They're livin' under the same roof, but they're not really tergevver. The only fing that's keepin' them apart – is Joe.'

'I don't know wot you're talkin' about,' said Sylvie, starting to close the door again.

Once again, Amy's pleas prevented her from doing so. 'If you could bring yerself ter let us take Joe ter meet 'er, I fink it would make a diff'rence.'

Sylvie stared at her. 'Are you kiddin'?' she growled, in disbelief. 'Yer want ter use *my* son ter 'elp your farver and muvver ter get tergevver again?'

'Please try to understand, M-Mrs Temple,' interceded Tim. 'You've got n-nothing to lose. You've practically s-said so yourself.'

''Ave I now?' Sylvie blurted. 'Well, I'm glad you know so much, young man. But you're right. I don't care a monkey's for Ernie Dodds. As a matter of fact, I'm moving on ter pastures new. Yer might like ter tell 'im that from me.'

'So then, there's n-not much point in hanging on, is there? If you've m-met somebody else, w-what harm can it d-do to let your son meet the r-rest of his family?'

'I know 'ow yer feel about Mum, Mrs Temple,' said Amy. 'If I was in your footsteps, I'd probably feel the same way too. But life 'as ter go on. Mum an' Dad mean a lot ter me an' my sisters and bruvver. As long as they stay apart, our life is in ruins.'

Sylvie hesitated before answering. 'An' wot about me?' she said. 'Wot about *my* life? I'm sorry fer you, Amy. I'm sorry fer you *an'* yer sisters an' bruvver. But I've got ter learn 'ow ter pick up the pieces of me own life, wivout worryin' about your muvver an' farver. As far as I'm concerned, they're goin' ter 'ave ter do the same as me – work fings out fer themselves. My son ain't no part of 'em.'

With that, she closed the door.

For a moment, Amy stared at the door, hardly able to believe that, no matter how hard both she and Tim had tried, that door would never be open to her or any member of the Dodds family. She wanted to cry, but the tears wouldn't come. Anger seemed the only alternative, but she was past that too. All that was left now was pity, pity for this woman who had allowed herself to be consumed with so much bitterness.

'It's all right, d-dear,' said Tim, gently putting his arms around her. 'One day she'll r-realise what she's d-done.'

He gently turned her round, and led her back towards the road. But before they had even reached the garden gate, they heard the front door opening behind them. They stopped, and turned. Sylvie was standing there, the door wide open.

''E's upstairs,' she called.

On the whole, Aggs was adapting pretty well. After more than a year living amongst the lost souls in the cold, open wastes of Hyde Park, she was now feeling more like a woman again. Wearing clean clothes, of course, made a great difference, but her gradually improving state of mind was also reflected in the fact that her fingernails were growing again, after such a long period in which she had consistently bitten them down to the quick. For the time being, however, she still had problems about being left alone in the house: the feeling of being shut away with a roof over her head was a constant fear. But, with Amy's help, she was taking everything one step at a time. The one remaining obstacle to a rational new existence, however, was Ernie. Every bone in her body told her that she must find a way to forget and forgive, and yet the prospect of doing so still filled her with doubt and apprehension. Her only way of dealing with it all was to bury herself in a sea of domestic work, and somehow hope that the anxiety would just go away.

On Good Friday afternoon, Aggs found herself alone in the house, for Arnold and Elsie had been taken by Thelma to a special children's matinée performance of a Walt Disney film at the Savoy Cinema in Holloway Road, and Ernie was in the front yard, trying to make sense of the few flowerbeds that had been neglected for so long. Aggs passed the time listening to the wireless in the front parlour, which, since her return home, had more or less become her own bedroom. Peering out discreetly through the fine mesh curtains, she could see Ernie, in his open-neck shirt and rolled-up sleeves, toiling in the cold afternoon air, his muscles rippling with energy. She was unable to prevent the feelings that had been aroused within her. Try as she may, she couldn't deny that he was just as ruggedly handsome as the day she'd first met him. Even so, it disturbed her.

When Amy came home with Tim, Aggs watched them become immediately engaged in what looked like an intense, animated discussion on the pavement outside. From time to time, Amy would give an adoring glance at Tim, who, to Amy's delight, had won Aggs over the moment she had set eyes on him again. But Aggs could tell that by the expressions on all their faces, that they were talking about her, for, every so often they would look towards the front parlour window, and quickly lower their voices. Despite all her efforts to keep out of sight, she felt frustrated that she couldn't hear exactly what it was they were talking about.

'I fink it's about time we put the kettle on!' Amy announced, brightly, the moment she and Tim came in to see her mum in the front parlour. 'We got yer some 'ot cross buns!'

Aggs could see that Amy was in a buoyant mood, and it slightly worried her. 'Where yer bin then?' she asked, warily.

'Oh, nowhere in particular,' returned Amy, perching on the arm of the sofa Put-u-up beside her mum. 'We went ter church.'

'Church!' gasped Aggs, astonished.

'It was a moving service,' said Amy. 'I didn't understand most of it, but it felt good ter sing the hymns.'

Aggs looked at her daughter as though she was now the mad one.

Tim had been sent off with Ernie to put on the kettle, which left Amy and Aggs alone.

'Yer know, Mum,' Amy said. 'When I woke up this

mornin', d'yer know the first fing I thought of?'

Aggs shrugged her shoulders.

'I thought of this same time last year. A cup of tea an' hot cross buns, just the same as always – except that we din't 'ave you wiv us ter share it. Don't leave us again, will yer, Mum?' she pleaded, gently stroking Aggs's hair. 'I don't fink I could bear it.'

Aggs smiled back weakly. She didn't quite know how to respond. 'I'll do me best,' was all she could say.

A short while later, they joined Tim and Ernie in the back parlour, where they all sat down at the table with their tea and hot cross buns, which Amy had warmed up in the oven. The conversation soon turned to the party. Aggs listened to Amy and Tim discussing with Ernie the handful of neighbours who were coming, how many bottles of booze they should get in, and whether the Dolly Sisters would keep their promise, and make one of their jam sponge sandwiches. Aggs listened to all this with trepidation. When Amy had first put the idea to her, she had had what amounted to a panic attack, and only Amy's assurance that getting to mix with people again would benefit her recovery convinced her that she should at least make the effort. Even so, she remained nervous.

Once tea was over, Amy announced that she and Tim were going to do the washing-up. Aggs was shrewd enough to know that this was merely a ploy to leave her alone with Ernie, so she quickly got to her feet as if to join them. But Amy would have none of it. 'Oh no, yer don't!' she commanded. 'I've got ter train my future 'usband 'ow ter look after me!'

Now alone with Ernie, Aggs desperately searched around in her mind for an excuse to leave the room. But the moment she started to rise up from her seat to go, Ernie stopped her.

'No, Aggs,' he said, calmly. 'Let's talk.'

'Wot's the use?' she asked, with obvious anguish.

Ernie persisted. 'If we don't talk, we'll become complete strangers.'

'Ain't that wot we are?' replied Aggs. 'An' that wot we've always bin?'

'No, Aggs,' said Ernie, sitting opposite her across the table. 'There was a time when you an' me were as close as anyone could be. A lot 'as 'appened since then – I know that. I don't blame you, Aggs. I never 'ave. But there's no reason now why we can't try all over again. We owe it ter the kids. We owe it ter each uvver.'

Aggs, her face staring distantly at the walls, had resisted the urge to look directly at him. 'I don't see 'ow we can do that, Ern,' she said awkwardly. 'I don't see 'ow we can ever make fings 'ow they used ter be, 'cos too much 'as gone on in between.'

Ernie had his hands clasped together on the table in front of him. 'There *is* a way,' he said assuredly.

She turned to look at him.

'By facin' up ter the truth,' he said.

Aggs replied, 'The truth is that you've got a fifteen-year-old son by anuvver woman. Just 'ow d'yer expect *me* ter face up to that?'

'By meeting 'im, Aggs.'

Aggs immediately turned away in disgust.

'By meeting 'im, an' gettin' ter know 'im,' pressed Ernie. 'Believe me, it's the only way.'

'It's *not* the only way,' insisted Aggs, again resisting the temptation to look him in the face. 'Can't yer understand? This is anuvver woman's son we're talkin' about, a son who

I didn't even know about fer over fourteen years! 'Ow can yer expect me ter shut me eyes an' pretend that the 'ole fing never 'appened?'

'No, Aggs,' replied Ernie, leaning across the table as far as he could towards her. 'I can't expect yer ter do that. But I love yer, Aggs, an' I fink yer still love me. So why do we 'ave ter go on torturin' ourselves.' He lowered his voice so that it was only just audible. 'This fing that's come between us, Aggs – ' he said, tentatively stretching his hand across to cover hers – 'the only way we can make a new start, is ter accept wot's 'appened, face up to it, and get on wiv our lives.' He squeezed her hand lovingly. 'Meet the boy, Aggs,' he pleaded. 'Don't let 'im be a thorn in yer flesh. Meet 'im, an' accept that 'e's there, that 'e's just as much a part of the family as Amy, Thelma, Arnold and Elsie. If yer can bring yerself ter do that, I promise yer, I'll never again let yer down.'

For a full minute, Aggs sat there quite impassively. She sat so still, she seemed to have turned to stone. Then, without further words, she gently pulled her hand away from Ernie, got up, and quietly left the room.

The Easter Monday 'do' may have started out as a fairly modest affair, but by the time some of the neighbours had got a few drinks inside them, it promised to turn into a right old booze-up. The real fun started when those two well-known teetotallers the Dolly Sisters decided to taste a glass of rum each, taken from a black-market bottle given to Ernie by a customer when he worked at the public baths. Mabel was the first to show the effects of what she called her 'pick-me-up', for, even after the first couple of sips, her eyes were rolling, and she was starting to giggle like a schoolgirl. Then her sister joined in, and when they started singing dirty songs that their late father had taught them years before, they brought the house down. Everyone enjoyed this impromptu entertainment, especially Arnold and Elsie, who joined in the words of the songs, fortunately without actually understanding what they meant.

For the first hour or so, Aggs seemed to be coping with the sudden invasion of her room quite well. She spent most of the time on the sofa, talking with Letty Hobbs, who had a way of making her feel perfectly natural and secure. Letty's husband, Oliver, was also there. A ticket-collector on the London Underground for almost twenty-five years, to some he appeared a rather dour man, mainly because he rarely had much to say, except when spoken to. But tonight he was on good form, amusing the kids with his boisterous version of 'Nellie Dean', and tapping the foot of his artificial leg in time to a gramophone record of Glenn Miller and his orchestra playing, 'Chattanooga Choo Choo'. Everyone was doing their best to make Aggs's homecoming a success. No one kept her chatting for too long, no one even mentioned her time in the park, or what had led up to it. Thanks to Amy, every attempt was made to play down the past; the emphasis tonight was only on having a good time.

For Amy, however, the celebration she had planned with such good intentions was in danger of turning into a disaster, for after carefully manipulating her mum into a position where she was left with her dad to talk things over, Aggs's determination not to compromise with Ernie about his son Joe was in danger of jeopardising the entire future of the Dodds family. With this in mind, Amy knew she had just one last card to play. But she was dreading the thought that the plan she had worked out with her dad would backfire, and cause her mum to crack up all over again.

Halfway through the evening, Ernie disappeared from the party, making the excuse that he'd run out of tobacco for his fags, and was going to buy some round the Enkel pub. Amy went out to the front doorstep to watch him go. Her stomach was churning.

A few minutes later, Marge Jackson came out to the scullery to help Amy lay out the sandwiches she'd got Mrs Bramley to make up in the tea shop. But there was another reason why she wanted to talk with Amy on her own.

'Amy,' she asked, whilst piling sandwiches on to a large serving plate, ''ave yer thought about wot you're goin' ter do – I mean now that yer mum's 'ome, an' yer don't 'ave ter look after the kids so much?'

'Not really, Marge,' replied Amy, busying herself by slicing the Dolly Sisters' jam sponge sandwich. 'I won't 'ave ter join up, so I expect I'll find somefin' ter do, sooner or later.'

'Does that mean when yer get married yer won't bother any more?'

Amy flashed her an astonished look. 'No, Marge!' she rebuked. 'Wotever makes yer fink that? I'd go mad stuck 'ome all day on me own. In any case, even if Tim does manage ter get a well-paid job, I couldn't afford to. We'll 'ave ter find somewhere ter live. We boaf said 'ow, when the war's over, we'd like ter save up an' buy an 'ouse of our own.'

'Amy!' gasped Marge. ''Ow yer goin' ter do that? People in our walk of life can't afford such fings.'

Amy stopped slicing the jam sponge sandwich, and looked up at her. 'Maybe not, Marge,' she said, 'but we'll try. If yer don't 'ave dreams, nuffin' ever comes true.'

Marge waited until Amy had gone to the gas cooker to boil a kettle for tea, then, without looking at her, asked, 'Amy, if yer really are serious about wantin' ter get a job, 'ow would yer feel about comin' back – round the corner?'

Amy turned with a start. 'Marge!' she exclaimed. 'Are yer serious? Come back ter work at the tea shop?'

Marge couldn't contain her smile. 'There's a job goin' at the end of the week. One of those two girls who took over from you an' Hilda 'as given in 'er notice. Not that I'm sorry. She's a real madam, that one!' She paused anxiously. 'So – wot d'yer fink?'

Amy came across to her, eyes gleaming. 'D'yer mean it, Marge?' she asked, eagerly. 'D'yer really mean it?'

Marge was beaming. 'I wouldn't ask if I didn't,' she replied. 'I've already asked Head Office, and they agreed. I'm not the only one who finks you're worth yer weight in gold.'

'Oh, Marge!' Amy threw her arms round her and hugged her.

'Do I take it this is "yes"?' Marge asked.

When Amy broke loose, her expression had suddenly changed to tense and sombre. 'I 'ope so, Marge,' she said, painfully. 'After wot's about ter 'appen, I 'ope so.'

When they returned to the front parlour, the party was in full swing. Mabel Hardy, one of the two sisters, had abandoned all caution to the wind and was dancing a frenzied tango with Tim, without music, but with her sister, Doris, yelling out '*Olé!*' at every twist and turn they made. Even Aggs had to laugh; all this was a revelation to her, and from now on she would see her eccentric neighbours in a new light!

A few minutes later, everyone tucked in heartily to the Spam and cheese sandwiches, which went down a treat, especially as they were accompanied by bitter and brown ale for the men, and a cup of tea for the ladies. Letty Hobbs had to keep a firm eye on her husband, Olly, for he was getting so merry, he kept breaking out into song all on his own.

'Wot's 'appened ter yer dad then?' asked Bert Farrar, in the middle of all the eating and boisterous humour. 'I bet yer 'e's 'avin' a crafty one round the pub!'

This provoked even more laughs and dirty comments, except that Amy was more concerned to see how her mum had reacted. Playing for time, she checked the clock on the mantelpiece over the tiled fireplace, and exchanged an anxious look with Tim. In desperation, she called, 'Ladies and gents. A quick word in yer ear, if you please!'

Oliver, who was still singing to himself, was quickly silenced by Letty.

'Hush fer the little lady!' called Bert.

Once there was complete silence in the room, Amy suddenly felt awkward, and didn't know what to do. 'I just wanted ter fank yer all fer comin',' she said. Then glancing again quickly at the clock, and nervously across at her mum, she continued, 'I know Mum's pleased ter see yer all. She was only sayin' just before yer came as 'ow lucky we are ter 'ave such good neighbours.' She paused briefly. When she looked around and saw all eyes turned towards her, it made her feel terribly self-conscious. 'This war,' she continued, 'it does terrible fings ter people. Our poor ol' street up 'ere 'as bin frough some 'ard times one way an' anuvver – bombs all round, our boys bein' whipped off ter fight Gord knows where, no money, no food, clothes, rationing –' she threw a meaningful look towards Elsie and Arnold – 'especially sweets an' chocolates!'

This brought a few laughs and the odd comment of 'Yer can say that again!'

'But all in all,' continued Amy, after flicking another anxious glance towards the clock, 'we're lucky ter live in a place like this, lucky ter be alive . . .'

Murmurs of agreement all round.

'But it ain't bin easy,' she said, aware that her mum was hanging on her every word. 'Some people 'ave found it more difficult ter cope than uvvers. I 'ate war. It turns people's 'eads, it leaves 'em feelin' as though there's no end in sight. But I 'ope there is an end in sight – for all our sakes. An' I 'ope that in years ter come, people know wot we've all 'ad ter go frough ter keep this world from goin' round the bend, 'cos if they don't, then none of it'll 'ave bin worf it.'

Calls of 'Hear! Hear!'

'So I want ter fank you again fer comin' round ter see Mum,' said Amy, looking across at Aggs. 'By just bein' 'ere, you're lettin' 'er know that there are always plenty of folk around who care for 'er, an' who never want ter see 'er be un'appy again.'

Everyone applauded, and turned towards Aggs, whose eyes were lowered. Meanwhile, Tim came across to give Amy a proud hug.

At that moment, Amy's heart missed a beat as she heard the front street door open, then close. She immediately flashed an anxious look across at her mum, then back to Tim. 'L-leave it to me,' he said. Whilst Aggs was being made a fuss of by Letty, Bert and Marge, Tim called discreetly to Thelma, Arnold and Elsie, then quietly led them out of the room.

A few minutes seemed like hours to Amy, as she waited for what was about to happen by handing round more sandwiches. And when Arnold and Elsie finally came bursting back into the room again, she found her whole body shaking from head to foot.

'Mum! Mum!' shouted Arnold and Elsie, excitedly, racing each other to see who could reach their mum first.

'Look who's here!' spluttered an ecstatic Arnold.

'Look! Look! Look . . . !' cried Elsie.

The room went silent, as through the door came the figure of a boy, aged fifteen, and looking very smart in a grey school uniform and cap, edged in mauve. Behind him came Thelma, who was half beaming, half crying. 'Mum,' she announced. 'There's someone 'ere ter see yer.'

The room fell utterly silent as the boy stood alone in the middle of the room, looking from face to face, trying to work out which of them was in fact his stepmother.

Tim held on to Amy, as she caught her mum's stunned look of disbelief.

Ernie appeared discreetly in the open doorway, and waited.

Aggs got to her feet, and stared at the boy with an impassive expression.

Thelma whispered into the boy's ear from behind, and he moved the remaining few steps towards Aggs. When he reached her, he stopped, took off his cap, and said, almost as though he had rehearsed it, 'Hello. I'm your stepson. My name's Joe.'

Aggs paused a moment. Her stony expression had changed to one of puzzled disbelief. The boy's face – there was more than a passing resemblance to at least two other members of her family.

Amy pressed hard against Tim, fearing the worst.

Aggs made a brief move. But just when it seemed that she

was going to sweep straight past the boy, she stretched her arms out slowly, and gently wrapped them round him.

The room erupted into applause and cheers.

Ernie's face cracked with tears.

Amy broke away from Tim, and joined her mum, who was now engulfed by Thelma, Arnold, Elsie, and her stepson, Joe.

Quite unaccountably, Oliver started singing all on his own again. It was a sentimental old song called, 'Always'. But it was a poignant sound, and one which prompted Ernie to come forward and hold out his hand to Aggs. She took it, and whilst everyone in the room joined in the chorus, he led her round the tiny space in a slow waltz.

Once the party was over, and everyone had gone home, the Dodds family eagerly settled down to getting to know Joe. He was, inevitably, bombarded with questions, and he had plenty to ask himself. He immediately struck up a friendship with Arnold, and he knew Elsie had accepted him, for she started hurling insults at him from the moment she set eyes on him. Thelma thought he looked a bit like her dad, but he had the same shape nose as his own mum.

With Ernie's encouragement, Aggs spent almost an hour talking to the boy, asking him about his school, and the things that interested him. Although she never once referred to his own mother, she said nothing about Sylvie Temple that would upset him. By the time Joe was packed off to spend the night sharing Arnold's room, to her amazement, she found that her stepson had made quite an impression on her.

When everyone had turned in for the night, Amy and Tim sat outside in the dark together for what seemed like hours. The air was cold and crisp with the gathering frost, so they snuggled up tight against each other, and stared up at the clear night sky. Jupiter was there again, so was Venus, and so was the red planet Mars. But tonight, they all seemed to be brighter than ever before, as though they wanted to say something, perhaps to send some kind of message, an assurance of better times ahead.

'D'yer know wot I'd like ter do right now?' asked Amy, her cheeks burning hot with the ice cold. 'I'd like ter take off all me clothes, and dance on top of the Anderson.'

'Amy!' cried Tim, in outraged disbelief.

Amy grinned mischievously. 'No, not really,' she added, before explaining. 'But that's wot 'Ilda would've done. She'd 'ave taken one look at wot's gone on 'ere ternight, an' rushed straight out an' done just that.'

'B-Bit cold,' suggested Tim.

'Not fer 'Ild,' replied Amy. 'She knew wot it was like to feel on top of the world. D'yer fink that's where she is now – on top of the world, up there, where she can keep an eye on us?'

Tim's eyes scanned the thousands of stars that were sprawled out across the entire sky.

'If yer are up there, 'Ild,' Amy called, softly, 'fanks fer all yer've done. Don't worry, mate,' she promised. 'Yer won't regret it.'

They were suddenly interrupted by the sound of Aggs calling to them from the back door.

'G'night, Tim!'

'Goodn-night, M-Mrs Dodds.'

'G'night, Mum!'

'G'night, Amy.'

* * *

A few minutes later, Aggs returned to her front parlour room, where she checked the Put-u-up bed that had just been made up for her. She paused a moment, put on her bedroom slippers, picked up her nightie, made for the door, and turned off the light. In the passage outside, she slowly made her way up the stairs in the dark to the first floor. When she came to the door of Ernie's bedroom, she waited a moment, and listened. From inside, she couldn't hear a thing. Ernie wasn't asleep. He was waiting for her.

She quietly turned the door knob, and went in.